JOHN DONNE

Ignatius His Conclave

Ignatius of Loyola, Campion Hall, Oxford. (Spanish school, early seventeenth century; wood carving 89 in. ✕ 74 in., painted and gilded on canvas and gesso. Formerly in the Allom Collection)

JOHN DONNE

Ignatius His Conclave

AN EDITION OF THE
LATIN AND ENGLISH TEXTS
WITH INTRODUCTION AND
COMMENTARY
BY
T. S. HEALY, S.J.

OXFORD
AT THE CLARENDON PRESS
1969

Oxford University Press, Ely House, London W. 1

GLASGOW NEW YORK TORONTO MELBOURNE WELLINGTON
CAPE TOWN SALISBURY IBADAN NAIROBI LUSAKA ADDIS ABABA
BOMBAY CALCUTTA MADRAS KARACHI LAHORE DACCA
KUALA LUMPUR SINGAPORE HONG KONG TOKYO

© OXFORD UNIVERSITY PRESS 1969

PRINTED IN GREAT BRITAIN

PREFACE

My residence at Oxford during the preparation of this edition was made possible by a generous grant from the Danforth Foundation. I wish to express here my gratitude to the Trustees of the Foundation.

In order to see as many copies of the text as possible I have imposed upon the kindness of many collectors and librarians. Sir Geoffrey Keynes, Mr. I. A. Shapiro, and Mr. John Sparrow were kind enough to allow me to use their copies. The librarians of the Chapter Library at Windsor, of Carlisle and York Cathedrals, and of the Innerpeffray Library deposited their copies at the Bodleian for my use. I would like to express my thanks to them and to the librarians of all the libraries listed on pages xlviii to l. It goes without saying that I am most indebted to the staff of Duke Humphrey's Library in the Bodleian.

Professor Gabriel Liegey of Fordham first suggested this edition to me. Miss Alice Walker of St. Hilda's College and Mr. Desmond Neill of the Bodleian helped me get started on the text. Dr. David Rogers, also of the Bodleian, assisted me in locating some of Donne's more arcane books. The late Professor William Jackson of Harvard led me to most of the seventeenth century copies of the text which were not listed by Sir Geoffrey Keynes. I must thank Frs. Anthony Levi and Basil Fitzgibbon of Campion Hall and Mr. Brian Daley of Merton College for their help with many points of latinity and history. Mr. John Sparrow, Warden of All Souls, and the Revd. Dr. T. M. Parker of University College both read this edition in its other incarnation and made many helpful suggestions. Fr. Edwin Cuffe of Fordham was also kind enough to read its every line and to share with me both his scholarship and his judgement. I am deeply indebted to Miss Elizabeth Wade-White for her generous kindness in helping me proof-read.

At every step in preparing this edition I have been able to rely on the help of Dame Helen Gardner, Merton Professor of English Literature at Oxford. To the generosity with which she has given of her time and learning it owes more than I can say. The only truly proprietary claim I can make is that all errors of fact or interpretation are strictly my own.

If it were appropriate to dedicate an edition, this would have borne on its dedication page the name of Joseph A. Slattery, S.J. I could thus have given some expression to my indebted affection for a great teacher and lifelong friend.

T. H.

Fordham
October 1967

CONTENTS

REFERENCES AND ABBREVIATIONS

QUOTATIONS from Donne's poems are from *The Divine Poems*, Oxford, 1952, and *The Elegies and Songs and Sonnets*, Oxford, 1965, both edited by Dame Helen Gardner; from *The Satires, Epigrams and Verse Letters*, Oxford, 1967, edited by W. Milgate; and from *The Poems of John Donne*, Oxford, 1912, edited by H. J. C. Grierson. These are referred to as

> *Divine Poems*
> *Songs and Sonnets*
> Milgate
> Grierson

I have used the following modern editions of Donne's prose works: *The Sermons of John Donne*, edited by G. R. Potter and Evelyn M. Simpson, 10 vols., University of California Press, 1953–61; *Essays in Divinity*, edited by Evelyn M. Simpson, Oxford, 1952; *Devotions Upon Emergent Occasions*, edited by John Sparrow, Cambridge, 1923; *Paradoxes and Problems*, edited by Sir Geoffrey Keynes, The Nonesuch Press, 1923; *The Courtier's Library or Catalogus Librorum Aulicorum*, edited and translated by Evelyn M. Simpson, Nonesuch Press, 1930. These are referred to as

> *Sermons*
> *Essays*
> *Devotions*
> *Paradoxes and Problems*
> *Catalogus*

Quotations from the other prose works are from the original editions, and the following forms of reference are used:

> *Pseudo-Martyr* *Pseudo-martyr*, 1610
> *Biathanatos* Βιαθάνατος (1646)
> *Letters* *Letters to Severall Persons of Honour*, 1651

Because of the frequency with which they occur in the Commentary, I have used abbreviated titles for two works by King

James I and two by Cardinal Robert Bellarmine. In 1608 James I published anonymously the *Triplici Nodo Triplex Cuneus*. In 1609 he reprinted this work under the title of *An Apology for the Oath of Allegiance* and added to it a new work, his *Premonition*. I have used this last printing and refer to the two works as

Apology

Premonition

Bellarmine's answers were his *Responsio*, first printed in 1608 under the name of his chaplain, Matthaeus Tortus and his *Apologia pro Responsione Sua*, printed under his own name in 1609. I have taken the texts from vol. xii of the edition of Bellarmine's works by Justin Fevre, *Opera Omnia Roberti Bellarmini*, 12 vols., Paris, 1874. They are referred to as

Responsio

Apologia

Other references:

Gosse   *The Life and Letters of John Donne*, by Edmund Gosse, 2 vols., 1899.

Keynes   *A Bibliography of Dr. John Donne*, by Geoffrey Keynes, 3rd edition, 1958.

Simpson   *A Study of the Prose Works of John Donne*, by Evelyn M. Simpson, 2nd edition, 1948.

Walton   *The Lives of John Donne, etc.*, by Izaak Walton (the reprint of the edition of 1675 in the World's Classics Series), Oxford, 1962.

D.N.B.   *Dictionary of National Biography*, Leslie Stephen and Sidney Lee (eds.), London, 1885–1900.

Sommervogel *Bibliothèque de la Compagnie de Jésus*, C. Sommervogel, Augustin de Backer, Aloys de Backer (eds.), Brussels, 1890.

INTRODUCTION

I. *The Two Versions*

ON 24 January 1611, *Conclave Ignati* was entered on the Stationers' Register to Walter Burre.[1] It was printed with no indication of the author or of the place and date of publication. It must have appeared shortly after the entry, since a copy was purchased for the Earl of Northumberland before 2 February 1611, and in the same month Pierre L'Estoile purchased a copy in Paris.[2] Further, a copy of the duodecimo which Robert Burton owned not only confirms its appearance in the early months of 1611 but shows that the author was known, since Burton has written on the title-page 'John Donne 1610'.[3] The same year an English duodecimo under the title *Ignatius His Conclave* was entered on the Stationers' Register by Nicholas Oakes for Richard More. The date of the entry was 18 May.[4] In this edition the author's anonymity is preserved, but the title-page is clearly marked 'London . . . 1611'.

The work must have been composed in the latter half of 1610. It refers to Ravaillac, whose notoriety dates from the assassination of Henri IV on 14 May 1610; and it contains a reference to Galileo's *Sidereus Nuncius*, published in Venice in March 1610,[5] which could hardly have reached Donne before the spring of that year.

There is little doubt possible that the Latin version was printed first. All the external evidence points to this: the first-recorded purchases of it; the note on the title-page that the English version was 'translated out of the Latin'; its entry in the

---

[1] Edward Arber, *A Transcript of the Registers of the Company of Stationers of London 1554–1640*, London, 1876, iii. 204.

[2] I. A. Shapiro, *Times Literary Supplement*, 6 Feb. 1953, p. 96.

[3] This copy is in the Library at Christ Church, Oxford.

[4] E. Arber, op. cit. iii. 208.

[5] The preface to *Sidereus Nuncius* is dated 11 Mar. 1610.

Stationers' Register almost four months before the English version. There is also at least one piece of internal evidence. On p. 10, the Latin is clearly in error in its reading 'Gregorii': the English corrects the text to read 'Boniface', the only possible name which can make sense of the passage.

But the priority of the Latin version in print does not necessarily mean that it was written first. To decide whether or not it was we must rely on internal evidence. There are several places in the text where verbal comparison points to the priority of the Latin. The marginal note 'Proculum and Posthumum' seems a deliberate echo of a pun which makes sense only in the Latin (p. 5). In the same manner, 'imaginarium' is put in the margin to explain the force of a remark which has lost its point in translation (p. 33). There are two long, complex, and confused English sentences (p. 41, ll. 23 to 26; p. 67, ll. 2 to 21) which can best be explained by seeing them as an unsuccessful effort to reproduce in English the smooth subordinations of the Latin. Finally, there is one instance where the English seems to have omitted entirely the summary sentence of a long development (p. 48, l. 18): 'Nunc nobis stellae fixae, & firmamento haerentes, nunc autem Planetae sunt Canones.' The result in the English is an awkward and unpleasant transition. In several instances puns or plays on words are weakened in the course of translation. 'For the most part we use her aversly and preposterously' suffers from the last word losing the literal meaning it has in the Latin's 'ea fere aversa praeposteraque utamur' (p. 16, l. 6). The same process is at work more clearly on p. 12: 'Modo enim veritas amittatur, quo id modo fiat non interest' puns on the word 'modo' and the English is incapable of catching this: 'For so the truth be lost, it is no matter how.'

In addition to these primarily verbal differences between the two texts, there is clear evidence that the Latin is more carefully structured than the English. It is continually conscious of rhythmic effect, of carefully built climaxes, and makes a far greater use of the range of verbal *schemata* than does the English. For example, in the Latin, Donne enjoys bringing a subordinate development to a climax by compacting verbs at the end of a sentence. Such climaxes as 'audiret, exierat, conspexerim' (p. 12, l. 13), and 'perlustrandi, invadendi, occupandi' (p. 16, l. 3) simply will not fit into understandable English. A better example is the snarling conclusion of the only rhetorical set piece in the work reminiscent of the great cumulative climaxes of the *Sermons*. This is the story of Pier Luigi which is built up, unsavoury detail after unsavoury detail, to terminate in:

Quod addi potuit, addidit. Virum, Clericum, Episcopum, non muneribus, non precibus aggressus est, sed vi stupravit, rapuitque.

The English version (p. 43, ll. 8–11) has none of the edge of the Latin. That Donne saw this is proved by his reworking of the same story in to far tauter form in the *Sermons*, twenty years later (*Sermons*, ix. 380). There he preserves the sequence intact, but instead of working out in English a Latin climax built on verbs, he has shifted to a series of nouns and made his climax out of the one swift clause 'he ravished a Cardinal'.

Granted the greater rhetorical polish of the Latin text, it seems fair to ask whether or not Donne did the English translation himself. What little external evidence we have claims that he did. His son in the edition of 1653 makes this claim; and such has been the supposition of all of Donne's critics from Walton to Mrs. Simpson. Once again, the internal evidence supports this supposition. It is difficult to translate one's own prose. Donne both conceived and wrote his text first in Latin. With his training and experience, there was no question of the language being 'foreign' to him. When it was written he obviously polished and worked it over and, most probably, saw it through the press. When he came to translate it, he faced the usual problems of fitting into English a work which had been both thought and written in Latin. Perhaps because of this, he felt free in his translation to change and expand the text. I have given a complete list of the differences between the two versions in Appendix A. Two things should be noted about that list. The first is the frequency of the translator's short-cut of clarification by expansion: 'odiosos' becomes 'odious and contemptible' 'inutilis' becomes 'infirmity and unfitness'. Secondly, these expansions, sometimes consisting of whole phrases and clauses, are much more frequent in the latter half of the text. Both these facts may suggest that the translation was hurried but they also demonstrate the translator's freedom with his text.

There is one final consideration. This is that ideas, phrases, and sometimes whole sentences from the English text of *Ignatius His Conclave* can be found in *Pseudo-Martyr* and *Biathanatos* which preceded it, as well as in both the poetry and the sermons. Each of these echoes has been noted in the Commentary. They are not very many, but the fact that any exist at all is a sound argument for Donne's authorship of the translation.

As an example of seventeenth-century English prose, *Ignatius His Conclave* has little to distinguish it. In its conception and structure the satire itself is interesting because of the way it works into prose the ironic detachment the classicists had already imposed on verse satire. But the prose in which this conception is worked out is weak. Donne clearly intended it to be 'pointed' in imitation of the Latin. It would probably have annoyed him to find himself ranked well below Bacon's *Advancement of Learning* (1605) in the 'pointed' or Senecan style; but such a judgement would be quite just. He has some good epigrams and one or two sharp paragraphs, but in 1610 he was a long way from the rich blend of Senecan and Ciceronian styles he was to use to such great effect in the sermons. By this early date he does not even seem to have decided what was to be the 'unit' of his prose. His carelessness about stops[1] makes it difficult to separate sentences one from another: while the 'unit' of the sermons, the paragraph, tends to get lost in the long cumulative tirades to which all the characters are given. Both these defects make the rhetorical organization difficult to follow. At times there simply is no rhetorical organization at all. In short, the English prose of *Ignatius His Conclave* suffers the full

[1] See Evelyn Simpson, 'A Note on Donne's Punctuation', *Review of English Studies*, iv (1928), 295–300: also, *Sermons*, i. 75–6.

range of faults we would expect to find in a hurried translation from the Latin.

The Latin prose presents another picture. It too suffers from the lack of rhetorical control. But the nature of the language forces Donne into greater clarity, and in its carefully punctuated sentences we can see much more of what he intended.

By the time Donne was a schoolboy at Oxford the great battle over Renaissance Latin style was almost over. It had begun with the complete domination of Cicero and through the work of men like Bembo in Italy, Camerarius in Germany, and Ascham and Cheke in England, Cicero's periodic 'Asiatic' style was the model for all those who sought in their prose to escape from the 'barbarous' Latin of the Middle Ages. The counterblast against the dominance of Cicero was sounded early in the century, by no one more loudly than Erasmus in his *Ciceronianus* (1528). For all its wit, *Ciceronianus* was not a textbook and not until Justus Lipsius did the anti-Ciceronians or 'Attics' have a theoretician to match the excellence of such practitioners of the style as Montaigne.[1] The publication of Lipsius' *Tacitus* in 1575 began the literary respectability of those who more or less rejected the Golden Age of Latin prose and sought their models among the authors of the Silver Latin period, above all Seneca and Tacitus.[2] In general, these authors aimed at force rather than sensual beauty; at accuracy in, and care for, detail and point rather than the architecture of periodic construction. They liked a prose of mordant concision and avoided as much as possible the generalizations and ceremonious pace of the Ciceronians. It

[1] The best studies of 'Attic' and 'Asiatic' prose in the sixteenth and early seventeenth centuries are the following articles by M. W. Croll: 'Juste-Lipse et le Mouvement Anti-Cicéronien', *Revue du Seizième Siècle*, ii (1914), 200–42; 'The Cadence of English Oratorical Prose', *Studies in Philology*, xvi (1919), 1–54; 'Attic Prose in the Seventeenth Century', *Studies in Philology*, xviii (1921), 79–128; 'Muret and the History of Attic Prose', *Publications of the Modern Language Society of America*, xxxix (1924), 254–309. The question is discussed in so far as it touches English prose in W. F. Mitchell's *English Pulpit Oratory from Andrewes to Tillotson*, New York, 1932. The most complete study in English is Professor George Williamson's, *The Senecan Amble*, London, 1951.

[2] M. W. Croll, 'Juste-Lipse et le Mouvement Anti-Cicéronien', *Revue du Seizième Siècle*, ii (1914), 215.

should be noted that while the 'Attics' prepared the way for the
individual neglect of all rhetoric which we call modern, this was
not their intention. Like the 'Asiatics' they both taught and
practised imitation: what changed was the model not the system.[1]

In the Latin *Conclave Ignati* Donne is clearly following Lipsian
style.[2] This does not mean that he succeeds completely in his
intention. From the very beginning, however, that intention is
relatively clear. The satire begins with a brief question and
briefer answer; this sets the tone of colloquial speech and
informality, despite the fact that the prose is smooth and carefully worked.

The careful but angular rhythms of this passage recall the
opening of Lipsius' own *Satyra Menippaea* (1605):

Quid hoc anno Romae in Senatu dictum, actum, cautum sit,
volo memoriae prodere. Frustra me respicis cum sublato digito,
Sigalion. Non debet silentio perire res tam magna. Dicam quae
vidi, quae audivi, quibus interfui. Quis vetat? Ego scio coactores
abisse, et niveam libertatem redisse. Si vera dicam, agnoscite: si
falsa, ignoscite.[3]

Both men here have gone out of their way to avoid rhetorical
fullness and formality. Donne is not as adroit as Lipsius in
avoiding all but the most essential conjunctions. He does follow
him closely in the frequency with which he uses parentheses.
And although he is far from completely successful with them,
Donne is manifestly striving for Lipsian *acumina* or 'points':

Damnari non vetuit, sed dominari eos noluit. (p. 14)

Irrisor semper est, qui adulatur, aut paedagogus. (p. 32)

Genus accusationis est parcius laudare . . . (p. 36)

Gaudent autem mutua sibi exempla esse *Papa & Lucifer*. (p. 72)

. . . non ibi diu degent *Iesuitae*, quin sponte sua nascatur et
Infernum. (p. 80)

[1] M. W. Croll, *op. cit.* 217.
[2] For a detailed description of the Lipsian style, see M. W. Croll, op. cit.
224–5.
[3] *Quatuor Clariss. Virorum Satyrae*, Leyden, 1620, p. 59.

... cui enim parum foeminae inerat, parum Innovationis satis erat. (p. 84)

All through his text Donne has the 'Acumen, Venustas, Dilectus, Ornatus vel nimius, . . . tum Schemata nullo numero, tandem verborum copia' which a violent anti-Lipsian described as the marks of Lipsian prose.[1]

In certain respects Donne does not follow Lipsius' lead. He does not use many neologisms nor is his vocabulary particularly difficult or archaic. *Conclave Ignati* has few of the sharp (usually visual) metaphors which characterize Lipsius' prose and which in an exaggerated form were to beget *concettismo*. Nor, for all its angularity, is the rhythm of Donne's prose as harsh or as full of surprises. In general, he avoids most (if not all) of the list of strictures the critic mentioned above attaches to Lipsian style:

... desunt autem Perspicuitas, Aequabilitas, Collocatio, Junctura et numerus Oratorius. Itaque Oratio est obscura, non paucis barbarismis et Soloecismis, plurimis vero Archaismis et Idiotismis, innumeris etiam Neoterismis inquinata; comprehensio obscura, compositio fracta et in particulis concisa, vocum similium aut ambiguarum puerilis captatio.[2]

This selectivity demonstrates what might have been concluded about Donne's Latin prose style *a priori*, that it is his own. He manifestly intended to write his satire in the 'aculeate' style, proper to Seneca and expounded by Lipsius. He also manifestly intended to write his own Latin, without slavish imitation and with a fine freedom to fall back on the accuracy and simple rhythmic effects of the medieval authors he had read. In Latin prose, as in everything else to do with the use of words, he is his own master.

II. *The Historical Setting*

In the current state of Donne's biography, there is little that can be said about the circumstances immediately surrounding

[1] Gaspar Scioppus ('Macer'), quoted in G. Williamson's *The Senecan Amble*, London, 1961, p. 122.
[2] G. Williamson, op. cit., p. 122.

the composition of *Ignatius His Conclave*. The black years after
his happy but financially disastrous marriage with Anne More
had been spent at Mitcham. In 1608 his reconciliation with Sir
George More, Anne's father, put an end to the poverty and social
exile which the poet and his growing family had suffered. With
the assurance of an income, even the modest one of Anne's
dowry, Donne was once again free to move in the only circles
which could promise him promotion. This year brought him
back into contact with powerful friends, such as Lady Bedford
who stood as godmother for his daughter Lucy. We know that
early in 1609 he endeavoured to secure the post of Secretary to
the Virginia Company but without success.[1] In 1610 an even
more important ally was found in the person of Sir Robert Drury
who became Donne's patron. It was while this relationship was
growing that *Ignatius His Conclave* was written.

Pseudo-Martyr is the work which immediately precedes
Ignatius His Conclave. It is a long and closely reasoned argument,
pointing out to the recusants that in risking their lives to avoid
taking the Oath of Allegiance they are committing suicide, not
earning for themselves a martyr's crown. Although the book is,
in general, less violent and bitter than was customary among
controversialists, it allows for no doubt at all about Donne's
position.[2] In addition, the work shows an impressive mastery of
the extensive and highly technical controversial literature both
of England and of the Continent. It is the intellectual quality of
Pseudo-Martyr which poses for most modern readers the basic
question about *Ignatius His Conclave*. Why did Donne write it?
He had just finished a long and serious book, with its statement
of irenic intention; now he launches into a light-hearted booklet

[1] Gosse, p. 209.
[2] It might be noted here that the standard critical comment about *Pseudo-
Martyr*, that it is a charitable work filled with irenic sweetness, is something of
an exaggeration. Donne certainly believed in 'composing all parties' and was able
to work more of this belief into his work than most of his contemporaries. But
chapter iv in *Pseudo-Martyr* is as far from irenicism as anything in William Cra-
shaw. This is the chapter on the Jesuits, in which Donne has harsher things to
say than anywhere else in his works, including *Ignatius His Conclave*. In these
pages it is evident that his 'composition' was quite willing to omit one part at
least.

in the manner and tone of the satirists who eleven years before had brought ecclesiastical censure down on their heads. In the first work Donne makes it clear that he is writing seriously on a complex legal question and as a layman in an area where he has real competence: in the second, he does not even acknowledge authorship and comes close to admitting that the book is a product of 'petulancy and lightness'. What did he hope to gain either before the serious and scholarly king or in the eyes of such honest battlers as Morton or such active ones as Andrewes?

Since what little biographical information we have does not answer this question, we have to look into the controversial exchanges of the time to see if the satire bears any relation to them. There are three controversies which suggest themselves immediately. The first is the long series handled first on the Catholic side by Allen and then Persons; and from the Anglican side by every divine in quest of controversial spurs.[1] But although many of the arguments and illustrations Donne uses occur in these works, *Ignatius His Conclave* does not belong anywhere in the series. The second possibility is the series of controversial works by Thomas Morton, eight of them in the five years between 1605 and 1610.[2] Although it seems probable that Donne worked with Morton from 1606 onwards, this work curiously enough does not belong in the Morton series. Finally, there is the long series of works generated by the two *Breves* of Paul V forbidding the English Catholics to take the Oath of Allegiance and the letter of Cardinal Bellarmine to the Archpriest Blackwell to the same effect. Of this series the star items (if not the most effective) were the two small works by James I, published together in 1609 under the title *An Apology for the Oath of Allegiance . . . together with a Premonition*. These two books,

---

[1] For lists of these controversies, see T. H. Clancy, S.J., *Papist Pamphleteers*, Chicago, 1964, pp. 235–43; and A. C. Southern, *Elizabethan Recusant Prose*, London, 1950, pp. 59–180.

[2] A full list of the Morton tracts involved is given in Appendix C. It should be noted that the *S.T.C.* lists another treatise for this period, 18188 *A Just and Moderate Answer*. This work is in answer to Morton and is manifestly not his.

and the two answers from Bellarmine, provide, as I hope to show, the context we need for *Ignatius His Conclave.*

The exchange between the King and Bellarmine has its origins in the *Oath of Allegiance*, 'for the better discovering and repressing of Popish Recusants' of May 1606.[1] The Oath is said to have been written by Bancroft and it was most shrewdly drawn. It contained among other protestations of loyalty the following affirmation:

. . . and I do further swear that I do from my heart abhor, detest and abjure, as impious and heretical, this damnable doctrine and position, that princes which be excommunicated or deprived by the Pope may be deposed or murdered by their subjects or any other whatsoever . . .[2]

The act also did not content itself with requiring attendance at the parish church, but imposed on recusants the obligation of receiving the Sacrament at least once a year in the parish church.[3]

At first the Archpriest, Blackwell, in the interest of peace, was inclined to accept the Oath as a purely civil document, despite a *Breve* from Paul V forbidding him or his priests or people to do so. In this he was joined by many of the party among Catholics, since labelled 'Appellants'.[4] The Jesuits flatly opposed the taking of the Oath as the government undoubtedly knew they would. Bancroft had done his work well and there was real confusion among Catholics. Despite the papal prohibitions of 22 September 1606 and of 23 August 1607, many English Catholics took the Oath, among them Blackwell himself. The motives behind this acceptance are as various as the men themselves, although there appears to have been a group of Benedictines and secular priests who felt that some agreement had to be reached with the

---

[1] G. W. Prothero, *Select Statutes and Other Constitutional Documents*, Oxford, 1954 (4th edition), p. 256.

[2] G. W. Prothero, op. cit., p. 259.

[3] G. W. Prothero, op. cit., p. 256.

[4] T. H. Clancy, *Papist Pamphleteers*, Chicago, 1964, pp. 6–7, 91–2.

government.[1] In such a situation, it was obviously to the government's advantage to separate the recusant body as much as possible from the Jesuits. This campaign lies behind many of the books and pamphlets published after 1606. Such efforts were only increased when a copy of the letter sent at the Pope's request from Bellarmine to Blackwell was received in England.[2] The letter urged the Jesuit position that the Oath was no merely civil act, but called into question one of 'the principal heads and foundations' of the Catholic faith.

The first answer to this letter was the publication in 1607 of: *A Large Examination Taken at Lambeth . . . of M. George Blackwell, upon Occasion of a certain Answer of his, without the Privity of the State, to a letter lately sent to him from Cardinal Bellarmine.* In the circumstances the 'without the privity of the State' was an exaggeration, witnessed by the name of the King's printer, the soon to be much overworked Robert Barker, on the title-page.[3] This was followed by James's opening gun, the anonymous *Triplici Nodo Triplex Cuneus*, in February 1608. The whole controversy was to be haunted by its nomenclature, and this title was a good start. The three knots at which the royal wedge was aimed were the letter from Bellarmine and the two *Breves* of Paul V. There seems to have been little doubt about the identity of the author. The book is relatively mild in tone and defends the Oath as a purely civil act. Its real harshness is reserved for the Jesuits as the fomenters of rebellion and regicide.

Rome felt, against the advice of Henri IV, that an answer should be made, and Bellarmine was chosen to make it. He too was given to unfortunate names, and published his answer, the

---

[1] In the summer of 1606, Augustine Baker, an English Benedictine, returned to England on family business. He relates how he was advised by men 'wise according to the world and esteemed so in divinity' in order to settle his affairs with greater ease to 'make haste and take the Oath before the Breve should come out and be published . . . many Catholics at that time and upon these and such other reasons did take the said oath and many priests did give the like timely warning and good advice (as they thought it) to their friends to hasten the taking of it'. Justin McCann and Hugh Connolly, O.S.B., *Memorials of Father Augustine Baker*, *Catholic Record Society*, xxxiii (London, 1933), 88–9.
[2] James Brodrick, *Robert Bellarmine*, London, 1961, p. 271.
[3] James Brodrick, op. cit., p. 276.

Responsio, under the name of his chaplain, Matteo Torti: which name gave rise to such a number of puns that they make the first part of Andrewes's answer almost unreadable. Bellarmine's work is along classical lines, arguing that the implications of the Oath would cut the English Catholics off from Rome and would, in fact, make the King so much the supreme head of the Church in England that every vestige of papal authority would be destroyed.

Since James's book had appeared anonymously, Bellarmine felt free to treat his adversary as roughly as the customs of the times allowed. James was crushed by the abuse, having somewhat foolishly supposed that his work would be welcomed with the deference his exalted rank demanded.[1] Not only did Bellarmine sharply disabuse him in this respect, but he had the bad grace to rake up the 1599 correspondence between James and Clement VIII, when in the grim days before he acquired the aid of Cecil, the King of Scotland was close to despair about his chances of inheriting the English crown and was willing to look for help in such far-off places as papal Rome.

The King was now deeply and personally involved and hastened to redress the balance. He first sacrificed his secretary, Lord Balmerino, in an attempt (which could have deceived only the most devoted courtier) to prove that the correspondence of 1599 had been entered upon without his knowledge.[2] Then he entered into consultation with his bishops to produce a reissue of his *Triplici Nodo Triplex Cuneus* under the new title *Apology*, with a long preface, called the *Premonition,* addressed to all the rulers of Christendom. After several false starts, this double volume, with the august name of its author prominently displayed, was finally published in May of 1609.

The part of it known as the *Apology* was in substance the same as *Triplici Nodo Triplex Cuneus* with only slight changes. The *Premonition* was new and was addressed to the Emperor Rudolph and the princes of Europe. Its reception was hardly enthusiastic:

The King of Spain, the Archduke in the Netherlands and the

---

[1] D. H. Wilson, *King James VI and I*, London, 1959, p. 238.
[2] D. H. Wilson, op. cit., pp. 234–5: J. Brodrick, op. cit., pp. 289–90.

Emperor curtly declined the copies presented to them. James
found himself engaged in ridiculous efforts to soften their in-
transigence. Nor did his Catholic allies give him any great satisfaction. Henri IV accepted the book but expressed ironical doubt
that it would achieve the desired results. In Venice, though its
circulation was banned, the Doge and Senate agreed reluctantly to
receive the copy sent them from England; but upon its presentation it was at once deposited unopened in the most secret archives
of the State where it has remained unmolested to the present day.[1]

In the text James does not reopen the question of his dealings
with Clement VIII.[2] He defends the clemency of his government
and attacks with more rhetoric than logic the pretensions of the
papal Antichrist.

Henri IV urged at Rome that the matter be left there. But
Paul V was not the man to lose the last word and Bellarmine
was again ordered to produce an answer. This he did through
the long, hot Roman summer and it appeared as his *Apologia* in
September 1609.

This quartet of books, the immediate exchange between the
King and the Cardinal, was only the visible part of the iceberg.
Three other works were begun under royal commission. The
Dean of Chester, William Barlow, was instructed to answer
Persons's contribution.[3] John Barclay was told to revise his
father's book *De Potestate Papae* (a good *politique* attack on papal
interference in secular government) and Lancelot Andrewes was
instructed to answer Bellarmine directly, which he did in *Tortura
Torti* in July 1609, and the *Responsio ad Apologiam Cardinalis
Bellarmini* in 1610. If the 'saintly' Bishop Andrewes proved
himself not above tampering with documents in the first of these
two books,[4] the second remains the best of the whole series
and the only one in which theology raises its weary head in the
midst of the abuse and counter-abuse. The controversy did not
stop in 1610, but went on to involve Abbot Casaubon and

---

[1] D. H. Wilson, *King James VI and I*, London, 1959, p. 238.
[2] J. Brodrick, op. cit., p. 290.
[3] P. A. Welsby, *Lancelot Andrewes*, London, 1964, p. 145.
[4] P. A. Welsby, op. cit., p. 150.

Cardinal du Perron.[1] But that part of it need not concern us here.

What does concern us is the correspondence of *Ignatius His Conclave* with James's two treatises, the *Apology* and the *Premonition*, and the almost as close correspondence with Bellarmine's two, the *Responsio* and the *Apologia*. It is not a simple reproduction of James's arguments: it is rather the opposite. Donne passes over major sections of James's work without so much as a nod; for instance, the endless diatribe proving the Pope to be Antichrist. Nor does his book attempt to answer the three major charges of Bellarmine against the Anglicans; on papal power, the Eucharist, and the worship of Saints. Donne's purpose seems to be to mention most of the major points at issue, but to mention them in passing. His attack is a series of deliberate feints and glancing blows, not a direct assault on Bellarmine or defence of James. He even largely ignores the points on which James has scored, and scored well, off his adversary, such as the discussion of the argument from prescription applied to English Church matters. His treatment of this issue is typical of the whole book: he does not mention prescription in its serious application to papal power, but mockingly applies it to sodomy at the papal court. So throughout the book: all the major issues are touched, but each of them is mocked and distorted in the process. Even the art of controversy itself is mocked. Minor points are made by citing huge (and otherwise significant) tomes; the citation itself becomes more biting than the text it supposedly justifies; or the citation makes a mockery both of itself and the point it makes.[2]

Despite this distortion, the echoes are unmistakable. All of them have been noted individually in the Commentary, but it might be well here to summarize them. Historical stories are the same: the Emperor Phocas and Boniface III; Alexander III walking on the Emperor's neck; Jesuit assassins; the novelty of Cardinals; the canon 'Alius'. Illustrative tales are repeated: the

---

[1] D. H. Wilson, op. cit., pp. 231–42.
[2] See in the Commentary, pp. 132, 126, 136.

ass worshipping the Host; Vasquez's justification of the worship of devils; the bad Latin of the verses on the *Agnus Dei*; Sixtus V's congratulations to Jacques Clement from the *Brutum Fulmen*. Serious points under which lie volumes of controversy are touched lightly: Henry VIII and his marriage; papal distrust of monarchy; the Roman distinction between local and general Councils; the sale of indulgences; the new articles of faith in the Council of Trent; the 'spiritual treasury' of the Church. There are echoes which are purely verbal: the *Manes* of Elizabeth; Gog and Magog; Lucifer the Calaritan Bishop; the Cardinals of Ravenna; the Roman tag 'pie credi potest' for covering weak arguments. Points which are almost personal to James are echoed: the harsh reflections on the influence of women in Church affairs; the baroque question of the meaning and function of Enoch and Elias; the resentment directed by James against Bellarmine (and by Donne against the Roman Church in general) for allowing personalities to enter into controversy.

There are even two passages in James's work which might well have given Donne's imagination the spark it needed to conceive *Ignatius His Conclave*. The first is from the *Premonition*:

. . . his style is nothing new but a Satyre and a heape full of iniurious and reprochefull speeches, as well against my Person as against my Booke . . . (p. 108)

The second is the concluding passage of the *Apology*:

. . . and I dare boldly affirm that whosoever will indifferently weigh these irreconcilable contradictions here set down will easily confess that Christ is no more contrary to Belial, light to darknesse and heaven to hell, then Bellarmine's estimation of Kinges is to God's. (p. 110)

There is little novelty in most of these arguments taken individually. They can be found in abundance in the ocean of controversy in England and abroad after the first break with Rome. Many of them can be found together in the more immediately involved works of Barlow, Barclay, Morton, Persons,

and Andrewes. What is striking in *Ignatius His Conclave* is that
so many of them and such specific ones are found in so short
a space. The only books that come close are Andrewes's two
400-page tomes and even in them I have been able to find fewer
direct echoes of James's arguments and his speech.

The conclusion I draw is that *Ignatius His Conclave* was written
as a satirical mockery of Bellarmine's two works against James,
and one which would employ, as far as possible, exactly those
arguments in its mockery which the King had used in all
seriousness.

The following passage in Walton's *Life of Dr. John Donne* is
tempting to anyone trying to find the occasion of *Ignatius His
Conclave*.

About this time, there grew many disputes that concerned the
Oath of Supremacy and *Allegiance*, in which the King had appeared,
and engaged himself by his publick writings now extant; and,
his *Majesty* discoursing with Mr. *Donne*, concerning many of the
reasons which are usually urged against the taking of these
Oaths; apprehended, such a validity and clearness in his stating
the Questions, and his Answers to them, that his Majesty commanded him to bestow some time in drawing the Arguments into
a Method and then to write his Answers to them: and, having done
that, not to send, but be his own messenger and bring them to him.
To this he presently and diligently applied himself, and, within
six weeks brought them to him under his own handwriting, as
they be now printed; the Book bearing the name *Pseudo-Martyr*,
printed anno 1610.[1]

Pseudo-Martyr could hardly have been written in six weeks, no
matter how diligently Donne set himself to work. The command
of the King, the six weeks, and the fact that Donne wrote
something, are the factual details Walton gives us to work with:[2]
and, if they do not fit *Pseudo-Martyr*, they certainly fit *Ignatius
His Conclave*. James took advice from every possible source in his
controversy with Bellarmine. Donne had already made a major

---

contribution in his legal attack on the Jesuit position on the Oath. He could easily have suggested to someone close to the King (for example, his chaplain, Morton) that it would be good tactics to attack Bellarmine as well by mockery as by serious argument: and that the material for such an attack lay to hand in the royal books already printed. At the first sign of encouragement, 'he presently and diligently applied himself and within six weeks' presented the finished work for royal approbation.

If this suggestion is accepted, it explains why the book was written in Latin. The originals in the controversy had been in that language (and the Roman parts stayed in it). Certainly the only audience capable of seeing the finesse of Donne's satire would have found the Latin a natural form. The little book must have had some success and was thus put into English for more general and less informed readers.

That it was considered effective can be seen from the dates of its various reprintings. That of 1626 corresponds to the first year of a new reign when, under a young monarch and his Catholic queen, there was a suspicion of a sharp rise in Catholic activity.[1] The second reprinting came when that suspicion had become a self-evident conclusion from the conduct of the Court and the arrival in London in 1634 of Gregorio Panzini as a papal observer.[2] The third and last reprinting of the century came in 1680 in the middle of the stirs provoked by Titus Oates. As Keynes notes, it appears to have had as its sponsor on this occasion Thomas Barlow, Bishop of Lincoln (and history's best candidate for the honour of being the original Vicar of Bray).[3] Once again, it was seen as a useful tool against Jesuits and Papists.

There is further evidence in support of the context into which I have placed *Ignatius His Conclave* in the copious *marginalia*

[1] *Sermons*, vii. 14–15.
[2] H. R. Trevor-Roper, *Archbishop Laud*, London, 1962, pp. 307–12. It was this edition immediately after the publication of the *Poems* that moved John Donne, Jr., to procure from the Archbishop of Canterbury a prohibition against the selling or printing of Donne's works without his son's approval. David Novarr, op. cit., pp. 27–8.
[3] Keynes, p. 20; *D.N.B.*, iii. 224–9.

Donne gives us. He makes fifty-six direct citations. For the most part they are indicated in the margin although some are not. It might be noted here that despite occasional errors, the marginal references are generally quite accurate.[1]

Among the authors referred to there is not one Englishman and not one Anglican. There are numerous references to Englishmen and English affairs in the text, but no English sources are used or cited. Some of the controversialists on both sides liked to quote extensively from opposition writers; but few, if any, carried this to the extreme of quoting none of their own countrymen or co-religionists. The only Protestant Donne quotes is Kepler, and he was hardly a theologian. In addition, he uses two ancients (Vegetius and Hippocrates) and one Arab (Mesues). The rest of his list is filled with Catholic names, and among them no fewer than fifteen Jesuits. The list demonstrates that Donne either had, or had access to, a well-stocked and up-to-date library of Catholic controversial and theological writers. The library also included such peripheral material as hagiography and history. Thirty-three of the books he quotes are theological, the great majority of them being clearly 'controversial'. Twelve of the books are historical or hagiographical. There is in them too an element of controversy. There is reason for doubting that the library belonged to Donne himself because only four references are made to books on the law.

Another reason for doubting that he owned the books involved is the dates they bear. *Ignatius His Conclave* quoted from nineteen books which had appeared before 1600: but from thirty-seven dated after 1600. Of those thirty-seven, no fewer than eighteen are dated either in 1609 or 1610. Someone was manifestly buying almost everything published under Catholic auspices and it is unlikely that in 1610 Donne himself could have afforded the expense of these books or that he would have had the necessary contacts abroad to arrange for their purchase.

---

[1] D. C. Allen, in 'John Donne's Knowledge of Renaissance Medicine', *Journal of English and German Philology* xlii (1943), 324, claims that Donne was a careless citer of texts. *Ignatius His Conclave* does not bear out this conclusion.

The fact that he had the run of such a controversial library, so generously and exactingly supplied, serves to confirm the conclusion about the quasi-official character of the work he was doing.

III. *The Satire and the Satirist*

The figures that Donne selects to people his Hell are an oddly mixed group. They are all men of the sixteenth century, all Catholics, and all in some way innovators. The first four treated, Copernicus, Paracelsus, Machiavelli, and Columbus could be called innovators on the grand scale, although one is tempted to find Columbus ill at ease in such company. The last two, Aretino and Philip Neri, hardly qualify as innovators at all and appear to be included simply because Donne disliked them.

The first claimant to the honours of Hell is Copernicus. He is also the least successfully satirized. Donne allows him to state his case, but despite the theological terms in which it is presented it is not a ridiculous one, nor does Donne treat it as such. I cannot escape the impression that Copernicus is included for reasons of pure topicality. The impact of *Sidereus Nuntius* barely six months before was still felt. Donne did not want to put its author or the other great living astronomer, Kepler, into his Hell: and Copernicus is a more deeply revolutionary figure than Brahe. So Copernicus summarizes himself in two statements: he has raised the earth and lowered the sun.

In this description Donne seems to be following one of the contemporary popular sketches. Koyré reprints one by Thomas Digges, dated 1576.[1] It shows the sun at the base with the orbiting planets set out in semicircles above it. Thus the sun is at the 'lowest part' and the earth half-way up 'the Heavens'. Also from the earth only the rear of Venus' orbital track can be seen, which explains Ignatius' comment about our seeing her only 'aversly'.

---

[1] Alexandre Koyré, *From the Closed World to the Infinite Universe*, Baltimore, 1957, p. 37.

Where Donne betrays his unwillingness to make Copernicus a figure of fun is in Ignatius' answer to him. Ignatius tries his hand (without either accuracy or conviction) at the usual Ptolemaic and Aristotelian answers. But as Donne had already recognized in *Biathanatos*, 'the pertinacity which is imputed to Aristotle's followers . . . seems now to be utterly defeated'.[1] Thus Ignatius mentions the opposition of Clavius; the three tired Pythagoreans are produced as mockery;[2] the moral indifference of scientific systems is alleged; and contemporary disagreements among astronomers are pointed out.[3] The significant comment is the remark, 'Those opinions of yours may very well be true.' This was, of course, Donne's own conclusion. If the excitement of *Sidereus Nuntius* made him include Copernicus, his own realization of its importance deprived him of any desire to attack him with vigour.[4]

The reader can almost feel Donne's relief as he turns to a figure made for fun and Paracelsus trumpets his entrance. He begins his self-indictment with his heroically proportioned name. He continues with a clinically exact (and deliberately indelicate) description of himself as 'Satan's organ and conduit'.[5] He then gives his four claims to glory as an innovator: his attacks on Galen and the medicine of the schools; his experiments; his

[1] *Biathanatos*, p. 146.
[2] C. M. Coffin, *John Donne and the New Philosophy*, New York, 1958, p. 94.
[3] I. A. Shapiro 'John Donne the Astronomer', *T.L.S.* 1937, 492. This brief but excellent article gives a summary of Donne's astronomical thinking both before and after *Ignatius His Conclave*. He was eventually, along with the majority of men of his time, to accept Tycho Brahe's compromise between the old and the new astronomies.
[4] Because of the two exact references Donne makes to astronomers, it is easy to conclude that he knew a great deal more about the subject than in fact he did. It should be noted that if Donne had been looking for a real astronomical villain, he could easily have found one in Giordano Bruno with his notions of the infinite universe. I don't think he had any such quest in mind; nor do I see evidence for his *expertise* as an astronomer in the lines from the poetry with which Professor Coffin deals. The new astronomy provided him with images and conceits; it did not make a scientist out of him. It is frightening to think of what critics 300 years from now will make of Eliot's use of Freudian terms.
[5] *O.E.D.*, s.v., 3a: 'any natural channel, canal or passage in the animal body'. Donne uses the word again in *Sermons*, iii. 235–6: '. . . all the other conduits and cisterns of the body . . .'.

supposed cure for the pox; and his use of poisons. Ignatius then adds three more for him: his claim to have made the 'homunculus'; his comments on the Scriptures; and his practice of alchemy.

We know that Donne owned a copy of Paracelsus' *Chirurgia Magna*,[1] but his knowledge goes beyond this single volume as can be seen from the extent of his criticisms. Paracelsus and his attacks on the established medical authorities were in the air,[2] and many of the charges are general enough. Certainly the name and bombastic style of the man, along with his ridiculous claims and alchemical hocus-pocus were enough to sharpen Donne's satiric tooth.

With Paracelsus as with Copernicus, Donne has a great deal of sympathy. For this reason, his irony is not very successful, We know that he found Paracelsus' attack on organized medicine refreshing:

. . . as Paracelsus says of that foul contagious disease which then had invaded mankind in a few places, and since overflown in all, that for punishment of general licentiousness God first inflicted that disease, and when the disease would not reduce us, he sent a second worse affliction which was ignorant and torturing physicians . . .[3]

And the passage with which Ignatius closes his refutation and speaks of a 'Legion of homicide-Physitians' has the authentic ring of Donne's own wit. He seems to recognize the two real contributions of Paracelsus which were an embryonic chemical knowledge and a refusal to accept the time-worn theories of the medical schools. Had Donne lived to see the greatest of satirists dissect medical pretensions once and for all in *Le Malade Imaginaire*, he would most certainly have both laughed and applauded.

The bite of the satire begins with Machiavelli's introduction, which would have made a first-class soliloquy for an Elizabethan

---

[1] Keynes, p. 218.
[2] Cf. *All's Well That Ends Well*, ii. iii. 11.
[3] *Biathanatos*, p. 215.

stage 'Machiavell'. He has the two characteristic stage traits—
underhanded cleverness and atheism; and he reveals them in
his tortuous approach to Lucifer and in his blasphemous parody
of the Trinity.[1] He proceeds swiftly to qualify himself as blood-
thirsty, devious, irreligious, dissembling, revolutionary, and
regicidal. In brief, he is so perfect a villain that he puts even
Ignatius into the shade.

With so complete a catalogue of villainies, for once we are in
a position to know Donne's sources. There are three works of
Machiavelli germane to his purpose and he manifestly knows all
three. The *History of Florence* he quotes in *Pseudo-Martyr*;[2] there
is at least one echo of the *Discorsi* in *Ignatius His Conclave*;[3] and
the whole of its presentation is based on *The Prince*. Donne is
clearly no victim of the 'myth of Gentillet'[4] and has not taken
his knowledge of Machiavelli from his critics, Catholic or
Protestant. The texts were easily available to him in Italian,
even in English printings.[5]

Donne must have been aware of the confrontation he was
producing, because Machiavelli had no worse enemy than the
Jesuits. Following Reginald Pole's attack on him,[6] the Jesuits
had him condemned by Paul V and by the Council of Trent,
as well as helping to burn him in effigy at Ingolstadt.[7] On this
last occasion the inscription affixed to the effigy is reminiscent
of Donne's description of Ignatius: 'homo vafer ac subdolus,

---

[1] Felix Raab, *The English Face of Machiavelli*, London, 1964, p. 57. Mario Praz,
'Machiavelli and the Elizabethans', *Proceedings of the British Academy*, xiii, 1928,
80.

[2] *Pseudo-Martyr*, B4 verso.

[3] See the Commentary, p. 115. The comments of Lucifer on what will happen
to the moon once the Jesuits get there (p. 81) seem to echo the passage in
Discorsi I. xi where, at the end of the chapter, Machiavelli remarks that if the
Roman court were transferred to Switzerland, it would in no time reduce the
purest and strongest people in Europe to its own degraded level.

[4] Raab, op. cit., pp. 55–6.

[5] A. Gerber, 'All the Five Fictitious Italian Editions of Works of Machiavelli
and Three of those of Pietro Aretino Printed by John Wolfe of London, 1584–1588',
Modern Language Notes, 1907, 2–6, 129–35.

[6] *Epistolarum Reginaldi Poli*, Brescia, 1744, i. 137–52. Selections from Pole's
attack are given in Raab, op. cit., pp. 30–2.

[7] P. Villari, *The Life and Times of Niccolo Machiavelli*, London, n.d., ii. 190–1.

diabolicarum cogitationum faber optimus, cacodaemonis auxiliator.' The Jesuit campaign continued up to Donne's time with books by Antonio Possevino, Pedro Ribadeneyra, and, in 1610, Thomas Fitzherbert.[1]

Donne's Machiavelli is not, however, merely the stage villain although he is that as well. His atheism is more subtle in that it involves 'dissembling of religion'. His bloodthirstiness recalls the 'murtherous Machiavell' but he ties it, in praise of Ignatius, to war and regicide. Perhaps most significant of all, Donne recognizes, as did few men of his time, the republicanism latent in so much of Machiavelli's work:[2] he makes him boast that he:

also did arme and furnish the people with my instructions, how when they were under this oppression, they might safeliest conspire, and remove a *tyrant*, or revenge themselves of their *Prince*, and redeeme their former losses;

and he concludes his speech:

so that from both sides, both from *Prince* and *People*, I brought an aboundant harvest, and a noble encrease to this kingdome.[3]

In all of this Donne has clearly recognized the basic conclusion to which Machiavelli's thought leads: that there is no place in the practical world of politics for a world view which claims to work out in statecraft the will of God. If Bacon is the one figure of the time who could accept Machiavelli's conclusions with relative ease and Raleigh an example of the tensions which resulted from half accepting him, Donne belongs with Hooker and, before him, Pole and the Jesuits. Neither in 1610 nor later could his mind accept a world of secular political activity in a city of man divorced from dependence on, and responsibility to, the city of God.

---

[1] Antonio Possevino, S.J., *De Nicholao Machiavelli*, Rome, 1592: Pedro Ribadeneyra, S.J., *Tratado de la Religion y Virtudes que Deve Tener el Principe Christiano . . . contra . . . N. Machiavelli*, Antwerp, 1597: Thomas Fitzherbert, S.J., *An Sit Utilitas in Scelere, vel de Infoelicitate Principis Machiavelliani*, Rome, 1610.

[2] Raab, op. cit., p. 68. Sources for this republicanism might be *Discorsi* ii. 2. 6; iii. 9. 41.   [3] p. 31.

Between the defeat of Machiavelli and the approach of Aretino, Donne sandwiches the amusing assault on Lucifer by 'all which had invented any new thing, even in the smallest matters': in short, the 'Table of Contents' of Pancirolli's collection of novelties.[1] Then Aretino is granted his brief appearance which is much more a discussion of Jesuit censorship and morals than of Aretino or his work. Ignatius begins by unfairly crediting him with 'licentious pictures'. In fact, they were done by Giulio Romano and all that Aretino provided was the descriptive and bawdy text. It is possible that Donne had not seen the little book in which both appeared. For the charge of being less than respectful to princes, he is on surer ground. It would have been very easy for him to have seen the rest of Aretino's work, particularly the plays and the letters.[2]

Despite the Elizabethan association of Aretino with Machiavelli,[3] it is hard to feel that Donne takes him seriously. He had said as much in a letter of 1600,[4] and effectively reveals through Ignatius the same attitude here when he remarks that Aretino's worst is milder than the Roman satirists and historians.[5] There is no reason to believe that Donne was annoyed by his work or that he gave it more importance than it had in *Satire IV*, 'Aretines pictures have made few chast.'[6] Thus he wastes on a weak opponent a good epigram: '. . . whatsoever Lucifer durst think, this man durst speake.'

The next claimant, Columbus, is also treated briefly. Like Aretino he serves Donne only as a peg on which to hang charges against the Jesuits. The identification of the Jesuits with Spanish policy enabled many of the controversialists to work on the equation; the crimes of Spain were the crimes of the Jesuits. As far as the New World was concerned, there was to hand a useful

---

[1] The best comic comment on *Ignatius His Conclave* is the one which Gosse makes (i. 256) on this point of the text. He refers to 'a skirmish of popes, embryos and friars'. Donne might well have used it had he thought of it.

[2] A. Gerber, op. cit. The second article (pp. 129–35) gives a complete list of Aretino's work which Wolfe published. To this might be added the Paris edition of *Lettres familières de Pierre Aretin* in 1609.

[3] Mario Praz, op. cit., p. 83.   [4] See p. 137.

[5] See p. 65.   [6] Milgate, 16.

catalogue of Spanish crimes in de las Casas's indictment of
colonial cruelty. Thus with a fine disregard for dates, the Jesuits
stood guilty of war, famine, slavery, idolatry, and the traffic
in gold.[1]

The final adversary Ignatius must face is, ironically enough,
his old friend Philip Neri. Here Donne seems angry, and Neri
is the only adversary treated with contempt. I suspect that what
had really stuck in Donne's imagination was the pious nonsense
which makes up so large a part of Neri's official biography. At
least half of it is filled with visions, ecstasies, and improbable
miracles. In the attack on Baronius Ignatius gives vent to a long
tirade made up entirely of medical metaphors which one suspects
should rather have gone to Paracelsus. There is one amusing
charge in the passage. Ignatius had indeed referred to Neri as
the 'bell which hung outside and summoned others to enter', but
what they entered was not the Church but the Jesuit Order.[2]

With Neri we come to the end of the adversaries and can turn
our attention to the two main figures in the satire, Lucifer and
Ignatius himself. Lucifer is a disappointment: nor is there any
of the standard infernal imagery in his treatment—not so much
as an echo even of James's *Daemonologie*. Lucifer's sole purpose
in the satire is to serve as a foil for the real villain, Ignatius. In
this function he is perfect. His emotional states are all those of
a born coward. Frightened, ashamed, perplexed, and jealous, he is
impressed by Copernicus and Machiavelli, shaken by Paracelsus,
and smothered by the crowds. He finally appeals for Ignatius'
help, but ends by fearing for his own throne. He is the only truly
comic figure in the piece.

Ignatius is very much the opposite. He has the 'advocate's
naïveté' but he is only comic in the sense that Gulliver, Claudius,
Julius II, and Master Gratianus' friends are comic, that is in the

[1] de las Casas's indictment was published in 1552 (see p. 139). By that time
there were few Jesuits in the New World. The Society's earliest mission work
had all been in the other direction. The Jesuit missions of Brazil were opened in
1549, but of these de las Casas makes no mention. Jesuits began working in Peru
in 1567 and in Mexico in 1572.

[2] Louis Bouyer, *The Roman Socrates; A Portrait of St. Philip Neri*, London, 1958,
p. 24.

blindness of his self-exposure. In what is exposed, Ignatius is pure villain. We see this villainy in two ways: first, in what he says of himself (or the rare times that the narrator speaks of him directly); secondly, in his refutation of the claims of his competitors.

Apart from the initial description, 'a subtile fellow and so indued with the Divell, that he was able to tempt . . . even to possesse him', Donne makes very few direct comments on his villain. He describes him as 'of the same temper as Lucifer' and 'the verier Lucifer of the two'. He comments on his ignorance, violence, and ambition but on little else. There are two reasons for this. The first is purely formal; in the device used by Donne Ignatius is meant to condemn himself and thus the less his author says about him the better. The second reason is the purpose of the work itself; Ignatius is not really a character, he is the spokesman of and for his Order. Donne's real target is not a long dead founder but the Order he founded. This is demonstrated by the restrained use Donne makes of biographical information which was surely known to him. Comments are made on the Saint's ignorance, his early career as a soldier, the wound which ended it, and his troubles at Paris. But there are other stories from Ignatius' life which would have annoyed Donne: the penances and isolation immediately after his 'conversion'; the stories of his visions, particularly one of which much was made by the early Jesuits;[1] his exaltation at Mass; his dealings with leading persons in Rome; and the long list of miracles given in such a biography as Ribadeneyra's. None of this is mentioned. It is possible to see here an element of fair play for a man whom Donne, when he was a child, must have been taught to admire. It is also possible to see two clear indications of Donne's structural sense: his realization that his central figure must speak his own doom; and that any personal attack on Ignatius would lessen the impact on the reader of the blanket condemnation of Jesuits and jesuitry.

---

[1] This is the vision at La Storta in 1537. It was frequently used to attack Ignatius; J. Brodrick, *St. Ignatius Loyola*, London, 1961, pp. 353–5.

One fact is evident. Donne knows more (and that in greater detail) about the Jesuits than most of the controversialists. His knowledge of the prelacies offered to Jesuits could have come from Ribadeneyra's *Catalogus*:[1] but he also knows that the prohibition to accept them falls under a vow and this is a more precise detail than Ribadeneyra gives. He is familiar with the rules of the Society, major ones such as the exclusion of any apostolate directed primarily to women and such a minor one as the instruction for the proper keeping of table silver. He knows legislative decisions, such as Ignatius' prohibition against attacks on the Sorbonne and the Parliament of Paris and the fact that the rules themselves are liable to change by proper authority.

There are also two areas of attack which he largely avoids. The first is on the name of the Society which was under regular assault for being presumptuous, blasphemous, or indiscreet— depending on the bias of the attacker. The second is on personal morality. To this he makes two glancing references: the amusing suggestion about the testing to which the cuts in Martial were really put; and the remark about the 'favours of women'. He never mentions Jesuit wealth, disguises, or orgies—all staples of invective controversy. He permits himself some of the standard range of charges. The Jesuits are cunning in theology, par- ticularly in the interpretation or reinterpretation of historic decisions. They are ambitious in search of power, and will 'be exceeded by none' even in crime. But there are really only two major charges which are made again and again in different forms and under different guises. These are that the Jesuits are avid innovators and anti-monarchists.

The first of these is the less important. Ignatius urges the novelty of the Gregorian Calendar. He prides himself on his men's ability to 'dish and dress their precepts' to the changing times. He boasts of the part they played in the innovations introduced by the Council of Trent and in such matters as confession by letters. Most topically he counters Machiavelli's

[1] See p. 113.

duplicity with the doctrines of Mental Reservation and Mixed Propositions which he claims are better because they are new. But even here, Donne is not at the heart of his attack: it is only when he comes to the Jesuit attitude towards monarchs and monarchy that he gets into his stride.

Regicide is the unifying theme of *Ignatius His Conclave*. Ignatius claims the superiority of Jesuits to all contestants on this point, and so, of course, does Donne. Jesuits have not only theorized on the matter (e.g. Bellarmine and Mariana) but have worked to put their theories into practice. They corrupt courtiers with gold and treachery, they possess themselves of the secrets of kings in confession, they hate the very name of monarch, they labour to upset kings and kingdoms, and they believe that no king is really theirs until they can see his heart—sliced or skewered as the case may be. In addition, they rewrite history to establish the papal dominion over kings and say, to change the text very slightly, that 'they are content that kings be damned, but not that they should rule'.

It should be noted that Donne's opinions about Jesuits and kings were not to change. As time went on they became less detailed but more settled. The notion of papal superiority over kings in any temporal matter he cannot accept, and even less can he accept any theory which justifies the removal of a king, no matter how much a tyrant, by any human means.

Even the most devoted of Donne students will not want to spend much time on his controversial prose works. These can only be of serious interest in their relation to his poetry and the sermons. There is, however, a basic continuity to Donne's mind and imagination which links a work like *Ignatius His Conclave* to his greater achievements in verse and prose. The first common element that strikes the reader is the 'outrageous wit'. We are asked in the first line to lay aside narrative and, indeed, logical continuity and are whisked into a wild world of improbable people and even more improbable rhetoric. 'I was in an ecstasy' he says, and with that word we leave behind the real world, even the real world of controversy, and enter into one that is as improbable as it is impossible. All the Aristotelian canons are shed and with gaiety—if not with complete success.

Three hundred and fifty years later we suffer from one great disadvantage: the references are lost to us and must be explained, and because they must, they lose their effrontery. On the other hand, we gain from not being involved in the actual subject, so that one aspect of this effrontery is probably clearer to us than it was to Donne's contemporaries. That is, the mockery of controversy itself, particularly of theological and scholastic controversy. When Donne quotes a *Corpus Iurium* of several thousand folio pages to substantiate a minor detail of papal procedure, or with solemn savagery quotes a victim of the *Ligueurs* about the acceptability of animal sacrifices, we can find a mockery that the learned King and his advisers probably missed. For us Henri IV is a figure over the Pont Neuf, so that we can laugh at the enshrining of his heart in the Jesuit Collège de la Flèche. Sir Henry Wotton probably shivered—or, if he laughed, it was because he knew the author.

Donne shows a consistent distrust of engaging in theological controversy. Time and again he reduces a major subject of religious brawling to a quick remark. Prescription is applied to sodomy, not the rule of kingdoms; the conflict about grace and free will is seen as a clever tactical shift; the endless and laborious identifications of the Antichrist are lopped off with one flash of Ockham's razor.

From this technique we might conclude that *Ignatius His Conclave* was Donne's last formal effort in print (*Pseudo-Martyr* having been the first) to prove to the King and his ministers that he should be granted secular and not ecclesiastical preferment. But there is a deeper dislike at work here; a dislike of 'all sophistications and illusions and forgeries'; a dislike for the world of those who 'write for religion without it'.[1]

> But snatch mee heavenly Spirit from this vaine
> Reckoning their vanities, lesse is the gaine

[1] Gosse, i. 221; in a letter to Sir Henry Goodyer.

Then hazard still, to meditate on ill,
Though with good minde; their reasons, like those toyes
Of glassie bubbles, which the gamesome boyes
Stretch to so nice a thinnes through a quill
That they themselves breake, doe themselves spill:
Arguing is heretiques game, and Exercise
As wrastlers, perfects them; Not liberties
Of speech, but silence; hands, not tongues, end heresies.[1]

Theological argument was a 'wrastle' in which Donne neither now nor later chose to exercise his skills.

The same is true of the curious learning that sprinkles both page and margin. He enjoyed the display of it, but enjoyed mocking it as well. The patronizing tone towards Galileo, the irrepressible sense of the ridiculous in Kepler and Machiavelli, the skill at dissecting medical mumbo-jumbo—all testify to his sense that learning, even his own, was always a fair target for mockery. His mind was agile and curious, but I cannot think that the 'new philosophy' loomed as large in it as its terminology did in his imagination. He realized that Galileo's station-keeping moons destroyed the best of the Aristotelian arguments against Copernicus: but there is a great deal of Donne's own thinking in Ignatius' neat reduction of astronomy to the moral order:

Hath your raising up of the earth into heaven, brought men to that confidence, that they build new towers or threaten God againe? Or do they out of this motion of the earth conclude, that there is no hell, or deny the punishment of sin? Do not men beleeve? do they not live just, as they did before?

There is in Donne a deeply conservative cast of mind. It was not the conservatism of the scholars who refused to look down Galileo's telescope. He had had in his own life to wrestle with great religious change and he made it slowly but honestly. His marriage proves that there were things he prized above the prudent care of his career. But God's will as he saw it blessed the sanctity of rest and continuity:

... Labour to find a testimony of God's love to you in your present

---

[1] Milgate, p. 31; stanza xii of *The Progresse of the Soule*.   [2] p. 17.

estate, and never put yourself either for temporal or for spiritual ammendement upon changes.[1]

This conservatism is what lies behind the structure of Donne's Hell. Unlike Dante, he reserves its choicest accommodations not for traitors but for innovators. He is correct in seeing the whole world of the 'counter-reformation' as a new thing, an innovation. Much more than on the Continent, in England this new thing was identified with the Jesuits. Later in his life he was to feel the same way about the Puritans. Even in 1611 he could link the two together—the extreme right and the extreme left of the religious spectrum. And he rejected them both for the same reason: they were extremes.

In 1611 one point at which this conservatism could be brought to focus was the 'divine right of kings'. In the first decade of the seventeenth century this had become something of a literary *locus communis* as well, particularly in England. James himself set what he felt to be the appropriate tone in his address to the Parliament of 1609:

The State of Monarchy is the supremest thing upon earth. For Kings are not only God's lieutenants upon earth and sit upon God's throne, but even by God himself they are called Gods. There be three principal similitudes that illustrate the state of monarchy: one taken out of the Word of God and the other two out of the grounds of Policy and Philosophy. In the Scriptures Kings are called Gods, and so their power after a certain relation compared to the Divine Power. Kings are also compared to fathers of families: for a King is truly *Parens Patriae*, the politic father of his people. And lastly Kings are compared to the head of this Microcosm of the body of man. . . .[2]

It is hard to think of Donne going quite as far as that, although many did.[3] Nor was he ever a theoretician of politics, following

---

[1] *Sermons*, i. 227–8.

[2] *The Kings Majesties Speech to the Lords and Commons, . . . at Whitehall, Wednesday the 21 of March 1609*. London, 1609, A4 verso.

[3] Serious discussions of the point can be found in George Carleton's *Jurisdiction Regall, Episcopall, Papall*, London, 1610 (Carleton was later Bishop of Chichester); and in Justus Lipsius' *Six Books of Politics*, London 1594. The wilder style of hectic

the tight subtleties of the *politiques* in his search for order. His comments seem to rise from convictions deeper than any argument. The best defence of the Church is the crown: and chaos, no matter how religiously motivated, is never to be preferred to order.

. . . And as in civil governments a tyranny is better than an Anarchy, a hard King better than none, so when we consider religion idolatry is better than atheism and superstition better than profaneness.[1]

For the student of Donne's work, this conservatism is the most interesting aspect of *Ignatius His Conclave*. It is the deepest link that ties this work to the great body of the *Sermons* and to the *Divine Poems*. The other aspects mentioned, the wit, the sense of the ridiculous, the outrageous effects of irony—these all look backwards. What is to carry Donne forward for the rest of his life is the abiding sense that man, even with the fullest help of God, can do very little good and had best hold on to what he has. He saw himself as he saw the fishermen of Galilee:

. . . [God] does not call them from their calling, but he mends them in it. It is not an innovation: God loves not innovations; Old doctrines, old disciplines, old words and forms of speech in his service, God loves best. . . .[2]

eulogy can be seen in John Colville's *Palinode*, London, 1600 (which being in the nature of a recantation of opposition to James had reason for exaggerations); Thomas Rosa's *Ideae: sive de Jacobi . . . enarratio virtutibus*, London, 1608 (which is simply fantastic); and George Marcelline's *The Triumphs of King James*, London, 1610.

[1] *Sermons*, ix. 145.
[2] *Sermons*, ii. 305.

BIBLIOGRAPHICAL NOTE

I. *The Latin Text*

Conclave Ignati survives in two forms: a duodecimo and a quarto. External evidence indicates that the quarto is a foreign printing. Keynes notes that the two Cambridge copies (ULC1 and ULC2) are 'bound up with other tracts that were printed at Hanau *apud Thomam Villerianum* (possibly a fictitious imprint) and it is probable, for typographical reasons, that this edition of *Conclave Ignati* was issued from the same press'.[1] Professor C. M. Coffin, after examining the two copies, advances the suggestion that they might have been printed by Conrad Biermann in Frankfurt.[2] Although both agree that the quarto is not an English printing, neither of them can prove it conclusively or establish where it was printed.

The relationship between the two editions can, however, be much more clearly established. From an examination of both it is clear that the duodecimo served as the copy text for the quarto. There are at least five instances where letters over-inked or under-inked in the duodecimo are responsible for errors in the quarto. In the duodecimo (A9 verso, l. 26) an under-inked 'si quid cui iuris' becomes 'si quid tui iuris' in the quarto (B1 recto, l. 3). In the margin of the duodecimo (B12 verso) an over-inked *Ribadeneyra*, where the bottom left foot of the 'R' has blurred (clearly seen in TCC and WAL), becomes *Libadeneyra* in the quarto (C1 verso). Again in the margin the duodecimo (C8 recto) blurs the 'o' in *Aphor.*, and the quarto (C3 verso) prints it as *Apher*. On the same page, the quarto takes the under-inked 'ti' in 'extispices' (12°, C8 verso, l. 22) and prints it as 'exuspices'. Finally, St. Frances's 'thorum genialem', with an under-inked 'o' in the

---

[1] Keynes, p. 14.
[2] C. M. Coffin, *Ignatius His Conclave* (Facsimile Texts No. 53) New York, 1951, pp. xi–xiv.

duodecimo (C11 verso, l. 2), is turned into 'therum' in the quarto (C4 verso, l. 34).

When the compositor of the quarto reaches the errata list he further demonstrates his originality. No corrections are made at all in the first three signatures, perhaps because while setting them he was unaware of the existence of an errata list. While setting the D signature he takes the trouble to correct one page in the outer form (D1 recto); 'inferendo' and 'extensa' according to the errata. He then corrects one page of the inner form (D3 verso) but incompletely: printing 'ni' for 'in' but ignoring the last item listed, 'eam' for 'eum'. He then prints no errata list for the entire signature. The duodecimo prints its errata in two columns, printing first the error and then the correction. The quarto prints its errata in a continuous paragraph and clearly intends to follow the same order. The compositor, however, manages to get nine of his twenty-one items reversed (7, 9, 10, 11, 12, 14, 15, 17, 19).

For all the above reasons, it is clear that the duodecimo was printed before the quarto. In addition, what evidence there is points to the quarto being a foreign edition. Consequently, I have worked on the conclusion that the duodecimo is the edition referred to in the Stationers' Register and must serve as the basic text for this edition.

The duodecimo text is quite good, with very few errors apart from those listed in the errata. It would be tempting to conclude from this that it had benefited from the author's supervision as it went through the press. Perhaps it is to Donne that we owe the lines addressed to the reader immediately before the errata list:

Jesuitarum Daemonem credo operae insedisse: unde alias tot errata? Nostra autem hic corrigimus: sed quando Jesuitae sua?

                                                        (E5 verso)

There is, however, no clear evidence that an autograph manuscript was used as the copy text. Some effort must have been made at proofing the sheets during printing. One correction was made in the outer form of A (A12 verso) and one in the inner form of D (D7 verso). The uncorrected form 'veris' survives in CCO, GK, and WAL: the other copies have the corrected form 'iuris' (A12 verso).[1] The uncorrected reading 'in' survives in BCO, BM, CCO, NLS, and YUL: the other copies have the corrected form 'ni' (D7 verso).[2]

The collation of all the copies is straightforward: A–D^{12}, E^6. The pages are numbered 1 to 94 from A4 recto to E2 verso. The title is on A1; *Typographus Lectori* A2 recto to A3 verso; the body of the text from A4 recto to E2 verso; *Apologia pro Jesuitis* E3 recto to E5 recto; and the Errata E5 verso. E6 is blank. There are no irregularities in numbering or cutting and all the copies are in good condition.

In 1680 another edition of the Latin text appeared (Wing B 837). This printing is usually found bound up with a later anti-papal tract of Bishop Barlow.[3] It is, however, nothing more than a reprint of the quarto, repeating thirty-six of the quarto errors and adding sixteen of its own.

II. *The English Text*

The first English printing, *Ignatius His Conclave*, retains its anonymity but bears the date 1611. It was entered in the Stationers' Register by Nicholas Oakes for Richard More on 18 May, 1611.[4] The work survives in several other printings: 1626, 1634–5, and 1653. All of them are derivative from the edition of 1611.

Keynes lists three items under the year 1611.[5] The first, his No. 4, is the one discussed here. His No. 5 and No. 6 are not really separate editions. No. 5 is an early and erroneous form of the title-page of No. 4: the error was noticed and the page was extracted: thus five copies of No. 4 begin with the title-page on A2. One copy of No. 4, HCL2, has an inserted title-page of

[1] See p. 22.   [2] See p. 82.
[3] Keynes, p. 20.
[4] E. Arber, *A Transcript of the Registers of the Company of Stationers of London 1554–1640*, London, 1876, iii. 208.
[5] Keynes, pp. 14–18.

a much later date. It is this copy which Keynes lists as No. 6. The erroneous title-page can be seen in BM G9 recto.

I have been able to examine only seven of the eight copies Keynes lists under his No. 4. The eighth copy, which he locates in the Chapter Library at Windsor, is not catalogued and the librarian informs me that he thinks it was disposed of several years ago.

The collation of all seven copies is A–G^{12}, with pages numbered 1 to 143, A6 recto to G5 recto. A1 is blank; the title is on A2; *The Printer to the Reader*, A3 recto to A5 verso; the body of the text from A6 recto to G5 recto; G5 verso is blank; *An Apologie for Jesuites*, G6 recto to G7 verso, G8 recto the errata; G8 verso to G12 verso are blank (except as noted above for BM). Page 59 is misnumbered 39. The 'irregularities in the signature numerals', noted by C. M. Coffin,[1] are the absence of 'D5' on p. 71 and the italics of E1 and G5. All copies are in excellent condition.

The text is a much more careless printing than the Latin. There are twenty-four errors listed in the errata (which manages to add another of its own) and sixteen more are to be found in the text. With a fine sense of balance the printer has also made sixteen errors in the marginal notes. Given this number of errors, it is probable that Donne did not see the translation through the press. There is no evidence of any proofing during the press run.

The other printing during Donne's lifetime is that of 1626. It is also a duodecimo containing 84 leaves, collated A–G^{12}. A1 and 2 are blank; A3 is the title-page; A4 recto to A6 verso *The Printer to the Reader*; A7 recto to G6 recto, the text with pages numbered 1 to 143; G6 verso is blank; G7 recto to G8 verso *An Apology for Jesuites*; G9 verso to G12 verso are blank. Two copies of this edition (ULE and KCC) preserve an error on B4 recto, 'peach' for 'peace', which has been corrected in the other two copies (BM and ULC). This text in general is a much better printing than that of 1611. The errors in 1611's errata

[1] C. M. Coffin, *Ignatius His Conclave* (Facsimile Texts No. 53) New York, 1951, p. xxii.

have all been corrected as have many of the unlisted ones. 1626 adds some of its own but these are very few. Unfortunately, it has no authority as a text, because the copy from which it was set was clearly the printing of 1611. The proof of this is the arrangement of the lines. 1626 follows 1611 almost exactly. In the one case where 1611 prints twenty-three instead of twenty-four lines on a page (p. 135) 1626 does the same. Where 1611 prints twenty-five lines, 1626 follows it in one case (p. 71) and in the other prints only twenty-four lines, but by crowding its lines catches up by line 9 of the following page (p. 51). When 1626 makes a correction the line is usually justified carefully to even it off. The less obvious mistakes in 1611, particularly those in the marginal notes, are left unchanged in 1626. And there are direct corruptions: 1611 has a blurred 'c' in the marginal note on 'Mosconius' which becomes 'Moseonius' in 1626 (p. 55).

There are only three reprintings in the seventeenth century after Donne's death. Since they are also all three derivative, they can be briefly discussed. Full bibliographical details are given in Keynes.[1]

As far as the text is concerned, 1634 and 1635 are the same. The date is altered on the title-page and was probably changed during the press run. In addition to nine copies of 1634 listed by Keynes, I have seen microfilms of three others. Keynes lists a tenth copy in the Library of Jesus College, Oxford, but the librarian there informs me that as far as he can determine the College has never owned one.

Both 1634 and 1635 show evidence of some proofing during the press runs, but both are careless printings with many errors. In general, they follow 1626 so closely that it is impossible to suppose that they had any other source. Where the errors in 1626 are obvious, 1634-5 will correct them. Where the error in 1626 is not obvious, 1634-5 reprints it. 1634-5 usually reprints those errors which 1626 has added to the original 1611.

The last seventeenth-century printing is dated (in its subtitle) 1653. It appears in a collection of *Juvenilia* published by Donne's

<hr>

[1] Keynes, pp. 18-19.

eldest son, John, and dated 1652.[1] On this title-page *Ignatius His Conclave* is described as 'A Satyr, Translated out of the Originall Copy written in Latin by the same *Author*; found lately amongst his own Papers.' As Keynes points out this description is 'evidently only for purposes of sale'. The note on Donne as translator is interesting; but the implication that a new manuscript source was available to the printer is simply false. The printing is a fair one and some effort has been made to organize the originally haphazard use of quotation marks. But the text itself is a copy of 1634–5. The *marginalia* alone prove this, since 1653 reprints errors that occur only in 1634–5. The entire section, *The Printer to the Reader*, is omitted.

III. *Copies Consulted*

The following is a list of seventeenth-century copies of the various printings, arranged by dates. I have added abbreviations only when they have been used in the text or the notes. Items marked with ★ are those not found in the latest edition (1958) of Keynes.

I. *CONCLAVE IGNATI*, 1611

   12° STC 7026 Keynes No. 2
   ★1. Balliol College, Oxford (BCO)
   2. Bodleian Library, Oxford (BLO)
   3. British Museum (BM)
   ★4. Christ Church, Oxford (ChChO)
   5. Corpus Christi College, Oxford (CCO)
   6. Harvard College Library (HCL)
   7. Sir Geoffrey Keynes (GK)
   8. National Library, Scotland (NLS)
   9. Trinity College, Cambridge (TCC)
   ★10. University Library, Cambridge (ULC)
   11. Yale University Library (YUL)
   ★12. Westminster Abbey Library (WAL)

[1] Keynes, pp. 79–82.

II. *CONCLAVE IGNATI,* 1611

    4° Keynes No. 3

    1. British Museum
    2. Sir Geoffrey Keynes
    3. University Library, Cambridge 1
    4. University Library, Cambridge 2

III. *IGNATIUS HIS CONCLAVE,* 1611

    12° STC 7027 Keynes No. 4

    1. British Museum (BM)
    2. Emmanuel College, Cambridge (ECC)
    3. Sir Geoffrey Keynes (GK)
    4. Harvard College Library (HCL1)
    5. Harvard College Library (HCL2)
    6. Huntington Library, California (HEH)
    7. University Library, Cambridge (ULC)

IV. *IGNATIUS HIS CONCLAVE,* 1626

    12° STC 7028 Keynes No. 7

    1. British Museum (BM)
  *2. University Library, Edinburgh (ULE)
    3. King's College, Cambridge (KCC)
    4. University Library, Cambridge (ULC)

V. *IGNATIUS HIS CONCLAVE,* 1634

    12° STC 7029 Keynes No. 8

    1. British Museum
    2. Bodleian Library, Oxford
    3. Folger Shakespeare Library, Washington D.C.
    4. Sir Geoffrey Keynes
    5. Harvard College Library
    6. Huntington Library, California
  *7. H. Bradley Martin, New York
  *8. National Library of Scotland
    9. Peterborough Cathedral Library
 *10. Robert S. Pirie, Massachusetts
  11. University Library, Cambridge

12. Yale University Library
*13. John Sparrow, All Souls College, Oxford

VI. *IGNATIUS HIS CONCLAVE*, 1635

12° STC 7030 Keynes No. 9

1. British Museum
2. Bodleian Library, Oxford
*3. Carlisle Cathedral Library
4. Corpus Christi College, Oxford
5. Folger Shakespeare Library, Washington D.C.
6. Sir Geoffrey Keynes
7. Harvard College Library
*8. Johns Hopkins University Library
9. Innerpeffray Library, Perthshire
10. Lambeth Palace Library
11. The Newberry Library, Chicago
12. Peterborough Cathedral Library
*13. Robert S. Pirie, Massachusetts
14. I. A. Shapiro, Birmingham
15. Theological Seminary, Princeton
*16. Trinity College, Dublin
17. Windsor Chapter Library
*18. The Wrenn Library, Texas
19. Yale University Library
*20. York Minster Library

VII. *IGNATIUS HIS CONCLAVE*, 1652

12° Wing D 1863 Keynes No. 10

The complete list of copies is given in Keynes, pp. 79–82.
The only copy I have consulted is the one in the Bodleian.

VIII. *CONCLAVE IGNATI*, 1680

8° Wing B 837 Keynes No. 11

The complete list of copies is given in Keynes, p. 20.
The only copy I have consulted is the one in the Bodleian.

There are two modern versions of *Ignatius His Conclave*. The
first occurs in Mr. John Hayward's *Complete Poetry and Selected*

Prose of John Donne, first published in 1929 by the Nonesuch Press. There have been eight subsequent issues. Mr. Hayward collated the 1611 and 1626 English texts. The other is a facsimile reproduction of the text of 1611 with an introduction by Professor Charles M. Coffin: *Ignatius His Conclave by John Donne*, Publication No. 53 of the Facsimile Text Society, New York, Columbia University Press, 1941.

IV. *The Text of this Edition*

The Latin text of this edition is based on the duodecimo of 1611, and my principal copy has been the one in the British Museum, collated with all the other known copies. All the corrections noted in the duodecimo errata list have been included in the text and noted in the apparatus. The duodecimo and quarto texts have also been collated, but quarto readings are noted in the apparatus only when they correct the duodecimo or when the quarto adds an error of its own to an error in the duodecimo.

When corrections have been made in the text of the principal copy, they are noted in the apparatus by the sign *Ed.* Such corrections have only been made when the text is in obvious error, and most frequently they have been justified by the English text. In several places, all of them noted, I have corrected errors in the *marginalia*, either in the spelling of proper names or the indications of chapters and pages. The latter has only been done when the work in question was either so much a classic that its interior divisions were fixed by Donne's time (e.g. the *Decretum* of Gratian), or when I have been sure that I have seen the only possible edition Donne could have been using.

For the English text, it is clear that only the edition of 1611 has any authority. All the others are derivative and are so in series: 1626 from 1611, 1634–5 from 1626, and 1653 from 1634–5. My principal copy has been the first of the two Harvard University Library copies (HCL1), collated with all the other known copies.

I have corrected this basic text from the edition of 1626 only when it is manifestly in error. In several places I have made corrections which were necessary to make sense out of the text. These are frequently based on the readings of the Latin text and they are noted in the same fashion as for the Latin text in the apparatus. All the corrections made in the errata list have been adopted into the text; each instance of this is also indicated in the apparatus. Since the edition of 1626 was printed during Donne's lifetime, I have noted all its significant differences from 1611. I have not extended the apparatus to include differences which merely reflect the compositor's practice in justifying his lines: e.g. 'me' and 'mee', 'thought' and 'thoght'. In correcting the *marginalia* I have followed the same practice as in the Latin text.

For both texts it seemed best to use the standard modern forms for 'u' and 'v', for 'i' and 'j', for ligatures and for the long 's'; all contractions have also been expanded. I have throughout preserved Donne's italics. The only major change I have made in punctuation is to regularize the use of quotation marks which, in both original copies, is careless and inconsistent. The spelling has been left in its original form and variety.[1]

---

[1] Since this Introduction was set in type I have learned that the late Professor R. C. Bald, in preparing a forthcoming biography of Donne, discovered an anonymous contemporary English translation of *Conclave Ignati: Ignatius his Closet, or his late Installinge in the Highe Courte of Parliament, summoned by generall consent of the chiefe governinge Furyes of the deepest Hell* (MS. Harl. 1019). He feels that although the translation must have been simultaneous with Donne's own, it is clearly not Donne's work. It does not appear ever to have been printed. I have not had the opportunity to see this manuscript.

LATIN AND
ENGLISH TEXTS

TYPOGRAPHUS LECTORI

Autorem quaeris? Frustra. Ignotior enim est Paparum olim Parentibus. Si tamen coniectandi pruritu labores, habe a me quod de illo amicus, cui librum legendum miserat, ad me scripsit: 'Evulgari ista noluerat Autor: indignum ratus tam re ipsa seria
5 gravique quam ea quam in alio, ante edito, libro sibi proposuerat, servaratque gravitate, ad hoc scriptionis genus descendisse. Ego contra, acies instruxi meas; hinc argumenta, inde exempla eduxi. Proposui ingentem *Erasmum*; quem etsi unum e nostris *Praedi-*

In contro. *cantibus* eum appellet *Scribanius Iesuita*, in suis tamen libenter
fol. 106
10 numerat Coccius. Eius autem Sarcasmis, huiusque generis velitationibus, non minus debere Ecclesiam nostram fatentur Adversarii, quam ipsi *Luthero* strenue in acie dimicanti. In mentem etiam ei revocavi, quam hoc sit ipsis *Papistis* familiare; quidque hoc in genere fecerat *Rebullus* transfuga, tam in illis libris
15 quos *Salmonees* appellare voluit, quam in altero *Cabale des Reformés* nuncupato, cuius si non Autor, certe Apologista fuit. Nec illo, hoc in genere, inferior, quisquis fuit, qui *Macer* dicitur: qui dissertationem de tremenda illa in *Venetos Pauli 5.* excommunicatione, aliisque rebus animarum salutem spectantibus,
20 *Risui & Lubentiae* consecravit. Uterque, non ut iste autor in re (si personas spectes) levi, (quid enim *Iesuita* futilius?) lusisse,

14 *Rebullus 12° errata: Rebuccus 12°*   15 *Cabale 12° errata: Cubale 12°*

THE PRINTER TO THE READER

Doest thou seeke after the Author? It is in vaine; for hee is harder
to be found then the parents of Popes were in the old times: yet
if thou have an itch of gessing, receive from me so much, as a
friend of his, to whom he sent his booke to bee read, writ to me.
'The Author was unwilling to have this booke published, 5
thinking it unfit both for the matter, which in it selfe is weighty
and serious, and for that gravity which himselfe had proposed
and observed in an other booke formerly published, to descend
to this kinde of writing. But I on the other side, mustred my
forces against him, and produced reasons and examples. I 10
proposed to him the great *Erasmus* (whom though *Scribanius* the *In Contro.*
Jesuit cal him *one of our Preachers*: yet their great *Coccius* is well *fol. 106.*
content to number him amongst his Authors). And to his bitter
jestings and skirmishings in this kinde, our enemies confesse,
that our Church is as much beholden, as to *Luther* himselfe, 15
who fought so valiantly in the maine battell. I remembred him
also how familiar a fashion this was among the *Papists* themselves;
and how much *Rebullus* that *Run-away*, had done in this kinde,
as well in those bookes, which he cals *Salmonees*, as in his other,
which he entitles, *The Cabal of the Reformed Churches*, of which 20
booke, if he were not the Author, hee was certainly the *Apologist*,
and defender. Neither was that man, whosoever hee bee, which
cals himselfe *Macer*, inferiour to *Reboul* in this kinde, when hee
dedicated to *Laughter*, & to *Pleasure*, his disputation of that
horrible Excommunication of *Paulus* 5. against the *Venetians*, and 25
of other matters concerning the salvation of soules. Both which,
not contenting themselves, as this Author doth, to sport and
obey their naturall disposition in a businesse (if you consider the
persons) light inough (for what can bee vainer then a *Jesuit*?)

12–13 *Preachers*: . . . Authors). *Ed.*: Preachers:) . . . Authors. *1611, 1626*
Margin *106 Ed.*: *160 1611, 1626*

genioque indulsisse contentus, in ipsos Principes, & unctos Domini petulantissime insurgit. Addidi etiam, longe longe modestiora haec esse, quam quae ab ipsis, in civilibus eorum bellis, cum *Paparum, Cardinaliumque* famam, per *Lucianum*
5 *Redivivum, Pasquillum* suum dilaniant lacerantque, quotidie evomuntur. Succubuit, librumque mei iuris fecit: quem tibi *Proculum* & (quod ipse valde vult) in hoc genere *Posthumum,* in exteras oras emittendum mitto. Ingenuitatem eius, candoremque, & animum ad partes conciliandas studiosum, alterum librum testari mavult.
10 Humanam imbecillitatem edoceat iste; quamque difficile sit, homini in *Iesuitarum* scriptis gestisque versato, ita *Iesuitam* penitus exuere, ut nihil de eorum sordibus, *Petulantia & Levitate* contrahat. Vale.'

ANGELIS TUTELARIBUS,
15   CONSISTORIO PAPALI, & COLLEGIO
SORBONAE *PRAESIDENTIBUS*

NOBILISSIMUM par Angelorum, ne nunquam vos convenisse diceretur, semper autem vos mutuo abhorrere, & semper *Aversa facie Ianum referre,* his saltem in cartulis meis vos unire
20 tentavi, non ut lites vestras componam, nec enim a vobis in me compromissum est; sed ut de communi vobis inimico caveatis, quae vidi referam. Eram in Ecstasi: &

> *Animula, vagula, blandula,*
> *Comes hospesque corporis,*

have saucily risen up against *Princes,* & the *Lords Anointed.* I
added moreover, that the things delivered in this booke, were
by many degrees more modest, then those which themselves,
in their owne civill warres, do daily vomit forth, when they
butcher and mangle the fame and reputation of their *Popes* & 5
Cardinals by their revived *Lucian, Pasquil.* At last he yeelded, &
made mee owner of his booke, which I send to you to be delivered
over to forraine nations, (*a*) farre from the father: and (as his *Proculum and*
desire is) (*b*) his last in this kinde. Hee chooses and desires, that *Posthumum*
his other booke should testifie his ingenuity, and candor, and 10
his disposition to labour for the reconciling of all parts. This
Booke must teach what humane infirmity is, and how hard
a matter it is for a man much conversant in the bookes and Acts
of *Jesuites,* so throughly to cast off the *Jesuits,* as that he contract
nothing of their naturall drosses, which are *Petulancy,* and 15
Lightnesse. Vale.'

TO THE TWO TUTELAR ANGELS,

PROTECTORS OF THE POPES CONSISTORY,
AND OF THE COLLEDGE OF SORBON

Most noble couple of *Angels,* least it should be sayd that you 20
did never agree, and never meet, but that you did ever abhorre
one another, and ever

> *Resemble* Janus *with a diverse face,*

I attempted to bring and joyne you together once in these
papers; not that I might compose your differences, for you have 25
not chosen me for *Arbitrator*; but, that you might beware of an
enemy common to you both, I will relate what I saw. I was in
an *Extasie,* and

> *My little wandring sportful Soule,*
> *Ghest, and Companion of my body* 30

15 *Petulancy 1626: Petulaucy 1611*   23 *face,*] *face; 1626*   30 *Ghest*] *Guest*
1626

Per omnia libere vagata est. Omnes Coelorum numerabat Contignationes & volumina. Omnes Insularum natantium, omniumque in firmamento haerentium, situs, dimensiones, naturas, populos etiam & politeias complexa est. De quibus tamen

5 adhuc silere, ingenuum videtur, ne aut *Galilaeo* fiat iniuria, qui

Nuncius Sydereus caeteros mundos, Astra scilicet nuper accersivit, sibique obnoxios

De Stella in Cygno fecit, aut *Kepplero*, cui (ut ipse de se testatur) a *Tychone Brahe* mortuo, *cura incessit, ne quid novi in coelis se inscio existeret.* Datur enim ex lege locus praeventioni: & quae prius didicerant,

10 edisserant prius. Hoc tamen a me non dedignentur accipere, nusquam *Enochum* inventum aut *Eliam*. Supera cum perlustrassem omnia, tum sicuti

— *operoso tramite scandens*
Aethereum montem, tangens vicinia solis,
15 *Hymnos ad Phoebi plectrum modulatur Alauda:*
Compressis velis, tandem ut remearet, alarum,
Tam subito recidit, ut saxum segnius iisset.

Ictu oculi, etiam & *Inferos* video in conspectu meo positos. Et perspicillis, nescio quibus, credo iisdem quibus *Gregorius Magnus*

20 & *Beda* animas amicorum, e corporum ergastulis egressorum, etiam & aliquando eorum, qui nec de facie iis noti erant, etiam & qui nunquam nati, tam feliciter semper dignoscebant, cum aut in coelos evolantes, aut vivis se immiscentes viderent, video omnes viscerum terrae meatus, omnes omnium gentium & saeculorum

---

15 *Hymnos 12° errata: Hymnus 12° Alauda 12° errata: Alanda 12°* 19 iisdem *12° errata:* iis deus *12°*: iis Deus *4°*

had liberty to wander through all places, and to survey and
reckon all the roomes, and all the volumes of the heavens, and
to comprehend the situation, the dimensions, the nature, the
people, and the policy, both of the swimming Ilands, the *Planets*,
and of all those which are fixed in the firmament. Of which, I 5
thinke it an honester part as yet to be silent, then to do *Galilaeo*
wrong by speaking of it, who of late hath summoned the other *Nuncius*
worlds, the Stars to come neerer to him, and give him an account *sydereus*
of themselves. Or to *Keppler*, who (as himselfe testifies of him- *De stella in*
selfe) *ever since* Tycho Braches *death, hath received it into his care,* 10 *Cygno*
that no new thing should be done in heaven without his knowledge.
For by the law, *Prevention* must take place; and therefore what
they have found and discovred first, I am content they speake
and utter first. Yet this they may vouchsafe to take from me,
that they shall hardly find *Enoch*, or *Elias* any where in their 15
circuit. When I had surveid al the Heavens, then *as*

> *The Larke by busie and laborious ways,*
> *Having climb'd up th'etheriall hill, doth raise*
> *His Hymnes to Phoebus Harpe, And striking then*
> *His Sailes, his wings, doth fall downe backe agen* 20
> *So suddenly, that one may safely say*
> *A stone came lazily, that came that way,*

In the twinckling of an eye, I saw all the roomes in Hell open to
my sight. And by the benefit of certaine spectacles, I know not
of what making, but, I thinke, of the same, by which *Gregory* the 25
great, and *Beda* did discerne so distinctly the soules of their
friends, when they were discharged from their bodies, and
sometimes the soules of such men as they knew not by sight,
and of some that were never in the world, and yet they could
distinguish them flying into Heaven, or conversing with living 30
men, I saw all the channels in the bowels of the Earth; and all
the inhabitants of all nations, and of all ages were suddenly made

  Margin *De stella*] *De Stello 1626*   10 *Braches 1626*: Brachcs *1611*
18 *th'etheriall 1611* errata, *1626*: *th'eternall 1611*   19 *Harpe*,] *Harpe; 1626*
20 *agen*] *agen, 1626*   21 *say*] *say, 1626*

incolas mihi repente familiares factos. Tali aliquo usum Organo,

Paleotus de
Sindone ca. 6.

sed ad aures accommodato puto *Robertum Aquinatem*, cum prolixam *Christi* in cruce pendentis Orationem excepit. Tali etiam,

4
Josephina di
Gieron.
Gracian.

qui Sermonem *Christi* in laudem patris sui *Iosephi* habitum, *Adriano Sexto* dedicavit. Surburbia autem Inferi (de utroque *Limbo* loquor & *Purgatorio*) fateor me ita negligenter praetergressum, ut nec viderem: ad nova enim, nec ante detecta, avide rapiebar. *Purgatorium* autem cum iam per annos fere 50, in Romanae Ecclesiae aliquibus angulis, a nonnullis credi videri

10 possit, (ab eo scilicet tempore, quo Vaticinia *Homeri, Virgilii*, caeterorumque *Papistarum Patriarcharum, Concilium Tridentinum* implere voluit, & non una Transubstantiatione contentum, aliam etiam statuere in animum induxit, ut *Fabulae* scilicet in *Dogmata* mutarentur) nimia diligentia indignum mihi prorsus

15 videbatur. Ad penitiora igitur progressus, vidi locum secretiorem, ipsique *Lucifero* fere proprium, ad quem ineundum iis tantum ius erat, qui ita aliquid novi in vita moliti fuerant, ut & antiquitati barbam vellerent, & dubia & anxietates, scrupulosque iniicerent, & post invectam quidvis opinandi licentiam, tandem prorsus

20 contraria iis quae ante statuta fuerant, statuerent. De quo loco,

Theo. Niem.
nemus unio.
Tra. 6. ca. 29.

aliqua nos noticia dignatus est *Lucifer*, cum abhinc annis amplius ducentis, in epistola sua ad *Cardinalem S. Sexti*, ei promittit *locum in inferiori parte sui aeterni chaos, palatio suo*. Hic de supremo loco adhuc litigare visi sunt *Bonifacius* Papa tertius, & *Mahomet*. Ille

25 de veteri religione expulsa, hic de nova inducta gloriatur: uterque magnum diluvium. Sed *Mahometum*, tum quia aliquid veteri Testamento dare videtur, tum quia quasi *Coepiscopo* usus est *Sergio*, in *Alcorano* concinnando, litem perditurum metuendum est; quia satis *Lucifero*, supremo iudici liquet, (quomodo enim id

familiar to me. I thinke truely, *Robert Aquinas* when he tooke
Christs long Oration, as he hung upon the Crosse, did use some
such instrument as this, but applied to the eare: And so I thinke
did he, which dedicated to *Adrian* 6, that Sermon which *Christ*
made in prayse of his father *Joseph*: for else how did they heare
that, which none but they ever heard? As for the *Suburbs* of Hel,
(I meane both *Limbo* and *Purgatory*) I must confesse I passed
them over so negligently, that I saw them not: and I was
hungerly caried, to find new places, never discovered before.
For *Purgatory* did not seeme worthy to me of much diligence,
because it may seeme already to have beene beleeved by some
persons, in some corners of the *Romane Church*, for about 50 yeares;
that is, ever since the Councell of *Trent* had a minde to fulfill the
prophecies of *Homer*, *Virgil*, and the other *Patriarkes* of the
Papists; and beeing not satisfied with making one *Transubstantia-*
tion, purposed to bring in another: which is, to change *fables*
into *Articles* of faith. Proceeding therefore to more inward places,
I saw a secret place, where there were not many, beside *Lucifer*
himselfe; to which, onely they had title, which had so attempted
any innovation in this life, that they gave an affront to all
antiquitie, and induced doubts, and anxieties, and scruples, and
after, a libertie of beleeving what they would; at length established opinions, directly contrary to all established before. Of
which place in *Hell*, *Lucifer* affoarded us heretofore some little
knowledge, when more than 200 yeares since, in an *Epistle* written
to the *Cardinall S. Sexti*, hee promised him a roome *in his palace, in*
the remotest part of his eternall Chaos, which I take to bee this place.
And here Pope *Boniface* 3, and *Mahomet*, seemed to contend about
the highest roome. Hee gloried of having expelled an old Religion,
and *Mahomet* of having brought in a new: each of them a great
deluge to the world. But it is to be feared, that *Mahomet* will
faile therein, both because hee attributed something to the old
Testament, and because he used *Sergius* as his fellow-bishop, in
making the *Alcoran*; whereas it was evident to the supreme
Judge *Lucifer*, (for how could he be ignorant of that, which

Paleotus de
Sindone ca. 6.

Josephina di
Gieron.
Gratian.

5

10

15

20

25

Theod. Niem.
nemus unio,
Tra. 6. ca. 29.

30

35

eum lateret, qui id Papae in mentem insinuarat?) *Bonifacium* non
solum politeiam *Israele ticam* in testamento veteri extructam,
demolitum fuisse, cum viam Pontificibus sterneret, super cervices
regum ambulandi, sed & ab omni exemplo & coadiutore absti-
5 nuisse, cum novum hoc, quod ipse *Gregorius* (Papa non adeo
insipiens, nec modestus nimis) nomen abhorruit, usurpare
satagebat. Adde etiam quod *Bonifacio* accedunt quotidie novi

Sedulius advocati: nam post emeritos fere *Franciscanos*, quorum in una
Apolog. pro
libro conform. acie, in uno capitulo, viderat eorum magister *Franciscus* 6000
li. 2. ca. 2. milites, qui cum adhuc eo vivo, in Tyrocinio militabant, 18000.

11 daemonum in auxiliis habuere, non parum *Iesuitae* ea damna
Harlay defence resarciunt; qui aliquando in suis castris 200000. alumnorum
des Jesuites fovent. Etsi enim ita semper foecundus fuerit ordo *Benedicti*, ut de

Valladerius de eo dicatur, *quotquot hodie ebulliunt novos ordines guttulas esse &*
Canoniza.
Franciscae *fonticulos, illum autem Ordinem, Oceanum, qui 52. Pontifices, 200.*
Rom. in Epist.
16 *Cardinales, 1600. Archiepiscopos, Episcopos autem 4000 emiserit,*
Sanctos autem ab Ecclesia approbatos 50000. Itaque ab eo Bonifacii
partes non mediocriter auctas fatendum sit: parum tamen est,
si ad *Iesuitas*, aut eorum Typos infirmiores, imperfectioresque,
20 *Franciscanos* conferantur. Etsi igitur *Mahometum* Novatoris
nomine dignum censent, eaque in re, nec *Bonifacio* fortasse
inferiorem, ab eo tamen ad nostra tempora, omnes fere qui eius
haeresin sequuti sunt, in unanimitate & concordia ociosa steriles
degunt, nec quid novi se produxisse gloriari possunt: cum a
25 *Bonifacio* excitati sui successores, foecundiores semper extiterint,
& nova peccata, novas Indulgentias, Idololatrias, & Regicidia
genuisse, nemine id negante, manifestum sit. Quamvis igitur ad
loca inferni vulgaria humiliaque *Turcas* aeque ac *Papistas* turmatim
descendere pie credi potest, ad locum tamen istum honorificen-

---

17 Bonifacii *Ed.*: Gregorii *12⁰*   20 *Franciscanos 12⁰ errata: Franciscanis 12⁰*:
Franciscanus 4⁰

himselfe had put into the Popes mind?) that *Boniface* had not
onely neglected, but destroyed the policy of the State of *Israel*,
established in the old *Testament*, when he prepared *Popes* a way,
to tread upon the neckes of *Princes*, but that he also abstained
from all Example and Coadjutor, when he took upon him that   5
newe Name, which *Gregorie* himselfe (a Pope neither very
foolish, nor over-modest) ever abhord. Besides that, every day
affoords new Advocates to *Boniface* his side. For since the *Fran-*
ciscans were almost worne out (of whome their General, *Francis*,   *Sedulius*
had seene 6000 souldiers in one army, that is, in one chapter   *Apolog. pro*
which, because they were then but fresh souldiers, he saw   *libro conform.*
lib. 2. cap. 2.
assisted with 18000 Divels), the *Jesuits* have much recompenced   *Harlay defence*
those decayes and damages, who sometimes have maintained in   *des Jesuites*
their Tents 200000 schollers. For though the order of *Benedict*   14
have ever bene so fruitfull, that they say of it, *That all the new*   *Valladerius de*
Orders, which in later times have broken out, are but little springs, or   *Canoniza.*
Francis. Ro. in
drops, and that Order the Ocean, which hath sent out 52 Popes, 200   *Epist.*
Cardinals, 1600 Archbishops, 4000 Bishops, and 50000 Saints approved
by the Church, and therefore it cannot be denied, but that
Boniface his part is much releeved by that Order; yet if they be   20
compared to the *Jesuits*, or to the weake and unperfect Types
of them, the *Franciscans*, it is no great matter that they have done.
Though therefore they esteeme *Mahomet* worthy of the name
of an Innovator, & therein, perchance not much inferiour to
Boniface, yet since his time, to ours, almost all which have   25
followed his sect, have lived barren in an unanimity, and idle
concord, and cannot boast that they have produced any new
matter: whereas *Boniface* his successors, awakened by him, have
ever beene fruitfull in bringing forth new sinnes, and new pardons,
and idolatries, and King-killings. Though therefore it may   30
religiously, and piously be beleeved, that *Turkes*, as well as
Papists, come daily in troupes to the ordinary and common
places of *Hell*; yet certainly to this more honourable roome,

    10-12 chapter . . . Divels), *Ed.*: chapter) . . . Divels, *1611, 1626*   Margin
Valladerius Ed.: *Volladerius 1611, 1626*   18 *50000*] *5000 1626*   33 *Hell;*]
Hell: 1626   roome,] roome *1626*

tiorem, & insignibus Novatoribus reservatum, frequentior sane
Papistis aditus est: ideoque desperandum *Mahometo* erit, nisi
Imperatores Christianos imitatus, subselliis a Papae pedibus contentus (ubi adhuc sedet) esse velit. Ad hunc autem locum accedere
5 laborant, non solum qui in rebus animam directe spectantibus
aliquid innovarunt, sed & qui in scientiis, aut moribus, aut
aliqua in re, qua animae facultates exerceri possunt, aut ad
pugnaces, & rixosas controversias excitari. Modo enim veritas
amittatur, quo id fiat modo non interest. Perraro autem aperiun-
10 tur huius loci portae, nec fere nisi intervallo saeculari. Tantum
autem mihi indulsit fatum, ut tum temporis adfuerim, & candi-
datos omnes, quique introitum ambiebant, ipsumque *Luciferum*,
qui in Cameram exteriorem, ut ipsos suas causas agentes audiret,
exierat, conspexerim. Protinus autem ut crepuit ianua, vidi
15 *Mathematicum* quendam, qui ante totus in hoc fuerat, ut *Claudium*
Ptolomaeum inveniret, irrideret, in tenebras detruderet, erecta
facie, constanti gressu, ad fores accedere: pedibus manibusque,
ipso pene neglecto *Lucifero*, pulsare, clamare, 'Mihine occlusae,
cui pervii omnes coeli? qui & ipsi terrae anima fui, motumque
20 dedi?' Novi autem ex hoc, *Copernicum* fuisse. Etsi enim de eius
vita nihil mali audieram, tamen dum in mentem venit, Paparum
asseclas, nomen & poenas *Hæresis* ad omnia fere extendisse, iisque
Bellar. de adhuc utebar ego perspicillis *Gregorianis & Bedanis*, per quae,
Purgat. li. 2.
c. 8. etiam *Origenes*, optime de Ecclesia Christiana meritus, ab aliquo
25 visus est in inferno fuisse, non haerebam amplius, quin statim
Copernicum esse agnoverim. Cui *Lucifer*, 'Quis tu? Etsi enim ex
hac ipsa audacia dignus ingressu videaris, & etiam in inferis
novum ausus es, tamen & caeteris hic adstantibus, paremque
sortem expectantibus, tibi erit satisfaciendum.' 'Nisi te ex genere
30 putarem coelestis *Luciferi* (respondit *Copernicus*) astri mihi per-
familiaris, non te dignarer hac allocutione, *Lucifer*. Is sum, qui tui

9 aperiuntur] reperiuntur 4⁰   14 Protinus 4⁰: Protinu 12⁰

reserved for especiall Innovators, the *Papists* have more frequent accesse; and therefore *Mahomet* is out of hope to prevaile, and must imitate the *Christian Emperours*, and be content to sit (as yet hee doth) at the Popes feet. Now to this place, not onely such endeavour to come, as have innovated in matters, directly 5 concerning the soule, but they also which have done so, either in the Arts, or in conversation, or in any thing which exerciseth the faculties of the soule, and may so provoke to quarrelsome and brawling controversies: For so the truth be lost, it is no matter how. But the gates are seldome opened, nor scarce oftner then 10 once in an Age. But my destiny favoured mee so much, that I was present then, and saw all the pretenders, and all that affected an entrance, and *Lucifer* himselfe, who then came out into the outward chamber, to heare them pleade their owne Causes. As soone as the doore creekt, I spied a certaine *Mathematitian*, which 15 till then had bene busied to finde, to deride, to detrude *Ptolomey*; and now with an erect countenance, and setled pace, came to the gates, and with hands and feet (scarce respecting *Lucifer* himselfe) beat the dores, and cried; 'Are these shut against me, to whom all the Heavens were ever open, who was a Soule to 20 the Earth, and gave it motion?'

By this I knew it was *Copernicus*: For though I had never heard ill of his life, and therefore might wonder to find him there; yet when I remembred, that the *Papists* have extended the name, & the punishment of Heresie, almost to every thing, and that as 25 yet I used *Gregories* and *Bedes* spectacles, by which one saw *Origen*, who deserved so well of the *Christian Church*, *burning in Hell*, I doubted no longer, but assured my selfe that it was *Copernicus* which I saw. To whome *Lucifer* sayd; 'Who are you? For though even by this boldnesse you seeme worthy to enter, 30 and have attempted a new faction even in *Hell*, yet you must first satisfie those which stand about you, and which expect the same fortune as you do.' 'Except, O *Lucifer*,' answered *Copernicus*, 'I thought thee of the race of the starre *Lucifer*, with which I am so well acquainted, I should not vouchsafe thee this discourse. 35

Bellar. de purgat. L. 2. cap. 8.

17 countenance,] countenance; *1626*

misertus, in centrum mundi detrusi, te una cum tuo ergastulo, hac terra, ad coelos ita evexi, ut nec *Deo* liceat sua vindicta frui. Ipsumque solem officiosum nimis speculatorem, & scelerum proditorem, tuique inimicum, in ima mundi abire iussi. Patebit

5 haec ianua aliquid in re aliqua novi molitis, mihi totam mundi machinam versanti, & pene novo Creatori, occludetur?' Nec quid praeterea addidit. Haesit autem meditabundus *Lucifer*, quid enim faceret? Introitum negare bene merenti, iniquum. Dare, ad summa aspiranti, periculosum. Nec enim maiora tentasse ante

10 lapsum, ipse sibi visus *Lucifer*. Habuit certe quod satis commode opponi potuit, noluit tamen eloqui, ne sibi metuere videretur. Animum autem eius perspexit, homo vafer, qui prope Cathedram stabat, *Ignatius Loyola*, ita Daemone imbutus, ut & ipsum tentasse potuit; nec id solum, sed & (quod vulgo dicitur) possidere.

15 Hic de ingressu suo certus, consciusque multarum Myriadum e sua familia, ad hunc locum anhelantium, caeteris omnibus se opposuit. Damnari non vetuit, sed dominari eos noluit. Etsi autem cum e vivis excessit, erat omnium literarum prorsus imperitus, ipsaque *Ptolemaei & Copernici* nomina ignoraret, utpote

20 cui persuaderi potuit, vocabula *Almagestum, Zenith, Nadir,* Sanctorum nomina esse, & in *Litaniam* reponenda, & *Ora pro nobis*, iis adiiciendum, postquam tamen in infernis versari coepit, a *Iesuitis* suis quotidie accedentibus, aliquid didicit. Etiam & dum in limine inferni haerebat, hoc est, a quo se Papae arbitrio manci-

25 paverat, non nihil delibavit. His instructus, ita *Copernicum* aggreditur. 'Itane *Luciferum* nostrum te tibi conciliaturum speras, si eum genere Astrorum dignatus fueris? qui ante astra condita,

I am he, which pitying thee who wert thrust into the Center of
the world, raysed both thee, and thy prison, the Earth, up into
the Heavens; so as by my meanes *God* doth not enjoy his
revenge upon thee. The Sunne, which was an officious spy, and
a betrayer of faults, and so thine enemy, I have appointed to go ₅
into the lowest part of the world. Shall these gates be open to
such as have innovated in small matters? and shall they be shut
against me, who have turned the whole frame of the world, and
am thereby almost a new Creator?' More then this he spoke not.
Lucifer stuck in a meditation. For what should he do? It seemed ₁₀
unjust to deny entry to him which had deserved so well, and
dangerous to graunt it, to one of so great ambitions, and undertakings: nor did he thinke that himselfe had attempted greater
matters before his fall. Something he had which he might have
conveniently opposed, but he was loath to utter it, least he ₁₅
should confesse his feare. But *Ignatius Loyola* which was got neere
his chaire, a subtile fellow, and so indued with the Divell, that
he was able to tempt, and not onely that, but (as they say) even
to possesse the Divell, apprehended this perplexity in *Lucifer*.
And making himselfe sure of his owne entrance, and knowing ₂₀
well, that many thousands of his family aspired to that place, he
opposed himselfe against all others. He was content they should
be damned, but not that they should governe. And though when
hee died he was utterly ignorant in all great learning, and knew
not so much as *Ptolomeys*, or *Copernicus* name, but might have ₂₅
beene perswaded, that the words *Almagest, Zenith, and Nadir,*
were Saints names, and fit to bee put into the *Litanie*, and *Ora
pro nobis* joyned to them; yet after hee had spent some time in
hell, he had learnt somewhat of his *Jesuites*, which daily came
thither. And whilst he staied at the threshold of *Hell*; that is, ₃₀
from the time when he delivered himselfe over to the Popes will,
hee tooke a little taste of learning. Thus furnished, thus hee
undertakes *Copernicus*. 'Do you thinke to winne our *Lucifer* to
your part, by allowing him the honour of being of the race of that

16 *Loyola Ed.*: Layola 1611, 1626   27 names,] names 1626   33 Do you
1611 *errata, 1626*: O you 1611

non solum in coelis fulserat, sed & eius gloriae satur, colonias suas & domicilium in hanc Monarchiam transtulit. Nobile nostro Ordini exemplum, regna longinqua perlustrandi, invadendi, occupandi. *Lucifero* nostro, eiusve asseclis honor esse possit, ex

5 Astro *Lucifero, Venere*? cuius faciem, quam dedignati semper fuimus aversatique ex hoc liquet, quod ea fere aversa praeposteraque utamur. Quin potius de *Lucifero Calaritano Episcopo*,

August. de Haeret. ca. 81. glorietur *Lucifer* noster: nec ideo tantum quia in *Haereticographis* locum invenit, ob solam animae propagationem asseveratam, sed

10 de hoc potissimum, quod primus omnium in dignitatem Imperatoriam insurgere ausus est, ipsique Imperatori nomina *Antichristi, Iudae*, aliaque stigmata inurere. Tu autem quid novi commentus es, quod *Lucifero* in lucrum cedat? Laboret, ocietur terra: quid interest? Nec enim hac confisi terrae evectione,

15 homines iterum ad Turres aedificandas, Deoque minitandum se accingunt, nec ex hoc motu terrae inferna non esse concludunt, poenasve peccantium inficiantur. Omnia ut ante credunt, peragunt. Adde quod & dignitati doctrinae tuae detrahit, & iuri tituloque ad hunc locum accedendi deroget, quod etiam vera esse

20 possunt, quae asseris. Si quid cui iuris igitur, si quid honoris, hac in re acquiratur, id totum *Clavio* nostro debetur, qui se tibi, & veritati in omnium animos gliscenti tempestive opposuit. Ille enim rixarum, ille pugnarum scholasticarum (nec quid amplius in hac re adhuc sperandum, quam ut magis necessaria, has ob

25 lites, negligantur) autor dicendus erit. Sed nec hoc nomine solum honore afficiendus, sed & ob labores eximios in *Calendario Gregoriano* exantlatos, quibus & Ecclesiae pacem, & civilia negotia

starre? who was not onely made before all the starres, but being
glutted with the glory of shining there, transferred his dwelling
and Colonies unto this Monarchy, and thereby gave our Order
a noble example, to spy, to invade, and to possesse forraine
kingdomes. Can our *Lucifer*, or his followers have any honour 5
from that starre *Lucifer*, which is but *Venus*? whose face how
much wee scorne, appeares by this, that, for the most part we
use her aversly and preposterously. Rather let our *Lucifer* glory
in *Lucifer* the *Calaritan Bishop*; not therefore because he is placed   *August. de*
amongst Heretiques, onely for affirming the propagation of the   *Hæret. cap. 81.*
soule; but especially for this, that he was the first that opposed 11
the dignity of Princes, and imprinted the names of *Antichrist*,
Judas, and other stigmatique markes upon the *Emperour*; But
for you, what new thing have you invented, by which our
Lucifer gets any thing? What cares hee whether the earth travell, 15
or stand still? Hath your raising up of the earth into heaven,
brought men to that confidence, that they build new towers or
threaten God againe? Or do they out of this motion of the earth
conclude, that there is no hell, or deny the punishment of sin?
Do not men beleeve? do they not live just, as they did before? 20
Besides, this detracts from the dignity of your learning, and
derogates from your right and title of comming to this place,
that those opinions of yours may very well be true. If therfore
any man have honour or title to this place in this matter, it
belongs wholly to our *Clavius*, who opposed himselfe opportunely 25
against you, and the truth, which at that time was creeping into
every mans minde. Hee only can be called the Author of all
contentions, and schoole-combats in this cause; and no greater
profit can bee hoped for heerein, but that for such brabbles,
more necessarie matters bee neglected. And yet not onely for 30
this is our *Clavius* to bee honoured, but for the great paines also
which hee tooke in the *Gregorian Calender*, by which both the
peace of the Church, & Civill businesses have beene egregiously

    14 have *1626*: hane *1611*   18 motion *1611 errata, 1626*: notion *1611*
33 peace] *1626 corrected*: peach *1626 uncorrected* (*ULE, KCC*); *see Introduction*
p. xlvi.
    812405   C

egregie perturbavit. Adde quod & coelum ipsum vim passum inde videtur, mandatisque eius obsecutum, adeo ut *S. Stephanus*,

Harlay defence des Jesuit. mesdi. 6.

Ioannes Baptista, caeterique qui certis diebus, statisque temporibus, ubi Reliquiae eorum asservantur, miracula edere iussi sunt,
5 iam non amplius festum ut solebant, expectant, sed decem ante
dies excitantur, & ad ea peragenda e coelis descendere coacti
sunt. Haec vere nova, & inaudita. Tua autem, non tua dicenda
sunt, cum ea, longe ante, *Heraclides, Ecphantus, Aristarchus* in
mundum protruserant, qui tamen cum caeteris Philosophantum
10 turbis inferius quiescentes, ad locum istum *Heroibus Anti-
christianis* reservatum, non aspirant. Nec adeo inter vos conveni-
tis, ut sectam ducere valeatis, cum & tu aliorum, *Tycho Brahe*
tuum, alii eius schemata ordinemque pervertunt & immutant.
Recedat igitur ad sua castra, *Horrende Imperator, Mathematiculus*
15 *iste.* Si quando patres nostri Ordinis *Decretum Cathedrale* a Papa
eliciunt, quo de fide credendum definiatur, *Terram non moveri*, &
contrariis *Anathema* infligatur, tum & Papae id statuenti, &
Copernici sectatoribus, si qui tum inter Papistas fuerint, huius loci
dignitas fortasse non denegabitur.' Annuit *Lucifer*: quiescit, ut
20 sol suus, *Copernicus*, nec verbum mussitat. Eius autem locum
occupat ab eo proximus: cui *Lucifer*, 'Et tu, quisnam es?' Ait
ille, '*Philippus Aureolus Theophrastus Paracelsus Bombast ab Hohenheim.*' Tremuit *Lucifer*, quasi a novo Exorcismo, putavitque esse
potuisse primum versum primi Ioannis capitis, qui semper in
25 Exorcismis decantatur, ex Bibliis *Hibernicis* aut *Wallicis* iam
excerptum. Cum autem nominis texturam esse agnoscit, se
colligit, & erectus, 'Quid ad *Imperatorem Satanam Luciferum
Belzebub Leviathan Abaddon* dicturus es', dixit. Subiungit ille,

troubled: nor hath heaven it selfe escaped his violence, but hath ever since obeied his apointments: so that *S. Stephen, John Baptist*, & all the rest, which have bin commanded to worke miracles at certain appointed daies, where their Reliques are preserved, do not now attend till the day come, as they were 5 accustomed, but are awaked ten daies sooner, and constrained by him to come downe from heaven to do that businesse; But your inventions can scarce bee called yours, since long before you, *Heraclides, Ecphantus*, & *Aristarchus* thrust them into the world: who notwithstanding content themselves with lower 10 roomes amongst the other Philosophers, & aspire not to this place, reserved onely for *Antichristian Heroes*: neither do you agree so wel amongst your selves, as that you can be said to have made a *Sect*, since, as you have perverted and changed the order and *Scheme* of others: so Tycho Brachy hath done by yours, and 15 others by his. Let therefore this little *Mathematitian* (dread Emperour) withdraw himselfe to his owne company. And if heereafter the fathers of our Order can draw a *Cathedrall Decree* from the Pope, by which it may be defined as a matter of faith: *That the earth doth not move*, & an *Anathema* inflicted upon all 20 which hold the contrary: then perchance both the Pope which shall decree that, and *Copernicus* his followers, (if they be Papists) may have the dignity of this place.' *Lucifer* signified his assent: and *Copernicus*, without muttering a word, was as quiet, as he thinks the sunne, when he which stood next him, entred into 25 his place. To whom *Lucifer* said: 'And who are you?' Hee answered, '*Philippus Aureolus Theophrastus Paracelsus Bombast of Hohenheim*.' At this *Lucifer* trembled, as if it were a new *Exorcisme*, & he thought it might well be the first verse of Saint *John*, which is alwaies imployed in *Exorcismes*, & might now bee 30 taken out of the *Welsh*, or *Irish Bibles*. But when hee understood that it was but the webbe of his name, hee recollected himselfe, and raising himselfe upright, asked what he had to say to the great *Emperour Sathan, Lucifer, Belzebub, Leviathan, Abaddon*.

Harlay defence des Jesuites mesdi. 6.

Margin *des Jesuites*] *dis Jesuite 1626*   19 faith] Faith *1626*   20 *Anathema 1626: Antahema 1611*   28 *Hohenheim 1611 errata, 1626: Bohenheim 1611*

'Iniuriosum tibi foret, *Gloriose Imperator*, facta mea coram te
enumerare, quasi non a te profecta fuerint omnia quae per me
Organum tuum & Canale fieri visa sunt. Cum autem potius tibi
praeco futurus sim, quam meorum facinorum buccinator, non
5 sunt silenda omnia. Praeterquam quod igitur *Medicos Methodicos*
artemque ipsam ita in contemptum adduxi, ut iam penitus
periisse videatur ipsa medicina: hoc mihi semper summum fuit
& antiquissimum, ne artem aliquam novam Canonesve certos
stabilirem. Volui enim ex incertis, laceris, lacunosis experimentis
10 meis omnia periculose hauriri. In quibus probandis, quot homines
cadavera effecti? Cumque in illa tempora inciderim, quae morbis
paradoxis abundabant, quorum fere omnium centrum erat &
cloaca, quae tum fremere incipiebat, lues venerea, certam eius
facilemque curationem omnibus spondebam, ne quenquam a
15 libidine absterrerem. Cumque omnia fere venenosa ita a natura
comparata sunt, ut sensibus ipsis ingrata se perfacile prodant, &
praecaveri possint, per me factum est, ut semota hac qualitate
proditoria, tuto exhiberi possint, nec tamen languidius officium
praestent suum. Haec omnia per Mineralia (fateor) tua exequu-
20 tus sum, ignibusque tuis; nec tamen de praemio desperandum,
quandoquidem harum innovationum primus tibi minister fuerim,
& instrumentum.' Observabat iam in fronte *Luciferi* exortam
tempestatem *Ignatius*. Erat enim ipse eiusdem cum illo tempera-
menti, & illi utique compatiebatur. Ut igitur illum a *Paracelso*
25 liberaret, 'Noli', inquit 'putare tibi hic licere ad nominis men-
suram Orationem protrahere. Fatendum est, te magna, & magno
Luciferi ministro digna ausum; cum & arte tua hominem in
Alembicis generari posse & confici gloriatus es, & etiam im-
mortalem fieri. Nec dubitandum est, quin ex Commentariis tuis,

---

3 Canale *12⁰ errata*: Cunale *12⁰*

Paracelsus replyed, 'It were an injurie to thee, ô glorious *Emperour*, if I should deliver before thee, what I have done, as thogh al those things had not proceeded from thee, which seemed to have bin done by me, thy organe and conduit: yet since I shal rather be thy trumpet herein, then mine own, some things may be uttered by me. Besides therfore that I broght all *Methodicall Phisitians*, and the art it selfe into so much contempt, that that kind of phisick is almost lost; This also was ever my principal purpose, that no certaine new Art, nor fixed rules might be established, but that al remedies might be dangerously drawne from my uncertaine, ragged, and unperfect experiments, in triall whereof, how many men have beene made carkases? And falling upon those times which did abound with paradoxicall, & unusuall diseases, of all which, the pox, which then began to rage, was almost the center and sinke; I ever professed an assured and an easy cure thereof, least I should deterre any from their licentious-nesse. And whereas almost all poysons are so disposed and conditioned by nature, that they offend some of the senses, and so are easily discerned and avoided, I brought it to passe, that that trecherous quality of theirs might bee removed, and so they might safely bee given without suspicion, and yet performe their office as strongly. All this I must confesse, I wrought by thy minerals and by thy fires, but yet I cannot dispaire of my reward, because I was thy first Minister and instrument, in these innovations.' By this time *Ignatius* had observed a tempest risen in *Lucifers* countenance: for he was just of the same temper as *Lucifer*, and therefore suffered with him in every thing and felt al his alterations. That therefore he might deliver him from *Paracelsus*, hee said; 'You must not thinke sir, that you may heere draw out an oration to the proportion of your name; It must be confessed, that you attempted great matters, and well becoming a great officer of *Lucifer*, when you undertook not onely to make a man, in your *Alimbicks*, but also to preserve him immortall. And it cannot be doubted, but that out of your *Commentaries* upon the *Scriptures*, in which you were utterly

30 name *1611 errata, 1626*: hammer *1611*

in libros sacros, in quibus prorsus ignarus eras, multi errandi
ansas & occasiones arripuerint. Ideone tamen ad penitiora haec
loca tibi patefaciendus aditus? Quid ex ipsa assecutus es medicina,
quod nos *Jesuitas* latet? Etsi enim a *Ribadeneyra* nemo e nostris
5 exhibeatur, qui de re medica scripserit, quantum tamen ea in
facultate valeamus, testem appello *Pontificem maximum*, qui nobis
privilegium concessit medicinam exercendi, eoque nomine
morientibus assistendi, quod aliis Monachis denegatum est.
Quibus enim animus tradiderat, corpus denegaret? Cum autem
10 & potestatem, ipsam quoque medicinae scientiam peritiamque
per Bullam suam omnipotentem in nos transtulisse iure putari
potest, cum praesertim qui finem alicui concedit, media etiam
ad finem necessaria, ex regulis iuris concessisse semper credatur.
Liceat autem vera coram te, *Imperator horrende*, profari. Metallis
15 istis, regni tui thesauris, visceribusque male abutuntur isti,
profanantque. Quid enim te medicamenta iuvant? Mollis certe
res est, & foeminea medicina. Cum enim *nulli Medicinae insit a*
natura, ut sanguinem educat, longe a studiis nostris amovenda erit.
Cur autem ad morbos propellendos, vitamve protrahendam, quae
20 tua sunt adhiberentur? Nonne aequum est, fratri & Collegae tuo
Pontifici Romano, qui in superficie terrae tuae dominatur, regnumque tuum quotidie auget, haec a te subsidia ministrari? Illi
debetur aurum, illi gemmae in gremio tuo delitescentes, quibus
Principes terrae per proceres magnatesque suos ad eius obsequia,
25 mandataque capessenda, illaqueare possit, & inescare: his praesertim temporibus, cum fere ubique pristina iura & vectigalia ei
passim denegentur. Illi ferrum, metallaque minus generosa, ad
machinas conficiendas, illi mineralia ad venena nata, illi nitrum

Bulla 18 in
Gretze. cont.
Hasenmull.

Mosconius de
Maiest. Eccl.
milit. cap. 7.

Mesues. Theor.
1. cap. 2.

---

13 iuris *12⁰ errata, 4⁰, 12⁰ corrected*: veris *12⁰ uncorrected (CCO, GK, WAL); see*
Introduction, p. xlv   Margin *Mesues Ed.*: *Mesnes 12⁰*

ignorant, many men have taken occasion of erring, and thereby
this kingdome much indebted to you. But must you therefore
have accesse to this secret place? what have you compassed,
even in Phisicke it selfe, of which wee *Jesuits* are ignorant? For
though our *Ribadeneyra* have reckoned none of our *Order*, which   5
hath written in *Physicke*, yet how able and sufficient wee are in
that faculty, I will bee tryed by that Pope, who hath given a
priveledge to *Jesuites* to practise *Physicke*, and to be present at
Death-beds, which is denyed to other *Orders*: for why should hee
deny us their bodies, whose soules he delivers to us? and since
he hath transferd upon us the power to practise *Physick*, he may   11
justly be thought to have transferd upon us the Art it selfe, by
the same *Omnipotent Bul*; since hee which graunts the end, is by
our *Rules* of *law* presumed to have graunted all meanes necessary
to that end. Let me (dread *Emperour*,) have leave to speake truth   15
before thee; These men abuse & profane too much thy mettals,
which are the bowels, and treasure of thy kingdome: For what
doth *Physicke* profit thee? *Physicke* is a soft, & womanish thing.
For since *no medicine doth naturally draw bloud*, that science is not
fit nor worthy of our study; Besides why should those things,
which belong to you, bee employed to preserve from diseases, or   21
to procure long life? were it not fitter, that your *brother*, and
colleague, the Bishop of *Rome*, which governes upon the face of
your earth, and gives dayly increase to your kingdome, should
receive from you these helps and subsidies? To him belonges all   25
the Gold, to him all the pretious stones, conceal'd in your entrailes,
wherby hee might baite and ensnare the *Princes* of the earth,
through their Lords, and counsellours meanes to his obedience,
and to receive his commandements, especially in these times,
when almost everywhere his auncient rights & tributes are   30
denied unto him. To him belongs your Iron, and the ignobler
mettals, to make engines; To him belong your Minerals apt for

Bulla 18 in
Gretze. cont.
Hasenmull.
Mosconius de
maiest. Eccle.
milit. cap. 7.

Mesues. Theor.
1. cap. 2.

5 *Ribadeneyra* Ed.: *Ribadenegra 1611, 1626*   9 *Death-beds*] *Deaths-bed 1626*
10 delivers] delivered *1626*   Margin *Mesues.* Ed.: *Mesnes 1611: Mosnes 1626*
20 study; Besides *1626*: study, Besides, *1611*   21 diseases *1626*: deiseases
1611   25 from you these *1611 errata, 1626*: from these *1611*   28 Lords
1626: Lord *1611*

debetur, & pulveris tormentarii elementa omnia, quo reges, regna, aulas, fora, tribunalia, demoliri possit, & devastare. Nec etiam *Novatoris* gloriam vere meretur *Paracelsus*, cuius doctrinam, ad antiquissima tempora refert *Severinus*, aliique eius sequaces.

5 Satis igitur tibi satisfactum putes, si legioni Medicorum Homicidarum, Principum in peccatis veneno sublatorum, mulierumque fucis & facierum medicamentis lascivientium, quorum quotidie ex *Academia* tua, ingens ad nos advolabit numerus, praeficiaris.' Sorte sua contentus, loco cedit *Paracelsus*; succedit *Machiavellus.*

10 Qui cum Ignatii procacitatem, proterviamque animadverterat, qui in *Advocati Regis* munus, non vocatus, se insinuarat, indignam *Florentino* ratus hanc stupidam *Copernici & Paracelsi* patientiam, hominum *Germaniam* suam redolentium, tela aliqua venenata in *Arsenati* suo *Italo* confecerat, in emeritum istum *Pampelunae*

15 militem, *Gallo-Spanicum Hybrida*, proiicienda. Cum autem videret, *Luciferum* semper eius dicta approbare, mutavit e re nata subito consilium; aliamque mentem induens, ad *Ignatium* ipsum uni *Lucifero* secundum, orationem vertere statuit; tam ut ea arte eum demulceret, quam ut *Lucifero* eum suspectum redderet, ne

20 per honores titulosque speciosos *Ignatio* oblatos, acceptosque, ipsius honor nubem aliquam aut eclipsin pateretur, aut ille homines politicos, & rerum civilium peritos, ad suas partes attrahendo, res novas in regno suo moliretur. Ita itaque locutus *Machiavellus*: 'Horrende Imperator, tuque eius Daemon vigilantis-

25 sime, *Ignati* pater, qui & huius Aulae Archicancellarius, & Praesul summus summae Synagogae,(nisi & hic quoque *Romana* Primatum suum obtinere credenda erit) liceat mihi antequam ad meipsum descendam, quaedam de stupenda vestra sapientia, huiusque regni politeia, meditari, profari, admirari. Meminisse digneris,

poyson; To him, the Saltpeter, and all the Elements of Gun-
powder, by which he may demolish and overthrow Kings and
Kingdomes, and Courts, and seates of Justice. Neither doth
Paracelsus truly deserve the name of an *Innovator*, whose doctrine,
Severinus and his other followers do referre to the most ancient 5
times. Thinke therefore your selfe well satisfied, if you be
admitted to governe in chiefe that Legion of homicide-Phisitians,
and of Princes which shall be made away by poyson in the midst
of their sins, and of woemen tempting by paintings and face-
phisicke. Of all which sorts great numbers will daily come 10
hither out of your *Academy*.'

Content with this sentence, *Paracelsus* departed; and *Machiavel*
succeeded, who having observed *Ignatius* his forwardnesse, and
saucinesse, and how, uncal'd he had thrust himselfe into the
office of *kings Atturney*, thought this stupid patience of *Copernicus*, 15
and *Paracelsus* (men which tasted too much of their *Germany*) unfit
for a *Florentine*: and therefore had provided some venemous darts,
out of his *Italian Arsenal*, to cast against this worne souldier of
Pampelune, this *French-spanish* mungrell, *Ignatius*. But when he
thought better upon it, and observed that *Lucifer* ever approved 20
whatsoever *Ignatius* sayd, he suddenly changed his purpose; and
putting on another resolution, he determined to direct his
speech to *Ignatius*, as to the principall person next to *Lucifer*, as
well by this meanes to sweeten and mollifie him, as to make
Lucifer suspect, that by these honors & specious titles offered 25
to *Ignatius*, and entertained by him, his owne dignity might bee
eclipsed, or clouded; and that *Ignatius*, by winning to his side,
politique men, exercised in civill businesses, might atempt some
innovation in that kingdome. Thus therefore he began to speake.
'Dread *Emperour*, and you, his watchfull and diligent *Genius*, 30
father *Ignatius*, *Arch-chancellor* of this *Court*, and highest *Priest*
of this highest *Synagogue* (except the primacy of the *Romane
Church* reach also unto this place) let me before I descend to my
selfe, a little consider, speake, and admire your stupendious
wisedome, and the government of this state. You may vouchsafe

19 *Pampelune 1611 errata, 1626: Pampelnus 1611*   30 Dread *1626*: Dtead *1611*

summe Imperator, quamdiu a passo *Nazareno* solitariam quandam sterilemque vitam, & Eremiticam degere coactus sis. Tandem autem (qui tuus in coelestibus imitandis semper mos fuit) ex nimio amore tuo, tibi genitus est filius dilectissimus, qui tibi stat

5 a dextra *Ignatius*. Ex utrisque autem procedit *Spiritus*, a vobis in mundum missus, qui *Mitra & Coronis* insignitus, Ecclesiam vestram militantem gubernat. Eius autem filii, quos aut in terra reliquit *Ignatius*, aut posthumi nati sunt, quam recte cum *Spiritu* tuo *Pontifice Romano*, viri *Aequivoci* dici possunt. Nec eo solum

10 sensu *aequivoci*, quo Legati Papae in tuo *Concilio Nicaeno* dicti sunt aequivoci, quia idem sentiebant, idem loquebantur, sed potius ob introductam in mundum novam Aequivocationis artem. O eximios & incredibiles *Hypercriticos*! qui non ex fragmentis marmoreis, sed ex ipsis Inferni Archivis, ex ipsa *Luciferi, Papae,*

15 *Ignatii*, virorum vere aequivocorum mente, linguam *Turris Babylonicae* diu obrutam, iterum resuscitarunt. Me autem quod attinet, O nobile par Imperatorum, etsi ut libere fatear, quaecunque a me facta sunt, ubi de *Iesuitis* erit mentio, puerilia certe dicenda erunt, (nec enim hoc mihi denegari spero, me saltem

20 Alphabetaria quaedam Elementa praestruxisse, & paedagogiam, viamque ad altiora praeparasse) taedet me tamen pudetque, una cum futili hoc chymericoque, *Copernico*, & cadaveroso vulture *Paracelso*, serie me collocari. Indignor, ianuas illas, quibus adeundis illis aliqua spes esse potuit, mihi non sponte aperiri. Mitius

25 tamen, de temeritate & societate *Paracelsi* doleo, quippe qui in lanienis & carnificinis humanis satis exercitatus, de *Iesuitarum*

to remember (great *Emperour*) how long after the *Nazarens* death, you were forced to live a solitarie, a barren, and an Eremiticall life: till at last (as it was ever your fashion to imitate heaven) out of your aboundant love, you begot this deerely beloved sonne of yours, *Ignatius*, which stands at your right hand. And from both 5 of you proceedes a spirit, whom you have sent into the world, who triumphing both with *Mitre* and *Crowne*, governes your Militant Church there. As for those sonnes of *Ignatius*, whom either he left alive, or were borne after his death, and your spirit, the Bishop of Rome; how justly & properly may they be called 10 *Equivocal* men? And not only *Equivocall* in that sence, in which the *Popes Legates*, at your *Nicene Councel* were called *Equivocal*, because *they did agree in all their opinions, and in all their words*: but especially because they have brought into the world a new art of *Equivocation*. O wonderfull, and incredible *Hypercritiques*, who, 15 not out of marble fragments, but out of the secretest Records of Hell itselfe: that is, out of the minds of *Lucifer*, the *Pope*, and *Ignatius*, (persons truly equivocall) have raised to life againe the language of the Tower of *Babel*, too long concealed, and brought us againe from understanding one an other. For my part (ô noble 20 paire of *Emperours*) that I may freely confesse the truth, all which I have done, wheresoever there shall be mention made of the Jesuites, can be reputed but childish; for this honor I hope will not be denied me, that I brought in an *Alphabet*, & provided certaine Elements, & was some kind of schoolmaister in pre- 25 paring them a way to higher undertakings; yet it grieves me, and makes me ashamed, that I should be ranked with this idle and Chymaericall *Copernicus*, or this cadaverous vulture, *Paracelsus*. I scorne that those gates, into which such men could conceive any hope of entrance, should not voluntarily flie open to mee: 30 yet I can better endure the rashnesse and fellowship of *Paracelsus*, then the other: because hee having beene conveniently practised in the butcheries, and mangling of men, hee had the reason to

gratia bene sperare potuit. Qua & ego via incedebam semper;
ideoque sacrificia *Gentium & Iudaeorum*, quae sanguinis effusione
fere peracta sunt, (quibus non solum populus, sed & ipsi Sacerdotes, ad res magnas animati erant) mollibus *Christianorum*
5 sacrificiis praeferebam. Vellem sane, si mihi optio daretur,
panem quam vinum, Romanam Ecclesiam a populo sustulisse,
cum in hoc aliqua saltem species sanguinis effingi poterat. Nec
tu *Reverende Antistes Ignati*, ab hoc abhorruisti, qui cum primam
aetatem bellis castrisque consecraras, post a vulnere recepto
10 inutilis redditus, & ineptus, non solum de bello spirituali
Ecclesiae inferendo serio cogitasti, sed & sicariis tuis vias in
regum cubicula aperuisti. Quam dignitatem, non soli ordini tuo
reservasti, sed (etsi fatendum sit fomitem & fundamentum huius
doctrinae apud vos manere, vobisque peculiare esse) tamen (qua
15 summa praeditus es liberalitate) non dedignatus es vicaria opera,
aliorumque manibus, his in negotiis aliquando usum fuisse. Vobis
igitur, animos suos, & fortitudinem debent tam illi qui toties
Angliam frustra aggressi sunt, quam qui in *Gallia*, ingentes ausus
suos ad finem perduxere. Si tamen nec nisi *Novatoribus*, iisque
20 solis in re *Christiana* versatis, idque magno cum eorum damno &
detrimento, aditus iste decernendus sit, non video quin proximus
a *Iesuitis* etiam accersitus introeam ego: qui non solum vias
edocui, quibus per perfidiam & Religionis simulationem, res-
publicae liberae ab uno aliquo occupari possint & usurpari, sed
25 & populum ea iniuria affectum, artibus meis armavi, quibus inter
se tutius conspirare, seque de Principe ulcisci, tyrannum tollere,

---

19 perduxere *12⁰ errata*: perducere *12⁰*   22 accersitus *12⁰ errata*: accersitis
12⁰

hope for favour of the Jesuites: for I my selfe went alwaies that way of bloud, and therefore I did ever preferre the sacrifices of the *Gentiles*, and of the *Jewes*, which were performed with effusion of bloud (whereby not only the people, but the Priests also were animated to bold enterprises) before the soft and wanton 5 sacrifices of *Christians*. If I might have had my choyce, I should rather have wished, that the *Romane Church* had taken the *Bread*, then the *Wine*, from the people, since in the wine there is some colour, to imagine and represent blood. Neither did you, (most Reverend *Bishop* of this *Dioces*, *Ignatius*) abhorre from this 10 way of blood. For having consecrated your first age to the wars, and growne somewhat unable to follow that course, by reason of a wound; you did presently begin to thinke seriously of a spirituall warre, against the *Church*, and found meanes to open waies, even into Kings chambers, for your executioners. Which 15 dignitie, you did not reserve onely to your own *Order*, but (though I must confesse, that the foundation, and the nourish-ment of this Doctrine remaines with you, and is peculiar to you,) out of your infinite liberalitie, you have vouchsafed sometime, to use the hands of other men in these imploiments. And there- 20 fore as well they, who have so often in vaine attempted it in *England*, as they which have brought their great purposes to effect in *Fraunce*, are indebted only to you for their courage and resolution. But yet although the entrance into this place may be decreed to none, but to Innovators, and to onely such of 25 them as have dealt in *Christian* businesse; and of them also, to those only which have had the fortune to doe much harme, I cannot see but that next to the Jesuites, I must bee invited to enter, since I did not onely teach those wayes, by which thorough *perfidiousnesse* and *dissembling of Religion*, a man might possesse, 30 and usurpe upon the liberty of free *Commonwealths*; but also did arme and furnish the people with my instructions, how when they were under this oppression, they might safeliest conspire, and remove a *tyrant*, or revenge themselves of their *Prince*, and

5 before *1611 errata, 1626*: befote *1611*   18–19 to you,) . . . liberalitie, *Ed.*: to you, . . . liberalitie,) *1611, 1626*

& damnum resarcire valeant: unde utrinque (tam a Principe quam a populo) messem uberem, & nobile huic regno incrementum attulerim.' Hac oratione non mediocriter permotum notavi *Luciferum*, & ad *Machiavellum* inclinare. Nam *Patriarcham* quen-
5 dam *Laicorum* (ut dicitur) eum agnovit. Viderat autem semper *Clerum Romanum* quotidie, facile, sponte, turmatim, ad inferos devolvere, utpote qui in conscientiam peccare sueti, *Laicos* autem ex desidia quadam & negligentia, sola omissione plaerunque delinquere. Praemia igitur ex aequo se debere *Machiavello*
10 putavit, qui eos ita sopitos implicitosque ad egregia cruentaque facinora excitasset. Adde etiam quod, cum *Ignatio* introitus negari non potuit, cuius ambitiones & molitiones perspectas habuit *Lucifer*, idoneus ei videbatur *Machiavellus*, & necessarius, qui cum altero componeretur; ut aequata per illos lance, ipse
15 tuto viveret, & venena inter se commista innocua redderentur. Hoc autem *Ignatium* latere non potuit, Daemone ipso solertiorem, & *Lucifero* Luciferiorem. Prodit igitur *Ignatius*, ad genua se devolvit, pronusque in terram *Luciferum* adorabat. Nec haec certe per *Vasquium* Idololatria dicenda erit, quia quem putavit
20 verum Deum, etsi in Daemonis specie adoravit. Clamavit autem, intonuitque *Ignatius*

Tanto fragore boatuque,
Ut nec sulphureus pulvis, quo tota Britanna
Insula, per nimbos Lunam volitasset ad imam,
25 *Si cum substratus Camerae, conceperat ignem,*
Aequando fremeret nostro fragore boatuque.

Haec tandem, cum articulatius loqui potuit, locutus est: 'In te, *Nefande Imperator, Pontificemque Romanum, Imaginarium* tuum, (sive

7 *Laicos* Ed.: *Laicis* 12⁰

redeeme their former losses; so that from both sides, both from *Prince* and *People*, I brought an aboundant harvest, and a noble encrease to this kingdome.' By this time I perceived *Lucifer* to bee much moved with this Oration, and to incline much towards *Machiavel*. For he did acknowledge him to bee a kind of *Patriarke*, of those whom they call *Laymen*. And he had long observed, that the *Clergie* of *Rome* tumbled downe to *Hell* daily, easily, voluntarily, and by troupes, because they were accustomed to sinne against their conscience, and knowledge; but that the *Layitie* sinning out of a slouthfulnesse, and negligence of finding the truth, did rather offend by ignorance, and omission. And therefore he thought himselfe bound to reward *Machiavel*, which had awakened this drowsie and implicite *Layitie* to greater, and more bloody undertakings. Besides this, since *Ignatius* could not bee denied the place, whose ambitions and turbulencies *Lucifer* understood very wel, he thoght *Machiavel* a fit and necessarie instrument to oppose against him; that so the skales beeing kept even by their factions, hee might governe in peace, and two poysons mingled might doe no harme. But hee could not hide this intention from *Ignatius*, more subtil then the *Devill*, and the verier *Lucifer* of the two: Therefore *Ignatius* rushed out, threw himselfe downe at *Lucifers* feet, and grovelling on the ground adored him. Yet certainly, *Vasques* would not cal this *idolatry*, because in the shape of the *Devil* hee worshipped him, whom hee accounted the true *God*. Here *Ignatius* cried, and thundred out,

> *With so great noise and horror,*
> *That had that powder taken fire, by which*
> *All the Isle of Britaine had flowne to the Moone,*
> *It had not equalled this noise and horror.*

And when he was able to speak distinctly, thus hee spoke. 'It cannot be said (unspeakable *Emperour*) how much this obscure *Florentine* hath transgressed against thee, and against the *Pope*

21. q. 4.
Omnis iactura
cum *Gratiano* verbum accipiatur, qui scripturas sanctas *Imagi-*
narias appellat, sive cum illis qui *Imaginarios* vocant qui Imaginem

Modest. in ver.
milit.
ferunt *Imperatoris*) in Ordinem denique nostrum, immane quantum peccare ausus est tenebrio iste *Florentinus?* Ecquis enim
5 ante illum hoc genus iniuriae, calumniaeve commentus est, ut
Luciferum adulari, captare, irretire se posse speraret? Certe quem
quis adulatur, laudesque, sua opinione non debitas offert, eum
longe semet inferiorem putat, eumque captivum ducere, & de eo
triumphum agere, sibi non iniuste videtur. Irrisor semper est,
10 qui adulatur, aut paedagogus. Subesse enim potest, & in ipsa
adulatione, honestum quoddam erudiendi genus. Cum enim viri
principes, iis virtutibus quae ad munus suum necessariae sunt,
imbui dicuntur & ornari, tacita inde adhortatione, ad eas
acquirendas excitantur. Tene autem iste irridere ausus, aut
15 (quae maior iniuria) docere? Illumve ex animo laudes tuas effari

32. q. 2. Pudor
credendum erit, & non potius *Gratiani* levitatem imitari, qui te
Principem mundi, ita ut *Rex Scacchorum,* & *Cardinalis Ravennae,* per
derisionem dici, scribit? Vir iste, cum nuper in vivis degeret,
tantum suo ingenio tribuebat, ut nihil se auxiliis insinuationi-
20 busque tuis debere putavit. Tantumque abfuit, ut te invocaret,
tibi immolaret, ut nec regnum tuum agnoverit, nec etiam te in
rerum natura esse crediderit. Fateor quidem eandem eum habuisse
& de Deo sententiam, eoque iure aliquem hic ei deberi locum;
Paganis etiam, & Gentilium Idololatris superiorem. Inest enim
25 in omni Idololatria falsoque cultu, aliqua Religio, aliquid etiam
perversae simplicitatis, & quod humilitatem sapit, a quibus iste
longe abfuit, cum penitus Deum esse animo negaverit. Quia
autem haec serio putavit, & vera esse quae affirmabat, credidit,

13 tacita *12⁰ errata:* tanta *12⁰*

thy *image-bearer*, (whether the word bee accepted, as *Gratian*
takes it, when he calles the *Scriptures*, Imaginarie Bookes; or as
they take it, which give that style to them who carrie the
Emperours image in the field;) and last of all against our Order.
Durst any man before him, thinke upon this kinde of injurie, and
calumnie, as to hope that he should be able to flatter, to catch,
to entrap *Lucifer* himselfe? Certainely whosoever flatters any
man, and presents him those praises, which in his owne opinion
are not due to him, thinkes him inferiour to himselfe and makes
account, that he hath taken him prisoner, and triumphs over
him. Who ever flatters, either he derides, or (at the best)
instructs. For there may bee, even in flattery, an honest kind of
teaching, if Princes, by being told that they are already indued
with all vertues necessary for their functions, be thereby taught
what those vertues are, and by a facile exhortation excited to
endeavour to gaine them. But was it fit that this fellow, should
dare either to deride you, or (which is the greater injury) to
teach you? Can it be beleeved, that he delivers your praises
from his heart, and doth not rather herein follow *Gratians* levity;
who saies, *That you are called Prince of the world, as a king at Chests,
or as the Cardinall of Ravenna, onely by derision?* This man, whilst he
lived, attributed so much to his own wit, that hee never thought
himselfe beholden to your helps, and insinuations; and was so
farre from invoking you, or sacrificing to you, that he did not so
much as acknowledge your kingdome, nor beleeve that there was
any such thing in nature, as you. I must confesse, that hee had
the same opinion of God also, and therefore deserves a place here,
and a better then any of the *Pagan* or *Gentile* idolaters: for, in
every idolatrie, and false worship, there is some Religion, and
some perverse simplicitie, which tastes of humilitie; from all
which, this man was very free, when in his heart he utterly
denyed that there was any God. Yet since he thoght so in
earnest, and beleeved that those things which hee affirmed were
true, hee must not be rancked with them, which having beene

Margin *Imaginarium 1611* errata, 1626: Imag. tuum 1611   21 q. 4 Omnis Ed.:
21. q. Omnis 1611, 1626
812405   D

non illis adaequandus erit, qui verum Deum satis edocti, in
eius inimici castris tamen militarunt. Nec nobis vitio verti

Flagel. Daemo.
Menghi.
debet, quod aliquando in *Exorcismis* male a nobis audias; *Haereti-*
cum, Ebriosum, Susurronem, Bestiam Scabiosam te vocemus, *Elementa*
5 *ne te recipiant coniuremus, indissolubilem damnationem, cruciatumque*
mille millies solito maiorem minitemur. Haec enim ex tacito pacto inter
nos fieri satis nosti, & ex mysteriis, huic *Neophytae* & in *Synagoga*
nostra, *Catechumeno,* minime patefaciendis. Quod etiam de *Aqua*
lustrali, & de *Agnis Dei,* quae te horrere prudenter fingis, agno-
10 scendum est. Quibus certe si inesset vis aliqua, corpora morbis,
animas peccatis, elementa Daemonibus, impressionibusque mali-

Summa Bul-
larii, verbo
Agnus Dei.
gnis purgandi (uti ex versibus *Urbani* quinti cum suis *Agnis* ad
Gregorium Imperatorem missis satis apparet) aequum certe fuisset,
ut in illos versus vires suas exercuissent, &, si non *Haeresibus,* at
15 saltem *Barbarie* purgassent & *Soloecismis,* ne nihil in illis verum
esse *Haeretici* dicerent, nisi quod in fine habetur,

Parsque minor tantum tota valet integra quantum.

Quae autem in *Exorcismis,* praeter alios, ausi sunt nostrae familiae
homines, privilegio speciali tribuendum est, quo nobis licentia
20 datur, Daemoniacos de re quavis interrogandi; cum alii omnes
ad ea solum quae rem natam spectant, negotiumque quod prae
manibus habent, misere obligentur. Quod privilegium, etsi nec
a *Vicario* tuo, *Pontifice Romano,* nec a te certe manasse puto,
laudandus tamen Cottonus noster, qui cum de quaestionibus
25 seditiosis Daemoniacae proponendis interrogatus esset, ut se
liberaret, tale privilegium ementiri ausus est, & audacia inaudita,

13 missis *12⁰ errata:* missi *12⁰*

sufficiently instructed of the true God, and beleeving him to be
so, doe yet fight against him in his enemies armie. Neither ought
it to be imputed to us as a fault, that sometimes in our *exorcismes*
wee speake ill of you, and call you *Hereticke*, and *Drunkard*, and   *Flagel. Daemon*
Whisperer, and *scabbed Beast*, and *Conjure the elements that they should*   *Menghi.*
not receive you, and threaten you with *Indissoluble Damnation, and*   6
torments a thousand thousand times worse then you suffer yet. For these
things, you know, are done out of a secret covenant and contract
betweene us, & out of *Mysteries*, which must not bee opened to
this *Neophite*, who in our *Synagogue* is yet but amongst the   10
Cathecumeni. Which also we acknowledge of *Holy Water*, and
our *Agnus Dei*, of which you doe so wisely dissemble a feare,
when they are presented to you: For certainly, if there were any
true force in them, *to deliver Bodies from Diseases, soules from sinnes,*
and the Elements from Spirits, and malignant impressions, (as in the   15
verses which *Urban* the fift sent with his *Agnus Dei* to the   *Summa Bullarii*
Emperour it is pretended), it had beene reason, that they should   *verbo Agnus*
first have exercised their force upon those verses, and so have   *Dei*
purged and delivered them, if not from Heresie, yet from
Barbarousnesse, and *solaecismes*; that Heretiques might not   20
justly say, there was no truth in any of them, but onely the last;
which is

> *That the least peece which thence doth fall,*
> *Will doe one as much good as all.*

And though our *Order* have adventured further in *Exorcismes*   25
then the rest, yet that must be attributed to a speciall priviledge,
by which wee have leave to question any possessed person, of
what matters we will; whereas all other Orders are miserably
bound to the present matter, and the businesse then in hand.
For, though I do not beleeve, that either from your selfe, or   30
from your *vicar* the *Pope*, any such priviledge is issued; yet our
Cotton deserves to be praised, who being questioned, how he
durst propose certaine seditious Interrogatories to a possessed
person, to deliver himselfe, fained such a priviledge; and with

---

17 pretended), it *Ed.*: pretended.) It *1611, 1626*

novoque falsificandi genere *Luciferi* Chirographum sigillumque
(ab eo enim solo proficisci potuit) effingere. Porro extra hanc
in *Exorcismis* libertatem, quam tibi semper nos exhibeamus
4 humiles & mancipatos, non aliunde quaerendum est, quam ex

Lettera di actis peruanis, ubi de *Barcena* nostro legitur, eum, cum profunda
Diego Torres.
nocte, sine teste eum in cubiculo salutarat aliquis e tuis Angelis,
protinus e Cathedra surrexisse, locumque illum Diabolo, quem
longe se digniorem praedicabat, resignasse. De iniuriis autem
Pontifici Romano, ab hoc *Florentino* illatis, etsi permulta dicenda
10 essent, satis tamen ex hoc uno animus eius dignosci potest, quod
crimina vulgaria, popularia, tantoque viro indigna ei attribuat.
Genus accusationis est parcius laudare: & eius dignitati detrahi-
tur, cuius cum laudes exiguas proferimus, omniaque tamen dixisse
videri volumus, maiora reticemus. Viderat fortasse iste Catalogos
15 aliquos *Casuum Reservatorum,* qui quotannis a Papis augentur;
putavitque ideo Papas ea peccata reservasse, ut ea soli patrarent.
Sed aut ignarus est, aut illis iniquus nimis. Illine licentiam pec-
Dist. 32. Is qui. candi populo ademisse censendi erunt, qui Concubinas non
tantum dari patiuntur, sed aliquando iusserunt: quique meretri-
20 cibus partem patrimonii sui *S. Petrum* debere volunt? Mulieres-
Ibid. Vidua que infami illo nomine meretricum onerari nolunt, donec 23000
Scappus de Iure hominum admiserint. Cuius etiam Religionis professi, Academicos
non Script. L.1.
ca. 54. meretrices in domo retinentes expelli vetant, quia *praesumendum*
24 (aiunt) *Scholares sine Meretricibus nolle vivere.* Illene a peccatis alios
Sum. Angel. absterrere velle putandus, qui ita illorum securitati prospicit, ut
ver. Papa N.1.
doceat in omnibus secundae tabulae praeceptis, totiusque legis
moralis posse a se dispensari: nec ea *Decalogi praecepta principia*
dici posse, nec conclusiones necessario a primariis deductas? Ideoque
(uti semper hoc docendi genus coluit) exemplo Regulam

3 tibi] *the 12⁰ errata gives* ubi *as an error to be corrected to* tibi; *but none of the*
copies examined reads ubi   Margin Diego *12⁰ errata:* Biego *12⁰*   17 Illine
12⁰ errata: Illinc *12⁰*   Margin *Dist. 34. Ed.: Dist.* 32 *12⁰*   22 Religionis *Ed.:*
Religionem *12⁰*   24 peccatis *12⁰ errata:* piaculis *12⁰*

an un-heard-of boldnesse, and a new kind of falsifying, did (in a
manner) counterfeit *Lucifers* hand and seale, since none but he
onely could give this priviledge; But, if you consider us out of
this liberty in *Exorcismes*, how humble and servile we are towards
you, the Relations of *Peru* testifie inough, where it is recorded, 5
that when one of your angels at midnight appeared to our *Barcena*
alone in his chamber, hee presently rose out of his chaire, and
gave him the place, whom he professed to bee farre worthier
thereof, then he was. But to proceed now to the injuries, which
this fellow hath done to the *Bishop* of *Rome*, although very much 10
might be spoken, yet by this alone, his disposition may bee
sufficiently discerned, that he imputes to the *Pope*, vulgar and
popular sinnes, farre unworthy of his greatnesse. Weake praising,
is a kind of Accusing, and wee detract from a mans honour, if
when wee praise him for small things, and would seeme to have 15
said all, we conceale greater. Perchance this man had seen some
of the *Catalogues* of *Reserv'd Cases*, which every yeare the *Popes*
encrease, and he might thinke, that the *Popes* did therefore
reserve these sinnes to themselves, that they only might com-
mit them. But either hee is ignorant, or injurious to them. For, 20
can they bee thought to have taken away the libertie of sinning
from the people, who do not onely suffer men to keepe *Concu-*
bines, but sometimes doe command them? who make *S. Peter*
beholden to the *stewes*, for part of his revenue: and who
excuse women from the infamous name of whore, till they have 25
delivered themselves over to 23000 men? The Professors of which
Religion teach, *that Universitie men, which keep whores in their*
chambers, may not be expeld for that, because it ought to be presumed
before hand, that schollers will not live without them. Shal he be
thought to have a purpose of deterring others from sinne, which 30
provides so well for their security, that he teaches, that he *may*
dispense in all the commaundements of the second Table, & in all moral
law, and that those commandements of the second table can neither be
called Principles, nor Conclusions, necessarily deduced from Principles?
And therefore, (as they ever love that manner of teaching) hee 35

Margin content:
Litera di Diego Torres
Dist. 34. Is qui.
Ibid. Vidua
Scappus de iure non script. L.1. cap. 54.
Summa Angel. verb. Papa. N. 1.

Margin *Dist. 34 Ed.*: *Dist. 32 1611, 1626*

illustravit, & de sorore ducta dispensationem dedit? quique in uno suo horreo, urbe *Roma* tot reposuit indulgentias, ut nemini difficile sit, una aliave hora 100000 annorum inde expromere

Privilegium remissiones? Quam luculentus huius liberalitatis Pontificiae
Mendican.
verbo. Indul. testis est *Leo 10.* qui dicentibus semel Orationem Dominicam, &

6 nomen *Iesu* (absit horror a verbo) ter iterantibus, 3000. annos concessit? Quam profusus aut *Dispensator* aut *Calculator Bonifacius,* qui tot in una *Lateranensi* Ecclesia Indulgentias agnoscit, ut *nisi a solo Deo numerari non possint.* Quid quod non solum plenaria

10 detur ipsis *Franciscanis,* sed & eorum parentibus; etiam & in eorum habitu morientibus, etiam & id petentibus, etiam & illo post mortem indutis, etsi non petierant; & quinque annorum indulgentia habitum osculantibus. Et tandem *Clemens 7* privilegio uni Ordini dato, (quod iam, ut & omnia alia, Iesuitis commune

15 factum est) locum aliquem iis subiectum visitanti, aut si eum locum nequeat alium quemvis, aut si nec id possit, etiam illud volenti, Indulgentias omnes impertit *concessas & concedendas in orbe universo.* Et quamvis verum sit si in illis Indulgentiis, certa pecuniae summa determinetur (quod plaerunque fit) pauperem

20 qui id praestare nequit, etsi satis de peccatis doleat, nullum tamen inde consequi beneficium, easque *Gerson* vocare ausus est fatuas & superstitiosas, quae pro una Oratione enunciata 20000. annorum largiantur, tamen Pontificum animum liberalem, nec in peccatis sibi reservandis adeo solicitum, satis superque

25 testatur. Si autem in centum annorum curriculo, aliquis e faece populi unus, ob *Sodomiam* ultimo tradatur supplicio, idque non tam ob admissam culpam, quam ob ius *Principibus Ecclesiasticis* debitum, ab illo ereptum & usurpatum, minus certe dolendum

23 largiantur *12⁰ errata*: largiatur *12⁰*

did illustrate his *Rule* with an Example, & dispensed in a mariage
between *Brother* and *Sister*, and hath hoorded up so many
Indulgencies in one barne, the citie of *Rome*, that it is easie for any
man in an houre, or two, to draw out Pardons inough for
100000 yeares. How cleare a witnesse of this liberality is *Leo* 10? 5
who only for rehearsing once the *Lords* praier, and thrise repeating the name of *Jesu* (bee it spoken heere without horrour) hath
given 3000 yeares indulgence. How profuse a *Steward* or
Auditor was *Boniface*, who acknowledges so many *Indulgences* to
be in that one *Church* of *Lateran*, *that none but God can number them?* 10
Besides these, plenary Indulgences are given, not only to the
Franciscans themselves, but to their *Parents* also: and to any which
dies in their habit; and to any which desire that they may do so;
and to those who are wrapped in it after death, though they did
not desire it; and five yeares *Indulgence* to those who doe but 15
kisse it. And at last, *Clement* 7. by a priviledge first given to one
Order, (which since is communicated to our Order, as the
priviledges of all other Orders are) gave to any who should but
visite a place belonging to them, or any other place, if hee could
not come thither: or if he could come to no such place, yet if he 20
had but a desire to it, *All indulgences which had beene graunted, or*
heereafter should be graunted in the universal world. And though it
be true, that if in any of these Indulgences a certaine sum of
money were limited to bee given (as for the most part it is;) a
poore man, which could not give that money, though he were 25
never so contrite for his sins, could have no benefit thereby: and
though *Gerson* durst call those Indulgences *foolish,* and *super-*
stitious, which gave 20000. yeares pardon for rehearsing one
praier, yet they do aboundantly testifie the *Popes* liberall disposition, and that he is not so covetous in reserving sinnes to 30
himselfe; But if perchance once in an hundred yeares, some one
of the scumme of the people be put to death for *Sodomy*; and that,
not so much for the offence, as for usurping the right of the
Ecclesiastique Princes, wee must not much lament nor grudge at

18 priviledges *Ed.*: priviledge *1611, 1626*   25 which] who *1626*
32 scumme *1611 errata, 1626*: sonnes *1611*

est aut queritandum, cum solum ad interrumpendam prae-
scriptionem fiat, in quam sibi vindicandam, proclives semper
Laici fuere. Nec enim ita avarus in hoc genere deliciarum *Papa*

Theo. Niem.
Nemus Unio
Trac. 6. c. 29.

est, quin id etiam delibent *Cardinales* sui, quos *Carpidineros*
(elegantia certe tuis *Secretariis, Monachis* scilicet, peculiari) in
6 Epistola tua ad eorum unum scripta tibi visum est nuncupare.

Rodol. Cupers.
de Eccles.
univer. fol. 4.

Cum enim ita in *Papam* compaginentur *Cardinales,* ipsumque eius
corpus fiant, ut *nec sanguinem in febre emittere possint, nisi eius licentia*
9 *prius impetrata,* quid illis denegandum erit? aut quod peccatum

Azor. par. 2.
L.4. c.1.
Mosconius de
Maiest. Eccl.
Militant. c. 5.
Ibid. Idem. c.6.
Scappus de Iure
non script. L.1.
cap. 25.

200. illorum speciosa privilegia effugere potest? *quos ex Ecclesiae*
Hierarchia, non magis quam ipsos Episcopos, Papa tollere potest, cum
& a Deo instituti fuerant, Apostolique prius Cardinales erant quam
Episcopi. Quos etiam in Creatione, *Fratres* appellat, & *Principes*
mundi, Orbisque terrarum *Coniudices*; &, ut nihil desit, *Tot Reges*
15 *sunt, quot Cardinales.* O corpus horrendum; & ut in multis, ita in
hoc insigniter monstrosum, quod speciem suam propagare non

Azor. ubi
supra.

valent; cum *nec omnes Cardinales, sede iam vacante, Cardinalem creare*
possint. His certe, peccatorum non magis invidet Papa, plurali-
tatem, quam beneficiorum. Etiam & *Borgiam,* hac dignitate
20 gaudere voluit, ut plura scelera uno actu, ingeniosa impietate
congesserit, quam, quod sciam, ex ipsis Pontificibus, aliquis
conatus sit. Non enim solum fibulam solvit, pudicitiaeque suae
fraena laxavit, sed secunda ambitione exardescens, sexum mutare
voluit. Iuvenem autem, & imberbem, ceu fructus agrestes
25 fastidivit. Nec enim satis a sexu muliebri discessisse alias sibi
videbatur, nisi virilem haberet, venerabilem, barbaque specta-
bilem Venerem. Nec ibi consistit: pergit ingeniosa libido.

that, since it is onely done to discontinue, and interrupt a
praescription, to gaine which Title, the *Layety* hath ever beene
very forward against the *Clergie*: for even in this kinde of his
delicacies, the *Pope* is not so reserved and covetous, but that he
allowes a taste thereof to his *Cardinals*, whom you once called
Carpidineros, (by an elegancy proper onely to your *Secretaries*,
the *Monkes*) in an *Epistle* which you writ to one of that Colledge:
For since, the *Cardinals* are so compacted into the Pope, and so
made his owne body: *That it is not lawfull for them, without licence*
first obtained from him, to be let bloud in a Fever, what may be
denied unto them? Or what kind of sin is likely to be left out of
their glorious priviledges, which are at least 200? *Which Order*
the Pope can no more remove out of the Ecclesiastique Hierarchy, then
hee can Bishops; both because Cardinals were instituted by God, and
because the Apostles themselves were Cardinals before they were Bishops.
Whome also in their creation he stiles *his brothers, and Princes of*
the world, & Co-judges of the whole earth: and to perfect all: *That*
there are so many Kings as there are Cardinals. O fearefull body; and as
in many other things, so in this especialy monstrous, that they
are not able to propagate their species: *For all the Cardinals in*
a vacancy are not able to make one Cardinal more. To these men
certainly the Pope doth no more grudge the plurality of sins,
then he doth of Benefices. And he hath beene content, that even
Borgia should enjoy this dignity, so that hee hath heaped up,
by his ingenious wickednesse, more sorts of sins in one Act,
then (as far as I know) any the *Popes* themselves have attempted.
For he did not only give the full reine to his licentiousnesse, but
raging with a second ambition, hee would also change the Sex.
Therein also his stomacke was not towardes young beardlesse
boyes, nor such greene fruit: for hee did not thinke, that hee
went farre inough from the right Sex, except hee had a manly, a
reverend, and a bearded Venus. Neither staied he there; but his

Margin notes:
Money-takers
Theod. Niem. Nemus unio Tract. 6. c. 29.
Rodol. Cupers de Eccles. uni- ver. fol. 4.
Azor. par. 2. L. 4. c. 1. Mosconius de maiest. Eccles. Milit. c. 5. Ibidem.
Idem. c. 6.
Scappus de Iure non script. L. 1 c. 25.
Azor. ubi supra.

6 *Secretaries 1626: Secritaries 1611*   Margin *Theod. Ed.: Theol. 1611, 1626*
Margin *Mosconius Ed.: Moseonius 1611, 1626*   17 perfect *1611 errata, 1626:*
profit *1611*   23 Benefices *1611 errata, 1626: Boniface 1611*   24 should
1626: shoud *1611*   24–6 so that hee . . . know) any *Ed.:* if hee . . . know) as
any *1611, 1626*

Paparum exoletos tamen solicitare non dignatur. Voluit ad
Civium *Sodomae* licentiam pertigisse, qui *Angelos* inire ambiebant:
quo potuit modo eos imitatus, e sorte & portione Domini,
hominem e *Clero* sumit. Maius quiddam se fecisse ratus, cum
5 etiam Dei Creatorem, Sacerdotem, sibi obnoxium fecisset. Nec
tamen hunc in choro quaesivit, aut claustro, sed ut satis mon-
strosam *Venerem*, haberet, *Mitratam* etiam voluit. Nec adhuc in
Auge prodigiosa eius lascivia; non certe. Quod addi potuit,
addidit. Virum, Clericum, Episcopum, non muneribus, non
10 precibus aggressus est, sed vi stupravit, rapuitque. Cum igitur
ex plenitudine potestatis, ad ea genera peccatorum deveniant

Plat. in vit. Papae, quae & exemplo carent & nomine, ita ut Papa *Paulus*
Adrian. I. *Venetus*, qui faciem fucis tingens, foemina videri maluit, *Dea*
Cybeles, diceretur (nec sine mysterio, cum huic numini Cinoedi
15 sacri sunt) nec nisi praeventionis privilegio usi, suam aliis
licentiam impertiunt, male indigneque praevaricatur loquaculus
iste cum Paparum dignitati satisfactum putet, si crimina aliis
communia illis imputentur. Imperiorum translatio, Regnorum
ruinae, Regum Excommunicationes, depositiones, incendia,
20 bella, eorum insignia, & characteres proferenda erant. Etsi enim
exempla de Imperiis a Papa mutatis, tam saepe a nostris decantata,
vera non sint, nec quid eiusmodi a Papis antiquis perpetratum
fuerit, cum tamen nostri Ordinis politici caeteris sagaciores,
perspectum habeant, quantum ad Ecclesiae incrementum con-
25 ducat, haec in principes iurisdictio temporalis, non solum id
sibi licere Papis persuademus, sed & etiam antiquitus ab illis
factitatum. Ideoque *Canones Historiasque* invitas quamvis ad hanc
sententiam detorquendas, curavimus. Etsi enim unus e nostris,

Apologia pro nobilem illum *Canonem, Nos Sanctorum*, enervet, quo saepe haec
Garneto.

23 Ordinis *Ed.*: Ordines *12⁰*

witty lust proceeded further: yet he sollicited not the *Minions*
of the *Popes*; but striving to equall the licentiousnesse of *Sodomits*,
which would have had the *Angels*; to come as neare them as hee
could, hee tooke a *Cleargy-man*, one of the portion and lot of the
Lord: and so made the maker of *God*, a *Priest* subject to his lust; 5
nor did hee seeke him out in a Cloyster, or Quire; but that his
Venus might bee the more monstrous, hee would have her in
a *Mitre*. And yet his prodigious lust was not at the height; as
much as hee could he added: and having found a *Man*, *a Cleargy-*
man, a Bishop, he did not sollicite him with entreaties, & rewards, 10
but ravished him by force. Since then the *Popes* doe, out of the
fulnesse of their power, come to those kindes of sinne, which
have neither *Example* nor *Name*, insomuch that Pope *Paulus*   *Plat. in vit.*
Venetus, which used to paint himselfe, & desired to seeme a   *Adri. I.*
woman, was called the *Goddesse Cibele* (which was not without 15
mysterie, since, prostitute boyes are sacred to that Goddesse,)
and since they do not graunt ordinarily that liberty of practising
sinnes, till they have used their owne right and priviledge of
Prevention and *Anticipation*, This pratling fellow *Machiavell* doth
but treacherously, and dishonestly prevaricate, and betraie the 20
cause, if hee thinke hee hath done inough for the dignity of
the *Popes*, when he hath affoorded to them sins common to all the
world. The transferring of Empires, the ruine of Kingdomes, the
Excommunications, and depositions of Kings, & devastations by
fire and sword, should have bene produced as their marks & 25
characters: for though the examples of the *Popes* transferring the
Empire, which our men so much stand upon, bee not indeede
true, nor that the ancient *Popes* practised any such thing; yet
since the states-men of our Order, wiser then the rest, have
found how much this *Temporal jurisdiction* over *Princes*, conduces 30
to the growth of the Church, they have perswaded the *Popes*,
that this is not only lawfull for them, but often practised heeretofore: And therefore they provide, that the *Canons* and *Histories*
bee detorted to that opinion: for though one of our *Order* doe   34
weaken that famous *Canon*, *Nos sanctorum*, which was used still   *Apologia pro*
                                                                    Garneto

23 the ruine *1626*: rhe ruine *1611*   34 opinion: *1626*: opinion. *1611*

probari solita sunt, id tamen tum fecit, cum & demulcendus rex *Britanniae*, legesque mitigandae, & ipse nomen *Eudaemonis* induerat. Ad se autem redeat, & *Cacodaemonem* profiteatur, nobis-

De Desperata cum sentiet, quo etiam nomine ignoscenda est & *Cudsemio* sua
Calvi. causa c.
11. temeritas, cum *Anglos Haereticos esse neget, quia in perpetua Episco-*
6 *porum successione permanent.* Videntur enim isti homines hoc in loco

Ro. 12. 11. eorum translationi favere, qui verba Paulina ita legunt, *Servite tempori*, non *Servite Domino*, Canonesque e re nata interpretantur. De iniuriis autem nostro Ordini, ab hoc homuncione illatis, cum
10 in nobis & tua & Papalis laedatur maiestas, quibus quasi Dictatoribus Republica iam nutante, ab utrisque mandatum est, *Videamus ne quid Respublica detrimenti capiat*, non est cur de vindicta dubitemus. Hoc tamen est quod me praecipue excruciet, quod cum me *Praesulem* vocet & *Antistitem*, nomine nobis horrendo
15 & abominando, novi illum ex intima sua malignitate, haec ad *Bellarmini*, *Toletique* votifragas ambitiones referre, qui *Cardinalatum* aliasque dignitates amplexati sunt. Sed errat homo miser, & in nostris rebus rudis, ignarus, eos non solum ex hoc quod in Papae corpus coalescunt, summo suo bono, finique ultimo,
20 centroque foelicitatis, huic *Luciferi* Camerae reddi proximiores, sed & etiam ex ipso periurio, votique iusti contemptu, novum ad eam ius iis acquisitum esse. Martyrium quippe nostrum Cardinalatus est: & quamvis non multi ex nostris iis polleant viribus, ut ita Martyres se fieri patiantur, gaudeantque Pontifices eam in
25 alias familias transferre persecutionem, iis tamen qui tantas vires assequuti sunt, utpote qui maioribus praelaturis aucti, ad maiora edenda facinora idonei evadant, in hoc eorum Coelo, novae

Ribadeneyra Coronae, novae aureolae contexuntur. Dolenda igitur semper
Catalog. fol. 60
& 100. erit infirmitas *Laynae*, & *Borgiae*, qui a *Paulo 4. & Iulio 3.* oblatum

---

5 *perpetua Ed.: perpetuo 12⁰*   14 nobis *12⁰ errata: vobis 12⁰*

to bee produced for this doctrine, yet hee did it then, when the King of *Great Britaine* was to bee mollified and sweetned towardes us, and the lawes to bee mitigated, and when himselfe had put on the name *Eudaemon*. But let him returne to his true state, and professe himselfe a *Cacodaemon*, & he will bee of our opinion. In which respect also wee may pardon our *Cudsemius* his rashnesse, when he denies the *English nation to be heretiques, because they remaine in a perpetuall succession of Bishops*: For herein these men have thought it fit, to follow, in their practise, that *Translation*, which reades the words of *Paul: Serve the time*, and not that which saies: *Serve the Lord*. As for the injury which this petty companion hath offered to our *Order*, since in our wrongs both yours, and the *Popes* Majesty is wounded; since to us, as to your *Dictators*, both you have given that large and auncient Commission: *That wee should take care that the state take no harme*, we cannot doubt of our revenge: yet this above all the rest, doth especially vexe me, that when he calls me *Prelate*, and *Bishop*, (names which wee so much abhorre and detest) I know well, that out of his inward malignity, hee hath a relation to *Bellarmines*, and *Tolets* sacrilegious Vow-breaking ambitions, by which they imbraced the *Cardinalship*, and other Church-dignities: but herein this poore fellow, unacquainted with our affaires, is deceived, being ignorant, that these men, by this act of beeing thus incorporated into the Pope, are so much the neerer to their *Center* and finall happinesse, this chamber of *Lucifer*, and that by the breach of a vow, which themselves thought just, they have got a new title therunto: For the *Cardinalship* is our *Martyrdome*: & though not many of our *Order*, have had that strength, that they have beene such *Martyrs*, and that the Popes themselves have beene pleased to transferre this persecution into the other *Orders*, who have had more *Cardinals* then wee; yet without doubt, for such of ours which have had so much courage, new Crownes, and new Garlands, appropriate to our *Martyrs*, are prepared for them in this their *Heaven*; because, being inabled by greater meanes, they are fitter for greater mischiefes. Wee therefore lament the weaknesse of our *Laynez*, & our *Borgia*, who refused the *Cardinalship*

De desperata Calvi. causa c. 11.

Rom. 12. 11.

Ribadeneyra Catalog. fol. 60 and 100

Cardinalatum respuebant: (digna enim hoc loco, & hoc conventu,

Brisson. de
formul. L.1.

ea assertio videtur) nam & in sacrificiis apud antiquos Romanos tibi immolatis, victima quae reluctabatur, semper reprobari credita est: ideoque meritis laudibus decorandus *Bellarminus*,

5 qui ex novo Cardinalatu, novum genium sumens, retractationes edidit, & loca omnia quae in eius scriptis in favorem Principum deflecti potuerunt, castigavit. Haec autem omnia missa faciamus. Satis enim nos novimus inter nos. Ea vero quae a se gesta esse gloriatur vir iste, in re politica omnes, antiquos, modernos,

10 praetergressus, pensiculatius perpendamus. Quamvis magnos in re aliqua eum progressus fecisse quis putabit, qui ita in primis mediiisque haerebat, ut cum *Pontificem Romanum* viderat, noverat, ad Daemonis tamen notitiam non pervenit. Scio autem quo se perfugio tueri conabitur: in infinitum scilicet dari non debere

15 progressum; alicubi consistendum, acquiescendum. Nec etiam plura admitti debere media, cum per pauciora res expediri possit. Cum igitur ei perspectum fuerat *Pontificem Romanum* omnium malorum causam extitisse, primumque motorem, maluit ibi acquiescere, quam Daemonem agnoscendo, novam Tyrannidem

20 introducere, faterique Papam etiam Daemonis iura usurpasse. Quam certe opinionem si quis adhuc tueri velit, per nos liceat. Erit tamen nobis argumentum ingenii non ita perspicacis, si quis ita Pontificem, neglecto Daemone, suspiciat, imaginemque sine relatione ad prototypum, colat. Quam autem futilia, quam nihili

25 sint, quae in libros suos congessit hoc manifestum reddit, quod in omni Religione, in omni disciplina aliquis in eum insurrexit, nec quis illum vindicare aggressus est. Nec hoc ideo dicimus,

offered by *Paulus* 4. & *Julius* 3; (for in this place and this meeting it is not unfit to say they did so) even amongst the auncient *Romans*, when they sacrificed to you those sacrifices, which offered any resistance, were ever reputed unaccepted: And therefore our *Bellarmine* deserves much praise, who finding a new *Genius* and courage in his new *Cardinalship*, set out his Retractations, & corrected all those places in his workes, which might any way bee interpreted in the favour of Princes. But let us pass over all these things: for wee understand one another well inough; and let us more particularly consider those things, which this man, who pretends to exceed all Auncient and Moderne *States-men*, boasts to have beene done by him. Though truly no man will easily beleeve, that hee hath gone farre in any thing, which did so tire at the beginning, or midway, that having seene the *Pope*, and knowne him, yet could never come to the knowledge of the *Divell*. I know what his excuse and escape wil be: that things must not be extended infinitly; that wee must consist and arrest somewhere, and that more meanes & instruments ought not to be admitted, where the matter may be dispatched by fewer. When therefore he was sure that the *Bishop* of *Rome* was the cause of all mischiefe, and the first mover therof, he chose rather to settle & determine in him, then by acknowledging a *Divel*, to induce a new *tyrany*, and to be driven to confesse, that the *Pope* had usurped upon the *divels* right, which opinion, if any man bee pleased to maintaine, we do not forbid him: but yet it must be an argument to us of no very nimble wit, if a man do so admire the *Pope*, that he leave out the *Divell*, and so worship the Image, without relation to the *prototype* and first patterne. But besides this, how idle, and how very nothings they are, which he hath shoveld together in his bookes, this makes it manifest, that some of every *Religion*, and of every profession, have risen up against him, and no man attempted to defend him: neither doe I say this, because I think

Brisson de formul L. 1.

1 by] be *1626*   (for] for *1626*   2 is not unfit *1611 errata, 1626:* is unfit *1611*   9 one another *1611 errata, 1626:* our Author *1611*   15 having] haning *1626*   17 wil] well *1626*   29 *prototype 1611 errata, 1626:* Pro-tolipe *1611*

quia ideo minus mala ea putanda censemus, sed quia minus
artificiosa, & ad finem in quem diriguntur, minus valida. Non
ita nos, non ita progressi sumus: ea enim arte praecepta nostra
his in rebus condita sunt, & condita, ut cum a nobis ad illaque-
5 andos stabiliendosque nostros proferantur, Ecclesiae doctrinae
& opinionis communioris speciem reverentiamque iis induamus.
Cum autem ab adversariis ad conciliandam nobis invidiam, aut
infirmiores absterrendos producantur, humiliori sorte contenta
sunt, & in locum seriemque privatarum opinionum secedere non
10 dedignantur. Canonesque ipsi nunc splendidi mitraque & tiara
insigniti incedunt, & ex ipsa Cathedra divinum sonant, vimque
oraculorum obtinent; nunc autem laceri oberrant, mutilique
claudicant, & claustrale quiddam aut Eremiticum murmure
incerto susurrant; aut quasi ex pulpitis in aures populi praecipi-
15 tati; aut a Conciliis producti quae vel abortus passa sunt, partus-
que ediderunt ante inanimationem, Papae scilicet assensum, aut
iam vita destituta sint, etsi diu sana fuerant vegetaque, ad
civilia negotia non pertrahenda iudicantur. Nunc nobis stellae
fixae, & firmamento haerentes, nunc autem planetae sunt
20 Canones. Nunc in omnibus loquitur ipse *Papa*, nunc autem
Autores, e quibus excerpti sunt. Inde varie de *Gratiano* nostro
philosophamur: nunc illi honorem dignitatemque Adamantum,
& gemmarum nobiliorum attribuentes, quae inde nitorem &
firmitatem consecutae sint, quod quasi ex Atomis, particulisque
25 minutissimis conflentur, nunc autem montem ex arena undique
congesta agnoscimus, & fundamento recipiendo prorsus

his doctrine the worse for that, but it is therefore the lesse artificially caried, and the lesse able to worke those endes to which it is directed. For our parts wee have not proceeded so: for wee have dished & dressed our precepts in these affaires, with such cunning, that when our owne men produce them to 5 ensnare and establish our puples, then we put upon them the majesty and reverence of the *Doctrine of the Church*, and of *the common opinion*: But when our adversaries alleadge them, either to cast envy upon us, or to deterre the weaker sort, then they are content with a lower roome, and vouchsafe to step aside into the 10 ranck of *private opinions*. And the *Canons* themselves are with us sometimes glorious, in their mitres & pontificall habits, & found nothing but meere *Divine resolutions* out of the Chaire it selfe, and so have the force of *Oracles*; sometimes we say they are ragged & lame, & do but whisper with a doubtfull and uncer- 15 taine murmure, a hollow cloistral, or an eremitical voice, & so have no more authority, then those poore men which writ them: sometimes we say they were but rashly thrown into the peoples ears out of pulpits, in the Homilies of fathers; sometimes that they were derived out of such *Councels* as suffered *abortion*, 20 and were delivered of their children, which are their *Canons*, before inanimation, which is the Popes assent, or out of such *Councels*, as are now discontinued and dead, (howsoever they remained long time in use and lively & in good state of health) and therefore cannot be thought fit to be used now, or applyed 25 in civil businesses; sometimes wee say the Popes voyce is in them all by his approbation; sometimes that onely the voyce of those authors, from whom they are taken, speakes in them. And accordingly we deliver divers and various *Phylosophy* upon our *Gratian*, who compiled them; sometimes we allow him the 30 honour and dignity of *Diamonds* and the nobler sort of stones, which have both their cleerenesse, and their firmenesse from this, that they are compacted of lesse parts, and atomes, then others are: and so is *Gratian*; whom for the same cause, sometimes we account but a hil of many sands cast together, and very unfit 35

ineptum. Fateor certe patres nostri ordinis, ex iuvenili quadam
ferocia, qua tum temporis omnia audebat, (vix enim ex Ephebis
excesserat) male *Concilium Tridentinum* adduxisse, ad regulas
certas, & definitiones statuendas, a quibus recedendum non
5 fuit. Sed certe recedendum est; nec dissimulari potest, tam

Vide Benium. nostri Ordinis scriptores, quam *Dominicani*, in hoc bello, tragoe-
diaque Romae excitata, *De Gratia & Arbitrio* a castris
Tridentinis transfugisse. Nec enim quae a nobis scripta
9 sunt ita firma rataque esse volumus, ut ab aliis, dum-

Apologia pro modo nostri sint Ordinis, immutari nequeant. Ita qua usus
Garnet. c. 3.
est *Daemon-Ioannes* licentia in liberando *Rege Regnoque Britanniae*
a periculo depositionis, (*quia nulla in eum lata sententia*) Canoni-
busque multis, quos alii in eum intonandos putarunt, cum
tandem regnum illud hoc opio nostro satis fuerit stupefactum,
15 licebit nobis eosdem Canones ad pristinum vigorem restituere,
regnumque ita sopitum, aut innato suo calore, id est, bellis
intestinis, aut externis remediis acquisitis, ex *letargia* sua
excitare. Securitatem enim omnem qua gaudent Principes, ex
nostra habent indulgentia, canonumque remissa interpretatione,
20 privilegia sunt, quae cum a nobis emanarint, vitamque acceperint,
a nobis imminui, revocari, iugulari possunt. Eodem prorsus
modo, quemadmodum *Marianae* licuit, a *Concilio Constantiensi*
recessisse, licuit etiam *Cottono, Marianae* partes relinquere. Quod
tamen solis nostris, quibus datum est tempora nosse, & arcana,
25 licere volumus. Videmus enim ipsos *Sorbonistas*, qui *Papatum*
Aristocraticum sibi constituere videntur, etsi opinionem *Marianae*
evertere satagebant, ab eius tamen nomine caeterisque *Iesuitis*
prudenter abstinuisse. Modestia sane quam in iis non sperabam,
qui dum & in terris fui, Decretum contra me ediderant. Nec

to receive any foundation. I must confesse, that the *fathers* of our *Order*, out of a youthfull fiercenesse, which made them dare and undertake any thing (for our *order* was scarce at yeares at that time) did amisse in inducing the *Councell* of *Trent* to establish certaine *Rules & Definitions*, from which it might not be 5 lawfull to depart: for indeed there is no remedy, but that sometimes wee must depart from them: nor can it be dissembled, that both the writers of our *Order*, and the *Dominicans* have departed *Vide Benium* from them in that great war and *Tragedy* lately raised at *Rome*, about *Grace & Free-wil*. For it is not our purpose, that the 10 writings of our men should be so ratified, that they may not be changed, so that they bee of our *Order* which change them: so by the same liberty, which Daemon-Joannes hath taken in delivering the *King* of *Britaine* from the danger of *Deposition*; *Apolog. Gar-* (*because as yet no sentence is given against him*) and also from many *net. c. 3.* other *Canons*, which others thinke may justly bee discharged 16 against him, it will be as lawfull for us, when that *kingdome* shal be inough stupified with this our *Opium*, to restore those *Canons* to their former vigor, and to awake that state out of her *Lethargy*, either with her owne heat, intestine warre, or by some *Medicine* 20 drawne from other places: for *Princes* have all their securities from our indulgence, and from the slacke & gentle interpretation of the *Canons*: they are but privileges, which since they are derived, & receive life from us, they may be by us diminished, revoked, & annulled: for as it was lawfull for *Mariana* to depart 25 from the doctrine of the *Councel* of *Constance*, so it was lawfull for *Cotton* to depart from *Mariana*: which, not withstanding, wee would have onely lawfull for our *Order*, to whom it is given to know times, and secrets of state: for we see the *Sorbonists* themselves, (which may seeme to have an *Aristocratical Papacie* 30 amongst themselves) though they laboured to destroy the doctrine of *Mariana*, did yet wisely forbeare to name him, or any other *Jesuit*, which was a modesty that I did not hope for at their *Gretzer.* hands; since, before I dyed, they made one *Decree* against me: *Examen speculi fol. 139*

14 *Britaine*] *Btitaine 1626*   21 drawne] draw *1626*   34 before I dyed
1626: before I I dyed *1611*

tamen nihil patientiae meae, providentiaeque tribuendum, qui

*Gretzer.
Examen.
speculi,
ol. 139*
vires eorum agnoscens, infantiamque nostram, responsionem
omnem & exagitationem meis interdixi. Nec enim tam Herculei
eramus, ut in incunabulis serpentes extinguere conaremur. Cum

5 autem ab illo tempore saepius a nostris provocati fuerint (nec
enim regulam praeceptaque adeo ferrea meis dedi, ac *Franciscus*,
qui noluit sua ad tempora, & rem natam accommodari) excu-
sandi certe erant, si in nos immitiores extitissent. Si *Parlamentum
Parisiense* ea modestia rem peragendam non censuit, sed librum,

10 opinionem, hominem, edictis suis infamem reddere maluit, quid
aliud de eo dicendum quam *Gigantem*, & *animal indomitum* esse,
quod nunquam a nostris cicurari potuit. Clamant enim semper

*L'Eschassier
fol. 25*
ululantque *Papae legitime & Canonice progrediendum*, idque mali-
tiose interpretantur, de legibus suis, & Canonibus antiquis, quos

Idem. fo. 32
per *Aresta* (ut vocant) sua, via insensibili, in usum revocare se

16 posse sperant. Hoc igitur est de quo Machiavellum reum statui-
mus, eum non ita tuto cuniculos suos egisse, quin ab omnibus
deprehensus fuerit. Nos autem qui Ecclesiam quasi Navem ac-
cepimus, alto mari libere fluctuamur. Anchoram certe habemus,

20 sed apud nos, nec adhuc fixam: figendam autem & retrahendam,
prout nobis visum fuerit. Et satis scimus ut & Navibus ipsis, ita
& naviganti Ecclesiae, scopulos, promontoria, quaecunque firma
sunt & fixa, periculosa esse, & naufragium minitari. Non tamen
adeo obstinate dicimus, nihil prorsus in eius Commentariis esse,

25 quod huic Ecclesiae inservire possit. Sunt certe eiusmodi multa;
sed non ii sumus, qui ab aliis quicquid emendicemus, aut qui
a nobis non profecta Elogiis nostris adornemus. Nobile huius
temperantiae abstinentiaeque exemplum nobis exhibuit *Senatus*

Margin *L'Eschassier* Ed.: *L'eschussier 12⁰*

but yet therein, I thinke somewhat may bee attributed to my patience, & providence; who knowing their strength, and our owne infancy, forbad all of my *Order* to make any answere to that *Decree* of theirs: neither were we so *Herculean* as to offer to strangle Serpents in our cradle. But yet since after that time, 5 they have beene often provoked by our men: (for I gave not so iron a *Rule & Precepts* to my *Disciples*, as *Francis* did to his who would have not his Rule applyed to times & to new occasions) certainly they might have bin excused, if they had beene at this time sharper against us. And if the *Parliament* of *Paris* thought it 10 not fit to carry the matter so modestly in their *Arrest* against *Mariana*, but made both the *Booke*, and the *Doctrine*, and the *Man*, infamous: What should wee say more of it, but that it is a *Gyant*, and a wilde beast, which our men could never tame: for still it 14 cryes and howles, *The Pope is bound to proceede lawfully, and* **L'Eschassier** *Canonically*; and this they malitiously interprete of their owne *fol. 25.* lawes, and of *auncient Canons*, which they hope to bring into use **Idem fo. 32.** againe, by an insensible way of *Arrest*, and *Sentences* in that *Court*. This then is the point of which wee accuse *Machivell*, that he carried not his Mine so safely, but that the enemy 20 perceived it still. But wee, who have received the *Church* to be as a ship, do freely saile in the deep sea; we have an *anchor*, but wee have not cast it yet, but keepe it ever in our power, to cast it, and weigh it at our pleasure. And we know well enough, that as to sailing shippes, so to our sailing Church, all rocks, all 25 promontories, all firme and fast places are dangerous, and threaten ship-wracke, and therefore to be avoyded, and liberty and sea-roome to bee affected; yet I doe not obstinatly say, that there is nothing in *Machivels commentary*, which may bee of use to this Church. Certainely there is very much; but wee are not 30 men of that poverty, that wee neede begge from others, nor dignify those things with our prayses, which proceede not from our selves. The Senate of *Rome* gave us heeretofore a noble example of this temperance and abstinence, which therefore

Romanus, qui ideo *Christum* inter Deos referre noluit, quia ab Impera-
tore res proposita fuit, nec ab ipsis Consilium emanavit. Id autem de
quo praecipue gloriatur iste, licentiam scilicet simulandi, mentien-
dique a se introductam, nullo nititur fundamento, nullo colore

5 decoratur. Nec enim solus *Plato*, caeterique Rerumpublicarum
Architecti, licentiam mentiendi Magistratibus, etiam & Medicis
tribuere, sed & Patres Ecclesiae, *Origenem, Chrysostomum, Hierony-*
mum, aestimantes, non solum eandem in illis doctrinam in-
venerunt nostri, sed eos etiam ab omni naevo reprehensioneque

10 hac via liberant, illis scilicet licuisse hanc opinionem tueri,
donec Ecclesiae aliqua definitio contrariam statuisset. Quod
certe (etsi non ita libere hoc profitendum sit) adhuc nunquam
fecit. Hanc autem doctrinam, quamvis usu receptam, a Patribus
excusatam, exemplis etiam *Prophetarum & Angelorum* in scri-

15 pturis roboratam, itaque iure Gentium, & quasi lege Naturae
stabilitam, quia tamen a nobis profecta non est, aliquantulum
declinavimus. Aliam autem minus obnoxiam, quae tamen eadem
omnia Ecclesiae praestaret, Reservationem scilicet Mentalem,
mixtasque propositiones substituimus. Mentiendi igitur licentia

20 nec tuta est, nec nova: sunt enim plaeraque ex *Machiavelli* praeceptis ita obsoleta, tritaque, ut non dubitaverit Serarius noster
(sua tamen licentia usus) *Herodem*, qui tamdiu ante vixerat
Machiavellistam vocare. Sed ut uno ictu spes eius omnes, omnes
rationes amputemus, hoc assero, hoc edico, omnia scripta eius,

25 actaque omnia huc spectare, ut ad ruinam interitumque regni
huius, id est, sedis Pontificiae, via praeparetur. Quid enim aliud
conatur, quam ut Rerumpublicarum formae immutentur, ut
populo (metallo molli, ductili, fusili, & ad nostras impressiones

Observationes in Cassianum 'ol. 736. ex collat. 17

Tribaeres. L.2. c. 4.

Margin *ex. collat. 17 Ed.: ex collat. 19 12⁰*
12⁰ c. 4 Ed.: c. 24 12⁰　　　　Margin *Tribaeres. Ed.: Tribares.*

refused to place *Christ* amongst their *gods*, because the matter
was proposed by the *Emperour*, and begunne not in themselves.
As for that particular, wherein *Machiavel* useth especially to
glory; which is, that he brought in the liberty of dissembling,
and lying, it hath neither foundation nor colour: For not onely 5
Plato, and other fashioners of *Common-wealths*, allowed the libertie
of lying, to Magistrates, & to Physicians; but we also considering
the fathers of the *Church*, *Origen*, *Chrysostome*, *Hierome*, have not
onely found that doctrine in them, but wee have also delivered
them from all imputation, & reprehension by this evasion: *That* 10
it was lawfull for them to maintaine that opinion, till some definition of
the Church had established the contrarie. Which certainely, (though
this should not be so openly spoken of) as yet was never done.
But yet wee have departed from this doctrine of free lying,
though it were received in practise, excused by the Fathers, 15
strengthened by examples of Prophets & Angels, in the Scriptures, and so almost established by the law of *Nations*, and
Nature; onely for this reason, because we were not the first
Authors of it. But wee have supplied this losse with another
doctrine, lesse suspitious; and yet of as much use for our *Church*; 20
which is *Mentall Reservation*, and *Mixt propositions*. The libertie
therefore of lying, is neither new, nor safe as almost all *Machivells*
precepts are so stale and obsolete, that our *Serarius* using, I must
confesse, his *Jesuiticall* liberty of wilde anticipation, did not
doubt to call *Herod*, who lived so long before *Machivell*, a 25
Machiavellian. But that at one blow wee may cut off all his
reasons, & all his hopes, this I affirme, this I pronounce; that all
his bookes, and all his deedes, tend onely to this, that thereby
a way may be prepared to the ruine & destruction of that part
of this Kingdome, which is established at *Rome*: for what else 30
doth hee endeavour or go about, but to change the forme of
common-wealth, and so to deprive the people (who are a soft, a
liquid and ductile mettal, and apter for our impressions) of all

Observationes
in Cassianum
fol. 736 ex
collat. 17.

Trihaeres.Li.2.
cap. 4.

Margin *ex. collat. 17.* Ed.: *ex collat. 19. 1611, 1626*   23 obsolete *1611 errata,*
1626: obsolute *1611*   23-4 using, . . . confesse, *1626*: using . . . confess
1611   27 pronounce;] pronounce, *1626*

accommodatiori) omnem libertatem eripiat, destructaque penitus
omni civilitate, ad Monarchias (nomen in rebus saecularibus
merito nobis abominandum) omnia reducantur. Cum lachrymis
dicendum, dicendum tamen, plane nullum ex Monarchis iam
5 inveniri, qui non aut penitus se a regno nostro subduxerit, aut
nos in re aliqua gravi laeserit, unde autoritatem Pontificis,
Incomparabiliter minorem esse quam fuerat, fatetur *Cottonus*
noster; Ecclesiamque Christianam (quod solum *Romanae* com-
petit) *Diminutivam* esse. Inde etiam est, quod non nisi semel
in *Hebdomada*, *Cardinales*, iam conveniant, quod saepius facere
11 soliti fuerant, quia negotia in Curia *Romana* pauciora sunt. Ut
enim Reges *Britanniae*, *Daniaeque*, ceterosque omnes primi generis
Monarchas taceam, in ipsa Gallia ita aucti sunt inimici nostri, ut
parum absit, quin etiam numero nostris pares evadant: viribus
15 autem in hoc superent, quod in doctrina sua unanimes sint,
vicinisque Ecclesiis adhaereant. Cum tamen nostri, qui Catholici
ibi dici volunt, ita a Catholicis Romanis dissentiant, ut non solum
Concilia, sed & Regem Papae praeferant; illosque suos Gigantes,
Gog & Magog, *Parlamentum* scilicet *Parisiense*, *& Collegium Sor-*
20 *bonae*, omni conatui, omni molimini nostro semper opponant.
Etiam & in *Hispania* misere languemus, ubi Clerici Dominis suis
infideles de proditione accusantur, Iudicio Regis personae Ec-
clesiasticae subiiciuntur, & Sacrilegi, igni a Iudice saeculari
traduntur. Et quamvis partem, paulo minus, dimidiam regni sui
25 Ecclesiae *Romanae* concessisse videri volunt, regnumque cum
Ecclesia divisisse, ita tamen pensionibus, aliisque oneribus,
quibus Aulici filiique procerum aluntur, & conditionibus vene-
nosis inficiuntur haec eorum dona, ut potius *Hydropisin* pati
videatur Ecclesia, quam ex alimentis bene concoctis sanitate

De la Messe fol. 358.

Synta. Tholosa L.15. c. 4. ver. 15.

Scappus de Iure non script. L.1. ca. 6. Ibid. c. 16. Ibid. c. 18.

6 laeserit, unde 4⁰: laeserit. unde *12⁰*   Margin *ver.* 15 *Ed.: v.* 7 *12⁰*   24 quamvis
partem *12⁰ errata*: quamvis Regni partem *12⁰*   dimidiam *12⁰ errata*: dimidium
12⁰   Margin *c. 18. Ed.: c.* 25 *12⁰*

their liberty: & having so destroyed all civility & re-publique, to reduce all states to *Monarchies*; a name which in secular states, wee doe so much abhor, (I cannot say it without teares,) but I must say it, that not any one *Monarch* is to be found, which either hath not withdrawne himselfe wholy from our kingdome, or wounded & endamadged us in some weighty point: hereupon our *Cotton* confesses, that the authority of the Pope is incomparably lesse then it was, and that now the *Christian Church*, (which can agree to none but the *Romanes*,) is but a diminutive. And hereupon also it is, that the Cardinals, who were wont to meete oftner, meete now but once in a weeke, because the businesses of the *Court* of *Rome* growe fewer. To forbeare therefore mentioning of the Kings of *Britaine*, and *Denmarke*, and the other *Monarkes* of the first sort, which have utterly cast off *Rome*; even in *France*, our enemies are so much encreased, that they equal us almost in number: and for their strength, they have this advantage above us, that they agree within themselves, and are at unity with their neighbour Refourmed *Churches*; whereas our men, which call themselves *Catholick* there, doe so much differ from the Romane Catholick, that they do not onely preferre Councels, but even the *king*, before the *Pope*, and evermore oppose those their two great *Gyants*, *Gog* and *Magog*, their Parliament of *Paris*, and their *Colledge* of *Sorbon*, against all our endeavours. Besides all this, we languish also miserably in *Spaine*, where *Cleargy men, if they breake their fealty to their Lord, are accused of treason*; where *Ecclesiasticall persons are subject to secular iudgement*, and, *if they be sacrilegious, are burnt by the Ordinarie Magistrate*; which are doctrines and practises, contrary, and dangerous to us. And though they will seeme to have given almost halfe the kingdome to the *church*, and so to have divided equally; yet those Graunts are so infected, with pensions, and other burdens, by which the kings servants, and the yonger sons of great persons are maintained, that this greatnesse of the Church there is rather a dropsie, then a sound state of health,

De la Messe fol. 358

Synta. Tholosa L. 15. c. 4. v. 15.

5

15

20

24

Scapp. de iure non script. L. 1. c. 6.

Ibid c. 16

Ibid c. 18.

30

6 endamadged us in *Ed*.: endamadged in 1611, 1626   Margin *v. 15. Ed.*: *v. 7*. 1611, 1626   Margin *c. 18. Ed.*: *c. 25*. 1611, 1626

frui, & ista omnia potius ad invidiam Ecclesiae, quam maiestatem conciliandam fieri. Sed & in iure Ecclesiae usurpando, non
solum Reges *Galliae*, sed & *Britanniae* post se reliquit Rex *Hi-*
De Regno *spaniae*. Novum enim (ait *Baronius*) exortum est *Caput*, pro *Mon-*
Siciliae
5 *stro & Ostento. Excommunicat enim & absolvit: quam etiam exercet*
potestatem, & in Episcopos & in Cardinales. Appellationes impedit, nec
sedem Romanam superiorem agnoscit, nisi in casu praeventionis. Exosum
igitur nobis nomen, *Monarcha*, & exitiosum: in quod, tanto
impetu, tanta ferocia & acerbitate intonuit *Baronius*, ut frustra
10 aliquid adiicere conarer ego, etsi tua (*nefande Imperator*) lingua
loquerer. Nomen enim *Adulterinum* vocat, & *Turrem Babel:*
Regique, cui ipse subditus, nisi a nomine abstineat, ruinam minatur.
Interim Tyrannum esse statuit, & Bulla Coenae quotannis excommuni-
Resp. ad Card. catum. Hoc autem uno erga omnes se tuetur, *Nescit zelus imperiosus*
Column.
15 *parcere saltem Deo.* Quem tamen zelum, & a *Mandato Papae*, & a
Iuramento Cardinalitio inflammatum dicit; quibus omnibus instructus, in Monarchas insurgit. Nec aliam fere ob causam,
Bellarminus noster regimen Monarchicum tantis laudibus effert,
quam ut a tanta dignitate saeculares omnes arceantur, solique
20 Ecclesiae ea vindicentur. Bene igitur *Rebullus* quidam, (qui iam
huic regno innotescere laborat, cum calumniarum in Ministros
Gallos Ecclesiasque ibi constitutas satur, etiam in *Regem exterum*
potentissimum calamum stringere, & signa conferre ausus est) bene
24 inquam, & perquam accommodate *Baronium & Bellarminum*,
Salmonees *Clypeum Ensemque Ecclesiae Romanae* vocat. Gratulor illi sane de
Titulo *Ensis* nostro Ordini indulto; tam quod post omnes illorum
verborum [*Ecce duo Gladii*] interpretationes, ad temporalem
iurisdictionem in Papa stabiliendam, a nostris acquisitas, ab

established by wel-concocted nourishment, and is rather done, to cast an Envy upon the Church, then to give any true Maiestie to it. And even in usurping *Ecclesiasticall Jurisdiction*, the kings of *Spaine* have not onely exceeded the kings of *Fraunce*, but also of *Britany*. For (says *Baronius* of that king) *there is now risen up a new Head, a monster, and a wonder.* He Ex-communicates, *and he Absolves: And he practiseth this power even against Bishops, and Cardinals: He stops Appeales, and he acknowledges no superiority in the sea of Rome, but onely in case of Prevention*: And therefore, the name Monarch, is a hateful and execrable name to us. Against which, *Baronius* hath thundred with such violence, such fiercenesse, and such bitternesse, that I could hardly adde any thing there-unto, if I should speake (unspeakable *Emperour*) with thine owne tongue: for he cals it an *Adulterine name*, and a *Tower of Babel*, and threatens destruction to that king (though himselfe were his subject) except he forbeare the name. In the meane time, he resolves him to be a *Tyrant*, and pronounces him to stand yearely Excommunicate by the *Bulla Coenae*. Neither doth he offer to defend himselfe with any other excuse, when a Cardinall reprehended his fiercenes towards the king, then this; *An Imperious zeale, hath no power to spare God himselfe.* And yet he confesseth, that this zeale was kindled by the *Popes speciall commaund*, and by his *Oath* taken, as Cardinall. Neither hath our *Bellarmine* almost any other cause of advauncing *Monarchicall* government so much as he doth, then thereby to remove all secular men from so great a dignitie, and to reserve it only to the Church. It was therfore well done of that *Rebullus* (who now begins to bee knowne in this state) when having surfeited with Calumnies against the *French* Church, and her Ministers, he hath dared of late to draw his pen, and to joyne battell against a most puissant foraine Prince: hee did well (I say) and fitly, when hee called *Bellarmine* and *Baronius, The sword and buckler of the Romane Church.* And I cannot choose but thanke him for affoording the Title of *Sword* to our *Order*: as well, because after so many expositions of those words, (*Behold, heere are two swords*) which our side hath gathered, to establish a temporall Jurisdic-

De Regno Siciliae 6

10

19

Resp. ad. Card. Colum.

25

30

Salmonees

35

adversariis autem sublatas, elisas, irrisas, novam suppeditasse
videtur, & per *duos Gladios* Papae *excommunicationem, & Iesuitarum*
Regicidia intimasse; quam quod nobis supremam illam dignitatem
reservavit, ut quemadmodum *Deus* Paradisum suum *Ense ignito*
5 munire voluit, ita & nos Ecclesiae nostrae finibus insistamus, non
solum ut *Cherubin* ille, flamma ferroque instructi, sed & nupera
inventione, pulvere bombardico: de cuius Autore, an Monachus
scilicet fuerit, Daemonve, miror cur litigarent *Antiquarii*, cum
unum sint. Ut autem (*nefande Imperator*) in plaerisque rebus id
10 semper conatus es ut *Deum* imitareris, ita in nobis id egregie
assecutus es. Cum enim Reformationem Ecclesiae suae aggre-
deretur ille, in tua etiam te idem tentare decuit. Ideoque *Fran-*
ciscanos tuos (operarios certe, artificesque ante nos natos, non
contemnendos), per *Capuchinos* reformasti: hos etiam per *Re-*
15 *coletos.* Cum autem & in ipsa Ecclesia Dei, nonnulli in hac Re-
formatione eousque progressi sunt, ut non solum humores cum
periculo peccantes, sed & omnem pulchritudinem, speciem, &
ornatum eximere, spiritus vitales cum sanguine vitioso simul
exhaurire, maciem inducere, & *spasmum tetanumque febre curare*

Hipocrat. L.4. tentarent, tu tibi deesse noluisti, sed antiquorum tam *Circum-*
Aphor. 57.
21 *cellionum*, quam *Assassinorum* ingenium in nobis reformasti,, &
ad altiora audenda excitasti. Nec enim in *Circumcellionum* ferocia
consistimus, cum alios ad mortem nobis inferendam lacessimus,
& provocamus, nec in *Assassinorum*, qui ad Reges qui per eos
25 transibant occidendos, operam vendebant: nam sponte, gratis,
ubique id perpetramus. Et quemadmodum reipsa, a nemine nos
vinci patimur, ita & *Mysticis Mystica* opponimus; & ne Canon

tion in the *Pope*, and which our Adversaries have removed, worne out, or scorned, this man hath relieved us with a new, and may seeme to intend by the *two swords, the Popes Excommunications,* and the *Jesuites Assassinates,* and *King-killings*; as also because he hath reserved to our *Order* that soveraigne dignity, 5 that as God himselfe was pleased to defend his Paradice with fire and sword, so we stand watchfull upon the borders of our *Church,* not onely provided, as that *Cherubin* was with fire and sword, but with the later invention of *Gun-powder*; about the first inventour whereof I wonder, why *Antiquaries* should contend, 10 whether it were the *Divell* or a *Frier,* since that may be all one. But as (O unspeakable *Emperour*) you have almost in all things endevoured to imitate *God*: so have you most throughly performed it in us: For when *God* attempted the *Reformation* of his *Church,* it became you also to reforme yours. And accordingly by 15 your *Capuchins,* you did reforme your *Franciscans*; which, before we arose, were your chiefest labourers, and workemen: and after, you Reformed your *Capuchins,* by your *Recolets.* And when you perceived that in the *Church* of *God,* some men proceeded so farre in that *Reformation,* that they endevoured to draw out, 20 not onely all the peccant and dangerous humours, but all her beautie, and exteriour grace and Ornament, and even her vitall spirits, with her corrupt bloud, & so induce a leannesse, and il-favourednes upon her, and thought to cure a rigid coldnesse *Hypocra. L. 4.* with a fever, you also were pleased to follow that Example, and *Aphor. 57.* so, in us, did Reforme, and awaken to higher enterprises, the 26 dispositions as well of the *Circumcellions,* as of the *Assassins*: for we do not limit our selves in that lowe degree of the *Circumcellions,* when we urge and provoke others to put us to death; nor of the *Assassins* which were hired to kill some Kings, which 30 passed through their quarter: for we exceed them both, because wee doe these things voluntarily, for nothing, & every where. And as wee will bee exceeded by none, in the thinge itselfe: so to such things as may seeme mysticall and significant, wee oppose

Carranza sta-
tut. Synod.
N. 40.

Regul. Jesuit.
Cap. Praefect.
Refectori.

ille, *Ne quis Clericus cultellum cum cuspide portaret*, prophetica
aliqua relatione nos respiceret, praeceptum nostris dedimus,
ut *Cultelli eorum frequenter acuantur*, & ad usus semper parati sint.
Extispices enim sumus, prophanis longe solertiores; nec enim
5 exta brutorum animalium inspicimus, sed ipsarum animarum
exta, in Confessionibus, & exta Principum in proditionibus;
quorum corda nobiscum esse non ante credimus, quam ea
videamus. Sileat igitur loquaculus iste Secretarius; librosque
suos eo honore affici, contentus sit, quo *Ephemeridas* & *Calen-*
10 *daria* anniversaria dignatur Mundus, quae certis locis tempori-
busque accommodata, ibi alicui brevi usui inservire possunt.
Eiusque Sectatorum regulae omnes, ceu *Synodorum Provincialium*
Canones, ubi condita sunt, recipiantur; nostrae autem, quae
universum mundum pervagantur, permeantque, *Conciliorum*
15 *Oecumenicorum* vicem habeant, vigoremque retineant. Loco
autem aliquo inter Gentiles insigni, potiatur iste, modo a
nostris abstineat. Nec solum de modernis loquor, cum nostros
dico; vix enim unquam in Romana Ecclesia defuere Monachi, qui
Machiavellum longe superarunt.' Longa certe mihi videbatur
20 *Ignatii* Oratio; & de corpore tamdiu relicto metuebam, ne aut
putresceret, aut certe fracescere, & sepulturae tradi posset.
Nolui tamen discedere e scaena, donec peracta fabula. Sperabam,
si quid corpori accideret, *Iesuitas*, quibus miracula familiaria sunt,
& quorum famae studiosus in hoc negotio mihi videbar, com-
25 miseratione erga me usuros. Ut autem aliquando videram

> *Aut plumam, aut paleam, quae fluminis innatat ori,*
> *Cum ventum ad pontem fuerit, qua fornice transit*
> *Angusto flumen, reiici tumideque repelli;*
> *Duxerat at postquam choreas, atque orbibus undae*

Margin *Carranza . . . N. 40* Ed.: *Carrauca . . . N. 41* 12⁰

mysticall things. And so, least that *Canon*; *That no Clergy-man should weare a knife with a point*, might seeme to concerne us, by some prophetical relation, we in our *Rules* have opposed this precept: *That our knife be often whetted*, & so kept in an apt readines for all uses: for our divination lies in the contemplation of entrails; in which art we are thus much more subtile then those amongst the old *Romans*, that wee consider not the entrails of *Beasts*, but the entrails of souls, in confessions, and the entrails of *Princes*, in treasons; whose hearts wee do not beleeve to be with us, till we see them: let therefore this pratling *Secretary* hold his tongue, and be content that his booke be had in such reputation, as the world affoords to an *Ephemerides*, or yearely *Almanack*, which being accommodated to certaine places, & certaine times, may be of some short use in some certaine place: and let the *Rules* and precepts of his disciples, like the *Canons* of *provincial Councels* bee of force there, where they were made, but onely ours which pierce, and passe through all the world, retaine the strength and vigour of *Universall Councels*. Let him enjoy some honourable place amongst the *Gentiles*; but abstaine from all of our sides: neither when I say, *Our side*, doe I only meane Moderne men: for in all times in the *Romane* Church there have bene *Friers* which have farr exceeded *Machiavel*.' Truely I thought this Oration of *Ignatius* very long: and I began to thinke of my body which I had so long abandoned, least it should putrifie, or grow mouldy, or bee buried; yet I was loath to leave the stage, till I saw the play ended: And I was in hope, that if any such thing should befall my body, the Jesuits, who work *Miracles* so familiarly, & whose reputation I was so careful of in this matter, would take compassion upon me, and restore me againe. But as I had sometimes observed

> *Feathers or strawes swimme on the waters face,*
> *Brought to the bridge, where through a narrow place*
> *The water passes, throwne backe, and delai'd;*
> *And having daunced a while, and nimbly plai'd*

Margin *Carranza* . . . *N. 40* Ed.: *Carrauca* . . . *N. 41* 1611, 1626

Carranza stat. synod. N. 40.

Regul. Jesuit. cap. praefect. Refector. 6

10

15

20

25

30

Luserat, a liquidis laqueis, & faucibus hausta
Fluminis in gremium tandem cedit, reditumque
Desperat spectator scaenae;

Ita *Machiavellus* saepe se erigens, saepe repulsus, tandem evanuit.
5 Ego autem in facie vultuque *Luciferi* haerebam. Deprehendi
illum ita erga *Ignatium* affectum, ac Principes, qui quamvis
Officiariis suis invident, eximiam opes conquirendi licentiam,
tamen de illis queri non audent, ne populo eos reddant odiosos.
Passus igitur *Lucifer* est Infernum novum, Diabolum scilicet
10 popularem, gloriosum, & sine dubio res novas moliturum.
Voluit igitur in Cameram interiorem secessisse, recepto praeter
Ignatium nemine, quem neque secludere potuit, eximie meritum,
nec tutum putabat amplius ei occasionem dare, suas laudes cele-
brandi, caeterosque omnes deiiciendi, in conspectu publico, &
15 vulgo Daemonum. Sed recedentem turba animarum obsidebat.
Confluunt omnes, introitum flagitant, qui quid in rebus etiam
minimis innovarant. Etiam qui aut in mundo muliebri aliquid
De rebus nuper novi induxerant, aut in *Pancirolli* Commentariis locum invene-
inventis
rant, *Porcellanae, Conspiciliorum, Quintanae, Staphiarum,* etiam &
20 *Caviari* inventores, turbam augent. Eorum autem qui *Circulum*
se quadrasse gloriati sunt, infinitus pene numerus: sed nubem
istam dispescuit *Ignatius,* imperando, increpando, irridendo,
propulsando. Nollem tamen certe *Petrum Aretinum* inter caeteros
tam male ab eo habitum. De picturis suis portentosis glorianti,
25 vere certe respondit *Ignatius,* eum, utpote non ita doctum, multa
latuisse in hoc genere, quibus scatent antiquae, tam Historiae
quam fabulae & poemata: ideoque *Aretinum* non solum nihil de
novo addidisse, sed & stimulos iuventuti ademisse, quae in eius

Upon the watry circles, Then have bin
By the streames liquid snares, and jawes, suck'd in
And suncke into the wombe of that swolne bourne,
Leave the beholder desperate of returne:

So I saw *Machiavel* often put forward, and often thrust back, and 5
at last vanish. And looking earnestly upon *Lucifers* countenance,
I perceived him to bee affected towards *Ignatius*, as *Princes*, who
though they envy and grudge, that their great Officers should
have such immoderate meanes to get wealth; yet they dare not
complaine of it, least thereby they should make them odious and 10
contemptible to the people: so that *Lucifer* now suffered a new
Hell: that is, the danger of a *Popular Divell*, vaine-glorious, and
inclined to innovations there. Therefore he determined to withdraw himselfe into his inward chamber, and to admit none but
Ignatius: for he could not exclude him, who had deserved so well; 15
neither did hee thinke it safe to stay without, & give him more
occasions to amplifie his owne worth, & undervalue all them
there in publique, and before so many vulgar *Divels*. But as hee
rose, a whole army of soules besieged him. And all which had
invented any new thing, even in the smallest matters, thronged 20
about him, and importuned an admission. Even those which had
but invented new attire for woemen, and those whom *Pancirollo*   *De rebus nuper*
hath recorded in his *Commentaries* for invention of *Porcellan dishes,*   *inventis.*
of *Spectacles*, of *Quintans*, of *stirrups*, and of *Caviari*, thrust themselves into the troupe. And of those, which pretended that they 25
had *squared the circle*, the number was infinite. But *Ignatius*
scattered all this cloud quickly, by commaunding, by chiding,
by deriding, and by force & violence. Amongst the rest, I was
sory to see him use *Peter Aretine* so ill as he did: For though
Ignatius told him true when he boasted of his licentious pictures, 30
that because he was not much learned, hee had left out many
things of that kind, with which the ancient histories & poëmes
abound; and that therefore *Aretine* had not onely not added any
new invention, but had also taken away all courage and spurres
from youth, which would rashly trust, and relie upon his 35

industria temere confisa, nihil ulterius quaerendum putaret, itaque infinitum praedivitemque Antiquitatis thesaurum amissuram. Addidit etiam, *Raderum* caeterosque sui Ordinis, qui poetas castrare soliti, aliosque autores, (interim autem mirebar

5 ego eos & *vulgatam editionem suam* non castrasse quae verbis adeo obscoenis alicubi abundat, quaeque lingua *Hebrea* (eo nomine *Sancta* nuncupata) adeo horret, ut nihil obscoenum effari possit; ita ut unus ex illis (admodum subtiliter) animadvertit, stellam

Harlay defence   *Veneris* perraro eo nomine in Scripturis appellatam) non eo animo
des Jesuit. fol.
12.   id fecisse, ut eorum memoria aboleretur, sed ut prius experti

11 ipsi an *Spintria Tiberii*, & *Martialis Symplegma*, aliaque huiusmodi, non potius Chimerae & luxuriantium ingeniorum speculationes, quam res certae & ad artem methodumque deliciarum reducendae extitissent, (nec enim in re aliqua *Theoria* contenti, nisi &

15 ad *praxin* accedant *Iesuitae*) discipulis tandem suis, & novitiis ea facerent communia. Est enim foecunda Sacramentorum haec Ecclesia, Divinis autem onerata, iam & Moralia gignit. In quibus, ut & in Divinis, una specie populum contentum esse volunt; varias autem formas, arcana sua mysteriaque sibi reser-

20 vare: cuiusmodi nonnulla subobscure mihi tum innuere videntur,

Valladerius   cum in vita novae Divae, *Franciscae Romanae* scribant, *Thorum*
fol. 24.
genialem ei perpetuum Martyrium fuisse & *Miraculorum Officinam.* Cum tamen is fuerit *Aretinus*, qui Principibus sugillandis, contumeliisque afficiendis diu assuetus, habitum inde contraxerit

25 talem, ut & ad supremam Dei Maiestatem parvifaciendam ascendisse potuit, miror certe *Archi-Iesuitam* istum, etsi non ad sedem in Ecclesia sua triumphanti eum admiserit, munus tamen aliquod

diligence, and seeke no further, & so lose that infinite & precious treasure of Antiquitie. He added moreover, that though *Raderus*, and others of his *Order*, did use to gelde *Poets*, and other *Authors*: (and heere I could not choose but wonder, why they have not gelded their *Vulgar Edition*, which in some places hath such 5 obscene words as the *Hebrew* tongue, which is therefore called *Holy*, doth so much abhorre, that no obscene things can be uttered in it insomuch, that (as one of them very subtilly notes) the starre of *Venus* is very seldome called by that name in the Scripture: for how could it be, the word being not *Hebrew*?) yet 10 (said hee) our men doe not geld them to that purpose, that the memory thereof should bee abolished; but that when themselves had first tried, whether *Tiberius* his *Spintria* & *Martialis symplegma*, and others of that kinde, were not rather *Chimeraes*, & speculations of luxuriant wits, then things certaine & constant, and such 15 as might bee reduced to an Art and methods in licentiousnes (for Jesuits never content themselves with the *Theory* in anything, but straight proceed to *practise*) they might after communicate them to their owne *Disciples* and *Novitiates*: for this Church is fruitfull in producing *Sacraments*; and being now loaded with 20 *Divine sacraments*, it produces *Morall sacraments*. In which, as in the divine, it bindes the *Layety* to one species; but they reserve to themselves the divers formes, and the secrets and mysteries in this matter, which they finde in the *Authors* whom they geld. Of which kind I thinke they give a little glimmering and 25 intimation, when in the life of their last made *Goddesse, Francisca Romana*, they say: *that the bed where shee lay with her husband, was a perpetuall Martyrdome to her, and a shop of miracles.* But for all this, since *Aretine* was one, who by a long custome of libellous & contumelious speaking against Princes, had got such a habit, 30 that at last he came to diminish and dis-esteeme *God* himselfe, I wonder truly, that this *Arch-Jesuite*, though hee would not admit him to any eminent place in his *Triumphant Church*, should

Harlay Defence des Jesuit. fol. 12.

Valladerius fol. 24

inferioris sortis ei denegasse. Dignus enim mihi videbatur, qui
aut *Ignatio A Voluptatibus*, aut *Lucifero A Voce* esset. Quicquid
enim vel *Lucifer* ipse animo concipere potuit, effari audebat iste.
Eum tamen *Ignatius*, satis sibi ad omnia munera visus, pro-
5 trusit; urgentique, baculum intentabat. Nec mitiorem certe
Christophoro Columbo se exhibuit: qui cum nihil ei in terra marive
impervium fuerat, in Inferno difficultatem minus timebat. Per-
gentem autem sistebat *Ignatius*. 'Meminisse te decet, inquit, si
9 quid huic regno emolumenti, ex detectis terris *Occidentalibus*

*Matalius
Metellus,
Praefat. in
Osorium.*

eveniat, id omne nostris acceptum referendum. Si enim obti-
nuisset *Dominicorum* sententia, *praedicatione sola, non vi inferenda
incolas reducendos*, vix certe tot saeculis, *vicies centena millia hominum
ad 150. perducerentur*; quod a nobis cito peractum. Si lex lata a
Ferdinando in solos *Canibales*, ut *qui fidem amplecti noluere, servitute*
15 *plecterentur*, in alias Provincias extensa non fuisset, defuissent
nobis viri, qui terrae beneficium eruissent. Nisi nos, sublata
eorum Idololatria, nova, nostra, id damnum iis compensassemus,
nisi nos, genti ignarae barbaraeque, res aliquando naturales,
aliquando confictitias, pro miraculis obtrusissemus; nisi nos
20 etiam, ex *Americano* pretioso stercore confectum *Pharmacum*,
Principibus *Europaeis*, eorumque proceribus, & Consiliariis in-
sinuare, applicare, parati semper essemus, parum certe ex his
locis detectis (quod fortunae referendum) effectum foret. Laudo
tamen pertinaciam tuam, patientiamque: cuius (quoniam ea tibi
25 praecipua virtus) & hic exercendae occasionem habeas & in loco
remotiore consistas.' Etsi autem *Lucifer* turba ista nimia &
candidatorum diluvio pene obrutus, concitatior factus, quasi

11 *inferenda 12⁰ errata, 4⁰: inferanda 12⁰*   15 *extensa 12⁰ errata, 4⁰*: extenta
12⁰

deny him an office of lower estimation: For truly to my thinking, he might have beene fit, either to serve *Ignatius*, as *maister of his pleasures*, or *Lucifer* as his *Crier*: for whatsoever *Lucifer* durst think, this man durst speake. But *Ignatius*, who thought himselfe sufficient for all uses, thrust him away, and when he offered upward, offered his staffe at him: Nor did he use *Christopher Columbus* with any better respect; who having found all waies in the earth, & sea open to him, did not feare any difficulty in *Hell*, but when hee offered to enter, *Ignatius* staid him, & said: 'You must remember, sir, that if this kingdome have got any thing by the discovery of the *West Indies*, al that must be attributed to our *Order*: for if the opinion of the *Dominicans* had prevailed, *That the inhabitants should be reduced, onely by preaching and without violence,* certainely their 200000 of men would scarce in so many ages have beene brought to a 150 which by our meanes was so soone performed. And if the law, made by *Ferdinando*, onely against *Canibals: That all which would not bee Christians should bee bond-slaves,* had not beene extended into other Provinces, wee should have lacked men, to digg us out that benefite, which their countries affoord. Except we when wee tooke away their old Idolatrie, had recompenced them with a new one of ours; except we had obtruded to those ignorant and barbarous people some-times naturall things, sometimes artificiall, and counterfeit, in steed of *Miracles*; & except we had ben alwaies ready to convey, & to apply this *medicine* made of this pretious *American* dung, unto the Princes of *Europe*, & their Lords, & *Counsellours*, the profite by the onely discovery of these places (which must of necessity bee referred to fortune) would have beene very little; yet I praise your perseverance, and your patience; which (since that seemes to be your principall vertue) you shall have good occasion to exercise heere, when you remaine in a lower and remoter place, then you thinke belongs to your merits.' But although *Lucifer* being put into a heate, and almost smothered with this troupe and deluge of pretenders, seemed to have

Matalius Metellus, Praefat. in Osorium.

vicariatum quendam, aut a latere legationem concessisse *Ignatio* videbatur, potestatemque paulo minus absolutam ex arbitrio omnia agendi, errorem tamen suum, periculumque deprehendit. Meminit enim quanto impetu *Canon Alius* vibrari ab iis solet, quo Rex *Franciae*, non quia flagitiosus, sed quia inutilis depositus a sede dicitur: Regesque a dignitate excidere, si aliis rebus dediti rempublicam officiariis administrandam relinquunt. Voluit igitur & ipse rei gerendae manus admovere suas, seque immiscere; ne *Ignatio* forte daretur *praescriptio*; quo titulo, satis novit quantum in alios Principes praevaluerat & adhuc se tuetur *Ecclesia Romana*. Etsi autem *Ignatio* gratulari se simulabat, de se ab ista importuna turba liberato, cum tamen illum vidit, hoc solum agere ne nemo admitteretur, maiori opus esse diligentia putavit. Nam quamvis de *Patriarchis* suis bene sperabat, qui diu ante locum interiorem adepti fuerant, & cum quibus (ut dixit *Abbas* quidam *Diabolo*, eum post longa intervalla tentanti) ipse *consenuerat*, eos scilicet ius suum retenturos, strenueque defensuros, seque aggerem, si quid novi moveret, *Ignatio* opposituros; si tamen solus in hoc saeculo induceretur, metuit, ne tam eius spiritus, quam eorum erga illum reverentia, in damnum suum augerentur. In omnes igitur angulos oculos coniecit; & longius remotum, vidit tandem *Philippum Nerium*; qui non satis sibi conscius, de egregio aliquo erga hoc regnum merito suo, a portis abstinuit. Animo autem recolebat suo *Lucifer*, *Nerium*, Ordinemque totum, cuius institutor fuerat, *Congregationem* scilicet *Oratorii*, ideo praecipue a *Pontifice Romano* erectos, auctos, privilegiis honoratos, ut assiduis de *Vitis Sanctorum*, *Antiquitatumque Ecclesiasticarum*, orationibus ad populum habitis, ita novus honos iis conciliaretur, ut inde *Iesuitarum* torrens, & communis erga illos superstitio languidior paulo, tepidiorque redderetur. Iam

Paris de Puteo. de syndicatu de excess. reg.

Sophronius ca. 45.

5

10

16

20

25

30

28 *Ecclesiasticarum* Ed.: Ecclesiasticarum *12⁰*

admitted *Ignatius*, as his *Lieutenant*, or *Legat a latere*, and trusted
him with an absolute power of doing what hee would, yet he
quickly spied his owne errour, and danger thereby. He began to
remember how forcibly they use to urge the *Canon Alius*; by
which the king of *Fraunce* is sayd to have beene deposed, not for 5
his wickednesse, but for his infirmity, and unfitnesse to governe:
And that kings do forfeit their dignity, if they give themselves
to other matters, and leave the government of the State to their
officers. Therefore *Lucifer* thought it time for him to enter into
the businesse, least at last *Ignatius* should prescribe therein; by 10
which title of prescription he well knew, how much the *Church*
of *Rome* doth advaunce and defend it selfe against other *Princes*.
And though he seemed very thankfull to *Ignatius*, for his delivery
from this importunate company, yet when he perceived, that
his scope and purpose was, to keepe all others out, he thought 15
the case needed greater consideration; For though he had a confidence in his owne *Patriarkes*, which had long before possest that
place, and in whose company (as an *Abbot* said to the *Divell*, who
after long intermission now tempted him) *hee was growne old*, and
doubted not but that they would defend their right, and oppose 20
themselves against any innovation, which *Ignatius* should
practise, yet if none but hee in a whole age should bee brought
in, hee was afraid, that this singularity would both increase his
courage and spirit, and their reverence, and respect towards him.
Casting therefore his eyes into every corner, at last a great way 25
off, hee spied *Philip Nerius*: who acknowledging in his owne
particular no especiall merit towardes his kingdome, forbore to
presse neere the gate; But *Lucifer* called to his remembrance,
that *Nerius* and all that *Order*, of which hee was the Author,
which is called *congregatio Oratorii*, were erected, advaunced, 30
and dignifyed by the *Pope*, principally to this end, that, by their
incessant Sermons to the people, of the lives of *Saints* and other
Ecclesiastique Antiquities, they might get a new reputation, and so
the torrent, and generall superstition towards the Jesuits, might
grow a little remisser, and luke-warme: for at that time the Pope 35

*Paris de puteo,
de syndicat., de
excess. regum*

*Sophronius ca.
45.Consenuerat.*

enim de illis metuere ipse Papa coeperat; coeperant enim & illi
paradoxon suum spargere, *De Confessione & Absolutione per literas,*
& internuncios exhibenda, eaque arte omnium Principum arcana ad
se trahere: tentaverant etiam & *Monarcham* magnum *Italiae*
5 inhiantem contra Pontificem solicitare, cui articulos quosdam, de
eo reformando obtulere. Gaudent autem mutua sibi exempla
esse *Papa & Lucifer.* Quod igitur fecerat ille in Medio, in Infero
regno hic tentare aggreditur. Accersivit igitur *Philippum Nerium,*
animique in illum propensi aliqua signa edidit. Stupidior autem
10 erat *Nerius,* quam ut ea rite interpretari potuit. Vidit tamen ea
Ignatius, & priusquam *Lucifer* ad apertiora descenderet, aut
tantos hac in re progressus faceret, ut (cum honoris eius con-
stantiaeque semper ratio habenda fuerit) nulla ratione a propo-
sito suo abduci posset, aut averti, cito opponendum, re adhuc
15 tantum non integra existimavit. Se iam videre, dixit, Luciferum
minus cum *Philippo* versatum, quam cum *Iesuitis,* qui nesciret

In vita Nerii. quam apertum ei hostem se professus fuerat. Nec enim solum
fol. 106. Fol.
108. Visiones omnes respuit, iussitque quendam conspuere in faciem
Fol. 212. B *Virginis,* cum ei apparuit, quia *Daemonem* esse putabat, aliumque
Fol. 229. Medici specie moribundo insidiantem depellebat, nec facile
21 adducebatur, ut quemquam a *Daemone* vexatum crederet, sed
Fol. 19. etiam cum ei tres *Daemones* in via occursabant, non exorcismis,
non signo Crucis eos dignatus est, sed simpliciter neglexit &
praeteriit. Alios fortasse ad Religionem excitabat, ipse autem in
Fol. 26. saeculo tum mansit; adeo ut me memini, eum *Campanam* seu
21 *Tintinnabulum* vocitare solitum, qui cum ipse foris maneret, alios
Fol. 313. alliceret. Nec qui *Congregationem,* eius sequuntur, *Voto* aut
Sacramenti vinculo se obstringunt; nec quidquam, de quo ei

himselfe beganne to bee afraid of the Jesuites, for they begunne
to publish their *Paradox of Confession and absolution to bee given by
letters, and Messengers,* and by that meanes to draw the secrets of
all Princes onely to themselves; And they had tried and sollicited
a great *Monarch,* who hath manie designes upon *Italy,* against 5
the *Pope,* & delivered to that prince diverse articles, for the
reforming of him. Now the *Pope* and *Lucifer* love ever to follow
one anothers example: And therefore that which the one had
done in the middle world, the other attempted in the lower.
Hereupon he called for *Philip Nerius,* and gave him many evi- 10
dences of a good inclination towards him. But *Nerius* was too
stupid, to interprete them aright. Yet *Ignatius* spied them, and
before *Lucifer* should declare himselfe any further, or proceed too
farre herein, least after he were farre engaged, there should be no
way, to avert or withdraw him from his owne propositions (for 15
he saw there must be respect had of his honour and constancy)
hee thought it fittest to oppose now at the beginning. He sayd
therfore, 'that he now perceived, that *Lucifer* had not bene
altogether so much conversant with *Philip* as with the *Jesuits,*
since he knew not, how much *Philip* had ever professed himselfe 20
an enemy to him. For he did not onely deny all visions, and
apparitions, And commaunded one to spit in *Maries* face, when
she appeared againe, because he thought it was the *Divell;* And
drove away an other that came to tempt a sicke man, in the shape 24
of a Phisition; And was hardly drawne to beleeve any possessings;
but when three *Divels* did meete him in the way, to afright him,
he neither thought them worthy of any *Exorcisme,* nor so much as
the signe of the Crosse, but meerely went by them, as though he
scorned to look at them, & so despighted them with that
negligence. It may be that hee hath drawne others into *Religion,* 30
but himselfe remained then in the *Layety;* in so much as I remember, that I used to call him, *The Saints Bell,* that hangs without,
and cals others into the *Church.* Neither doe they which follow
this *Order,* bind themselves with any *vow* or *oath;* Neither do

*Vita Nerii fol.
106. Fol. 108.*

Fol. 212.

Fol. 229.
Fol. 19.

Fol. 26.
Fol. 313.

Margin *fol. 106.* Ed.: *fol. 107.* 1611, 1626   27 Exorcisme] *Exorcismes*
1626

gratias referat hoc regnum novi, nisi quod *Baronium ad scribendos Annales impulit. Nerius* autem ad haec omnia mutus, quasi de alio dicta. Historiae certe suae, eorumque quae de illo scribuntur, ignarus prorsus aut oblitus. Ausus autem est ipse *Lucifer*
5 (patientia *Ignatii* vix impetrata) eius partes suscipere, eousque progredi, ut dicere non vereretur, *Baronium, Bozium,* aliosque ex hoc alveo *Nerii* profectos, liberiori, apertiori, duriori in Principes stilo usos, Papae in regna omnia directae Iurisdictioni, melius consuluisse, fortius propugnasse, quam qui meticulosius quam par est,
10 maiestatique tantae causae conveniat, rem aggressi, vias obliquas, ambages perplexas, & ex variis rarisque circumstantiis inutiles, Haeresin sectantes *Bellarminianam,* sunt commenti. Omnia autem ista ab alumnis suis edita, *Nerio* deberi, ut radici poma. *Ignatius* autem cum eum videret partes omnes agere, Iudicis, Advocati,
15 Testis, priori insistens consilio, rumpendam Orationem putavit, ne cum merita *Nerii* decantasset, ad praemia obligaretur. 'Quid autem', clamat *Ignatius,* 'fecit iste, quid perpetravit, eiusve sequaces, in speculationibus, in praeparatoriis semper exercitati? Libri isti de Iurisdictione Papae scripti, quid aliud sunt, quam
20 *Medicorum* de morbis disputationes, aut de medicamentorum componendorum modis; qui cum in libris delitescunt, dum nemo ad aegrum pergit, morboque medicinam accommodat, quid ex illis boni, quid emolumenti? quam partem, quod membrum corporis languentis aggressi sunt isti? quo in Regno humores in
25 Papam peccantes, igne ferrove expulerunt? Quam Rempublicam in Anatomiam dissecuerunt? quod sceleton ad posteros erudien-

I know any thing for which this kingdome is beholding to him, *Fol. 163.*
but that *he moved Baronius to write his Annals.*'

To all this *Nerius* sayde nothing, as though it had beene spoken
of some body else. Without doubt, either he never knew, or had
forgot that he had done those things which they write of him. 5
But *Lucifer* himselfe tooke the boldnesse (having with some
difficultie got *Ignatius* leave) to take *Nerius* his part: and proceeded so farre, that he adventured to say, 'that *Baronius, Bozius,*
and others, which proceeded out of the *Hyve* of *Nerius,* had used
a more free, open, and hard fashion against *Princes,* and better 10
provided for the Popes *Direct Jurisdiction* upon all Kingdomes,
and more stoutly defended it, then they; which undertaking the
cause more tremblingly, then becomes the Majestie of so great
a businesse, adhered to *Bellarmines* sect, and devised such crooked
wayes, and such perplexed intanglings, as by reason of the 15
various, and uncertaine circumstances, were of no use: And that
whatsoever *Nerius* his *schollers* had performed, must be attributed
to him, as the fruit to the roote.' *Ignatius* perceiving that *Lucifer*
undertooke all offices for *Nerius,* and became Judge, Advocate,
and witnesse, pursuing his former resolution, determined to 20
interrupt him, least when hee had enlarged himselfe in *Nerius*
commendation, hee should thereby bee bound to a reward. He
therefore cried out, 'What hath *Nerius* done? what hath he, or
his followers put in execution? have they not ever bene onely
exercised in speculations, and in preparatory doctrines? Are 25
these bookes which are written of the *Jurisdiction* of the *Pope,* to
any better use then *Phisitians Lectures* of diseases, and of Medicines? whilest these *Receits* lie hid in *Phisitians* bookes, and no
body goes to the *Patient;* no body applies the medicine to the
disease, what good, what profit comes by all this? what part, 30
what member of this languishing body have they undertaken?
In what *Kingdome* have they corrected these humours, which
offend the *Pope,* either by their *Incision* or *cauterising*? what state
have they cut up into an *Anatomy*? what *Sceleton* have they

dos confecerunt? Hosce morbos, verbis praedicationibusque, ceu carmine & incantationibus curari posse sperant? Si autem hoc honore inde dignus putabitur, quia ex eorum scriptis aliquid decerpi posse videtur, quod ad hoc negotium accommodari 5 queat, cur *Bezam*, cur *Calvinum*, caeterosque eius generis hic in Infernis non haberemus? in quorum libris nonnulla inveniuntur, quae huc torqueri possunt. Sed cum nec ad *Monarchias* extirpandas collimarunt, nec *Canones* aut *Aphorismos* ad res omnes accommodandos, sed circumstantiis incertis obnoxios ediderunt, 10 nec quid alias in Principes durius statuerunt, nisi ubi supremam potestatem in *populo*, aut *Ephoris* resedisse opinati sunt: nec hanc etiam potestatem in principem irruendi, aut a privato arripi, aut ei delegari posse dicant, nec ideo quisquam ex eorum discipulis in vitam principis sui aliquid peregisse se glorietur; videmus hunc 15 locum iis semper fuisse occlusum. Fuere sane ex illis (etsi illis hunc honorem invideam, ut cum *Knoxio*, *Goodmanno*, *Buchanano* numerentur) qui nostros aemulati, reipublicae tranquillitatem perturbarunt, Principibusque iniquiores extiterunt, nec suo apud nos in hoc regno aliquo loco carent. Sed cum nihil, nihil 20 suis manibus peregere, nec inde se excusare possunt, quia minus valebant, (quid enim aut *Clementis* aut *Ravillaci* viribus tribuendum est, aut quid, eius ausibus, qui vitam suam negligit, in mediis castris impervium?) ad hanc secretam sacratamque Cameram vix aspirant.' Subiunxisse voluit *Lucifer*, non omnes 25 fortasse quae in regum viscera grassatae sunt manus, a *Iesuitis* ita armatas fuisse, ut ipsi omnibus Consiliis, omni definitioni, semper interfuerint: (quod tamen, non ut testis iuratus, sed ut *Lucifer* ipse, paterque mendaciorum, dicturus erat). Satis autem esse, quod & Confessarii ita animos imbuant ea doctrina, ut iam

provided for the instruction of Posterity? Do they hope to cure their diseases, by talking and preaching, as it were with charmes and enchantments? If *Nerius* shall bee thought worthy of this Honour, and this place, because out of his *schollers* writings something may be gleaned, which may be applied to this purpose, why should we not have *Beza* and *Calvin*, and the rest of that sort here in Hell, since in their bookes there may be some things found, which may be wrested to this purpose? But, since their scope was not to extirpate *Monarchies*, since they published no such *Canons* and *Aphorismes* as might be applied to all cases, and so brought into certaine use & consequence, but limited theirs to circumstances which seldome fall out, since they delivered nothing dangerous to Princes, but where, in their opinion, the *Sovereignty* resided in the *People*, or in certaine *Ephori*, since they never said, that this power to violate the person of a prince, might either be taken by any private man, or committed to him, & that, therefore, none of their disciples hath ever boasted of having done any thing upon the person of his soveraigne: we see that this place hath ever bene shut against them: there have bene some few of them (though I can scarce affoord those men the honour to number them with *Knox*, and *Goodman*, and *Buchanan*) which following our examples have troubled the peace of some states, and beene injurious to some princes, and have beene admitted to some place in this Kingdome; but since they have performed nothing with their hands, nor can excuse themselves by saying, they were not able: (for wherein was *Clement*, or *Ravillac* more able then they: or what is not he able to doe in the middest of an Army, who despiseth his owne life?) they scarce ever aspire, or offer at this secret and sacred *Chamber*.' *Lucifer* had a purpose to have replied to this: 'that perchaunce all their hands which had bin imbrued in the bowels of Princes, were not so immediatly armed by the Jesuits, as that they were ever present at all consultations and resolutions: (and yet he meant to say this, not as sworne witnesse, but as *Lucifer* himselfe, & the father of lies, in which capacitie he might say any thing) But that it was inough that *Confessours* do so possesse them with

non quasi medicina sed ut alimentum a natura accommodatum
proponatur: nec magis ad res istas peragendas, *Iesuitae* personam
iam requiri, quam cordis humani, quod spiritus per omnes artus

Brisson. de emittit, in omnibus artubus praesentiam. *Consulibus Romanis*, qui
formul. L. 1.

5 pro patria & exercitu se devovere Diis inferis soliti sunt, licuisse
ipsis a morte abstinere, & quemlibet e legione sacrum facere. Ita

Rensinck. & *Iesuitis*, quemlibet e populo, (gaudent enim & illi *Franci-*
Manual.
Franciscano. *scanorum* privilegiis, apud quos *nomen populi, omnes extra eorum*
ca. 9.
ordinem continet) ad sua facinora perpetranda excitare. Hoc autem

10 si concessum fuerit, *Nerianos* nemini inferiores, quorum libris (si
quid *Iesuitis* omnibus humanitus contingeret) Ecclesia contenta
esse potuit, nec de penuria macieve ei metuendum foret. Haec
loqui voluit *Lucifer*. Tacere autem satius visum, tutiusque.
Animadvertit enim *Ignatium* signum dare, omnesque eius co-

15 hortes, numerosas, vafras, rerum novarum avidas, cristas erigere,
fremere, in corpus unum coalescere, omnia eorum monumenta,
quanta fecerant, quanta passi fuerant, conquirere, producere,
aestimare. Legio autem *Anglicana*, quae *Capistrata* dicta, quam
ducebat *Campianus*, claudebat (ni fallor) *Garnetus*, prae caeteris

20 ferociebat. Et quasi secundum aliquod Martyrium subeundum,
aut ipsa immortalitas exuenda esset, ad quidvis paratissima.
Nerium igitur ut se subducat tacite monet *Lucifer*; nec quid de eo
addidit. De alio autem inducendo iam desperans, de excludendo
ipso *Ignatio* serio cogitat. Ita igitur eum aggressus: 'Doleo, mi

25 *Ignati*, nec in aliis merita, hoc loco, nec hic locum tuis meritis
dignum me invenisse. Mihi si mori licuisset, de successore video
non fore litigandum. Quod enim in Coelis primum facinus per-
petravi ego, quo Imperium hoc adeptus sum, si & a te factum non

that doctrine, that it is not now proposed to them as *Phisicke*, but as naturall food, and ordinarie diet; and that therfore for the performance of these things, a Jesuits person is no more requisite, then that the heart of a man, because it sends forth spirits into every limbe; should therefore bee present in every limbe: that when it was in use for the *Consuls* of *Rome* for the safety of their Country and army, to devote themselves over to the infernall *god*, it was lawfull for themselves to absteine and forbeare the act, and they might appoint any *Souldier* for that *Sacrifice*: and that so the Jesuites for the performance of their resolutions, might stirre up any amongst the people: (for now they enjoy all the priviledges, of the *Franciscans*, who say: *That the name of people comprehends all which are not of their Order*:) And that if this be granted, *Nerius* his schollers are inferiour to none; with whose bookes (if all the *Jesuites* should perish) the Church might contente herselfe, and never feare dearth nor leanenesse.' This *Lucifer* would have spoken; but hee thought it better and easier to forbeare: for hee observed, that *Ignatius* had given a signe, & that all his troupes which were many, subtile, & busie, set up their bristles, grumbled, and compacted themselves into one body, gathered, produced, and urged all their evidence, whatsoever they had done, or suffered. There the *English Legion*, which was called *Capistrata*, which *Campian* led, and (as I thinke) *Garnet* concluded, was fiercer then all the rest. And as though there had beene such a second *martyrdome* to have beene suffered, or as though they might have put off their *Immortalitie*, they offered themselves to any imploiment. Therefore *Lucifer* gave *Nerius* a secret warning to withdraw himselfe, & spoke no more of him; and despairing of bringing in an other, began earnestly to thinke, how he might leave *Ignatius* out. This therefore he said to him: 'I am sorry my *Ignatius*, that I can neither find in others, deserts worthy of this place, nor any roome in this place worthy of your deserts. If I might die, I see there would be no longe strife for a successour: for if you have not yet done that act which I did at first in *Heaven*, and thereby got this Empire, this may excuse

5

Brisson de for-mul. L. 1.

10

*Rensinck.
Manual.
Franciscan.
ca. 9.*

15

20

Haltered

25

30

35

est, inde excusari potes, quod quid fuerit, ignorant omnes. Si enim quis veterum, cum superbiam alius, alius luxuriam, aut mendacium fuisse autumet, vera dicat, aut si in *Casuistis*, qui artem peccandi profitentur, inveniri potest, certe de eo peccato 5 omisso, accusandus non eris. Iam autem cum nec a me deseri, nec in partes scindi potest hoc regnum, hac via succurrendum puto. Ad *Pontificem Romanum* literas dabo. Ille *Galilaeum Florentinum* ad se vocabit: qui *novum Mundum, Lunae* scilicet *astrum*, montes, *Nuntius* nemora, urbes iam satis perscrutatus est. Qui cum primis suis *sydereus*
10 perspicillis id effecerit, ut illum tam ex propinquo intueretur, ut de eius facie, formaque, & rebus minimis sibi satisfecerit, novis (cum iam in arte sua maiores progressus fecisse credendus sit) confectis, & a *Pontifice Romano* benedictis, *Lunam*, ceu ratem quandam in aethere fluitantem, ad terram proprius trahere 15 valebit. Illuc *Iesuitae* omnes, (ad illos enim id negotium spectare semper vociferantur) transfretabunt, Ecclesiamque *Lunaticam Romanae* conciliabunt. Certe non ibi diu degent *Iesuitae*, quin sponte sua nascatur & *Infernum*. In id tibi erit Imperium; ubi regnum, ibi domicilium statues. Et quemadmodum ex terra 20 in *Lunam*, ita & ex hac in caetera astra quae etiam & Mundi creduntur, *Iesuitis* tuis semper facilis erit transitus, eoque modo *Inferna* propagabis, imperiumque tuum dilatabis, propiusque ad sedem quam reliqui ego, ascendes.' Non expectavit dum peroraret *Lucifer, Ignatius*. Quamprimum enim eum respirare vidit, 25 vultum *Ignatii*, si quae in ea mutatio, exploraturum, moxque oculum ad alium Inferni locum, ubi ingens exortus rumor, convertere, hanc arripuit occasionem *Ignatius*, quasi finem dicendi fecerat. Respondit itaque, de eius tam erga *Romanam Ecclesiam*, quam Ordinem suum benevolentia, nova singulos dies producere 30 testimonia. Hoc etiam ultimum inprimis numerandum. Nosse se *Pontificem Romanum* eximia devotione, omnia a *Lucifero* profecta

you, that no man hath beene able to tell you what it was: For
if any of the *Auncients* say true, when they call it *Pride*, or
Licentiousnesse, or *Lying*: or if it be in any of the *Casuists*, which
professe the Art of sinning, you cannot be accused of having
omitted it. But since I may neither forsake this kingdome, nor 5
divide it, this onely remedy is left: I will write to the Bishop of
Rome: he shall call *Galilaeo* the *Florentine* to him; who by this time
hath throughly instructed himselfe of all the hills, woods, and
Cities in the new world, the *Moone*. And since he effected so much 9
with his first *Glasses*, that he saw the *Moone*, in so neere a distance, *Nuncius*
that hee gave himselfe satisfaction of all, and the least parts in *Sydereus*
her, when now being growne to more perfection in his Art, he
shall have made new *Glasses*, and they received a hallowing from
the *Pope*, he may draw the *Moone*, like a boate floating upon the
water, as neere the earth as he will. And thither (because they 15
ever claime that those imployments of discovery belong to them)
shall all the Jesuites bee transferred, and easily unite and recon-
cile the *Lunatique Church* to the *Romane Church*; without doubt,
after the Jesuites have been there a little while, there will soone
grow naturally a *Hell* in that world also: over which, you *Ignatius* 20
shall have dominion, and establish your kingdome & dwelling
there. And with the same ease as you passe from the earth to the
Moone, you may passe from the *Moone* to the other *starrs*, which
are also thought to be worlds, & so you may beget and propagate
many *Hells*, & enlarge your *Empire*, & come nearer unto that high 25
seate, which I left at first.' *Ignatius* had not the patience to stay
till *Lucifer* had made an end; but as soone as hee saw him pause,
and take breath, and looke, first upon his face, to observe what
changes were there, and after to cast his eye to an other place in
Hell where a great noyse was suddenly raysed: he apprehended 30
this intermission, and as though *Lucifer* had ended, he said:
'That of *Lucifers* affection to the *Romane Church*, and to their
Order, every day produced new Testimonies: and that this last
was to bee accounted as one of the greatest. That he knew well
with how great devotion the Bishop of *Rome* did ever embrace 35

3 *Casuists* Ed.: *Casuistis 1611, 1626*   18 *Church*; Ed.: *Church, 1611, 1626*

Consilia semper amplexatum, obsequutum. Sperare inde se, illum negotium hoc *Iesuitis*, Imperium autem sibi reservaturum. Nec non & *Pontificem*, se credere ante de hoc cogitasse. Et cum *Personio Anglo* de Cardinalatu spem ingessit, hunc locum, hanc 5 novam Ecclesiam eum in animo habuisse. Brevi futurum, ut omnia quae in terris nuper passa est *Romana Ecclesia*, ibi resarciantur. Hoc etiam aperto refugio, si iam in maiores angustias reduceretur, aut ei ultima impenderet exterminatio, minus mundo universo dolendum esse. De Receptione autem *Iesuitarum* 10 non esse dubitandum (etsi & invitis regibus se penetraturos profitentur) nunc praesertim, cum omnes terrae Principes non solum licentiam abeundi, sed & Apostolos suos libentissime & alacriter iis concessuri sint. 'Nec nimium reluctaturi putandi sunt, si & ipse *Pontifex* eos comitari dignaretur, & vaticinium sui 15 *Gersonis De Auferibilitate Papae*, hoc saltem modo implere vellet. Adde etiam quod foemina ibi regnare dicitur, quibus semper foeliciter usi sunt, qui quid in Religione innovare tentarunt. Quanta diligentia *Pulcheria & Eudoxia* Imperatrices, de *Paschate* statuendo a Papa solicitatae sunt? Quam obnixe de Imperatrice 20 ad suas partes trahenda tam Pelagius, quam *Papa* literis contendebat? Si enim is *Iuliae* honos tributus fuerit, ut in Numis publicis *Mater Castrorum*, & *Deum mater*, & *Augustorum*, & *Senatus* & *Patriae Mater* diceretur, quid ni foeminae a nobis imbutae *Matres Ecclesiae* dici possint? Cur non ingenio foeminarum fidendum 25 dum nobis fuerit, cum & aliquando Ecclesia nostra *Foeminae Pontifici* se crediderit? Qui autem ita felices in foeminarum gratia aucupanda putamur, ut ideo *nec foeminis liceat domos nostras ingredi*, *nec nobis, Curam Monialium suscipere*, quique per omnes *Indias* gratiam earum & benignitatem experti sumus, aut saltem (tam

Regul. Jesuit. *Fol. 73.* *Ibid. Fol. 47.*

---

23 quid ni *12⁰ errata, 4⁰, 12⁰ corrected*: quid in *12⁰ uncorrected* (BCO, BM, CCO, NLS, *TUL*); *see Introduction, p.* xlv.

and execute all counsels proceeding from him: And that therefore
he hoped, that hee would reserve that imployment for the
Jesuits, and that *Empire* for him their founder: and that he beleeved the *Pope* had thought of this before; and at that time when
he put *Parsons* the *English* Jesuite in hope of a *Cardinalship*, hee had 5
certainly a reference to this place, and to this *Church*: That it
would fall out shortly, that all the damages, which the *Romane
Church* hath lately suffered upon the earth, shall bee recompenced
onely there. And that, now this refuge was opened, if she should
be reduced into greater streights, or if she should be utterly 10
exterminated, the world would not much lament and mourne
for it. And for the entertainment of the Jesuites there, there can
be no doubt made at this time, when, (although their profession
bee to enter whether Princes will or no) all the Princes of the
world will not onely graciously affoord them leave to goe, but 15
willingly and cheerfully accompany them with Certificates, and
Dimissory letters. Nor would they much resist it, if the *Pope*
himselfe would vouchsafe to go with them, and so fulfill in some
small measure, that prophecy of his *Gerson, De Auferibilitate
Papae*. Besides this a woman governes there; of which Sex they 20
have ever made their profite, which have attempted any *Innovation* in religion; with how much diligence were the two *Empresses
Pulcheria* & *Eudoxia* sollicited by the *Pope* for the establishing of
Easter? how earnestly did both *Pelagius* and the *Pope* strive by
their letters to draw the *Empresse* to their side? For since *Julia* 25
had that honour given to her in publique coines, that she was
called *the mother of the Armie, the Mother of the Gods, and of the
Senate, and the Mother of her Countrie*; Why may not woemen
instructed by us, be called *Mothers of the Church*? Why may not
wee relie upon the wit of woemen, when, once, the Church 30
delivered over her selfe to a woman-*Bishop*? And since we are
reputed so fortunate in obtaining the favour of woemen, *that
woemen are forbid to come into our houses*; and we are forbid, *to take
the charge of any Nunnes*; since we have had so good experience of
their favour in all the *Indies*, or at lest have thought it fit, that 35

Reg. *Jesuit.
fol. 73.
Ibid. fol. 47.*

quia is mos antiquis *Haereticis* in opinionibus suis insinuandis, quam quod iis qui artes nostras norunt valde credibile illud semper putavimus) in literis suis anniversariis de hoc gloriandum putarunt & aliquid vero addendum, quibus id muneris datum
5 est, cur de hac Regina male nobis ominaremur, quae etiam motibus est & passionibus non infrequenter obnoxia? Saepe in absentia solis languet, saepe in Eclipsi deliquium patitur, & in articulo mortis posita videtur. Tum peragendae erunt partes nostrae, tum artes exercendae, & quicquid volumus extorquen-
10 dum. Experiendum etiam quid Carmina & Incantationes in eam valeant. Quae enim poetae dictabant, nec vera ipsi putavere, nos vera esse & mysteriis referta saepe experti sumus. Nec certe aliquam in mentem revocare possum foeminam, quae aut spem nostram fefellit, artesve elusit, una dempta *Elizabetha Angla.*
15 Cui etiam id ignoscendum fuit, quia foeminam penitus exuerat; cuius praecipuam dignitatem, scilicet, ut mater fieret, cur exoptaret, cui sine uxoris, matrisque, aut aliis ea indignis titulis foemininis, is aliunde successor praeparatus fuerat, qui diutius a regno detineri non debuit. Horum autem Principum de honore
20 cum haec loquor, homo iis inimicissimus, non alio me furore impulsum sentio, quam cum bruta animalia hostiam adorasse, a nostris dicuntur. Nec certe volens *Elizabethae Manibus* lito; (a quo verbo irridendo, cum a Rege *Britanniae* prolatum fuit, utinam
Heissius ad Aphor. Jesuit. Fol. 135. abstinuisset *Personius* noster, cum & idem verbum usurpaverit alter e nostris, dum *Garneti* inimicos increpans, *Beati Garneti*
26 *Manibus* eos insultare dicit). Nec tamen ab omni innovatione libera *Elizabetha* fuit; adeo enim obsoleverat antiqua Religio, ut eam ad pristinam dignitatem reducere, eam renovare, quaedam innovatio fuit. Eaque arte, sexus infirmitatem (si quid in hac re
30 patiebatur) eludebat; cui enim parum foeminae inerat, parum

10 in eam *12⁰ errata*: in eum *12⁰*

they which have the charge to write our anniversary letters from thence should make that boast, and adde something to the Truth, both because the Auncient *Heretiques* helde that course in insinuating their opinions, and because they which are acquainted with our practises will think any thing credible, which is 5 written of us in that behalfe, why should wee doubt of our fortune in this *Queene*, which is so much subject to alterations, and passions? she languishes often in the absence of the Sunne, and often in *Ecclipses* falles into swounes, and is at the point of death. In these advantages we must play our parts, & put our 10 devises in practise: for at these times any thing may be drawne from her. Nor must we forbeare to try, what verses, and incantations may worke upon her: For in those things which the *Poets* writ, though they themselves did not beleeve them, we have since found many truths, and many deep mysteries: nor can I 15 call to minde any woman, which either deceived our hope, or scaped our cunning, but *Elizabeth* of *England*; who might the rather be pardoned that, because she had put off all affections of woemen. The principall Dignity of which sex, (which is, to be a *Mother*) what reason had she to wish, or affect, since without 20 those *womanish* titles, unworthy of her, of wife, & mother, such an heire was otherwise provided for her, as was not fit to be kept any longer from the inheritance. But when I, who hate them, speake thus much in the honour of these two *Princes*, I finde myselfe caried with the same fury, as those *Beasts* were, which 25 our men say, did sometime adore the *Host* in the *Masse*. For it is against my will, that I pay thus much to the *Manes* of *Elizabeth*; from scorning of which word *Manes*, when the king of great *Brittaine* writ it, I would our *Parsons* had forborne, since one of our owne *Jesuits* useth the same word, when reprehending our 30 Adversaries, he says, *That they do insult upon Garnets Manes.* And *Heissius ad* yet this *Elizabeth* was not free from all *Innovation*: For the *Aphor. Jesuit.* ancient *Religion* was so much worne out, that to reduce that to *fol. 135.* the former dignity, and so to renew it, was a kinde of *Innovation*: and by this way of innovating shee satisfied the infirmity of her 35 Sex, if shee suffered any: for a little *Innovation* might serve her,

Innovationis satis erat. Sed nec etiam proprie Innovationem
dicere hanc ausim, ne *Luthero*, caeterisque procul a nobis in
coelis exultantibus, aliquid in hunc locum iuris deberi faterer.
Procliviorem autem, ad Innovationes nostras, *Reginam Lunaticam*
5 fore speramus. Diu enim cum illa perquam familiariter versatus
est Clavius noster; quid ab initio fecerit, quid factura sit, quo
modo erga vicina regna, caetera astra, mundosque tam vagantes,
quam firmamentarios se gerat, quibuscum foedera, coniugia,
societates ineat, quos aversetur, (modo ei adsint *Ephemeridae*)
10 perspectum habet. Maior autem est, quam qui *Reginae Lunaticae*,
aut a Consiliis inserviendae, aut a Confessionibus (quod nobis
utilius) donari possit. Nec in re tantilla tantus homo deperdendus.
Nec enim alium habemus, ad Solem, Mundosque alios transmun-
danos delegandum. Illum igitur ad maiora reservabimus. *Her-*
15 *bestus* noster, aut *Busaeus*, aut *Voellus* (qui soli ex nostris aliquid in
Mathematicis se valere, scriptis testantur) quamvis insipidi
putantur & pueriles, indigni tamen non erunt, qui & *Lunaticae*
huic Ecclesiae *Catechismos* accommodare, eiusque progressus

Eudaemon. Io. aspectusque observare possint. Etsi enim & *Garnetus Clavium*
Apolog. pro
Garnet. c. 9. magistrum habuit, parum tamen in scientiis profecit, sed
21 *Bellarmino* (altero etiam eius praeceptore) imbutus, eiusque
Dictatis plenus, ad politica anhelavit. Sedibus ibi defixis, hoc
certe non parum dignitatem nostram augebit, quod in literis ad
terram demittendis (si tamen non tota ad nos evanescat Ecclesia
25 *Romana*) miracula quaevis effingere semper nobis licebit. Quod &
Acosta de pro- ex Indiis (nec infeliciter certe) tentavimus; donec unus e nostris,
cur. Indo. Salu.
Li. 2. c. 9. simplicitate & ingenuitate *Christiana* magis quam *Iesuitica*,
miracula ibi non fieri dolendo agnoscit. Certe satius nobis
fuisset, omnes quinque fratres *Acostas* ex nostro Ordine expuisse,
30 quam unum eorum hoc in nos opprobrium evomuisse. De his

17 putantur *Ed.*: putentur, *12⁰*

who was but a little a woman. Neither dare I say, that this was properly an *Innovation*, lest thereby I should confesse that *Luther* and many others which live in banishment in *Heaven* farre from us, might have a title to this place, as such *Innovators*. But we cannot doubt, but that this *lunatique Queene* will be more inclin- 5 able to our Innovations: for our *Clavius* hath beene long familiarly conversant with her, what she hath done from the beginning, what she wil do hereafter, how she behaves herselfe towards her neighbour kingdoms, the rest of the starrs, & all the planetary, & firmamentary worlds; with whom she is in league, & amity, 10 and with whom at difference, he is perfectly instructed, so he have his *Ephemerides* about him. But *Clavius* is too great a per-sonage to be bestowed upon this *Lunatique Queene*, either as her Counsellour, or (which were more to our profit) as her Confessor. So great a man must not bee cast away upon so small a matter. 15 Nor have we any other besides, whom upon any occasion we may send to the Sunne, or to the other worlds, beyond the world. Therefore wee must reserve *Clavius* for greater uses. Our *Herbestus*, or *Busaeus*, or *Voellus* (and these bee all which have given any proofe of their knowledge in *Mathematiques*) although 20 they bee but tastelesse, and childish, may serve to observe her aspects, and motions, and to make *Catechismes* fit for this *Luna-tique Church*: for though *Garnet* had *Clavius* for his *Maister*, yet he *Eudaem. Ioan.* profited little in the Arts, but being filled with *Bellarmines* *Apol. pro Gar-* *net. c. 9.* Dictates, (who was also his *Maister*) his minde was all upon 25 *Politiques*. When wee are established there, this will adde much to our dignity, that in our letters which wee send downe to the earth, (except perchaunce the whole *Romane Church* come up to us into the *Moone*) we may write of what miracles wee list: which we offered to doe out of the *Indies*, and with good successe, till *Acosta de pro-* one of our *Order*, in a simplicity, and ingenuity fitter for a *cur. Indo. Salu.* *lib. 2. c. 9.* Christian, then a Jesuite, acknowledged and lamented that there 32 were no *miracles* done there. Truly it had bin better for us to have spit all those five *Brothers*, *Acostas*, out of our *Order*, then that any one of them should have vomited this reproach against us. 35

26 are] ate *1626*

De stud. Jesuit. abstrus. ca. 4. viris enim e nostris, qui scilicet vera, nimis tamen cruda fatentur, vere *Gretzerus* noster dixit, *Nullum corpus sine suis excrementis esse.* Huic autem Contemplationi, futurique Imperii politeiae consti-tuendae, non est nunc nobis (etsi admodum gratum sit) indulgen-
5 dum, nec tu in his occupationibus amplius detinendus. Scribat *Amplitudo* vestra; Consilium exequatur *Pontifex*; accedat *Luna*, quandocunque vobis visum fuerit. Interim quasi diversorio, mihi

Bellarm. de Purgat. L. 2. ca. 8. uti liceat interiori ista camera. Etsi enim *Gregorius* Papa perpetuo dolore stomachi, & pedum ab Angelo percussus est, quia precibus
10 suis, Deum ipsum ad *Traianum* ex inferis liberandum, & ad coelos transferendum compulerat, ideoque *Deus*, ex ore *Gregorii*, omnium successorum sponsionem accepit, neminem eorum id amplius ausurum, in me tamen revocando, nullum Pontifici imminere potest periculum, tum quia nec de me cogitasse in hoc pacto
15 putari potest *Deus*, de quo ipse nunquam cogitaverim, pactumque inde irritum reddatur, tum quia nec ita violetur sponsio, si non in Coelum, sed ab *Inferno* terreno, ad *Infernum Lunaticum* trans-ferendus sim.' Plura addere vetuit rumor, de quo dixi, undique increbescens: *Luciferoque* percontanti quid causae, responsum,
20 Animulam ad oras Inferni appulisse, qui *Pontificem* tandem exoratum dixit, ut *Ignatium* inter Divos referret; eiusque Canoni-zationem eum maturare. Iniquum enim esse, cum omnes artifices, laniique prophani, peculiares quos invocarent Divos haberent, solis laniis spiritualibus, & Regicidis suus deesset. Cum autem
25 *Iesuita Cottonus* in quaestionibus suis, ex invisibili privilegio Daemoniacae exhibendis, hanc inter alias, tam *Angliae* quam *Galliae* perniciosas, posuerat, *Quid pro Ignatii Canonizatione mihi faciendum?* tandem animadvertit, Regem *Hispaniae Philippum*, & *Henricum Galliae* per Legatos suos *Romae* contendere de hoc
30 negotio, quo scilicet eorum solicitante *Ignatius* proveheretur, (uterque enim eum sibi honorem deberi fingebat, cum uterque

It is of such men as these in our *Order*, that our *Gretzer* saies: *De studiis* *Jesuit.*
There is no body without his Excrements, because though they speake *Jesuit.* *abstrus. cap. 4.*
truth, yet they speake it too rawly. But as for this contemplation,
and the establishing of that government, (though it be a pleasant
consideration) we may neither pamper our selves longer with it   5
now, nor detaine you longer therein. Let your *Greatnesse* write;
let the *Pope* execute your counsell; let the *Moone* approach when
you two think fit. In the meane time let me use this Chamber, as
a resting place: For though *Pope Gregory* were strucken by the *Bellarm. de*
Angell with a perpetuall paine in his stomach and feet, because *Purgat. L. 2.* *c. 8.*
hee compelled *God* by his praiers, to deliver *Trajan* out of *Hell*,   11
and transferre him to *Heaven*; and therefore *God*, by the mouth of
Gregorie, tooke an assurance for all his *Successours*, that they
should never dare to request the like againe: yet when the *Pope*
shall call mee backe from hence, hee can be in no danger, both   15
because in this contract, *God* cannot bee presumed to have
thought of me, since I never thought of him, and so the contract
therein void; and because the Condition is not broken, if I bee
not removed into Heaven, but transferred from an Earthly *Hell*,
to a *Lunatique Hell*.' More then this he could not be heard to   20
speake: For that noise, of which I spoke before, increased
exceedingly, and when *Lucifer* asked the cause, it was told him,
that there was a soule newly arrived in *Hell*, which said that the
Pope was at last entreated to make *Ignatius a Saint*, and that hee
hastened his Canonization, as thinking it an unjust thing, that   25
when all artificers, and prophane Butchers had particular *Saints*
to invocate, only these spirituall Butchers, and *King-killers*,
should have none: for when the Jesuite *Cotton* in those questions
which by virtue of his invisible priviledge he had provided for
a possest person, amongst others, dangerous both to *England*   30
and *France*, had inserted this question: *What shall I do for* Ignatius
his Canonizing? and found out at last, that *Philip, King of Spaine*,
and *Henry, King of Fraunce*, contended by their Ambassadors at
Rome, which of them should have the honour of obtaining his
Canonizing (for both pretending to be King of *Navarre*, both   35

Margin *De studiis . . . cap. 4.* Ed.: *De studiis . . . cap. 5. 1611, 1626*

Rex *Navarrae,* & ea arte uterque *Iesuitas* eludebat: nam &
Pierre Matheu
Li. 1. Nar. 4.
D'*Alcala* e *Francisci* familia, & *Penaforte Iacobita, Philippo Rege* id
agente, in Coelum, neglectis Iesuitis, missi fuerant) tandem de
Regibus desperavit. Nec iis certe *Iesuitas* tantum debere decorum
Litera eius ad
Philip.
ei videbatur, cum & ipse *Baronius* ad eam constantiam pro-
6 gressus est, ut de iniuria Regi suo illata postulatus, se literis ad
Regem excusare non ante dignatus est, quam *Conclave* perage-
retur; ne si tum Pontifex creatus fuisset, id beneficio Regis ei
contigisse aliquis putaret. *Papam* igitur ipsi aggrediuntur.
10 Fatentur malle se in ea omnia a *Papa* restitui, quae in *Galliae*
Regno, & *Venetorum* Republica amiserant, quam *Ignatium*
in coelis collocari: idque potius Papam facere debere, ex Ordine
Gen. 2. 4.
quem in Creatione *Deus* ipse secutus videtur, qui prius Terram
ornavit quam Coelum: & hoc etiam argumento se *Israelitis* pro-
Gen. 17. 8.
bavit eorum Deum esse, quia scilicet *Canaan,* & alia beneficia
16 temporalia eis impertitus fuerat. Cum autem illud Papae omni-
potentiam iam superaret, in Coelis quid possit, aequum esse
illum experiri. Voluit autem ille titulo *Beati* (quem & *Aloisio*
Vita eius Episto-
la ad Paul. 5.
Gonsagae a Principibus eius Familiae, magna importunitate
solicitatus, concesserat) illis satisfecisse. Voluit etiam *Xaverium,*
21 qui miraculis claruisse dicitur, honore isto decorasse. Quidvis
voluit, dummodo *Ignatium* ei praeterire licuisset. Victus tamen
tandem est; & tam ipso Papa, quam Coelo ipso invito, nec etiam
24 annuente ipso *Lucifero, Ignatius* in *Divorum* turbam detrudendus
L. XLV. de
ver. oblig.
erit. Haec omnia, *Doctore Nello Gabriele* (de quo *Bartolus*) factus

pretended that this right and honour belonged to him: and so both deluded the Jesuits: For *D'Alcala* a *Franciscan*, and *Penafort* a *Jacobite*, were by *Philips* meanes canonized, and the Jesuite left out.) At last hee despaired of having any assistance from these Princes: nor did he thinke it convenient, that a Jesuite should be so much beholden to a King, since *Baronius* was already come to that heighth and constancy, that being accused of some wronges done to his King, hee did not vouchsafe to write in his owne excuse to the King, till the *Conclave* which was then held, was fully ended, least (as himselfe gives the reason) if hee had then beene chosen *Pope*, it should bee thought hee had beene beholden to the King therein. For these reasons therefore they labour the *Pope* themselves. They confesse, that if they might choose, they had rather hee should restore them into all which they had lost in *Fraunce*, and *Venice*, then that *Ignatius* should be sent up into *Heaven*; and that the *Pope* was rather bound to do so, by the Order which *God himselfe* seemes to have observed in the *Creation* where he first furnished the *Earth*, and then the *Heavens*, and confirmed himselfe to be the *Israelites* God by this *Argument*, that he had given them the land of *Canaan*, and other temporall blessings. But since this exceeded the Popes omnipotence in Earth, it was fit he should try, what he could do in *Heaven*. Now the Pope would faine have satisfied them with the title of *Beatus*, which formerly upon the intreaty of the Princes of that *Family*, he had affoorded to *Aloisius Gonzaga* of that *Order*. He would also have given this title of *Saint* rather to *Xaverius*, who had the reputation of having done *Miracles*. Indeed he would have done anything, so hee might have slipped over *Ignatius*. But at last hee is overcome; and so against the will of *Heaven*, and of the *Pope*, *Lucifer* himselfe being not very forward in it, *Ignatius* must bee thrust in amongst the *Saints*. All this discourse, I, beeing growne cunninger then that Doctor, *Gabriell Nele* (of whom *Bartolus* speaketh) that by the onely motion of their lippes,

Pierre Matheu
L. 1. Nar. 4.

5

Litera eius ad
Philip. 3.

10

15

Gen. 2. 4.

Gen. 17. 8.
21

25

Vita eius
Epistol. ad
Paul. 5.

30

L. XLV. de
ver. oblig.

2–4 Jesuits: . . . left out.) *Ed.*: Jesuits:) . . . left out *1611, 1626*   Margin
Matheu Ed.: *Mathieri 1611, 1626*   Margin L. XLV. *Ed.*: L. I. *1611, 1626*
33 their *Ed.*: his *1611, 1626*

peritior, qui ex motu labiorum, sine voce edita, omnium ser-
mones intelligebat, in omnium vultu legere mihi visus sum.
Ea (cum iam a *Lucifero* deprehensa) litem terminabant: nec
amplius haerendum de *Ignatio* inducendo putavit. Cui iam ex
5 Canonizatione, novum ius, novus titulus acquisitus erat. Metuit-
que, ne de mora eum Papa increparet; cum Canonizatio fere
quaedam declaratio iam sit, qua hominem de Ecclesia *Romana*
bene meritum, summorum iam in Inferno honorum participem
fieri, omnibus innotescat. Amare enim ubique *Augustinum*, plae-
10 runque fingunt isti viri: nec volunt illum ne tum quidem menti-
tum, cum dixerat, *Multorum corpora in terris honorari, quorum*
animae torquentur in Gehenna. Manum igitur *Ignati* praehendit
Lucifer, & ad portas ducit. Ego autem de eius Canonizatione
adhuc dubius, ad veritatem perquirendam proficiscor. Vix enim
15 credendum putavi, *Paulum 5.* qui nuper urbem Romam, Ecclesiamque tot impensis oneraverat, cum *Franciscam Romanam* Divis
immiscuit, ad *Ignatium* provehendum, cum iam nemo Regum
aut impensas faceret, aut sollicitaret, tam facile accessurum:
nec simul Thesauros Ecclesiae utrosque aperturum. Vix enim a
20 *Leone 3.* qui 800. a *Christo* annis, primus aliquem in Canonem
retulisse legitur, id factum esse animadverteram. Nec puto
Paulum 5. ad hanc foeminam sanctis adcensendam alia ratione
Valladerius ductum, quam quod illa, quam societati suae indixerat, Regula,
Fol. 57.
a Sancto Paulo dictata fuerat & scripta. Etsi enim ei scribendae
25 interfuerint etiam *Petrus, Magdalena,* alii, *Paulus* tamen autor
fuit. Cum autem veteres *Pauli* Epistolae huic Ecclesiae officiant
nimis, perquam cupide certe arrepturi erant, si quid ille tandem
scriberet, quod ab illis staret, & secundam iam conversionem ad

without any utterance, understood all men, perceived and read
in every mans countenance there. These thinges, as soone as
Lucifer apprehended them, gave an end to the contention; for
now hee thought he might no longer doubt nor dispute of
Ignatius his admission, who, besides his former pretences, had 5
now gotten a new right and title to the place, by his *Canoniza-*
tion; and he feared that the *Pope* would take all delay ill at his
handes, because *Canonization* is now growne a kinde of *Declaration*
by which all men may take knowledge, that such a one, to whom
the Church of *Rome* is much beholden, is now made partaker of 10
the principall dignities, and places in *Hell*: For these men ever
make as though they would follow *Augustine* in all things, and
therefore they provide that that also shall bee true which he said
in this point: *That the Reliques of many are honoured upon earth*
whose soules are tormented in Hell. Therefore he took *Ignatius* by the 15
hand, and led him to the gate. In the meane time, I, which
doubted of the truth of this report of his Canonizing, went a
little out for further instruction: for I thought it scarce credible,
that *Paulus 5.* who had but lately burdened both the *Citie* of
Rome, and the *Church*, with so great expences, when he canonized 20
Francisca Romana, would so easily proceed to canonize *Ignatius*
now, when neither any prince offered to beare the charge, nor
so much as sollicited it: for so he must bee forced to waste both
the *Treasures* of the Church at once. And from *Leo 3.* who 800
yeares after Christ, is the first Pope which Canonized any, I had 25
not observed that this had ever beene done: Neither do I think
that *Paulus 5.* was drawne to the Canonizing of this woman by
any other respect, then because that Rule which shee appointed *Valladerius*
to her *Order*, *was Dictated and written by Saint Paul*: For though *fol. 57.*
Peter, and *Magdalene*, and others, were present at the writing 30
thereof, as witnesses, yet *Paul* was the *Author* thereof. And since
Saint *Pauls* old *Epistles* trouble and dis-advantage this Church,
they were glad to apprehend any thing of his new writing, which
might be for them, that so this new worke of his might beare
witnesse of his second conversion to *Papistry*, since by his first 35

Papismum (cum ex eius prima ad Christianismum nihil illis
lucrosum adveniat) scriptis testari vellet. Nam certe *Paulum 5.*
hoc in negotio, *Deum, Deum esse opportuisse, cum Divinitate vixisse*
4 *familiariter, praedestinationem insusurrantem audivisse, in Concilio*
Fol. 5. *Divinissimae Triados assedisse,* (quae de illo dicit *Valladerius*) non
ita necessaria mihi videntur, cum *Pontifices Romani,* ista, ut
homines, & humanis passionibus plaerunque ducti, peragunt.
Comperi autem tandem, a *Gazettero* quodam, qui vulgi rumores
Romae corradere solitus, unde literas venales, ipsis *Iesuitarum*
10 *Iaponicis Indicisque* futiliores, mendaciores, conficeret, hoc ad
inferos delatum, & ab animula Iesuitula, novitia, credula, im-
plicita fide acceptum, sparsumque. Risi certe *Luciferi* creduli-
tatem, nec amplius de Infidelitate accusandum putavi. Reversus
autem sum, ut si forte ianuae occlusae non essent, aliquid de
15 Ignatii caeterorumque qui ante eum eo loco gavisi fuerant, mutuo
affectu annotarem. Ille autem adhuc fere in limine haerens, novam
litem intentarat. Protinus enim in locum supremum, & a
Luciferi solio proximum, oculos coniecerat; eum occupatum
cernens, *Luciferum* sistit; rogat, 'Quisnam ille, qui eam sedem
20 usurparet?' Dictum ei est, *Bonifacium* esse; cui, *Nouatori* eximio,
quique primus nomen *Episcopi Universalis* sibi vindicavit, id
honoris tributum. 'Illene *Novator,*' intonuit *Ignatius*? 'Aut hoc a
me ferendum, cuius in hoc laborarunt Alumni omnes, ut omnes
ante illum *Papas* id nomen retinuisse, probatum redderent?
25 *Gregoriumque* Papam non de nomine *Antichristiano* assumendo, sed
de Iure Pontifici Romano debito, usurpando, *Ioannem* Patriarcham redarguisse. Tene etiam decuit, *Lucifer,* aut Ecclesiae
Romanae immemorem certe, aut eius Imperii Arcanis imparem,
minusque capacem, sententiae iudicioque in inferno ferendo
30 favere, quod etsi veritati consentire potuit, non tamen esset

conversion to *Christianity*, they got nothing: for to say, that in
this business *Paulus* 5. *could not choose but be God, God himselfe,* to
say, *that hee must needes have lived familiarly with the God-head: and
must have heard Predestination it selfe whispering to him: And must
have had a place to sit in Councell with the most Divine Trinitie,* (all 5
which *Valladerius* sayes of him) is not necessary in this matter, Fol. 5.
wherein the Popes, for the most part, proceed as humane affections leade them. But at last, after some enquiry, I found that
a certaine idle *Gazettier*, which used to scrape up Newes, and
Rumours at *Rome*, and so to make up sale letters, vainer, and 10
falser, then the Jesuites Letters of *Japan*, and the *Indies*, had
brought this newes to *Hell*, and a little Jesuiticall *Novice*, a
credulous soule, received it by his implicit faith, and published
it. I laughed at *Lucifers* easinesse to beleeve, and I saw no reason
ever after, to accuse him of infidelity. Upon this I came backe 15
againe, to spie (if the gates were stil open) with what affection
Ignatius, and they who were in auncient possession of that place,
behaved themselves towardes one an other. And I found him
yet in the porch, and there beginning a new contention: for
having presently cast his eyes to the principall place, next to 20
Lucifers owne *Throne*, and finding it possest, he stopt *Lucifer*,
and asked him, who it was that sate there. It was answered, that
it was *Pope Boniface*; to whom, as to a principall Innovator, for
having first chalenged the name of *Universall Bishop*, that honour
was affoorded. 'Is he an Innovator?' thundred *Ignatius*. 'Shall I 25
suffer this, when all my Disciples have laboured all this while to
prove to the world, that all the *Popes* before his time did use that
name? And that *Gregory* did not reprehend the *Patriarch John*
for taking to himselfe an Antichristian name, but for usurping
a name which was due to none but the *Pope*. And could it be 30
fit for you, *Lucifer*, (who in this were either unmindfull of the
Romane Church, or else too weake and incapable of her secrets
and mysteries) to give way to any sentence in *Hell*, which
(though it were according to truth,) yet differed from the

25 'Is . . . Innovator?' . . . *Ignatius*. 'Shall *Ed*.: Is . . . Innovator . . . *Ignatius?*
shall *1611, 1626*

Iesuitarum Oraculis analogum consentaneumque?' Advolat igitur *Ignatius*; in *Bonifacium* irruit; & sede exuit. Eum autem pari passu comitatur *Lucifer*, auxiliumque ei praestat; ne si eum desereret, ipse sua sede periclitaretur. Ego autem ad corpus redeo, quod

5   *Qualis hesterno madefacta rore,*
    Et novo tandem tepefacta sole,
    Excutit somnum, Tremulam Coronam
       Erigit Herba.
    Quae prius languens, recidens, recurva,
10   *Osculum terrae dederat, Iubarque*
    Denegatum tamdiu, nunc refulgens
       Solis anhelat.

Animae adventu satis refotum est. Haec autem quae videram, saepe mente recolens, quam scilicet eleganter & concinne in
15 omnibus sibi mutuo respondent *Roma* & *Infernum*, cum videram Papam in inferno a *Iesuita* sede spoliatum, suspicatus sum idem eos & *Romae* conaturos.

APOLOGIA PRO IESUITIS

Tandem ad Apologiam *pro Iesuitis accedendum: id est, de illis,*
20 *silendum. Favet enim illis, quisquis de illis tacet. Nec certe cuiquam, diutissime locuto (etsi ei Oceanus Clepsydra esset) unquam deerit, quod de eorum flagitiis addere possit. Si cui quid huic Apologiae subtexere visum fuerit, per me liceat: tribus quatuorve versibus spatium relictum videt. Paradoxo tali satis. Nec totum, Iungius, Scribanius, Gretzerus,*
25 Richeomus, Cydonius, *aliive* Apologiis *assueti, belloque (quod aiunt) defensivo pene macerati (modo* Vera *&* Bona *de Iesuitis dicant)*

Bonar. in Amphithe. *occuparent: nec se hoc solamine tutentur, ipsum* Catonem, *quadragies & quater, causam dixisse. Nam & toties absolutus est: Quod de Iesuitis negant Parlamenta tam* Anglica, *quam* Gallica. *Cui autem brevior*

Jesuites *Oracles?*' With this *Ignatius* flyes upwardes, and rushes
upon *Boniface*, and throwes him out of his Seate: And *Lucifer*
went up with him as fast, and gave him assistance, least, if hee
should forsake him, his owne seate might bee endangered. And
I returned to my body; which   5

> *As a flower wet with last nights dew, and then*
> *Warm'd with the new Sunne, doth shake off agen*
> *All drowsinesse, and raise his trembling Crowne,*
> *Which crookedly did languish, and stoope downe*
> *To kisse the earth, and panted now to finde*   10
> *Those beames return'd, which had not long time shin'd,*

was with this returne of my soule sufficiently refreshed. And
when I had seene all this, and considered how fitly and propor-
tionally *Rome* & *Hell* answered one another, after I had seene
a Jesuit turne the *Pope* out of his *Chaire* in *Hell*, I suspected that 15
that *Order* would attempt as much at *Rome*.

AN APOLOGY FOR JESUITES

Now is it time to come to the *Apology* for *Jesuites*: that is, it is
time to leave speaking of them, for hee favours them most, which
saies least of them; Nor can any man, though hee had declaimed
against them till all the sand of the sea were run through his 20
houre-glasse, lacke matter to adde of their practises. If any man
have a mind to adde any thing to this *Apology*, hee hath my leave;
and I have therefore left roome for three or foure lines: which is
enough for such a paradox: and more then *Jungius, Scribanius,*
Gretzerus, Richeomus, Cydonius, and all the rest which are used 25
to *Apologies,* and almost tyred with defensive warre, are able to
employ, if they will write onely *good* things, and true, of the *Bonar. in*
Jesuites. Neither can they comfort themselves with this, That *Amphithe.*
Cato was called to his answere foure and forty times: for hee was
so many times acquitted, which both the *Parliaments* of *England* 30

quam par est, haec videatur Apologia, *totum librum pro* Apologia *interpretari potest, ex illa ipsorum Regula,* maximum Innocentiae argumentum esse, accusari ab Evangelicis. *Hac autem, dum adhuc*
5 *alicubi viribus ad nocendum polleant, gaudeant* Apologia. *Futurum brevi, ut, cum quemadmodum a* Venetis *spoliati, detrusi, in Galliis ventilati, & exagitati fuerint; ita & a reliquis Principibus deserantur, ipsa eorum imbecillitas eis fiat* Apologia, *reddanturque necessario*

Li. 1. c. 24. *innocui; quodque de Curribus falcibus instructis dixerat* Vegetius Iesuitis *accommodetur,* primo terrori fuisse, post derisui.

and *France* deny of the *Jesuites*. But if any man thinke this *Apology* too short, he may thinke the whole booke an *Apology*, by this *rule* of their owne *That it is their greatest argument of innocency to be accused by us.* At this time, whilst they are yet somewhat able to do some harme, in some places, let them make much of this Apology. It will come to passe shortly, when as they have bene dispoyled and expelled at *Venice*, and shaked and fanned in *France*, so they will bee forsaken of other *Princes*, and then their owne weakenesse will bee their *Apology*, and they will grow harmelesse out of necessity, and that which Vegetius sayd of chariots armed with sithes and hookes, will be applied to the Jesuites, *at first they were a terror, and after a scorne.*

Spongia pro Jesuit. cont. Equit. polon. fol. 2.

Li. 1. ca. 24.

FINIS

COMMENTARY

PAGE 3

l. 8. *an other booke formerly published.*[1] This is a reference to *Pseudo-Martyr* which Donne had written in 1609 and published in 1610. In it he attacked the Jesuits (particularly in Chapter IV) more harshly than he does anywhere in *Ignatius His Conclave*; but the attack is based on seriously handled argument and the book is Donne's major work of controversy.

l. 11. *the great Erasmus.* The work noted in the margin is the *Controversa Fidei* by the Belgian Jesuit, Carolus Scribanius, published at Antwerp in 1609. Coccius was a German theologian, author of the huge *Thesaurus Catholicus* (Cologne, 1600–1) which ranked second only to Bellarmine's *Controversiae* as a target for English controversialists. It figured largely in the Morton–Persons dispute, where Morton attacked it for falsifying patristic texts (see *An Encounter Against M. Persons*, pp. 126–57). The point of the reference was a dispute among Catholics: Coccius lists Erasmus among the Catholic authors; Scribanius, referring to the lack of miracles among the heretics, speaks of '. . . de vestris novi aetatis nostrae Evangelii praeconibus Roterodamus'. He quotes with particular ire Erasmus' quip '. . . nullus illorum adhuc exstitit qui vel equum claudum sanare potuerit' (p. 106). Jesuits generally were not publicly enthusiastic about Erasmus. Ignatius had disliked his work, particularly the *Enchiridion Militis Christiani* and had urged his followers not to use it (see Ribadeneyra, *Vita Ignatii Loyolae*, 1589, pp. 49–50).

l. 18. *Rebullus that Run-away.* Guillaume de Reboul was born of a French Huguenot family, but was excommunicated by the Huguenots in 1595. At the same time he was accused by his employer of misuse of funds. He fled to Avignon and then to Rome, and on the way became a Catholic. There he wrote a series of controversial works against the Huguenots, among them the two Donne seems to know, *Salmonées* and *Cabale des Reformés*. He also tried his hand at satire against the papacy, but these works do not

---

[1] The passages cited for comment are printed in italics with no attention paid to the typography of the original.

seem to have found a publisher. He was imprisoned for his pains, and must have been still in prison when Donne was writing. Scarcely the type of colleague of whom Bellarmine and the other Catholic apologists could have been very proud, he was finally hanged in 1611.

l. 23. *Macer*. Nicodemus Macer was the pen-name of the German Kaspar Schoppe. He published in 1607 a defence of Baronius against the Venetians: *Disceptatio de Paraenesi Card. Baronii*. This book begins with a patronizing fourteen-page brag, studded with classical lore, and as offensive as it is pompous. It finished with the claim that the author is working 'risui ac lubentiae'. Donne had used these same phrases before in *Pseudo-Martyr* (p. 90).

There was great interest among Anglicans in the Venetian controversy with the papacy. A spate of books came out on the subject, most of them translations (e.g. Vignier's *Concerning the Excommunication of the Venetians*, London, 1607). Donne had personal reasons for following the developments in Venice with interest because of his friendship for Sir Henry Wotton, the English ambassador to the Venetians during the troubles. Wotton was deeply involved himself, and his activities during the Interdict were manifold and can be qualified as zealous or indiscreet according to the bias of the historian (see Frances A. Yates, 'Paolo Sarpi's History of the Council of Trent', *Journal of the Warburg and Courtauld Institutes*, vii. 123–43). There is no proof that Donne and Sarpi were or ever became friends, but Donne in his will left a portrait of Sarpi to Henry King (see Gosse, ii. 360).

PAGE 5

l. 7. *their revived Lucian, Pasquil*. The word 'Pasquil' comes from the custom of attaching satires and libels to the statue of Pasquil in Rome. From the context it is evident that Donne is not referring to the English authors, such as Nashe or Breton, who wrote under the name Pasquil. And the choice among continental satires is too vast to permit a guess. By the seventeenth century the word had come to mean any sarcastic (and usually broad) satiric attack. Donne himself ironically calls the Roman Catholic histories 'pasquills' in *Sermons*, ii. 327.

l. 17. *The Two Tutelar Angels*. Throughout this passage Donne is playing with the traditional opposition between the Church in France, protecting its Gallican liberties, and the See of Rome (see

note on p. 130). He also enjoyed satirizing the traditional angelo-
logy. Cf.

... they afford a particular Tutelar Angel to every College and Corpora-
tion, and to the race of flies and of fleas and of ants, since they allow such
an Angel to every infidel kingdom, yea to anti-christ, yea to Hell itself...
(*Pseudo-Martyr*, p. 248)

See also *Biathanatos*, p. 20; *Sermons*, x. 45–6.

l. 23. *Janus*. The point of the allusion is that, like the two faces of
Janus, the papacy and the French Church will never see eye to
eye.

l. 27. *I was in an Extasie*. Cf. 'Satire IV':

> ... a trance,
> Like his, who dreamt he saw hell, did advance
> Itself on mee, Such men as he saw there,
> I saw at court, and worse, and more; ...
> (Milgate, p. 19)

l. 29. *My little wandring sportful Soule*. Mrs. Simpson says that
'this must be the earliest English rendering of Hadrian's famous
lines' (Simpson, p. 196).

PAGE 7

Margin. *Nuncius sydereus*. *Sidereus Nuncius* by Galileo, was pub
lished at Venice in 1610. (The dedication is dated 11 March.)
This book communicated Galileo's news of the irregularity of the
moon's surface, the composition of the galaxy, and the discovery
of the moons of Jupiter. It also gives the details of the telescope
with which the observations were made.

Margin. *De stella in Cygno*. *De Stella Tertii Honoris in Cygno* . . .
Narratio Astronomica, published by Kepler in Prague in 1606.
'Tychone iam mortuo, equidem haec me cura incessit, ne quid
fortasse novi existeret in coelo, me inscio' (p. 154). Donne made
fun of this same pompous phrase in his 'Problem VIII' (*Paradoxes
and Problems*, p. 51).

l. 15. *they shall hardly find Enoch, or Elias*. This cryptic remark is a
reference to a minor exchange of shot between James I and Bellarmine. It had long been pious custom to identify the two prophets
who would do battle against Antichrist (Rev. 9) with Elias and
Enoch. James, arguing quite rationally that prophecies are seldom

understood until they are accomplished, calls this a Jewish fable, claims the two prophets are already in Heaven, and identifies the apocalyptic warriors as the Old and New Testaments (*Premonition*, pp. 67 ff.). Bellarmine objects to this theory and points out that it ill accords with James's repeated protestations of respect for the Fathers (*Apologia*, p. 172). The substance of the discussion was whether or not the pope is Antichrist, on which subject James and Bellarmine were unlikely to concur. Donne's comment that Enoch and Elias are not floating about in some celestial middle distance supports James's position.

l. 17. *The Larke by busie and laborious wayes.* Donne here puts into verse the description of the lark which Albertus Magnus gives in his *De Animalibus*, xxiii. 5:

Alauda . . . cantat ascendendo per circulum volans, et cum descendit, primo quidem paulatim descendit, et tandem alas ad se convertens in modum lapidis subito decidit et in illo casu cantum dimittit.
(*Beati Alberti Magni Opera Omnia*, ed. A. Borgnet (Paris, 1891), xii. 437)

l. 24. *by the benefit of certaine spectacles.* The absurdities of the martyrologies were a frequent source of controversial ammunition, particularly since the simpler Roman writers used visions and private revelations as proofs of doctrine. James objected to the tales of the 'legended saints' and calls them 'Dii Penates or Tutelares, these Courtiers of God' (*Premonition*, p. 38). Morton devotes a whole chapter of his *Apologia Catholica I* to them, singling out the entries on St. Catherine and St. George for his especial scorn (pp. 110–13). He returns to the subject in *Apologia Catholica II* to indicate Bede and Gregory as the worst offenders (pp. 217–19).

In this passage Donne manifestly objects to the idea of souls leaving their bodies and appearing to the survivors. Cf. 'Resurrection':

> Had one of those, whose credulous pietie
> Thought, that a Soule one might discerne and see,
> Goe from a body . . .
> (*Divine Poems*, p. 28)

In general, Donne's 'rectified devotion' found little place for private revelations and visions. He linked them with the excesses of private interpretation.

. . . howsoever these Revelations and Inspirations seem to fall upon us from heaven, they arise from the earth, from ourselves, from our own *melancholy* and *pride*, or our too much *homeliness* and familiarity in our

accesses and conversation with God, or a *facility* in beleeving, or an often
dreaming the same thing . . . so ordinary were these apparitions *then*, as that
any son or nephew or friend could discern his fathers, or uncles, or companions soul, ascending out of *Purgatory* into heaven, and know them as
distinctly as if they kept the same haire, and beard, and bodily lineaments
as they had upon earth. . . . We see a great author of theirs (*Coccius*)
attribute so much to these apparitions and revelations, that when he
pretends to prove all the controversies by the *Fathers* of the Church, he
everywhere intermingles that reverend *Book, of Brigid's Revelations* . . . A
book of so much blasphemy, and impertinency, and incredibility, that if
a Heathen were to be converted, he would sooner be brought to beleeve
Ovid's Metamorphoses, then *Brigid's Revelations*, to conduce to Religion.

(Sermons, x. 145-6)

l. 31. *channels in the bowels of the Earth.* Cf. . . . 'th' earth's inward,
narrow, crooked lanes' *Songs and Sonnets*, p. 52. These channels
were thought to account for the filtration of salt out of sea water
so that inland lakes and rivers were fresh. The notion is derived
from Aristotle (*Meteorologia*, 354b and 355b) and was accepted by
Seneca (*Quaestiones Naturales*, III. v). Donne uses the same phrase
in *Sermons*, iii. 302.

PAGE 9

Margin. *Paleotus de Sindone. Jesu Christi Crucifixi Stigmata Sacrae
Sindoni Impressa . . . Explicata*, by Alphonso Paleoti, Douai, 1607.
This book is a large compendium of meditations, prayers, and information about the Passion of Christ. What probably most
annoyed Donne in it was the heavy reliance it places on the
'revelations' of St. Brigid. The passage he quotes here could have
caught his eye for its ceremonial language.

. . . Robertus Aquinas . . . insinuat . . . quod Christus antequam cruci sese
extenderet, vestibus nudatus atque genuflexus, oculos manusque ad coelos
extulerit, dicens haec aut similia verba: Suscipe Sancte Pater Aeterne me
dilectum filium tuum, quem tibi offero sacrificium immaculatum pro
salute humani generis et remissione omnium peccatorum. Ecce iam non
tibi offerentur legalia sacrificia hircorum aut agnorum, sed caro innocentis
filii tui (p. 119).

The same work is referred to in *Pseudo-Martyr*, pp. 107 and 331,
and in *Biathanatos*, p. 203.

Margin. *Josephina di Gieron. Gratian.* This is one of Donne's own
books, *Josephina: Summario de las Excelencias del Glorioso S. Joseph*, by
Gieronimo Gracian, Brussels, 1609. The passage which draws
Donne's fire is actually a quotation from Isidore. It is mostly a

narrative of a pious death, rather modestly done considering the date (pp. 116 recto–117 verso).

l. 6. *the Suburbs of Hel.* 'Schoolmen . . . have invented new things and found out or added suburbs to Hell . . .' (*Essays in Divinity*, p. 27). The same subject arises many times in the *Sermons* (cf. *Sermons*, vii. 165–89 and 190–214). It also led to a lively exchange between Bellarmine and James I. Bellarmine seems angry at James's claim that there were no texts to justify the Roman position on Purgatory (*Apologia*, p. 163). James's only answer is his query whether or not Purgatory would be large enough for him to go hawking (*Premonition*, p. 43).

l. 14. *Patriarkes of the Papists.* The allegation that the Roman Church found support for its teachings in the classical authors was fairly common. Book vi of the *Aeneid* was usually advanced by the Reformers as the Roman source for the doctrine of Purgatory. Donne uses the same charge in his *Catalogus*, no. 30 and in *Sermons*, vii. 177. Cf. Thomas Morton's '. . . the question is not who first conceited of Purgatory, for then a man may fetch it from Plato among the philosophers, from Virgil among the poets, and from Origen . . . among the Fathers . . .' (*A Catholicke Appeale*, p. 498). The basis of the charge is that the Roman Church was 'unscriptural'.

. . . And in this politicall Divinity, *Machiavel* is their Pope; And after they had perplexed understandings with Philosophicall Divinity in the Schoole, and in that Divinity, *Aristotle* is their Pope; they thought themselves in courtesie, or conscience bound, to recreate the world with Poeticall Divinity, and in this Divinity, *Virgill* is their Pope . . . (*Sermons*, vii. 131)

l. 18. *I saw a secret place.* This description echoes the inner circle in Hell, inhabited by the three great traitors, Judas, Brutus, and Cassius, in the *Inferno* (Canto 34). Mrs. Simpson has pointed out the relation between this passage and item no. 30 in the *Catalogus*: 'The Quintessence of Hell; or the private apartment of Hell, in which is a discussion of the fifth region passed over by Homer, Virgil, Dante and the rest of the papists . . .' (cf. note on p. 73 of the *Catalogus*). In commenting on Purgatory, James remarks, 'How many other rooms there be, I am not on God his Council . . . how many chambers and anti-chambers the devil hath, they can best tell who go to him' (*Premonition*, p. 43).

Margin. *Theod. Niem. nemus unio.* Donne is here using *De Schismatibus inter Pontifices Romanos* by Dietrich of Niem. It is usually known by the subtitle of its last volume, *Nemus Unionis*. First written in 1407, it outlined proposals for Church reform and the ending of the papal schism. Because of its sharp attacks against a divided papacy, it was popular among the Reformers, and was printed in 1536 at Nürnberg and in 1566 at Basle. The passage Donne quotes is entitled: 'Epistolae Sathanae Johanni Dominici . . . titulo S. Sixti Cardinali . . .' 'Nam pro remuneratione tuorum operum apud nos intime acceptaberis: tibi non in inferiori parte nostri aeterni chaos locum foetidissimum et ardentissimum praeparari fecimus in medio praefatorum Arrii et Mahometi . . .'

l. 28. *Pope Boniface 3.* Donne's probable source for the charge that Boniface III was the first Pope to claim Roman primacy was Platina's *de Vitis Summorum Pontificum.* Boniface reigned from February to November 607. According to Platina, who quotes Bede, Boniface's good relations with the Emperor Phocas had induced the latter to grant the title of *episcopus universalis* after Gregory I had rebuked John, the Patriarch of Constantinople, for employing it. The story is a commonplace of the controversialists. A strong statement against Boniface is given in Bernadino Ochino's *Of the Usurped Primacy* (1549) where Boniface, like Julius II, is made to trumpet his own iniquities. Cf. Jewel's *Apology* (pp. 25–6, 72), Morton's *Apologia Catholica I* (pp. 242–3), and *A Catholicke Appeale* (pp. 490–3). By the first decade of the seventeenth century this historical argument was familiar enough to fit easily into a summer sermon by George Cresswell, *The Harmonie of the Law and the Gospel* (1607). James urged the argument against Bellarmine (*Apology*, p. 92), who answered, as did all the Roman writers, that Boniface was far from the first to claim the primacy.

l. 31. *Mahomet . . . used Sergius as his fellow-bishop.* There was a legend that Mohammed as a child had been taught by a Nestorian monk named Sergius. Donne probably found the story in the *Cribratio Alcorani* by Nicholas of Cusa. He refers to the work in a letter to Robert Ker (*Letters*, p. 308). Cusa makes Sergius a Nestorian and a bishop (pp. 34 and 114).

PAGE II

l. 2. *the policy of the State of Israel.* Jewel gives a good summary of the 'policy of Israel' as Tudor polemicists understood and used it. In showing how the kings and rulers in Israel controlled religious affairs, he instances Moses, Joshua, David, Solomon, Hezekiah, Jehoshaphat, Josiah, and Jehu (*Apology*, pp. 115–16). James was fond of falling back on the Old Testament to support his claim to be the head of the Church in England. Besides the usual references to 'the Lord's anointed', he used against Bellarmine the sentence applied to Jehoshaphat, 'And he brought them back to the Lord God of their fathers' (2 Chron. 19: 4; *Apology*, pp. 106–7). Bellarmine's answer is in *Responsio*, p. 250.

l. 4. *to tread upon the neckes of Princes.* The story of Pope Alexander III putting his foot on the neck of the Emperor Frederick Barbarossa arose frequently when controversy ceased and personal abuse began. Bellarmine handles it in answer to James by denying it ever happened (*Apologia*, p. 200).

Margin. *Sedulius.* The Franciscan Sedulius is the author of *Liber Apologeticus adversus Alcoranum Franciscanorum (auctore Erasmo Alber) pro Libro Conformitatum*, Antwerp, 1607. Alber's attack was at first credited to Luther in its original German: *Barfüßer Mönche Eulenspiegel und Alcoran.* Under its French title, *L'Alcoran des Cordeliers* it became the major French borrowing from the German reforming press. It provoked many answers, of which Sedulius' is typical.

The legendary nonsense of the *Liber Conformitatum* was a natural target for Donne. He uses the work in *Biathanatos* (p. 123) and in *Pseudo-Martyr* (pp. 123, 126). Morton attacks it in *A Catholicke Appeale* (p. 240). In all of this section and later Donne may well be attacking the Jesuits with the Appellant argument that they were the direct heirs of the Franciscan tradition of unrest and social protest (see T. H. Clancy, S.J., *Papist Pamphleteers*, Chicago, 1964, pp. 84–7).

Margin. *Harlay defence des Jesuites. La Défence des Pères Jésuites en Response aux Médisances . . .* Paris, 1609, by François de Harlay (the elder). 'Ces Pères ont en leur charge deux cent mille escoliers dont la France en voit quarante mille' (p. 13). Jesuit numbers have a way of growing in direct proportion to the distance from Rome. Antoine Arnauld's attack was published in England as *The Arrainment of the Jesuites in France* (1594). From the past growth of the Order he estimated that by 1610 there would be 120,000 Jesuits (p. 8).

Margin. *Valladerius.* The *Speculum Sapientiae Matronalis ex vita Sanctae Franciscae Romanae* was published by Jean Valladier in Paris in 1609. Donne actually abbreviates the catalogue. In addition to the figures given here, Valladier adds 5 patriarchs of Jerusalem, 5,000 learned men, 43 emperors and empresses, 44 imperial children, 96 kings and queens, and 700 royal children. He carefully

notes how many in each category were French. Donne enjoyed
the listing and uses it again, in almost the same form, in *Sermons*,
ix. 337.

l. 26. *unanimity, and idle concord.* Speaking of the disunity of all
heresies (a point much urged by Roman writers) Donne remarks
in 1624, '. . . and that one Sect of Mahomet, was quickly divided,
and sub-divided into 70 sects . . .' (*Sermons*, vi. 157).

l. 30. *it may religiously, and piously be beleeved.* This technical
theological phrase, *pie credi potest*, was used by Bellarmine to qualify
the moral certainty one might have that a particular pope was not
a heretic. James picked it up and applied it, somewhat disingenu-
ously, to the primacy itself (*Premonition*, p. 14), which Bellarmine
held to be a matter of faith. Bellarmine called him sharply, and
fairly, to order by citing chapter and verse (*Responsio*, p. 232).
Donne here is mocking Bellarmine's preciseness in a burlesque
parallel of the two kinds of certitude.

PAGE 13

l. 9. *For so the truth be lost, it is no matter how.* 'Contemplative and
bookish men must, of necessitie, be more quarrelsome then others,
. . . But as long as they go towards peace, that is Truth, it is no
matter which way' (*Biathanatos*, p. 20).

l. 16. *to finde, to deride, to detrude Ptolomey.* This statement is
unfair to Copernicus. In the Preface to the *De Revolutionibus
Orbium Coelestium* he finds fault with Ptolemy's reasoning, but
without the usual scholarly vaunting.

l. 20. *a Soule to the Earth.* Copernicus is here made to use the
scholastic notion of the 'soul' as the moving principle of anything
that moves.

l. 27. *Origen . . . burning in Hell.* Origen taught that damnation
was temporary and that even the devils would ultimately be saved.
For this most of the orthodox theologians from the fifth century onward, condemned him as a heretic. In *Biathanatos* (pp. 20,
207), and in *Essays* (p. 8), Donne appears to agree with Origen.
This agreement would account for his sarcasm here. Later in his
life he rejected Origen's position (see *Sermons*, v. 86, vii. 217). The
Roman extension of the 'name and punishment of Heresie', particularly in the Council of Trent, was a frequent charge in Donne's
later sermons (see *Sermons*, x. 155–6). At the place cited in the

margin Bellarmine rejects Origen's position on damnation, but does not comment on his ultimate fate.

PAGE 15

l. 2. *raysed both thee, and thy prison, the Earth.* This and the following sentence echo the letter from Cardinal Schönberg, Archbishop of Capua, which opens the *De Revolutionibus*: '. . . te novam mundi rationem constitisse qua doceas terram moveri solem imum mundi adeoque medium locum tenere . . .' The notion manifestly interested Donne: cf. 'Copernicus in the Mathematiques hath carried earth farther up from the stupid center; and yet hath not honoured it, because for the necessity of appearances, it hath carried heaven so much higher from it' (*Letters*, p. 102). The adjectives applied to the sun are echoed in the opening lines of 'The Sun Rising' (*Songs and Sonnets*, p. 72).

l. 14. *Something he had which he might have conveniently opposed.* I am unable to suggest what it was that Lucifer might have said here.

l. 23. *when hee died he was utterly ignorant in all great learning.* Ignatius of Loyola (1491–1556) neither was nor claimed to be a scholar. He began his formal schooling in 1524 at the age of thirty-three and proceeded Master of Arts from Paris at the age of forty-four. Comments on his early lack of schooling are common in the controversies of the time. Étienne Pasquier in his *The Jesuit Displayed* (London, 1594) has a long passage on the ignorance of the Jesuits from Ignatius to his own day (B3–B4).

PAGE 17

l. 7. *we use her aversly and preposterously.* If one follows Copernicus' sketch of the universe, Venus orbiting between the earth and the sun would thus show only its back-side to the earth. The poet in Donne finds this 'preposterous' in both senses.

l. 9. *Lucifer the Calaritan Bishop.* The reference here is to Augustine's rejection of the notion of Lucifer of Cagliari that the soul is material. What Donne really objects to is the attack against the Emperor and the imperial prerogative to be found in Lucifer's defence of Pope Liberius against the Emperor Constance (see *Letters*, p. 91 and *Sermons*, x. 91; by the time this sermon was preached there was renewed interest in Lucifer because of the alleged discovery of his tomb in 1623).

l. 14. *what new thing . . . by which our Lucifer gets any thing?* Ignatius'
argument in this section (to l. 5 of the next page) that Copernicus
has done nothing for Lucifer's kingdom, since men behave just
as they did before, and the calmness with which he grants that
Copernicus' opinions 'may very well be true', suggest that Donne
was not, as is so frequently urged, disturbed by the new astronomy.

l. 25. *our Clavius . . . the Gregorian Calender.* Clavius is the German
Jesuit Christopher Klau who for twenty years was Professor of
Mathematics at the Roman College. In 1603 he published the
work which reflected his part in the reform of the calendar; *Romani
Calendarii a Gregorio XIII restituti explicatio.* The Gregorian Calendar came into force in 1582 in all Catholic countries, ten days
being cut out of that year. This made continental dates ahead of
English dates and thus provoked difficulties in 'Civill businesses'.
The adaptability of saints to the new calendar was seriously
advanced by Catholic apologists and just as seriously refuted by
the Reformers. Harlay gives a good example of this solemn
trifling:

> Chacun scait le miracle ordinaire des reliques de S. Estienne qui se
> faict tous les ans . . . ce miracle a rompu son cours accoustume et recivant
> la reformation du Pape Gregoire 13 s'est avance de dix jours et preserve
> encore ceste seconde merveille en la feste de l'invention de ses Reliques.
> Et de peur qu'il n'y demeurast du doute et que les opiniastres ne peussent
> plus couvrir leur incredulite de quelque excuse, le mesme se rencontre
> au Sang de S. Jean Baptiste et en plusieurs autres qui ont donne de sem-
> blables exemples au diverses parties qu'habitent les Chrestiens.
>   (*Défence des Jésuites*, p. 29; for Harlay see note on p. 107)

PAGE 19

l. 9. *Heraclides, Ecphantus, & Aristarchus.* Aristarchus of Samos
was generally held to be the first defender of the heliocentric
universe (J. L. E. Dreyer, *A History of Astronomy from Thales to
Kepler*, New York, 1953). Donne has added to his name those of
two ancient philosophers cited by Copernicus in the preface to his
De Revolutionibus: Heracleides of Pontus (*fl.* 320 B.C.) and Ecphantus
of Syracuse (*fl.* 300 B.C.). Copernicus had taken the last two
names from Plutarch. All three names were used by Copernicans
to lend an air of antiquity to their theories: the same names were
used by the Aristotelians to prove that Copernicus was a dis-
credited Pythagorean. See C. M. Coffin, *John Donne and the New
Philosophy*, New York, 1958, pp. 66–7, 94.

COMMENTARY III

l. 29. *the first verse of Saint John.* The opening verses of the Gospel according to St. John were a regular part of exorcisms. Erasmus uses the same furniture in his burlesque colloquy, 'The Exorcism', where the duped priest prepares for his encounter with 'a holy stole upon which hung the beginning of St. John' (*Desiderii Erasmi Roterodami Opera Omnia*, Leyden, 1704, i, p. 750). The first Bible in Welsh was printed in 1588. By 1611 only the New Testament had appeared in Irish (T. H. Darlow and H. F. Moule, *Historical Catalogue of Printed Editions of Holy Scripture*, London, 1903, iii. 791; iv. 1660).

PAGE 21

l. 6. *I brought all Methodicall Phisitians ... into ... contempt.* The 'method' was a medical system elaborated in the first century B.C. at Rome by Asclepiades. It was formally codified by his pupil Themison. Its main tenets were based on Epicurean atomism and displayed an opposition to Hippocrates, a dislike of anatomy, and a refusal to search out the causes of disease. By the seventeenth century the name had lost its precision, until it could be applied, as Donne applies it here, to the formal teaching of the conservative medical faculties which Paracelsus attacked. In substance these faculties either were Galenists or derived their medicine from Arabic sources which ultimately relied on Galen. Paracelsus resembled the 'methodists' in his dislike of anatomy: he resembled their opponents in his respect for Hippocrates. Donne gives a summary of what he feels to be Paracelsus' real position in the history of medicine in a letter to Sir Thomas Lucey:

... Physick, which for a long time considering nothing, but plain curing and that but by example and precedent, the world at last longed for some certain Canons and Rules, how these cures might be accomplished; And when men are inflamed with this desire, and that such a fire breaks out that rages and consumes infinitely by heat of argument, except some of authority interpose. This produced *Hippocrates* his Aphorismes; and the world slumbred or tooke breath, in his resolution divers hundreds of years: And then in *Galens* time, which was not satisfied with the effect of curing, nor with the knowledge how to cure, broke out another desire of finding out why those simples wrought those effects. Then *Galen* rather to stay their stomachs then that he gave them enough, taught them the qualities of the four Elements, and arrested them upon this, that all differences of qualities proceeded from them. And after (not much before our time) men perceiving that all effects in Physick could not be derived from these beggerly and impotent properties of the Elements, and that therefore they were driven often to that miserable refuge of specifique form, and of antipathy and sympathy, we see the world hath turned upon new principles which are attributed to *Paracelsus*, but (indeed) too much to his honor.   (*Letters*, pp. 14–16)

l. 11. *my uncertaine, ragged, and unperfect experiments.* Some of Paracelsus' comments on 'experimental' medicine can be found in *De Morbis Metallicis* (Tr. II, lib. ii, cap. 5, in *Paracelsi Opera*, Geneva, 1669, i. 718). Paracelsus does not mean what modern scientists would mean by 'experimental' medicine. His chemicals know how to purge or cure. The physician must enter into sympathy with them, understand them, 'overhear them': thus he enters into them experimentally. The basis of his capacity to do this is his own innate possession of the knowledge which he must by experience make active.

l. 14. *the pox, which then began to rage.* Donne owned a medical book on the pox, *Le Traicté de Verole*, by Guillaume Rondelet (Bordeaux, 1576). It begins with the statement, 'Tous ceux qui ont tracte la verole confessent qu c'est une nouvelle maladie . . .' (p. 3). A marginal note testifies to the durability of popular lore: 'La verole connue en France depuis 83 ans lors que Charles VIII Roi de France faisait guerre en Italie.' Pancirolli (see note on p. 137) goes one step further and blames Neapolitan soldiers who had accompanied Columbus (p. 87).

l. 15. *I ever professed an assured and an easy cure.* The several treatises in which he discussed his cure of syphilis were summed up either by Paracelsus or by his editor into the one volume, *De Causis et Origine Lues Gallicae* (*Paracelsi Opera*, iii. 173–212). In essence the cure was a tincture of mercury which proved effective. This would seem to lie behind Donne's comments on Paracelsus' use of poisons below. He admits to having had much trouble in getting the right tincture: one can conclude that the patients on whom he tried straight mercury did not survive to witness the effect.

l. 33. *to make a man, in your Alimbicks.* The creature in question is the 'homunculus' which Paracelsus discusses in *De Homunculis et Monstris* (*Der Bücher und Schrifften*, ed. Huser, Basle, 1589, pp. 311 ff.). Pagel gives the formula in brief: take human semen, keep it under heat for forty days, then feed it also under heat with the *arcanum* of human blood. At the end of this period there will be a real human child, slightly smaller than normal, but quite satisfactory in all other respects (W. Pagel, *Paracelsus, an Introduction to Philosophical Medicine*, Basle, 1958, p. 117; cf. *Sermons*, ix. 136).

l. 34. *your Commentaries upon the Scriptures.* What is meant here, I think, is Paracelsus' incessant references to the Scripture and his habit of looking on himself as a prophet. '. . . Bible study was one of the preoccupations of his later years and in his writings we have constant witness not only to his mastery of its language, but of its deepest spiritual significance' (Anna M. Stoddart, *The Life of Paracelsus*, London, 1911, p. 40). One of the problems one meets in discussing Paracelsus is that he has infected most of his biographers and commentators with his own extravagance.

PAGE 23

l. 5. *none of our Order, which hath written in Physicke.* The book to which Donne is referring is Pedro Ribadeneyra's *Illustrium Scriptorum Religionis Societatis Jesu Catalogus* (2nd edition), Lyons, 1609. The work is the source of several remarks on the Jesuits (see notes on pp. 149 and 153). Ribadeneyra gives no listing of Jesuit writers on medicine.

Margin. *Gretze. cont. Hasenmull.* The book in question is the *Historia Ordinis Jesuitici . . . ab Elia Hasenmullero . . . nunc vero . . . correcta et refutata a Jacobo Gretsero*, Ingolstadt, 1594. Gretzer includes a Bull of Gregory XIII allowing Jesuits in the Indies and Japan to practise medicine short of surgery and cautery, 'quando medici saeculares commode haberi non possunt' (p. 211). The comments here are taken from *Pseudo-Martyr*, p. 130, where Donne adds the speculation: 'I wonder that they have not procured a Bull that they might be midwives.'

Margin. *Mosconius.* The book is the *De Maiestate Militantis Ecclesiae*, Venice, 1602. 'Nec ad medendum admittuntur clerici aut monachi . . .' This prohibition is still in force in Roman canon law.

l. 19. *no medicine doth naturally draw bloud.* Donne is here quoting from a medical book which he owned: *Joannis Mesuae Damascini de re medica libri tres, Jacobo Sylvio medico interprete*, Paris, 1561. 'Nullum enim medicamentum facultatem habet primam et per se haemagogam, id est qua sanguinem abigat et vacuet' (p. 8).

l. 5. *Severinus*: A Danish humanist and scientist, Peder Sorensen (1540–1602). He was a disciple of Paracelsus and physician at the Danish court for thirty years. His major work was *Idea Medicinae Philosophicae*, Basle, 1571.

l. 9. *woemen tempting by paintings and face-phisicke*. Donne genially refers to cosmetics in *Paradox*, no. 2: '. . . love her who shows her great love to thee in taking this pains to seem lovely to thee.' Cosmetics were, however, a frequent target for contemporary moralists even less distinguished than Hamlet. William Rankins criticizes the practice in what may be one of the first attacks on the affluent society, *The English Ape and the Italian Imitation*, 1588 (p. 23). Robert West devotes seven of his poems to the same subject in *Wits A B C*, 1608 (see no. 35). Donne himself satirized Sir Hugh Plat, an English writer on cosmetics, in *Catalogus*, no. 1. He also has some harsh remarks on the use of 'paints' in Satire IV (Milgate, p. 14). A complete catalogue of the offending cosmetics is given by Edward Guilpin in *Skialetheia* (1598) C6 recto and verso.

l. 18. *this worne souldier of Pampelune, this French-spanish mungrell*. Ignatius Loyola was a Basque and received the wound in his legs which changed his life at the defence of Pamplona against the French in 1521. Donne had referred to Ignatius' wound in *Pseudo-Martyr* (p. 142).

l. 21. *and putting on another resolution*. Cf. 'For a man may oppress a favorite or officer with so much commendation, as the Prince neglected and diminished thereby, may be jealous, and ruine him' (*Essays in Divinity*, p. 34). This whole passage may also be a parody of Machiavelli's analysis of the proper use of discontented nobles in the conquest of a feudal kingdom (*The Prince*, chap. iv).

l. 12. *the Popes Legates, at your Nicene Councel*. Donne is here in error. What he means is the Council held at Carthage in 418. The charge of 'equivocal legates' was based on the story that the papal legates claimed that appeals could be made from the Council to Rome and advanced forged canons from Nicea in support of their claim. William Whittaker gives the story in detail in his *Answer to the Ten Reasons*, 1606 (pp. 175–6). Thomas Morton uses it in his *Preamble to an Incounter* (pp. 51–4) and again in *Apologia*

Catholica I (p. 288). He goes into great detail in *A Catholicke Appeale* (pp. 468–76).

l. 1. *For I my selfe went alwaies that way of bloud.* Donne is giving in this passage a general translation of Machiavelli's own words from Book II, chapter ii of the *Discorsi.*

Perchè avendoci la nostra religione mostra la verità e la vera via, ci fa stimare meno l'onore del mondo; onde i Gentili stimando assai, ed avendo posto in quello il sommo bene, erano nelle azioni loro più feroci. Il che si può considerare da molte loro costituzioni, cominciandosi dalla magnificenza de' sacrifici loro alla umiltà dei nostri, dove è qualche pompa più delicata che magnifica, ma nessuna azione feroce o gagliarda. Qui non mancava la pompa, nè la magnificenza delle cerimonie, ma vi si aggiungeva l'azione del sacrifizio pieno di sangue e di ferocia, ammazzandovisi moltitudine di animali: il quale aspetto, essendo terribile, rendeva gli uomini simili a lui.

l. 21. *they, who have so often in vaine attempted it in England.* Catalogues of assassins were a favourite controversial device. Andrew Willet's *Catholicon* (1602) gives a fairly complete one: Morton, Saunders, Parry, Arden, Sommerfield, Lopez, Babington, Yorke, Williams, Stanley, Squire. Thomas Morton adds Guy Fawkes and Clement in *A Full Satisfaction* (p. 64). By the time we come to James and Bellarmine, Chastel and Ravaillac can be added. James implies that all of them were inspired, if not directly armed, by Jesuits (*Premonition,* p. 104) while Bellarmine denies that 'sicariis sit spes aeternae vitae' and refers to the Council of Constance (*Apologia,* p. 182).

l. 1. *both from Prince and People.* Donne would appear to refer here to *The Prince* for the usurpation 'upon the liberty of free Commonwealths', and to either the *Discorsi* or the *History of Florence* for the removal of tyrants. The latter operation was frequently referred to as Machiavellian. Attacking Roman theorists who favoured elective monarchies, Morton remarks, 'this position, *people, as subjects, were before their governors,* doth taste too much of Machiavellisme . . .' (*A Full Satisfaction,* p. 28).

l. 8. *accustomed to sinne against their conscience.* In his 'John Donne and the Casuists' (*Studies in English Literature,* ii (1962), pp. 57–76), Professor A. E. Malloch points out that this whole passage is a direct attack on the moralists, Jesuit and others, who were called 'probabilists'. The phrase Donne uses could be taken from Ludovico Carbo's *Summa Casuum* (Venice, 1606) where the question is put, 'an liceat agere contra propriam opinionem'. Donne's position in 1611 and later can be found in the verse letter to Lady Carey: 'He that beleeves himselfe doth never lie' (Milgate, p. 107). This does not mean that he disapproved of casuistry. Cf. '. . . for all that perplexity and entangling, we may not condemn too hastily, since in purest antiquity there are lively impressions of such a custom in the Church, to examine with some curiosity the circumstances by which sins were aggravated or diminished' (*Pseudo-Martyr*, 144).

l. 19. *two poysons mingled might doe no harme*. Professor Praz says that this image is taken from Gentillet. I have been unable to find it in the place he cites ('Machiavelli and the Elizabethans', *Proceedings of the British Academy*, xiii (1928), p. 90). Cf. Ben Jonson, *Sejanus*, III. iii:

> I have heard that aconite,
> Being timely taken, hath a healing might
> Against the scorpion's stroke; the proof we'll give:
> That, while two poisons wrestle, we may live.

l. 23. *Vasques would not cal this idolatry*. Cf. 'Vasquez holds it be not idolatry to worship the devil in an apparition which I think to be God. It can be no offense to believe him after I have used all means to discern and distinguish' (*Biathanatos*, p. 144). The same argument is turned into a graceful compliment in the verse letter to the Countess of Salisbury (Milgate, p. 108). Gabriel Vasquez, the Jesuit theologian and moralist, was one of the most frequently quoted authors in Donne's library. James cites this passage as an example of papal idolatry (*Premonition*, p. 87). Bellarmine answers by putting the statement into the full context given above (*Apologia*, p. 178).

PAGE 33

l. 1. *as Gratian takes it*. The marginal citation is from the *Decretum Gratiani*, Pars II, Causa 21, q. 4. 'Imaginarias scripturas' is glozed as '. . . in quibus imaginamur et respicimus conditionem nostram'.

Margin. *Modest. in verb. Milit.* This work, *Modesti Libellus de Vocabulis rei militaris*, is part of the compilation by Flavius Vegetius (see note on p. 154) and the passage Donne quotes is on p. 106.

l. 11. *Who ever flatters . . . instructs.* Cf. the verse letter to the Countess of Huntingdon, 'oft, flatteries worke, as farre as Counsels, and as farre th'endeavour raise' (Milgate, p. 87). Almost the same words are used in a sermon: '. . . as the *Orators* which declaimd in the presence of the *Roman Emperors* in their Panegyrics tooke that way to make those *Emperors* see, what they were bound to doe, to say . . . that those *Emperors* had done so . . .' (*Sermons*, iv. 281). See also *Sermons*, i. 278 and v. 200. Ben Jonson uses the same idea in 'Flattery'.

> I have too oft preferred
> Men past their terms, and praised some names too much
> But 't was with purpose to have made them such.
> (*Underwood*, xiv)

l. 19. *Gratians levity. Decretum Gratiani*, Pars II, Causa 32, q. 2. Explaining the derisive use of *Princeps Mundi* for the devil, Gratian says, '. . . vel ad derisionem dicitur princeps talium sicut dicitur Rex schaccorum vel Cardinalis ravennae.' The last title deserves some note. Mosconius (see note on p. 113) has the following to say: 'Ravennatenses Cardinales dicti sunt ex privilegio Caroli tempore Leonis . . . et tale nomen adeo crevit ut etiam dicerentur Cardinales Ecclesiae Mediolanensis et Neapolitanae in Italia; praeterea Pius V in suo diplomate 1586 talia privilegia . . . abrogavit' (p. 115). In arguing against the institution of cardinals, James had correctly called the title, '. . . a style given at first to all priests and deacons of any cathedral church' (*Premonition*, p. 111).

l. 31. *in his heart he utterly denyed that there was any God.* Donne is here echoing the Elizabethan dramatists who had unanimously decided that the proper 'machiavell' was an atheist. This was also the opinion of both the Protestant and Catholic theologians who commented on Machiavelli.

PAGE 35

Margin. *Flagel. Daemon. Menghi.* This work by Hieronymus Mengus is *Flagellum Daemonum: exorcismos terribiles potentissimos et efficaces remediaque probatissima complectens* (Bologna, 1577). The edition of 1608 gives two long catalogues of appropriately insulting names for the devil (pp. 14–16; 1245–6).

Margin. *Summa Bullarii*. Stephanus Quaranta, *Summa Bullarii . . .
SS. Pontificum Constitutionum . . . ad Paulum V*. Venice, 1609. In
the article on 'Agnus Dei' (p. 6) we read:

Legimus Urbanum V Pont. Max. misisse ad Imperatorem Gregorium
tres Agnos Dei cum versibus infrascriptis:

> Balsamus et munda cera cum chrismatis unda
> Conficiunt Agnum, quod munus do tibi magnum
> Fonte velut natum, per mystica sanctificatum
> Fulgura desursum depellit, et omne malignum
> Peccatum frangit, ut Christi sanguis et angit
> Praegnans servatur simul et partus liberatur;
> Munera defert dignis virtutem destruit ignis
> Portatus munde de fluctibus eripit undae,
> Morte repentina servat; Satanaeque ruina
> Si quis honoret eum, retine super hostis trophaeum
> Parsque minor tantum tota valet integra quantum
> Agnus Dei miserere mei
> Qui crimina tollis, miserere nobis.

Controversialists delighted in poking fun at these verses of which
the Latin does indeed merit Donne's strictures. The small wax
images of the lamb and the cross, known as Agnus Dei, which were
enormously popular with Elizabethan recusants, seem to have
left their mark as well in the imagination of the time as on innumerable public houses. James attacks them with vigour (*Premonition*, p. 88) and Bellarmine defends them (*Apologia*, p. 178).

l. 25. *though our Order have adventured further in Exorcismes*. There
were famous cases of exorcism in which Jesuits were involved, for
example, Peter Canisius and the possessed members of the Fugger
family.

l. 31. *yet our Cotton deserves to be praised*. Pierre Coton was a French
Jesuit and controversial writer who was also the friend and confessor of Henri IV. The work mentioned here is *Quaestiones Spiritui
Immundo . . . propositae a P. Cottono*. It is a pamphlet of ten pages,
first published in Paris in 1609. Modelled on Rabelais's catalogue
of books it presents a series of questions which Coton is supposed
to have put to a possessed person in the course of exorcism. The
questions range from 'Quota pars recideret angelorum?' to 'Quid
circa honorem mearum reliquiarum?' The seditious one must
have been 'Quid circa regis sanitatem?' Donne may also have
looked at the introduction in which we are told that Coton 'nec
contentus vulgari effectu, suam hic occasionem ratus, Dei mysteria,

creationis arcana, abdita naturae, Principum, Magnatum, etiam (ut est homo nihil a se humani alienum putans) muliercularum secreta, de Mundi principe ... mendacii patre Diabolo, cognoscere aggreditur'. The copy of this work I have been able to see was printed at Lyons in 1610 as part of a compilation by Peter de Wangen, *Physiognomonia Jesuitica* (pp. 169–79).

PAGE 37

l. 5. *the Relations of Peru.* Donne is referring to the *Brevis Relatio Historica Rerum in Provincia Peruana apud Indos a Patribus Societatis Jesu Gestarum*, by Diego Torres, Mainz, 1604. The story Donne tells is on pp. 54–5. It manifestly appealed to him. He tells it fully in *Pseudo-Martyr* (p. 178) and again in a sermon: 'An undiscerning stupidity is not humility, for humility itself implies and requires discretion . . . when the Devil inticed the Jesuit at his midnight studies, and the Jesuit rose and offered him his chair, because howsoever he were a Devil, yet he was his better: this was no regulated humility' (*Sermons*, i. 316).

l. 17. *the Catalogues of Reserv'd Cases.* Reservation in the Church is a legal act by which a superior authority (in this case the pope) limits the normal power of inferior authorities to absolve in cases concerning certain sins (see Canon no. 893). The first official reservation was imposed in 1139 when an attack on the person of a cleric was reserved to the pope. The practice of so reserving certain cases grew and in the sixteenth century the augmented list of reservations was attacked by the reformers. Donne repeats here a popular, and useful, misapprehension of the term. In his sermons he uses it quite correctly (*Sermons*, x. 82; 156–7), and in one of them (*Sermons*, iii. 310) he gives a detailed explanation of the sins reserved in the Anglican Church.

Margin. *Dist. 34. Is qui. Decretum Gratiani*, Pars I, Distinction 34. 'Is qui non habet uxorem et pro uxore concubinam habet, a communione non repellatur tamen ut unius uxoris aut concubinae aut mulieris sit contentus.'

l. 23. *S. Peter beholden to the stewes.* The papal revenue from the stews of Rome is a constant element in the controversy of the time. Tyndale uses it in *Practise of Prelates* (1562: D7) as does Jewel in the *Apology* (p. 52). Agrippa devotes most of Chapter 64 to it in *De Vanitate* (1575). John Nichols gives the details of the numbers involved. He was an ex-seminarian who published the irenically entitled *Lives of the Proud Popes, Ambitious Cardinals, Lecherous Bishops, Fatbellied Monks and Hypocritical Jesuits*. He puts the number of women involved at 20,000 and their annual payments at 20,000 ducats. Persons disposed of him rather neatly (*D.N.B.* xliii. 413). Donne had used the same attack in *Pseudo-Martyr* (D recto) and it occurs once in the *Sermons*, viii. 102.

l. 26. *23,000 men.* Donne is here quoting Gratian again as well as a sixteenth-century moral handbook, *De His Quae Usu, Stylo, Praxi et Consuetudine Observantur*, published in Venice in 1586 by Antonio Scappus. It is interesting to note that Scappus further qualifies his heroically liberal allotment: '. . . non tamen meretrix appellatur quae sui ipsius copiam facit amore ducta non premii . . .' (lib. i, cap. 54, no. 1). He also includes the immemorial observation '. . . scholares sunt luxuriosi et nolunt stare sine meretricibus.' Donne had already used both quotations in *Pseudo-Martyr* (p. 272). The other major moral treatise Donne cites, Tholosanus (see note on p. 132) does not indulge in these monstrous numbers. But it supports the strictures on students with the comment, 'scholaris qui loquitur cum puella non praesumitur dicere pater noster' (p. 203). In the same section it adds a comment on University landladies: 'mulierem viduam cui habitatio relicta est posse a domo repelli si in eam hospitem induxerit scholarem'.

Margin. *Summa Angel.* This was a popular casuistry text, *Summa Angelica de Casibus Conscientiae*, by Angelo de Clavasio, first published in 1488 and republished a dozen times before 1650. Donne's quotation can be found on p. 619 of the edition of 1615. But he is somewhat less than fair in his handling of it. Clavasio does remark that the last seven commandments are not 'conclusiones necessario a primis principiis deductae'. He then qualifies his answer: '. . . Et in ipsis quantum ad rationem ipsarum non potest cadere dispensatio sed bene quantum ad observationem sanctionum.' Donne had made good use of just this qualification in *Biathanatos* (pp. 47–8).

PAGE 38

Margin. *Privilegium Mendican.: Compendium privilegiorum fratrum minorum et aliorum mendicantium et non-mendicantium*, by Alphonso de Casarubios, Brescia, 1599. This book is the source for the entire catalogue of indulgences given on pp. 32–3. Such compendia came in for a considerable pounding by the Reformers. Erasmus comments on them: 'Thou thinkest it a special thing to be put in thy grave in the cowl or habit of St. Francis. Trust me, like vesture shall profit thee nothing at all when thou art dead, if thy living and manners be found unlike when thou were alive' (*Desiderii Erasmi . . . Opera*, Leyden, 1704, v. 31). In the *Colloquies* he returns to the same point: once in passing (i. 744) and at much greater length in 'The Seraphic Funeral' (i. 866–73). Joseph Hall attacks this practice in *Virgidemiarum* (1599), IV. vii. 45–6.

PAGE 39

l. 1. *dispensed in a mariage between Brother and Sister.* The case in question was the marriage of Henry VIII to his brother's widow, Catherine of Aragon. Catherine and Prince Arthur (1486–1502) were engaged in 1497 and married in 1501. A dispensation was granted by Pope Julius II in 1509 for Henry to marry Catherine. Catherine claimed that the first marriage was never consummated. Henry claimed it was and that the dispensation was thus illegitimate. Donne gives his detailed reflections on the famous case in *Sermons*, viii. 265. The validity of the dispensation was defended by Bellarmine against James (*Responsio*, p. 250).

l. 17. *which since is communicated to our Order.* The word 'communication' is here used in its canonical sense (see Canons, nos. 63–5, 613). Since the time of the Franciscan Pope, Sixtus IV (1471–84), privileges granted by the Holy See to one mendicant order were automatically shared by all the others.

l. 23. *a certaine sum of money.* In this swift aside Donne touches on the standard reformation attack on the sale of indulgences. Cf. 'The Litany':

> From bribing thee with Almes, to excuse
> Some sinne more burdenous
> . . . Lord deliver us.
>   (*Divine Poems*, p. 22)

and the verse letter from Amiens in 1611:

> Pardons are in this market cheaply sold.
>   (Milgate, p. 105)

Several times in the *Sermons* Donne speaks harshly of the practice. See *Sermons*, v. 259 and x. 127. James makes the same charge: 'For they were now sure that to do what they would, their purse would

procure them pardons from Babylon. Omnia venalia Romae . . .'
(*Premonition*, p. 77). Bellarmine's answer is distinctly an uneasy one
(*Apologia*, p. 178).

l. 27. *Gerson durst call those Indulgences foolish.* Donne's translation
here is accurate but somewhat round. Gerson attacked indulgences
'tot dierum et annorum mille millium' and calls them 'enormitates'.
What he objects to is not the power to grant them but the state
of mind which he calls 'quantificatio' (*Joannis Gersonii Opera*, Paris,
1606, ii. 349). Comment on indulgences could be savage. '. . . etiamsi
Christum ipsum spoliassem, ac decollassem; tam largas habent
indulgentias, et auctoritatem componendi' (*Desiderii Erasmi . . .
Opera*, Leyden, 1704, i. 643).

PAGE 41

l. 6. *Carpidineros* (for Dietrich of Niem, see note on p. 105). In this
passage, Dietrich is addressing both Popes: 'O quam bene stabit
Ecclesia . . . quando vos ambo tunc Carpidinares gubernatis
illam cum hypocrisi, symonia, superbia, avaritia et luxuria . . .'

Margin. *Rodol. Cupers de Eccles univer.* This reference is to an
enormous apologetic tract *De Sacrosancta Universali Ecclesia* published by the Belgian Rudolph Cupers in 1588. '. . . quia cardinalis
aegrotans sanguinem minuere non potest nisi Papa assentienti'
(p. 4). Donne was struck by this piquant detail and uses it again
(see *Sermons*, iv. 188).

Margin. *Azor.* Donne is here quoting one of his favourite moralists
as the numerous references to Azorius in *Biathanatos*, *Pseudo-
Martyr*, *Essays in Divinity*, and the *Sermons* will show. Usually he
treats him with respect, but in this passage he plainly aims at
parody. In his *Institutiones Morales* (Pars II, lib. 4, cap. 3) Azorius
admits that some theologians hold that the Cardinals exist *iure
divino*, but he denies it himself. He also denies that the Apostles
could be called cardinals in any sense and specifically proposes that
the Pope might well do without cardinals. He scouts the number
200 applied to their privileges and says that there are in fact about
thirteen. He does note that *sede vacante* no new red hats are delivered.

l. 14. *because Cardinals were instituted by God.* Even Mosconius (see
note on p. 113) hesitates to go this far: '. . . illorum [Cardinalium]
considerabimus originem quam . . . omnes potius divinam

(saltem figurative) quam humanam appellant' (p. 103). He reports the reasoning of several theologians that '. . . apostolos prius Cardinalatus quam Episcopatus munere functos esse' (p. 104). He calls them 'iudices totius orbis' (p. 121), but is more cautious in saying '. . . sicut non licet tollere episcopos ita nec cardinales' (p. 121). Donne had used this same series of charges in *Pseudo-Martyr* (p. 120) as had Morton in his *Apologia Catholica I* (p. 242). James refers to the cardinalate as 'only a new papal erection, tolerated by the sleeping connivance of our Predecessors' (*Premonition*, p. 5).

l. 18. *there are so many Kings as there are Cardinals.* Donne finds this indiscretion in Scappus (lib. i, cap. 25; see note on p. 120). 'Privilegium immunitatis Ecclesiae . . . in favorem delinquentium extenditur ad domos et palatia Cardinalium . . . quia tot sunt reges quot Cardinales.'

l. 23. *even Borgia should enjoy this dignity.* The following lines recount the dark tale according to which Pier Luigi, the son of Paul III, assaulted the Bishop of Fano and caused his death. The story was popular among polemicists and had as its basis the immoral conduct of Pier Luigi. It seems, however, to be completely false (L. Pastor, *History of the Popes*, xi. 317 and note). Donne errs in calling him Borgia. Both father and son were Farnese. The error may have arisen from a play by Barnabe Barnes, *The Devil's Charter*, produced in 1607. In it Pope Alexander VI, who was a Borgia, tries to seduce and then murders a young man of his court. However opposed to Alexander's tastes this may have been, Borgia remains a more frightening epithet than Farnese. The story enjoyed considerable currency and Donne used it again in *Sermons*, ix. 380, telling the story in the same rhetorical structure with the same climax. Time had, however, dimmed his memory: the ravisher is only the Pope's nephew and his victim has been promoted to Cardinal.

PAGE 42

l. 8. *Auge prodigiosa.* The curious word 'auge' is not Latin but Italian and Spanish. It is a technical astrological term meaning the highest point of the apparent course of the sun, moon, or a planet. John Searle uses it in *An Ephemeris for nine years* (1609). Donne uses it again: '. . . this is *Beatitudo in Auge*, blessedness in the Meridionall height' (*Sermons*, ix. 129).

PAGE 43

l. 1. *witty lust.* Cf. 'We sin wittily, we invent new sins, and we thinke it an ignorant, a dull, and an unsociable thing not to sin' (*Sermons,* ix. 258). The pejorative use of the word (translating *ingeniosa*) is preceded in the *O.E.D.* by only one usage in 1602, 'Now doth the world begin to take sole pleasure in a witty sin' (*The Return from Parnassus,* Part ii).

l. 13. *Paulus Venetus.* Peter Barbo, Bishop of Venice, elected Pope in 1464 as Paul II. Donne's source for this description is Platina, *De Vitis Pontificum Romanorum*: '. . . qui adeo his muliebribus delinimentis delectatus est, conquisitis undique magno pretio gemmis et exhausto paene Romanae Ecclesiae aerario, ut quotiescumque in publicum prodiret, Cybele quaedam Phrygia ac turrita non mitrata videretur.' Platina could make little claim to objectivity in his treatment of his persecutor, Paul II. In his *Apologia Catholica I,* Thomas Morton cites the same passage (p. 365).

l. 19. *Prevention and Anticipation.* Both of these words are technical legal terms which Donne is using accurately. Prevention is 'the right which a superior person or officer has to lay hold of, claim or transact an affair, prior to an inferior one, to whom otherwise it immediately belongs'. Anticipation is 'doing or taking a thing before the appointed time . . . the act of assigning, charging or otherwise dealing with income before it comes due' (Earl Jowett, *Dictionary of English Law,* 1959). Both terms are also used in canon law: see Canons, nos. 1553–68.

l. 23. *The transferring of Empires.* In 1566 Mathias Flaccus Illyricus published his *De Translatione Imperii Romani* in Basle. In it he maintained that Charlemagne was made Emperor by divine authority and ruled by divine right. The papacy did nothing but recognize a *fait accompli.* In 1584 Bellarmine answered this with a book of the same title, published in Antwerp. His sharp attack on Flaccus' reading of history (Chapter viii) is repeated in the controversy with James (*Apologia,* pp. 140–1). He also attacks the notion that there was anything new in the papal power to crown the Emperor. It was this controversy that Donne had in mind in this cleverly organized passage.

l. 30. *this Temporal jurisdiction over Princes.* Donne here touches one of the major controversies of the time. It raged as hotly among

Roman theologians as between the reformers and Rome. Following St. Bernard and Boniface VIII, there was a school which took the metaphor of Luke 20, 'Behold two swords', quite literally. The two swords they claimed were the temporal and spiritual jurisdiction which belonged to Peter. Donne obviously sides with the opposing school, best represented among the Anglicans by William Barclay's *Of the Authority of the Pope* (1611; the Latin edition appeared in 1609). It is Bellarmine's answer to this book, *De Potestate Summi Pontificis in Temporalibus* (Rome, 1609), which Donne probably has in mind here. His own unqualified support of the royal prerogative and the sanctity of royal authority is too well known to need annotation. This authority was one of the major issues between James and Bellarmine. The Cardinal attacked the King for holding that Jesuits taught rebellion (*Apologia*, p. 197) and attacked the story of Pope Alexander III putting his foot on the neck of Barbarossa (*Apologia*, p. 200). James uses the classic arguments, basing his authority on the Old Testament (*Apology*, pp. 106–7).

l. 35. *that famous Canon Nos sanctorum. Decretum Gratiani*, Pars II, Causa xv, q. 6. 'Nos sanctorum predecessorum nostrorum statuta tenentes, eos qui excommunicatis fidelitate aut sacramento constricti sunt, apostolica authoritate a juramento absolvimus, et ne sibi fidelitatem observent omnibus modis prohibemus quousque ipsi ad satisfactionem veniant.' The case which gave rise to the canon was the dispute between Gregory VII and the Emperor Henry IV. Donne used the same case and canon in *Pseudo-Martyr* (pp. 301–2).

Margin. *Apologia pro Garneto.* This book by the Cretan Jesuit Eudaemon-Joannes (André l'Heureux) was published in Cologne in 1610. He argues that the canon suspended but did not destroy the rights of excommunicated kings: '. . . nihil est igitur quod regnis aut rei publicae ex eo canone metuant principes. Nam si ne in privatos quidem quicquam agi liceat quod revocari non possit, quanto minus in principem . . .' (p. 68).

l. 6. *Cudsemius his rashnesse.* Donne is disappointed in an adversary who is willing to praise the learning of James and of the divines at Oxford and call the Church of England schismatical rather than heretical (*De Desperata Calvini Causa*, Maintz, 1609, pp. 121–2).

l. 10. *Serve the time.* Erasmus, Tyndale, and Cranmer follow the Alexandrian reading: the Authorized Version and Douay follow the Vulgate's 'Domino servientes'. Catholics used the text to point out that the Anglicans were willing to follow the Vulgate when it suited them. The Anglicans answered, correctly, that there was good Greek authority for both readings (see Morton, *Apologia Catholica II*, pp. 40–1).

l. 27. *the Cardinalship is our Martyrdome.* Donne's knowledge is quite accurate. Jesuits still vow that they will neither seek nor accept any prelacy or other ecclesiastical dignity unless commanded to do so by the pope. In the sixteenth and seventeenth centuries, Jesuit writers made much of their martyrs and it is this propaganda Donne is satirizing. He refers in *Biathanatos* to '. . . Jesuits hunting out martyrdom in the new worlds . . .' (p. 71). And in 'The Litany' he remarks:

> . . . for, Oh, to some
> Not to be Martyrs is a martyrdome.
> (*Divine Poems*, p. 20)

He is also using this passage to point up the well-known opposition between Bellarmine and Francisco de Toledo (see *Pseudo-Martyr*, p. 121). The latter's elevation to the cardinalate in 1593 seemed to cause him few pangs of conscience, despite the fact that he was the first Jesuit cardinal. Bellarmine on the other hand so effectively resisted his own elevation that Clement VIII threatened him with excommunication unless he yielded (see J. Brodrick, *Robert Bellarmine*, London, 1961, p. 157).

Margin. *Ribadeneyra Catalog* (see note on p. 113). Ribadeneyra notes that Julius III had offered a red hat to Francisco Borgia and that Paul IV had made the same offer to Diego Laynez (pp. 58, 100). Both men refused the honour.

PAGE 47

Margin. *Brisson de formul. Barnabus Brissonius de formulis et sollemnibus populi romani verbis*, Paris, 1583. The passage Donne cites is on p. 17. He quotes this work again in *Essays* (p. 45). There is a savage irony to this citation. Brisson was executed in Paris by the *Seize* because of his activities in the *Parlement* on behalf of Henri IV.

l. 6. *his Retractations.* In 1607 Bellarmine published at Rome his *Recognitio*, essentially a list of corrections he wished made in the text of his enormous *Controversiae*. He was dissatisfied with previous editions, particularly that of Venice in 1596. In the *Premonition*, James had attacked this work of Bellarmine, remarking: 'He doth in place of retracting any of his former errors . . . not retract but recant indeed: I mean sing over again . . . a number of the grossest of them.' He goes on to specify that the grossest of the errors was Bellarmine's support for the theory of popular election of kings (pp. 116–22). In this passage Donne assigns to Bellarmine the same motives that James did; which Bellarmine resented and answered sharply (*Apologia*, p. 134). Thomas Morton repeats the charge in the *Encounter against M. Persons* (p. 8). See also *Pseudo-Martyr*, pp. 147–8, 255.

PAGE 49

l. 4. *we have dished and dressed our precepts in these affaires.* In this passage (which continues to line 1 on p. 51) Donne is satirizing the efforts of Jesuit theologians to employ historical analysis in the interpretation of the Fathers and the Councils. Nowhere was this work of discrimination more necessary than in the vast body of law, custom, and accretion which went under the name of Gratian. Both sides felt free to draw on the collection in much the manner Donne describes. Both sides also became adept at 'interpretations' which favoured the conclusions they desired to prevail. Morton in his *Preamble unto an Incounter* gives an example of such interpretation when he lists the Councils which the Jesuit theologians, particularly Vasquez and Bellarmine, wish to regard as 'particular' and not 'general', and thus not binding on the Church. Jewel had marked the way for him in his spirited defence of the value of local and provincial Councils (*Apology*, pp. 123–5). James quotes against Bellarmine a long series of provincial Councils at Toledo, each outdoing the other in protestations of loyalty to the royal authority (*Apology*, pp. 53–6).

l. 31. *Diamonds . . . compacted of lesse parts, and atomes.* Anselm Boethius de Boodt in his *Gemmarum et Lapidum Historia* (Hanover, 1609) explains the theory Donne is advancing here:

. . . diaphanitas aut perspicuitas gemmarum . . . propter terrae exactam in minima resolutionem, talemque partium unionem ut totum corpus nullis poris aut atomorum terminis discretum sit efficitur. Continuitas enim omne corpus diaphanum facit, quae in terra fieri non potest, nisi ipsa in corpuscula atomis longe minora redigatur, ac illis terrestre quippiam transparens addatur, ut vinculum minimarum partium sit, ac earum terminos obliteret, atque ex illis continuum corpus faciat.   (p. 9)

Thus the 'lesse atomes' of the text should be either 'fewer atoms of size' or 'more closely compacted atoms'.

l. 4. *inducing the Councell of Trent to establish certaine Rules.* The Council of Trent met for twenty-five formal sessions during the pontificates of Paul III, Julius III, and Pius IV, from 1545 to 1563. At its opening the Jesuits had been recognized as an Order for only five years. The rules and definitions to which Donne refers are the long series of reform and controversial decisions which formed the theological base of the 'counter-reformation'. The Jesuits most influential in the Council's discussions were Alphonso Salmeron (1515–85) and James Laynez (1512–65). The latter succeeded Ignatius as Superior of the Order. Throughout his *Sermons* Donne objects time and again to the imposition of 'new articles of faith' by the Council of Trent. This was also one of the main points in the controversy between James and Bellarmine (*Apology*, p. 27).

l. 9. *that great war and Tragedy lately raised at Rome.* Both of Donne's terms are applicable to the *disputatio de auxiliis* to which he refers. It began with the publication of the Jesuit Molina's *De Concordia Liberi Arbitrii cum Gratiae Donis* in Lisbon in 1588. His great opponent was the Dominican Dominic Bañez. The Jesuits claimed that their opponents destroyed the free will of man; the Dominicans that the Jesuits espoused a Pelagian liberty which denied efficacious grace. In 1598 Clement VIII summoned the controversy to Rome where it raged in wordy exchanges until 1607. In that year Paul V ended the meetings with the announcement that he would personally issue a decision; in the meantime each side was to refrain from calling the other's opinion heretical. He never found time to issue any such decision, nor have any of his successors. Donne refers to this dispute with the amused patronage of an outsider in *Pseudo-Martyr*, p. 100, *Essays*, p. 50, *Letters*, p. 16, and several times in the *Sermons*. Like most Anglicans he agreed substantially with the Jesuit position (see *Sermons*, i. 260–2 and vii. 122–6).

l. 15. *because as yet no sentence is given against him.* (For Eudaemon-Joannes, see note on p. 125.) He remarks that after the excommunication of princes, '. . . non possent populi rebellare aut debitam iis fidelitatem denegare antequam pronuntiaretur expresse in eos sententia' (p. 69).

COMMENTARY 129

l. 19. *awake that state out of her Lethargy.* In addressing the other kings of Europe and urging them to resist the encroachments of papal power, James says: 'it is my humble prayer to God that he will waken us up out of that lethargic slumber of security wherein our predecessors and we have lien so long' (*Premonition*, p. 131).

l. 25. *Mariana . . . the Councel of Constance . . . Cotton.* In 1415 the Council of Constance, at the insistence of John Gerson, condemned the proposition that 'quilibet tyrannus potest et debet licite et meritorie occidi per quemcumque vasallum vel subditum suum', as heretical, erroneous, and scandalous. Moralists generally accepted the condemnation, although most of them distinguished carefully between a lawful sovereign and a usurper.

A Spanish Jesuit, Juan Mariana (1536–1624) published his famous *De Rege et Regis institutione* in Toledo in 1599. In it he held that the king holds the delegated authority of the people and can thus be removed, by force if necessary, by the people. There are many reservations to his theory, but in general it authorizes the conclusion that in extreme cases a simple citizen may kill a king. His work was censured by Bellarmine and by the then Jesuit Superior, Aquaviva. It caused an enormous stir in France where, after the murder of Henri IV it was condemned by both the Parliament and the Sorbonne and was publicly burned by the executioner.

Pierre Coton (1564–1626) was the confessor of Henri IV and had persuaded him to revoke the 1594 expulsion of the Jesuits from France. After the death of the King he published his *Lettre Déclaratoire de la Doctrine des Pères Jésuites* (26 June 1610) in which he points out that the Jesuit General and fifteen Jesuit theologians had all condemned the teachings of Mariana. Donne writes an account of Coton's intervention in 1611 to Sir Henry Wotton (*Letters*, p. 123). See also *Pseudo-Martyr*, p. 145.

Margin. *Gretzer. Examen speculi.* The *Examen Speculi* is an appendix to the work *De Studiis Jesuitarum Abstrusioribus* which the German Jesuit controversialist, Jacob Gretser, published in 1609. In it he quotes Ribadeneyra's *Vita B. Ignatii*, where Ignatius forbids his people to enter into controversy with the Sorbonne. The latter had refused to recognize the Jesuits as a religious Order and thus had denied them permission to teach publicly in Paris (p. 139).

PAGE 53

l. 6. *I gave not so iron a Rule . . . as Francis.* Donne most probably
took this note from his copy of Rensinck (see note on p. 144) which
contains the *Testamentum* of St. Francis. He has a pencil mark
against the passage where the Saint urges his followers, 'ut non
mittant glossas in regula . . . sed sicut Dominus dedit mihi . . .
cum sancta operatione observetis usque in finem'. He had given
a more rhetorical rendering of the same passage in *Pseudo-Martyr*,
p. 130.

l. 12. *made both the Booke . . . and the Man, infamous.* The action mentioned here is the condemnation of Mariana's book on 8 June 1610.
The fact, however, was not what bothered Donne. What he
objects to is the blanket condemnation which he felt, rightly, to
be a Roman specialty. In *Biathanatos* he remarks,

> It is not just nor ingenuous to condemn all that a condemned man says
> (for even a leprous man may have one hand clean to take and give withal).
> And S. Hieronym is inexcusable in that point of his slippery zeal, in his
> behaviour towards Vigilantius, yea the Trent Council itself is obnoxious
> therein, for condemning Names of Authors and not Books. (p. 163)

In the 'Epistle' prefixed to 'Metempsychosis' he says,

> I forbid no reprehender, but him that like the Trent Councell forbids
> not bookes, but Authors, damning whatever such a name hath or shall
> write. None writes so ill, but that he gives not something exemplary,
> to follow, or flie.   (Milgate, p. 26)

Although James, after having royally insulted Bellarmine (*Premonition*, p. 108), pouts at Bellarmine's attacks 'as well against
my Person as against my Book', this notion is not in any sense
a commonplace of the controversialists. It seems to be another
instance where Donne is strikingly modern in his reactions.

l. 15. *The Pope is bound to proceede lawfully.* This quotation and the
following one are taken from *De la Liberté Ancienne et Canonique
de l'Église Gallicane*, by Jacques L'Eschassier (Paris, 1606): 'Cest
ainsi que l'église gallicane a tousiours dit qu'elle recognossoit les
papes légitimement et cannoniquement' (p. 25). L'Eschassier
urges that it is the duty of France to recall the Church to 'la sainc-
teté de ses anciens reglemens. Aussi cela se peut il plus aisément
faire par la voye insensible des arrests ramenens peu à peu l'ancienne discipline' (p. 32). The book is a defence of Gallican liberties against the encroachments of Roman canon law.

l. 33. *The Senate of Rome gave us . . . a noble example.* This story is told by Platina (see note on p. 124).

Admonitus Tiberius a Pilato de Christi morte ac dogmate, ad senatum retulit, censuitque Christum in deos referendum, ac templo honorandum. Fieri id non modo senatus vetuit, quod non ad se primum sed ad Tiberium scripsisset Pilatus . . .   (p. 5)

PAGE 55

Margin. *Observationes in Cassianum.* The author of these observations is Peter Ciaconius whose remarks in the edition of Cassian's works of 1628 are printed with the text. Ciaconius cites Plato, Origen, Jerome, and Chrysostom in support of the proposition that 'virum prudentem posse officioso mendacio non secus uti quam medicamento'. The section concludes with the defence, 'Horum itaque sententiam secutus est Cassianus priusquam ecclesia contrarium decerneret' (p. 948). Thomas Morton takes up this argument in several places of his *Encounter Against M. Persons* (pp. 52–6). Donne had used it twice in *Pseudo-Martyr*, pp. 119, 278.

l. 21. *Mentall Reservation, and Mixt propositions.* This tortured area of controversy involved the Jesuits because of their sponsorship of equivocation and mental reservation. The moral problem arises when one is forced to answer a question but is obliged not to reveal the truth. Theologians on both sides taught that a lie was always evil: hence the development of theories which would justify an answer by which one was not obliged to convict oneself or others. Equivocation is the generic term, which is divided into verbal equivocation and mental reservation. Verbal equivocation requires that the words used be capable of bearing two meanings, the classic example being the oracle's, 'Aio te Aeacida Romanos vincere posse.' Mental reservation involves the suppression of part of a statement or proposition. Thus the proposition is mixed; partly spoken and partly silent. The usual example is the phrase 'I am not a priest' spoken out loud, with the silent completion 'in order to reveal it to you'. When one remembers that to admit to ordination was, in certain cases, as good as a confession of guilt of treason, the notion of a mixed proposition comes very close to the plea of 'Not Guilty' in a modern court. As Persons remarked to Bagshawe, 'He that sticketh not at lies never needeth to use equivocation' (see T. H. Clancy, *Papist Pamphleteers*, Chicago, 1964, p. 178). Persons's defence of the practice is given in his *Treatise on Mitigation*: the best Anglican answer is in Morton's *Encounter Against M. Persons*. The whole of Book II of this work is taken up with this dispute. Donne himself gives a clear statement of the dilemma which gave rise to the various theories in 'The Litany':

> Good Lord, deliver us, and teach us when
> We may not, and we maye blinde unjust men.
>
> (*Divine Poems*, p. 23)

l. 23. *our Serarius*. The Jesuit theologian, Nicholas Serarius, was a friend of Morton (see Baddily, *Life of Morton*, 1669, p. 13) and, like Azorius, is one of the authors most frequently used by Donne in *Biathanatos*, *Pseudo-Martyr*, and the *Sermons*. He is also mentioned in a letter to Henry Goodyere (*Letters*, p. 35). In this passage Donne is quoting his *Trihaeresium* (Mainz, 1604). Speaking of Herod's success at playing off one opponent against another he remarks, 'Herodes tyrannus magnus erat, ut ex ipsius rebus gestis liquet Machiavellista' (p. 159).

PAGE 57

l. 7. *our Cotton confesses* (for Pierre Coton see note on p. 118). The work quoted here is his *Du Tres Sainct et Tres August Sacrament et Sacrifice de la Messe* (Avignon 1600). Discussing the papal powers, Coton remarks, 'son auctorité a esté incomparablement de plus grande autres fois . . . veu que l'Eglise Chrestienne n'est auiourd' huy qu'un diminutif de ce qu'elle a esté' (p. 358). Donne was annoyed by the assumption that Christianity and Roman Catholicism are convertible terms.

l. 10. *the Cardinals . . . meete now but once in a weeke*. It must have amused Donne to cite this huge folio of over a thousand pages to support so minor a point. The work is *Syntagma Iuris Universi atque Legum paene Omnium Gentium*, by Petrus Tholosanus (Frankfurt, 1599). Donne quotes from him again in *Biathanatos* (p. 54). Tholosanus was one of the French jurists who wrote on behalf of the independence of the State from ecclesiastical control.

l. 16. *they have this advantage . . . they agree within themselves*. No accusation the Roman controversialists made annoyed the reformed Churches more than the charge of sectarianism and disunity among Protestants. The only effective answer, given the facts, was the retort. Jewel's *Apology* gives a long summary of disputes, major and minor, among Catholics (pp. 45–7). William

Fulke in his *Confutation of Popish Discourses* (1581) lists the differences between French and Italian Catholics (p. 35). Morton also gives an extended list in *Apologia Catholica I* (pp. 301–11). And the subject was hotly controverted between Bellarmine (*Apologia*, p. 189) and James (*Premonition*, pp. 132–3). In 1609 Joseph Hall published a handbook of some three hundred disputed points in Roman theology and practice called *The Peace of Rome*.

Donne followed this line of argument in *Sermons*, iv:

> Let me see a Dominican and a Jesuit reconciled, in doctrinal papistry, for freewill and predestination, Let me see a French papist and an Italian papist reconciled in State-papistry for the Pope's jurisdiction, Let me see the Jesuits, and the secular priests reconciled in England, and when they are reconciled to one another, let them press reconciliatione to their Church.
>
> (p. 302)

See also *Sermons* ix. 343–4 and x. 173–4.

l. 24. *we languish also miserably in Spaine.* In no country of Europe was the Church more closely under the control of the monarchy than in Spain (see J. Lynch, *Spain under the Habsburgs*, Oxford, 1964, pp. 257–70). Donne's quotations from Scappus (see note on p. 120) are accurate, with the exception of the second one. What Scappus points out is that clerical immunity is enjoyed in Spain except for the case where 'Rex ipse cognoscit de vi et iniuriis inter ecclesiasticas personas'.

PAGE 59

Margin. *De Regno Siciliae: Resp. ad Card. Colum.* Caesar Cardinal Baronius wrote in 1609 an attack on the Sicilian crown's claim to ecclesiastical jurisdiction, the *Tractatus de Monarchia Siciliana*. Donne has taken phrases from it (pp. 14–19) to illustrate Baronius' position. In fact, Baronius was not attacking monarchy but what he felt to be an abuse of its powers; above all he argued against what he felt to be false documentation in support of the Sicilian claims. Baronius would, of course, hardly have agreed with Donne's position on the sanctity of royal authority. He claims openly that the Church is responsible for the salvation of the King's soul and must from time to time attack him spiritually (pp. 196–200). Cardinal Colonna attacked Baronius' strictures and Baronius includes both Colonna's letter and his answer to it in his book. In this answer he applies the Bull *In Coena Domini* to Sicily (pp. 176–8). He also claims to write in sorrow and adds, 'nescit zelus imperiosus parcere saltem Deo.' He claims that, 'ad scribendum impulit iussio Pontificia et ad hoc ipsum praestandum iuramento devincta dignitas Cardinalatus' (p. 65).

l. 25. *to remove all secular men from so great a dignitie.* Donne's memory fails him here. In *Pseudo-Martyr* he used the identical phrase, correctly, of Baronius not Bellarmine (pp. 52–3). The shrewdness of the observation, however, is valid no matter which cardinal it is applied to. The Roman position on the 'limited' rights of monarchs was specifically that they should be limited from above, that is by a superior spiritual authority. The best of them would have held that this limitation was on behalf of the people. But operatively the Roman position was hardly more democratic in the modern sense than James's own. It was ultimately to aid in the development of democracy; an historical irony little appreciated when, under Pius IX, it arrived.

l. 32. *The sword and buckler of the Romane Church.* These words are taken from *Les Salmonées du Sieur Reboul*, Lyons, 1597 (see note on p. 100). 'Ne pouvez vous pas reconnoistre ce grand Baronius couvert de ceste nouvelle pourpre . . . ou bien ce Bellarminus, qui d'un seul regard vous faict transir de peur . . . l'un le bouclier, l'autre l'espée de l'Église' (p. 191).

PAGE 61

l. 3. *the Popes Excommunications, and the Jesuites Assassinates.* In this remark Donne is mocking the efforts of the French Jesuits to separate the two. Even in England, after the accession of James, there was a tendency among Catholics to play down the papal deposing power, hence the remark of Eudaemon-Joannes that James was not under any personal sentence of excommunication. Louis Richeome, the Provincial of the French Jesuits, answered Pasquier and Arnould in the same sense (see T. H. Clancy, *Papist Pamphleteers*, Chicago, 1964, pp. 207 and 217).

In the dreary wastes of the Antichrist controversy, there are moments when Bellarmine actually sounds amused. Apropos of James's comment that papal excommunications are the 'fulmen quo Pontifex . . . ipsos etiam Reges percellit', he answers that according to the Book of Revelation it is only one of the lesser beasts that thunders over men and that consequently it cannot be that the Pope is Antichrist (*Apologia*, p. 180).

l. 9. *the later invention of Gun-powder.* For most of the men of the Renaissance the inventor of gunpowder was, like Dr. Johnson's first Whig, a devil. Don Quixote implies the work of the devil in the invention (Book iv, chap. 11) and Pancirolli (see note on p. 137) quotes Melanchthon and Polydore Vergil as the originators of the notion that the terrible weapon came 'monacho ministro et fabro, diabolo architecto' (p. 673). James says much the same as Donne (*Premonition*, p. 96) as does George Herbert in his 'Triumphus Mortis' (*The Works of George Herbert*, ed. F. E. Hutchinson, Oxford, 1953, p. 420). Donne had already used this charge against the Jesuits: 'As the inventor of gun-powder was a contemplative monk, so these practique monks thought it belonged to them to put it into use and execution to the destruction of a State and a Church' (*Pseudo-Martyr*, D4 recto).

l. 16. *by your Capuchins you did reforme your Franciscans.* As he does in the *Sermons* (ii. 297–8 and iii. 115) Donne here simplifies history. The 'Capucini' were authorized by Clement VII in 1528 not primarily as a reform of the Franciscans but as a group of hermits living under the authority of the local bishop, and limited to Italy. By 1643 they had grown so numerous that Urban VIII gave them recognition as an Order. The 'Recolets' were a reform group within the Franciscan family, first organized in 1532. In 1579 Gregory XIII granted them their independence from Franciscan control.

l. 21. *all her beautie, and exteriour grace.* In this passage Donne is repeating a commonplace of English controversial writers and one about which he felt deeply. He saw the Jesuits as representing on the Roman side the same harsh radicalism that the Puritans represented on the Anglican side. Frequently in the *Sermons* he calls the Jesuits Puritans (see *Sermons*, iv. 106–7). James refers to Jesuits as 'Puritan-Papists' in the *Premonition* (p. 44) and later in the same work, while calling for a General Council, he insists on 'all the incendiaries and novelist fire-brands on either side being debarred from the same, as well Jesuits as Puritans' (p. 113).

l. 24. *cure a rigid coldnesse with a fever.* Donne is referring to *Opera Hippocratis Coi et Galeni Pergameni*, Paris 1589. The same work is cited in *Biathanatos* (p. 171) and *Pseudo-Martyr* (C4 recto).

l. 27. *Circumcellions . . . Assassins.* Donne most probably learned of the Circumcellions from his reading of Augustine's *de Haeresibus*. They were claimed to be the storm troopers of the Donatists, particularly in the Province of Numidia. These vagabonds (hence their name, 'circum cellas rusticorum vagantes') flourished in the third and fourth centuries until finally suppressed by the Emperor Honorius. They believed that martyrdom in their cause assured salvation and should be deliberately sought out. Donne refers to them in *Biathanatos*, p. 69, *Pseudo-Martyr*, pp. 9, 134, and *Sermons*, x. 168-9. Meredith Hanmer seems to have been the first to apply the name Circumcellions to the Jesuits in his answer to Campion's *Brag* in 1581. It became a commonplace after Campion's death.

Assassins were members of a powerful rebel group in Persia and Syria in the twelfth and thirteenth centuries. Word of their activities came to Europe through the Crusaders. Their chief was the 'old man of the mountains' and he and his tribe haunted the medieval imagination. Dante was the first to use the word in the sense of professional secret murderers (see *O.E.D.* s.v.). The 'king' they killed was Conrad of Montferrat.

PAGE 63

l. 1. *no Clergy-man should weare a knife with a point.* This understandable rule can be found in Bartholomeo Carranza's *Summa Conciliorum et Pontificum*, Lyons, 1600. 'Prohibetur districte ne sacerdotes cultellum portent cum cuspidi nec clerici eorum' (p. 646). Against this text Donne puts the quotation from the Jesuit Constitutions, scrupulously taking care to identify it (line 20). The full text, from the rules for the refectorian or custodian of the dining-room, reads: 'Curet ne vasa et cetera in refectorio necessaria desint, et ut quam maxime munda sint, eaque caute tractet ne frangantur: curabit quoque ut cultelli debito tempore acuantur' (*Regulae Societatis Jesu*, Lyons, 1606, p. 212).

l. 9. *whose hearts wee do not beleeve to be with us.* After his death, the heart of Henri IV was given to the Jesuits to be enshrined in the Collège de la Flèche. In an anonymous pamphlet *A Copie of a Late Decree of the Sorbonne* (London, 1610) a rhyme, called a Pasquil, comments on the same event. It is given in both French and English:

> Ce n'est qu'a vous (trouppe sacree)
> Qu'on doibt bailler le Coeur des Roys.
> Quand les grands Cerfs sont aux abboys
> On en doibt aux chiens la Curee.

> 'Tis you alone, you sacred crue
> To whom the hearts of kings are due.
> When the great Harts are hunted hard
> The entrails are the Hounds reward.

l. 31. *Feathers or strawes swimme on the waters face*, etc. As far as I can determine, these verses are Donne's own. Cf. in 'Recusancy':

> So, carelesse flowers, strow'd on the waters face,
> The curled whirlepooles suck, smack, and embrace,
> Yet drowne them . . .
>
> (*Songs and Sonnets*, p. 11)

See also 'Satyre III', lines 103–8 (Milgate, p. 14).

PAGE 65

l. 7. *Princes . . . envy and grudge.* This comment, indirect as it is, was appropriate in the England of 1611. Estimates place Robert Cecil's 'ordinary' income at £25,000 a year and his total income at almost £50,000. Even Cecil's honest actions, such as the proposed Great Contract of 1610 and his 'gift' of Theobalds to the King three years earlier, were open to misinterpretation. The charges of 'corruption' were to grow through the years of James's reign and barely ten years later were to be used to topple Francis Bacon. Donne could well have intended a reference to both of these men who together had helped destroy Essex (L. Stone, 'The Fruits of Office', in *Essays in Economic and Social History . . . in Honour of R. H. Tawney*, Cambridge, 1961, pp. 89–116; A. L. Loomie, S.J., *The Spanish Elizabethans*, New York, 1962, pp. 118–19).

l. 22. *those whom Pancirollo hath recorded.* Donne is here using Guido Pancirolli's second book, *Nova Reperta sive Rerum Memorabilium Recens Inventarum . . .*, Hamburg, 1602. All the items listed have chapters to themselves. Donne quotes the same work in the *Catalogus* (no. 17) and Dame Helen Gardner has pointed out that Pancirolli is the source of Donne's remarks on the 'specular stone' in 'The Undertaking', and of the lamp 'in Tullias tombe', in 'Epithalamion'; *Songs and Sonnets*, p. 57 and Grierson, i. 140.

l. 28. *I was sory to see him use Peter Aretine so ill.* Peter Aretino, the poet and essayist, was born in Arezzo in 1492. He lived at Rome under the patronage of Leo X, then at Florence under the Medici and finally at Venice. He died in 1556. Donne had a strong enough stomach for licentious verse and was not seriously annoyed at the *Sonnetti Lussuriosi*, published in 1523. In a letter written in 1600 he remarks:

he [Aretino] is much less than his fame, and was too well paid by the Roman Church in that coin which he coveted most where his books

were by the council of Trent forbidden: which if they had been permitted
to have been worn by all, long ere this had been worn out.

(Quoted in Simpson, p. 316)

The second charge he makes against Aretino for his 'long custome
of libellous and contumelious speaking against Princes' (p. 67,
l. 29) is probably based on the squibs and satires Aretino published
against Frederico Gonzaga, the Duke of Mantua (E. Hutton,
Pietro Aretino, London, 1922; R. Roeder, *The Man of the Renaissance*,
New York, 1958, pp. 485–533).

PAGE 67

l. 2. *He added moreover, etc.* In this long sentence which runs to
line 21, Donne's structure breaks down completely. Even with the
effort to punctuate it correctly, it makes little sense and points
to hasty composition.

l. 2. *Raderus . . . did use to gelde Poets.* Matthew Rader was a Jesuit
philologist who brought out in 1599 an edition of Martial. He
followed the general custom of leaving out of his text, which was
intended for school use, the more salacious of the epigrams. He
marks his omissions and plainly states in his 'Praefatio', 'Nihil ad
haec templa et sacraria sapientiae nisi castum, sanctum integrum-
que aspiret; ne iuventus dum scientiam quaerit perdat innocentiam.'
Donne manifestly sympathized with the small boys who were
thus forced to find their own *legenda selecta*. He had already attacked Rader in his *Epigrams*; see Milgate, p. 54.

Margin. *Harlay Defence des Jesuit.* For Harlay, see note on p. 107.
'La langue des Hebrieux a esté nomme saincte disent quelques
docteurs de leur theologie, pour n'avoir point de mots qui peussent
offenser la chastité . . . l'éscriture ne parle que fort peu souvent de
l'estoille de Venus, et encore soubs le nom de Lucifer et en termes
empruntés' (p. 12).

l. 13. *Tiberius his Spintria & Martialis symplegma.* The exercises
mentioned are taken from Martial: 'quo symplegmate quinque
copulentur' (*Epigrammata*, xii. 43.8); and from Suetonius: 'sedem
arcanarum libidinum in quam undique conquisiti puellarum et
exoletorum greges monstrosique concubitus repertores, quos
spintrias appellabat, triplici serie conexi, invicem incestarent
coram ipso ut aspectu deficientis libidines excitaret' (*Tiberius*, 43).

l. 21. *it produces Morall sacraments.* Donne is referring to the objects
and actions known in the Roman Church as 'sacramentals'.

Originally the term meant the subsidiary rites used in administering the Sacraments (e.g. the blessing at a marriage) but it was later expanded to include a great variety of pious practices to which the reformers objected.

l. 26. *their last made Goddesse, Francisca Romana.* Frances of Rome was canonized by Paul V in May 1608. Valladier (see note on p. 107) remarks, 'nihil illi aliud thorum genialem fuisse quam perpetuam adumbrati martyrii et miraculorum officinam' (p. 24). The hyperboles of seventeenth-century hagiography were equalled only, if at all, by the eulogies addressed by churchmen to reigning monarchs. Donne quotes the source Valladier was using when he says, 'As *S. Hierome* says of Chastity, *Habet servata pudicitia martyrium suum,* Chastity is a continuall Martyrdome' (*Sermons,* ix. 166). Commenting on the exaggeration of miracles attributed to the Blessed Mother, he calls her a 'shop of Miracles' (*Essays,* p. 85).

PAGE 69

l. 12. *the opinion of the Dominicans.* The work Donne is using is *Hieronymi Osorii . . . de rebus Emmanuelis Regis Lusitaniae . . . domi forisque gestis,* Cologne, 1576, to which Matalius Metellus wrote the preface. I have been unable to discover where Donne found the numbers 200,000 and 150.

l. 16. *the law, made by Ferdinando.* The law in question was first promulgated in 1503, and repeated in the 'Laws of Burgos' in 1512 (see Acosta, *de Natura Novi Orbis,* Cologne, 1596, p. 213). Donne refers to it again in *Biathanatos* (pp. 40, 56). See also the verse letter to Henry Wotton:

> If they stand arm'd with seely honesty,
> With wishing prayers, and neat integritie,
> Like Indians 'gainst Spanish hosts they bee.
> (Milgate, p. 73)

In all this section Donne is probably relying on Fray Bartolome de las Casas's *Brevissima Relacion de la Destrucyon de las Indias,* N.S. 1552. This harsh attack on Spanish brutality in the New World was popular in England. The controversialists made much of the depopulation las Casas reported.

Christopher Hill adds a proper grain of salt to the complacency of the Englishmen of the seventeenth century about their own colonists (*Puritanism and Revolution,* London, 1962, p. 149).

l. 20. *wee tooke away their old Idolatrie*. In Problem no. 3, Donne
asks, 'Why did the devil reserve Jesuits till these later days?' He
continues, '. . . knowing that our times should discover the *Indies*
and abolish their *Idolatry*, doth he send these to give them
another for it?', *Paradoxes and Problems* (p. 43).

l. 25. *medicine made of this pretious American dung*. Since this description can hardly fit the two classic 'American' medicines, quinine and
guaiacum, I am drawn to take Donne's use of the word 'medicine'
as a sarcastic metaphor and conclude that what he is talking about
here is gold. The corrupting influence of Spanish gold was a
commonplace of the times. Raleigh in his *Discovery of Guiana*
(1596) remarks that it is the King of Spain's '. . . Indian gold that
endangereth and disturbeth all the nations of Europe: it purchaseth
intelligence, creepeth into councils and setteth bound loyalty at
liberty in the greatest monarchies of Europe' (*Works*, ed. Oldys
and Birch, 1829, viii. 388). Donne himself made the same reflec-
tion in 'The Bracelet':

> . . . Spanish Stamps, still travailing,
> That are become as Catholique as their King,
> Those unlick'd beare-whelps, unfil'd Pistolets
> That, more then canon shot, availes or lets,
>
> (*Songs and Sonnets*, p. 2)

For a modern study of the enormous reach of Spanish gold in
diplomatic affairs, see A. J. Loomie, S.J., 'Toleration and Diplo-
macy', *Transactions of the American Philosophical Society*, liii, part 6,
Philadelphia, 1963. The Spanish ambassador in 1603 carefully
logged the amounts which were to be paid as pensions to leading
English courtiers (pp. 30–7).

PAGE 71

l. 1. *Lieutenant, or Legat a latere. Legati a latere* were prelates,
almost always cardinals, who enjoyed extensive delegation of
papal authority in lands to which they were sent. By 1610 the
last legates in England, Wolsey, Pole, and Campeggio would
have been distant memories. Donne more probably has in mind
the influence of the papal legates on the affairs of the League in
France. Cf. *Sermons*, x. 127.

l. 4. *Canon Alius. Decretum Gratiani*, Pars II, Causa xv, q. 6. 'Alius
Romanus Pontifex, Zacharias, Regem Francorum non tamen pro
suis iniquitatibus quam pro eo quod tantae potestati erat inutilis,

a regno deposuit. . . .' The gloss on this canon reads, '. . . non intelligas inutilis id est insufficiens, . . . sed dissolutus erat cum mulieribus effoeminatus'. The case in question is the alleged deposition of Childeric III by Pope Zachary in 751. Donne had used the same case in *Pseudo-Martyr* (pp. 300–1) and it was a favourite of the Roman controversialists.

Margin. *Paris de puteo.* The *De Syndicatu Tractatus* was published at Frankfurt in 1605. Donne refers to the passages on pp. 17, 21, and 24 where the offences for which kings should be deposed are listed. He refers to Paris de Puteo frequently in *Pseudo-Martyr*.

l. 10. *by which title of prescription.* When a right, immunity or obligation exists by reason of a lapse of time, it is said to exist by prescription (Earl Jowett, *Dictionary of English Law*, 1959). Prescription is a major area of canon law, see Canons, nos. 63, 1446, 1470, 1508–12, 1725. James uses the legal argument against prescription by claiming that while English kings for centuries had allowed and acknowledged the papal authority in their domains, during the same centuries the same authority was frequently and successfully contested (*Premonition*, p. 32).

Margin. *Sophronius.* Donne is quoting here from the work, *Pratum Spirituale*, which was attributed, probably falsely, to the seventh-century Patriarch of Constantinople, Sophronius. He had used it earlier in *Biathanatos* (p. 191).

l. 30. *congregatio Oratorii.* Philip Neri received the brief of Gregory XIII authorizing his congregation in 1575. He set down in its rules that there were to be frequent sermons and that they were to deal with the lives of Saints and Church history. At the end of the sixteenth and the beginning of the seventeenth centuries the Oratorian Church in Rome enjoyed considerable popularity. Donne repeats the charge he had made in *Pseudo-Martyr* in almost the identical terms: '. . . that the world which in such a rage of devotion ran towards the Jesuits, might be arrested a little upon the contemplation of an Order which professed Church-knowledge as the other did State-knowledge' (p. 261). See also *Pseudo-Martyr*, pp. 50–1.

PAGE 73

l. 2. *Confession and absolution to bee given by letters.* The case to which Donne is referring involved the Portuguese Jesuit Emmanuel Sa

(1528–96). A late work of his, *Aphorismi Confessariorum*, appeared in Venice in 1595. The book was a dictionary of moral cases and solutions which, because of its simplicity, was very popular and had gone through fourteen editions by 1602. Sa had maintained in it that 'posse absentem etiam per scriptum absolvi aut per nuntium'. This proposition was condemned by Clement VIII in 1602 and removed from subsequent editions. In his text, Donne is quoting from the decree of the Holy Office (20 June 1602) 'per litteras et internuntios'. He refers to confession by letter in *Pseudo-Martyr*, pp. 129 and 279, and in *Sermons*, vi. 58. He speaks of the use of the Sacrament for 'spying into the counsails of Princes' in *Sermons*, ix. 310.

l. 5. *a great Monarch, who hath manie designes upon Italy.* With the genius they had for stirring up quite unnecessary trouble, the Spanish Jesuits at Alcalá debated in March 1602 whether or not it was an 'article of faith' that any individual was the true pope. The question was of no real significance, but when delated to Rome it was interpreted as the preface to an attack on Clement VIII by questioning his title. Bellarmine and James both make reference to the issue (see note on p. 108) and Vasquez, as head of the theology faculty at Alcalá, spent six weeks in the gaols of the Inquisition. The intervention of Philip III on behalf of the Spanish Jesuits confirmed the worst Roman suspicions, and what had originally been a superfluous scholastic nicety became for a time a subject of bitter controversy. Donne makes his point by bluntly stating what the more nervous Romans had actually suspected at the time (see L. Pastor, *History of the Popes*, xxiv. 341–6).

Margin. *Vita Nerii. De Vita et Rebus Gestis Beati Philippi Nerii*, by Antonio Gallonio, Mainz, 1606. Donne quotes the same edition in *Biathanatos*, p. 122, and in *Sermons*, vii. 334. The book itself is another good example of baroque hagiography, giving little picture of the man and whole chapters to catalogues of marvels.

l. 30. *hee hath drawne others into Religion.* One of the essential aspects of Neri's foundation was that its members remained secular priests and did not pronounce the usual three vows of the formal religious. Among other things, Donne is here making fun of the use of the Roman word 'religion' to describe a religious Order. The 'religion' in question in these remarks of Ignatius was, in historical fact, the Jesuit Order.

PAGE 75

l. 2. *he moved Baronius to write his Annals*. Baronius (1538–1607) was the author of the *Annales Ecclesiastici*, an enormous history of the Church meant as a counterblow to the Centuriators of Magdeburg. He succeeded Philip Neri as Superior of the Oratorians and served as confessor to Clement VIII. Donne refers to his revisions of the *Martyrologium* (1586) in *Biathanatos* (p. 66), and continually cites the *Annales* in *Pseudo-Martyr*.

l. 8. *Bozius*. Donne is probably thinking of the less well known of the two Oratorian brothers by this name. He was Francis, who wrote in 1602 a book entitled *De Temporali Ecclesiae Monarchia* which was answered at King James's request by William Barclay in 1611.

PAGE 77

l. 6. *Beza and Calvin*. By 1610 the democratic element in Calvinism could be quite openly attacked. David Owen in *Herod and Pilate*, along with his attack on Beza (the Epistle) feels free to cite the passage in Calvin's *Institutes* which Donne has in mind here (lib. iv, cap. 20, no. 22) with complete disapproval (p. 47). He also attacks Knox, Goodman, and Buchanan (pp. 48–9) (see following note). Morton tries to avoid the argument by accusing Persons of denying Calvin in theory but practising him in effect (*A Preamble unto an Incounter*, p. 76). In *A Full Satisfaction* he uses almost the same words Donne does here: '. . . Neither doth he ever restrain the outward power of any king except in those states where there is customably ordained for that purpose the magistracy of those who are called *Ephori* or *Tribuni Plebis*' (p. 109). Bellarmine had great sport with James reminding him of the 'magna multitudo Puritanorum' in his domain and listing passages from Calvin which dealt harshly with kings (*Apologia*, p. 182). The addition of Beza's name was doubly ironic. Among the Romans he was the least respected of the Reformers.

l. 21. *Knox, and Goodman, and Buchanan*. All three of these men were British reformers whose republican sympathies derived from Geneva. John Knox (1505–72) was the great Scots polemicist, historian, and reformer. His was the most indiscreet title in history: *The First Blast of the Trumpet Against the Monstrous Regiment of Women* (1558), sounded at Mary, but mortally offending the ears of Elizabeth. His ideas about the election of kings were highly unpleasing to James as they had been, indeed, to his mother. George Buchanan (1506–82) was a scholar and had been tutor to Montaigne and to James I. The King referred to him later, sometimes with respect, most frequently with fear. His inclusion here is justified by his *De Jure Regni*, 1579, advocating election of kings and allowing tyrannicide. Christopher Goodman (1520–1603) was an Oxford Puritan and a friend and associate of Knox at Geneva. In 1558 he published a series of offensively democratic pamphlets. Donne had linked Buchanan with Cade's Rebellion in the *Catalogus*, no. 17. All three men were an embarrassment to the Anglican controversialists (see Morton's *A Preamble unto an Incounter*, pp. 73–6).

l. 26. *Clement, or Ravillac.* Jacques Clement was the Dominican who assassinated Henri III in 1589. François Ravaillac murdered Henri IV in 1610. Clement was killed instantly by the King's guard: Ravaillac was horribly executed. The irony of putting the two names together was that while the Jesuits might have approved the killing of Henri III, their best friend and protector in France had been Henri IV.

The Anglican controversialists made much of the alleged exultation of Sixtus V when news of Henri III's death reached Rome. Donne is repeating here a phrase from the speech the Pope is reported to have made, 'in the midst of an army' and which James hurled at Bellarmine. Bellarmine's answer is not too convincing (*Responsio*, p. 233).

PAGE 79

l. 2. *as naturall food, and ordinarie diet.* This image pleased Donne and he used it in a letter: '. . . so many doctrines have grown to be ordinary diet and food of our spirits, and have place in the pap of our catechisms which were admitted but as physic in that present distemper . . .' (Gosse, i. 174). The substance of the point Donne is making had been strongly urged by James: '. . . and what difference there is between the killing or allowing the slaughter of kings, and the stirring up and approbation of practices to kill them, I remit to Bellarmine's own judgement' (*Apology*, p. 68). See also *Sermons*, i. 196.

l. 12. *the name of people comprehends all . . . not of their Order.* This reference is to a book which Donne owned, John Rensinck's *Manuale Franciscanorum* (Cologne, 1609), p. 57.

l. 23. *which Campian led, and . . . Garnet concluded.* Edmund Campion (1540–81) and Robert Persons (1546–1610) were the first two English Jesuits to return to England. They arrived in June 1580. Campion's brilliance and style captured the imagination of English Catholics, and the government did all in its power to capture him. They succeeded in July 1581. After a trial which was a travesty even by sixteenth-century standards he was executed at Tyburn on a charge of treason in December 1581. Henry Garnet (1555–1606) came to England with Robert Southwell in 1586. The next year he was made Superior of the Jesuits in England and held that post for eighteen years. He was captured in December 1605 and charged with implication in the Gunpowder Plot. His defence was that his only real information had come to him under the seal of confession. He was executed in May 1606.

l. 25. *such a second martyrdome.* The Jesuits in Hell manifest the same eagerness to rush at death or to accept dangerous employment that they had shown in life. The Jesuit Scribanius (see note on p. 100) remarks that his brethren surpassed the heroes of antiquity who had lacked the courage for 'multas mortes' (*Amphitheatrum Honoris*). It may be that Donne also has this boast in mind. See *Pseudo-Martyr*, p. 150 and *Sermons*, ii. 360.

l. 34. *that act which I did at first in Heaven.* The usual interpretation of the sin of the Angels was that it was one of pride. (See *Sermons*, ix. 377–8.)

PAGE 81

l. 3. *Casuists, which professe the Art of sinning.* Donne's attitude to casuistry was complex. Walton tells us that after his death there were found in his study 'cases of conscience that had concerned his friends, with his observations and solutions of them' (Walton, p. 68). This book has since been lost, but *Pseudo-Martyr* testifies to his thorough familiarity with the casuistry of his time. *Biathanatos* is simply an extended exercise in casuistry as Mrs. Simpson has pointed out (*Sermons*, v. 16). He seems, however, to have been of two minds on the whole subject, as this remark reveals. Some of the implications of the enormous growth of casuistical literature in the sixteenth and seventeenth centuries have been discussed in A. E. Malloch's 'Donne and the Casuists' (*Studies in English Literature*, 1962, pp. 57–76). As in many other things, Donne here eludes analysis. He proclaims his dislike of casuistry, and yet is willing to use it expertly. (See the almost contradictory statements in *Biathanatos*, pp. 30 and 33.)

Margin. *Nuncius Sydereus* (see note on p. 102). The mockery here is not a quotation from Galileo. The idea of 'he may draw the *Moone*' is echoed in *The First Anniversary*:

> Man hath weav'd out a net, and this net throwne
> Upon the Heavens, and now they are his owne.
> Loth to goe up the hill, or labour thus
> To goe to heaven, we make heaven come to us.
> (Grierson, i. 239)

Several lines later Donne refers to 'the floating Moon'.

PAGE 83

l. 5. *Parsons the English Jesuite in hope of a Cardinalship.* Robert Persons, the 'arch-Jesuit' of both fact and fiction, was Edmund Campion's companion on the first Jesuit mission to England. He left England in 1581 and never returned. He was instrumental in the founding of St. Omer's as well as in the founding of seminaries at Valladolid, Seville, and Madrid. He served long years as Rector of the English College in Rome and was all his life an indefatigable controversialist. In 1594 when Cardinal Allen died, Persons was accused of intriguing for a red hat. His biographer remarks that the accusations were most probably unjust (T. G. Law, *D.N.B.* xliii. 411–18).

l. 19. *Gerson, De Auferibilitate Papae.* Jean le Charlier de Gerson (1363–1429) was Chancellor of the University of Paris and one of the most famous of the Gallican theologians caught in the troubles of the Avignon papacy. Protestant theologians quickly adopted him as a precursor. He supported the superiority of a council over the pope as the only possible solution to schism, and in the work mentioned he discussed the crimes for and the procedures by which a pope could be deposed. Donne may not have actually read the work (first printed in 1494) although he mentions it again in *Sermons*, iv. 248. He could have found it in Rabelais's catalogue of books (*Pantagruel*, chap. vii). James uses it as an example of Gallican liberty and independence and Bellarmine offers no answer (*Premonition*, p. 27).

l. 22. *the two Empresses, Pulcheria & Eudoxia.* Donne is here collapsing history. The correspondence between Pope Leo I and the two

empresses concerned not the Paschal controversy but the monophysite heresy and the condemnation of Eutyches in the years
which led up to the Council of Chalcedon (A.D. 451) (see *The
Cambridge Medieval History*, i. 506).

l. 24. *Pelagius . . . the Pope . . . the Empresse.* The only thing I have
been able to determine about this reference is that the Pelagius
involved is not the heresiarch. Professor Gerhard Ladner of the
University of California at Los Angeles informs me that the Pelagius in question must be the Roman deacon (later Pelagius I) and
the Pope would be either Vigilius or else his predecessor Silverius.
But there is no evidence of their correspondence with the only
possible empress, Theodora. In addition, her monophysite
sympathies would make such a correspondence unlikely. It is possible that Donne meant the Emperor Justinian I; this would make
sense. But he doesn't say 'Justinian' and the whole context calls
rather for an empress than an emperor. In addition, I have not
been able to find the story in any of the historians Donne is
known to have used (see L. Duchesne, 'Vigile & Pelage', *Revue des
questions historiques*, xxxvi (1884), 369–84).

l. 25. *Julia.* This is Julia Domna, the mother of Caracalla and
Geta.

l. 30. *the Church delivered over her selfe to a woman-Bishop.* Donne
objected strongly to the credence given to feminine visionaries
whom he calls 'mothers of the Church'. He makes this clear in
Sermons, i. 253 and *Devotions*, p. 32 (see note on p. 103). He adds
here the baroque episode of Pope Joan, an English woman who
supposedly ruled for two and a half years and was discovered
when she gave birth to a child on the Via Tibertina. Fortunately
the good lady did not survive the exertion. Nor has her story
survived the historians. All the controversialists, however, used
it, including such respectable ones as Jewel and Morton. One of
the few who has the grace to recognize its falsity is Donne himself in *Sermons*, vii. 153.
    The serious reason for all this may be the irony with which
Bellarmine attacks the notion of a woman (Elizabeth) as supreme
head of the Church (*Responsio*, p. 219). James appears more than
half in agreement with him, although he cannot admit it (*Apology*,
p. 100). For the extent and effectiveness of this anti-feminine
attack from the Roman side, see T. H. Clancy, *Papist Pamphleteers*,
Chicago, 1964, pp. 36–9.

Margin. *Reg. Jesuit.* The two rules quoted are from those written for the superior of a local community (nos. 73 and 47). The first of them is standard for all religious Orders whose houses are under cloister. The second is peculiar to the Jesuits; Ignatius' intention having been that his Order avoid exactly the charge Donne makes against it.

PAGE 85

l. 13. *in those things which the Poets writ, . . . we have since found many truths.* I believe this reference is to Pierre Coton's *De la Messe* (see note on p. 132):

> . . . les saints Peres et l'eglise se sont servis non seulement des temoi-gnages mais aussi des fables et fictions poetiques . . . avec combien plus de raison nous croyons du Fils de Dieu et de sa Mere ce qu'ils disoient de leur Minerve et de Vulcain . . . puis de Venus, Castor, Pollux, Hercule, Deucalion, Pyrrha et autres materiaux d'impieté à ceux-la et de pieté . . . à tous ceux qui se scavent aider de la mythologie . . . (p. 178).

l. 25. *Beasts . . . which . . . did sometime adore the Host.* This story could have come from any one of innumerable medieval collections of eucharistic miracles, of which Chaucer's Prioress gives us a sample. Its most likely source, however, is Bellarmine's *De Sacramento Eucharistiae* (lib. iii. cap. 8). Here the story is told of the ass which left its hay to worship the Host by kneeling before it. James picked up the story and refers to 'Bellarmine with his hungry mare that turned her tail to her provender and kneeled to the Sacrament' (*Premonition*, p. 55). Bellarmine's answer is to present James with a brief bestiary taken from the Old Testament (*Apologia*, p. 169). Not to be outdone by his royal master, Morton repeats the story but piquantly changed the animal to a lamb (*A Catholicke Appeale*, p. 435).

l. 27. *the Manes of Elizabeth.* James (*Apology*, p. 18) had referred to the 'Manes (if I may say so) of my late predecessor'; both Persons and Bellarmine had objected to this as pretentious (*Responsio*, p. 217). Donne ties this to a remark of Sebastian Heissius in his *Ad Aphorismos Doctrinae Jesuitarum*, Ingolstadt, 1609 (p. 135). The book to which Heissius is responding is one of the innumerable versions of the *Jesuit's Catechism* which were current in England after the Gunpowder Plot.

l. 6. *our Clavius hath beene . . . conversant with her.* I have not been able to find why Donne should credit Clavius with any particular knowledge of the moon: unless he is here implying general lunacy. The remark about his 'Ephemerides' is a different matter. These Ephemerides or Almanacs were the popular source of weather information in Donne's time. Their basis was largely folklore and their predictions were founded on astrology and related pheno- mena such as animal behaviour, tides, transmission of sound, or the bites of fleas. Donne is thus having fun by saying, equivalently, 'Clavius is an accurate forecaster, provided he has heard the weather report.' See S. K. Heninger, *A Handbook of Renaissance Meteorology*, Durham, North Carolina, 1960, pp. 30–2, 217–24.

l. 18. *Our Herbestus, or Busaeus, or Voellus.* These names come from Ribadeneyra's *Catalogus* (see note on p. 113) where they and Clavius are the only ones listed as mathematicians, in Section XVII. They are almost complete unknowns, so that we might conclude that here the epithets 'tasteless and childish' reflect Donne's general opinion of mathematicians or, at least, teachers of mathematics.

l. 23. *Garnet had Clavius for his Maister.* (For Eudaemon-Joannes and his book, see note on p. 125.) At the end of the passage Donne mentions here the author goes on to say that Garnet was scheduled to remain at the Roman College and replace Clavius as the Pro- fessor of Mathematics, but that at his own request he was sent back to England (pp. 243–4). Donne contents himself with lateral references to Garnet as a man. It may be that he recognized the justice of the defence of Garnet's integrity which Bellarmine, in one of his rare flashes of anger, had urged against James's criticisms (*Apologia*, p. 186).

l. 32. *there were no miracles done there.* Donne is referring to Joseph Acosta's *De Natura Novi Orbis . . . sive de procuranda Indorum salute*, Cologne, 1596. The chapter in question is entitled, 'Cur miracula in conversione gentium non fiant nunc ut olim a Christi praedica- toribus'. The explanation is good sociology. No longer are an illiterate band of Christians preaching to a powerful empire, but missionary work now sends civilized men as the representatives of powerful kingdoms to preach to savages. Thus the only miracle required is patience. This kind of thinking recommended itself to Donne and he cites this work approvingly in *Pseudo-Martyr*, p. 126; *Essays*, p. 84; *Sermons*, iv. 278–9, viii. 366, and x. 173.

PAGE 89

l. 2. *There is no body without his Excrements.* In 1609 Jacob Gretser (see note on p. 129) published at Ingolstadt his *Relatio de Studiis Jesuitarum Abstrusioribus* in answer to a pamphlet by John Cambilhon attacking Jesuit formation. Cambilhon claimed to be an ex-Jesuit, and Gretser remarks of him in good controversial style, 'Quodnam corpus tam sanum est quod excrementis careat?' (p. 32).

l. 9. *Pope Gregory were strucken by the Angell.* This delightful fable was one of Donne's favourites. He uses it three times in his *Sermons* and each time in detail (iv. 80; vi. 59; vii. 86). But he does Bellarmine less than justice in his attribution of it to the passage cited from the *de Purgatorio*. Bellarmine says the story originated with John Damascene and, although he offers a defence, he carefully adds 'si haec historia defendi debeat'. He concludes by joining Cano and Soto in calling it a fiction. He also quotes the Roman author of the Life of Gregory who says that, 'hanc historiam de Traiano repertam esse in ecclesia quadam Anglorum nec fidem certam illi habitam a Roma'. Thomas Morton uses the story in *A Full Satisfaction*, A5 verso; *Apologia Catholica II*, pp. 180–6; and in *A Catholicke Appeale*, p. 429.

l. 28. *the Jesuite Cotton in those questions* (for Coton and his questions, see note on p. 118). The question involved was: 'Quid circa canonizationem, utrum urgere me velit?' In the original version the canonization involved was supposed to be Coton's own. Donne neatly transfers the query to Ignatius. Ignatius was beatified in 1609, but not canonized until 1622.

l. 32. *Philip, King of Spaine, and Henry, King of Fraunce.* In this section Donne is probably echoing Ribadeneyra's *Flos Sanctorum*, Madrid, 1609. Speaking of Ignatius' 'cause' he says that, 'los mayores y mas poderosos Principes de la Cristiandad se lo piden y supplican con grande instancia' (ii. 58).

PAGE 91

l. 2. *D'Alcala a Franciscan, and Penafort a Jacobite.* Diego d'Alcala, a Franciscan lay brother who died in 1463 was canonized by Sixtus V in 1588. Raymond of Penafort, a Dominican canonist who died in 1275, was canonized by Clement VIII in 1601. Donne is here quoting Pierre Mattheu, *Histoire de France . . . du Regne de Henri IIII*, Paris, 1605. 'On y parle de canonizer Ignace de Loyola, chef de l'ordre des Jesuites. Si le Roy l'entreprend comme il s'en parle, ce fera un acte digne de la pieté des descendans de S. Louys. Il semble qu'il en ait plus de suiet que nul autre Prince, estant vray qu'Ignace est né dedans les Estats de ses ayeux maternels et qu'il ait plus faict pour ces disciples que tous les Princes du monde ensemble' (ii. 355 verso). This whole section occurs in *Pseudo-Martyr* almost verbatim (pp. 124–5).

Margin. *Litera eius ad Philip.* This letter is part of the book mentioned on p. 133. Donne quotes Baronius accurately, but he omits the last phrase of the section which might have first caught his eye: '... procul absit a me ut me Regum favor et non potius Regis Regum Christi gratia in thronum provehat altiorem.' Baronius was undoubtedly quite sincere in this unfortunate comment.

l. 12. *therefore they labour the Pope themselves.* The change of subject from the singular (presumably Coton) to the plural (the Jesuits) is unexplained in the English as it is in the Latin.

l. 23. *the title of Beatus.* Aloysius Gonzaga (1568–91) was the son of the princely house of Mantua. He entered the Jesuits in 1585 and died six years later while attending the plague-stricken in Rome. He was beatified in 1605. The work Donne quotes is Ceparius, *Vita Beati Aloisii Gonzagae*, Cologne, 1608. It is in the worst hyperbolic hagiographical style. But Donne's knowledge of Roman politics is quite accurate. The biography was dedicated to Francisco Gonzaga, brother of Aloysius. He accepted it and then added a letter, backed by his name and marquisate, to Paul V, urging the speedy canonization of his brother. The Jesuits had twice to request the postponement of this honour (1620 and 1671), so that Ignatius, Xavier, and Borgia should precede Aloysius to the altars (see C. C. Martindale, *The Vocation of Aloisius Gonzaga*, London, 1927). Ceparius is twice quoted in *Pseudo-Martyr* (pp. 100, 175–7).

l. 25. *He would also have given this title . . . rather to Xaverius.* Francis Xavier (1506–52) was one of Ignatius' original companions in the founding of the Jesuits. He spent the last ten years of his life as a missionary in the Orient and died trying to reach China. He was canonized with Ignatius in 1622. Thomas Morton has a scornful section on Xavier's miracles in *A Catholicke Appeale* (pp. 421–4).

l. 32. *that Doctor, Gabriell Nele.* It would be tempting to say that Donne took this story and its reference from Rabelais's *Tiers Livre*, chap. xix. If he did, he got the reference wrong, as did

Rabelais. It is from *Bartoli Interpretatum Iuris Civilis Coryphaei* (Basle, 1562), p. 423. The good doctor appears to have been the first recorded lip-reader.

l. 14. *the Reliques of many are honoured upon earth.* This tag was used by many of the polemicists. Bellarmine picks it up in *Controversiae VII*, I. ix, and says, '. . . locum hunc fortasse non esse Augustinum; nusquam enim in eius operibus eum reperire potui'. Morton in *Apologia Catholica II* adds to the quotation, '. . . quicumque dixit (tribuitur autem a multis Augustino) . . .' (p. 333).

l. 23. *both the Treasures of the Church.* Frances of Rome was canonized with great solemnity by Paul V in May 1609. The first treasure Donne mentions here is the wealth of the papacy. The second treasure is the spiritual one to which he refers in *Sermons*, i. 229–30. It is the subject of a famous passage where he fully speaks his mind:

> Other mens crosses are not my crosses; no man hath suffered more then himselfe needed. That is a poor treasure which they boast of in the Romane Church, that they have in their Exchequer, all the works of supererogation of the Martyrs of the Primitive Church, that suffered so much more then was necessary for their owne salvation, and those super-abundant crosses and merits they can apply to me. If the treasure of the blood of Christ Jesus be not sufficient, Lord what addition can I find, to match them, to piece them out!   (*Sermons*, ii. 300)

In his *Premonition* (p. 39) James attacks the same notion.

l. 24. *Leo 3 . . . the first Pope which Canonized any.* Donne shares this remark with Morton, who gives Bellarmine as his source. See *Apologia Catholica I*, p. 249 and *A Catholicke Appeale*, p. 236. The Roman argument was that Leo had only regularized an already existing practice. Regularization was perhaps an inexact word until the Constitutions of Urban VIII in 1625. Donne had used this argument in *Pseudo-Martyr*, p. 197.

l. 29. *Dictated and written by Saint Paul* (for Valladier, see note on p. 107). Donne is understandably annoyed at Valladier who refers to 'leges ei sacrae societatis a Beato Paulo Apostolo dictatas' (p. 57), and continues to relate that Frances had a great devotion to Peter and Magdalen. Out of this Donne sets his amusing legal scene of the signing of a formal document. The passage he quotes on p. 95 (ll. 2–6) is taken from one of the rather less hysterical parts of Valladier's introduction (pp. 5–6).

PAGE 95

l. 9. *a certaine idle Gazettier*. Ignatius was beatified by Paul V on 27 July 1609 and Jesuits all over the world celebrated in high baroque style. A full account of some of these celebrations can be found in the *Annuae Litterae Societatis Jesu Anno 1609* (Dillingen, 1610). Mock naval battles, Trojan horses full of pitch and powder, parades, plays, speeches—all are involved. At Manresa in Spain the festivities closed with '. . . mille admodum ex reliquo discipulorum coetu *Io Ignati* ingeminantes' (p. 5).

l. 11. *the Jesuites Letters of Japan, and the Indies*. From their first regular publication in 1578 the Jesuit '*Annuae Litterae*' were enormously popular on the Continent. It would appear that they had some currency in England as well. Donne mentions them in another context and tone in a letter to Sir George More. Speaking of letters, he says, 'No other kind of conveyance is better for knowledge or love. What treasures of moral knowledge are in Seneca's letters . . . and what of natural in Pliny's? How much of the history of the time is in Cicero's letters? And how much of all these times in the Jesuits Eastern and Western epistles?' (*Letters*, p. 105).

l. 23. *Pope Boniface*. This is the standard reference to Boniface III, used by almost all the controversialists in the same terms Donne employs here (see note on p. 106).

PAGE 97

l. 6. *As a flower wet with last nights dew*. As far as I can determine, these verses, like those on p. 63, are Donne's own.

l. 15. *I suspected that that Order would attempt as much at Rome*. William Watson in *Decacordion* (1602) uses this notion of a Jesuit pope as the end of his series of charges that the Jesuits wish to take over the government of the world (p. 324). Donne amuses himself in *Pseudo-Martyr* by speculating on the exaggerations that would follow on the election of a Jesuit pope (pp. 119–25). See also *Sermons*, viii. 330.

l. 20. *till all the sand of the sea were run through his houre-glasse*. A *clepsydra* is a water clock, used in ancient times to limit public speakers (cf. Martial, *Epigrams*, vi. 35).

l. 24. *Jungius, etc.* Donne took all these names from Ribadeneyra's *Catalogus* where, in Section XXIV, they are listed in this order. All were controversial writers. Jungius was a Polish Jesuit, Scribanius (p. 100) and Gretzerus (p. 113) have already been mentioned. Richeome was the Jesuit Provincial of France and an important figure in the controversy that broke out on the death of Henri IV. Cydonius is the Eudaemon-Joannes (p. 125) who wrote in defence of Garnet.

Margin. *Bonar. in Amphithe.* Clarus Bonarcius is the pen-name of Carolus Scribanius (1555–1609). The work referred to is his *Amphitheatrum Honoris in quo Calvinistarum in Societatem Jesu Criminationes Iugulatae*, Naples, 1606. 'Smothered' would be better than 'slaughtered' for what this wild and disorganized tract does to arguments. Donne refers to it again in *Biathanatos*, p. 72.

l. 29. *Cato was called to his answere foure and forty times.* This tag is from Aurelius Victor, *De Viris Illustribus* (no. 47) where Cato the Censor is said to have been acquitted *quadragies et quater*.

PAGE 99

l. 3. *their greatest argument of innocency to be accused.* The work cited for this commonplace statement is Jungius, *Pro Spongia Stanislai Rescii adversus Haereticum Polonum.* Donne mentions him three times in *Pseudo-Martyr* (pp. 142, 162, and 350).

l. 7. *expelled at Venice, and shaked and fanned in France.* The Jesuits were expelled from Venice on 14 June 1606, because of their refusal to ignore the interdict laid on the Republic by Paul V. They remained excluded for fifty years. In France, the Jesuits had been banished in 1595 and remained out of the kingdom until recalled by Henri IV in 1604. Immediately after his death in 1610, agitation began again for their expulsion.

l. 10. *Vegetius.* The reference is to *Flavius Vegetius de re militari*, 1607 (p. 75). This must have been one of Donne's handbooks, since he refers to it in *Pseudo-Martyr*, twice in *Biathanatos*, and twice in *Essays*.

APPENDIX A

Differences between the Two Texts

I N any list such as this there is bound to be an element of choice. I have noted only those differences which strike me as significant and which do not make a normally strict translation. Minor readjustments and changes, necessarily involved in suiting English to Latin, I have not noted.

In the two columns below I have marked the page and line of the Latin text, even in cases where the English simply omits or adds to it. Omissions are indicated by lines (——).

	LATIN TEXT	ENGLISH TEXT
2: 16	Apologista	*Apologist* and defender
4: 3	haec	the things delivered in this booke
4: 12	sordibus	naturall drosses
6: 2	——	the *Planets*
6: 11	——	in their circuit
6: 18	Inferos	all the roomes in Hell
8: 5	——	for else how did they heare that, which none but they ever heard
8: 23	——	which I take to bee this place
12: 20	——	and therefore might wonder to find him there
18: 7	Haec vera nova et inaudita	—
20: 24	——	and felt al his alterations
22: 2	——	and thereby this kingdome much indebted to you
24: 15	——	But when he thought better upon it
26: 16	——	and brought us againe from understanding one an other
28: 15	vicaria opera	—
30: 7	conscientiam	conscience and knowledge
30: 24–5	per nimbos . . . substratus camerae	—

	LATIN TEXT	ENGLISH TEXT
32: 13	——	be thereby taught what those vertues are
34: 1	——	and beleeving him to be so
34: 9	——	when they are presented to you
34: 13	Gregorium	—
40: 22	fibulam solvit	—
42: 8	non certe	—
44: 8	canonesque e re nata interpretantur	—
44: 25	——	who have had more *Cardinals* then wee
48: 14	——	and so have no more authority than those poore men which writ them
48: 14	——	which are their *canons*
48: 17–19	nunc nobis stellae fixae . . . planetae sunt Canones	—
50: 5	——	for indeed there is no remedy
52: 15	——	and *Sentences* in that *Court*
52: 23	——	and therefore to be avoyded and liberty and sea-roome to bee affected
54: 22	sua tamen licentia usus	using I must confesse his *Jesuitical* liberty of wilde anticipation
56: 12	——	which have utterly cast off *Rome*
56: 24	——	which are doctrines and practises, contrary, and dangerous to us
58: 14	erga omnes	when a Cardinall reprehended his fiercenes towards the king
58: 16	quibus omnibus instructus in Monarchas insurgit	—
60: 25	——	for we exceed them both
66: 9	——	for how could it be, the word being not *Hebrew*
66: 20	——	which they finde in the *Authors* whom they geld
68: 26	——	then you thinke belongs to your merits
70: 5	inutilis	infirmity and unfitnesse
76: 9	——	and so brought into certaine use & consequence
76: 28	——	in which capacitie he might say anything

	LATIN TEXT	ENGLISH TEXT
80: 17	conciliabunt	unite and reconcile
82: 2	sibi	for him their founder
82: 9	dolendum	lament and mourne
86: 3	——	as such *Innovators*
90: 5	constantiam	heighth and constancy
90: 8	——	as himselfe gives the reason
90: 19	magna importunitate solicitatus	upon the intreaty
90: 20	——	of that *Order*
92: 4	——	besides his former pretences
92: 25	——	as witnesses
94: 7	ut homines	—

APPENDIX B

A Note on Sources

THERE is one contemporary continental satire with which *Ignatius His Conclave* is linked by several critics. Like Donne's work, the *Satyre Menippée* was born out of a precise controversy.[1] It recounts the meeting of the Estates General in Paris in 1593 at the summons of the League and against the interests of Henri IV. Its six authors wished to discredit the League and all its partisans; a task in which they admirably succeeded.

Like *Ignatius His Conclave*, although at much greater length, the *Satyre Menippée* begins with a complicated ritual disclaimer which describes how the anonymous report of the sessions arrived, via Italy, at the printer's. It then goes on to describe both the solemn entry of the Estates and the hall where they met. As in Donne, all the principal figures are allowed to condemn themselves in their ludicrous speeches. The final speaker, the *politique* d'Aubray, pronounces a long and narrative condemnation of the whole history of the League. This is followed by a *Supplement* called *Nouvelles de la Region de la Lune* which (one suspects because of its title and dedicatory epistle) some critics have connected with *Ignatius His Conclave*.

There are many similarities between the two works. Both are politically conservative in tone and purpose. Both focus on a political enemy and are willing to sacrifice individual characters to the attack on the general foe. Both employ the device of allowing the offenders to condemn themselves, although both can and do descend to straight invective. There are some *loci communes* of contemporary controversy which they both share. Finally, both are written in a colloquial prose, with some verse attached, always willing to sacrifice logic and argument for a good point or epigram.

---

[1] There are dozens of *Satirae Menippeae* in the sixteenth century. Most of them have the basic Lucianic pattern: mixed verse and prose; a vision, usually in heaven or hell; dialogue; an ironic point. The *Satyre Menippée* is the most famous and one of the best.

In general, however, the differences between them are more important than the similarities. First, the *Satyre Ménippée* allows its final section, fully one-third of the work, to break completely out of its ironic structure. The speech of d'Aubray is simple invective which presents the ideas of its authors. Second, the *Satyre Ménippée* has a central situation, but no central figure. The presiding officer, the duc du Mayenne, speaks first, but he hardly dominates the action of the piece. If in this sense the *Satyre Ménippée* is less dramatic than *Ignatius His Conclave*, in its descriptions it is much more detailed and visual. There is nothing in Donne's work like the description of the Leaguers in procession or of the tapestries that hang the hall. There is also nothing to equal the French taste for boisterous vulgarity—particularly having to do with smells. Finally, the *Satyre Ménippée* burlesques not only the characters but their speech as well. The pedantry of M. de Rose and the execrable Latin of the Cardinal de Pelvé may confirm their stupidity, but the speeches are gems of parody. Donne tries to imitate this, particularly in the character of Paracelsus, but never quite succeeds.

Only one place in the French work gives us any verbal echoes of *Ignatius His Conclave*. The letter which introduces *Les Nouvelles de la Region de la Lune* is from an anonymous Jesuit to the King of Spain. In it are many of the charges Donne makes against the Jesuits: their subjection to Spain; their cruelty in the Indies; their attempts to assassinate Henri IV.[1] All of these items are, however, commonplaces of French as of English *anti-jesuitica*.

A second possible source is discussed by Miss Marjorie Nicolson when she suggests that Donne took at least the envelope of his work from Kepler's *Somnium*. The *Somnium* was written in the late summer of 1610.[2] In order for it to reach Donne by December of that year, Miss Nicolson argues that it must have been taken in manuscript to Thomas Hariot; passed by him to Henry Percy who was in the Tower; and seen by Donne on a visit to Percy. By this time Donne had already written *Ignatius His Conclave* as a set of dialogues in strict imitation of Lucian's *Dialogues of the Dead*. He simply took the introduction and conclusion from Kepler. Thus

[1] *Satyre Ménippée*, ed. Charles Nodier, Paris, 1824, ii. 235–43.
[2] Marjorie Nicolson, 'Kepler, the Somnium and John Donne', *Journal of the History of Ideas*, i (1940), 259–80; *Voyages to the Moon*, New York, 1960, pp. 49–52.

the work begins as a cosmic voyage, then falls into dialogues, and at the end, returns to the cosmic voyage form again. (My understanding is that the two break points would occur on pp. 5 and 97 of this text.) This would have made it possible for Kepler to remark in his *Notes*, written between 1620 and 1623:

Fallor an author Satyrae procacis, cui nomen Conclave Ignatianum, exemplar nactus erat huius opusculi; pungit enim me nominatim etiam in ipso principio. Nam in progressu miserum Copernicum adducit ad Plutonis tribunal, ad quod ni fallor, aditus est per Heclae Voragines . . .

Miss Nicolson's point of departure is the disunity she feels to exist between the opening and closing sections of the work and its central dialogues. Since this is a matter of individual judgement, I feel I must disagree. There does not seem to me to be any break in the structure. Moreover, if I am interpreting correctly the points at which she feels these breaks occur, it should be pointed out that elements mentioned in the opening and concluding sections are also mentioned in the text.[1] In addition, I feel that the historical argument is open to the objection that it is too complex. It does not seem to me to be certain that Kepler's memory of the terrible year 1611 (when his mother's long suffering on a charge of witchcraft began) would be in perfect chronological order some ten to twelve years later. For these reasons and despite his complaint, his accusation that Donne borrowed from him seems improbable.

There is no English poet around whom the game of source hunting can less easily be played than around Donne. Even this very minor work shares with his major works the exclusive parentage of his own imagination. He could have taken the title from an illustration on a London broadside, dated 9 November 1605 and dealing with the Gunpowder Plot. A small lunette gives a picture of the devil, holding aloft a scroll and surrounded by evil spirits under the rubric 'Ignations Conclave'.[2] He could have been inspired by the hyperbole of a Jesuit sermon, preached by John Osorius and printed in Venice in 1601. Osorius identifies Ignatius as the terror of Hell, foretold by the prophet Jeremy, and as the

---

[1] The spectacles of p. 7 return on p. 13; Galileo and the *Sidereus Nuncius* are found on p. 81; and the abandoned body to which Donne returns on p. 97 is clearly mentioned, as abandoned, on p. 63.

[2] *Catalogue of Prints and Drawings in the British Museum*, i. 36, no. 67.

fifth angel of *Revelations*.[1] Among the mock battles, fireworks, speeches, and plays that marked the Order's celebration of Ignatius' beatification in the summer of 1609[2] we can be sure that someone (most probably a Spanish Jesuit living in Antwerp) preached and published a description of Ignatius' apotheosis: the *Beatus* striding into glory over the prostrate forms of Benedict, Francis, Dominic, and Bruno. The *frontispiece* to this edition is an example of such Jesuit rhetoric translated into carving. It shows Ignatius holding his cloak over a group of figures, most of whom are cowled and tonsured. The scene is celestial, but Ignatius is plainly cast as the new-found protector of the older monastic and mendicant orders. Donne could easily have read, seen, or heard such flourishes and decided to repeat them with a change of setting and personnel.

All of these are merely possibilities: but the leap from what might have been, to what Donne actually wrote, is a long one indeed. Certainly he needed no source. With equal certainty, if he had one, I have been unable to find it.

For the convenience of readers an alphabetical list follows of the less familiar authors from whom Donne quotes. I have added a few basic biographical details. The list does not include authors casually mentioned in the text. For all Jesuit authors the appropriate reference to Sommervogel is given.

ACOSTA   Joseph de Acosta (1539–1600), Spanish Jesuit missionary and Superior of the Jesuits in Peru. He returned to Spain and died as Rector of the Jesuit house in Salamanca. His works all concern the history of the Jesuits in Peru (Sommervogel, i. 31).

AZORIUS   Juan Azor (1533–1603), Spanish Jesuit and moral theologian at Alcalà and Rome. His *Institutiones Morales* was one of the most popular books of moral theology in the seventeenth century and is frequently cited by Donne. It was also attacked by Pascal (Sommervogel, i. 738).

BARONIUS   Caesar Baronius (1538–1607), Italian Oratorian, friend and follower of St. Philip Neri. He was made cardinal

---

[1] John Osorius, S.J., *Tomi Quinque Concionum de Sanctis*, Venice, 1601, Lib. iv, pp. 153–62.

[2] *Annuae Litterae Societatis Jesu Anno 1609*, Dillingen, 1610. The entire book is a collection of these *fasti*.

BARONIUS(*cont.*) in 1591. He is best known for his revision of the *Martyrology* (1586) and his monumental *Annales Ecclesiastici* which he had brought up to A.D. 1198 by the time of his death.

BARTOLUS   Bartolus (1313–55), Italian lawyer. At the age of twenty-five he was Professor of Law at Pisa. He was a Councillor to the Emperor, Charles IV.

BELLARMINE   Roberto Bellarmino (1542–1621), Italian Jesuit and controversial theologian. He was made cardinal in 1599 and served from 1602 to 1605 as Archbishop of Capua (Sommervogel, i. 1151).

BENIUS   Dominic Bañez (1528–1604), Spanish Dominican and for most of his active life a Professor of Theology at Salamanca. He was the main Dominican spokesman against the Jesuits in the *de auxiliis* controversy.

BRISSON   Barnabé Brisson (1531–91), French lawyer and Premier Président of the *Parlement* of Paris. His works are mainly on Roman law and history. Because of his moderation, he was hanged by the *Seize* in 1591.

CARRANZA   Bartolomeo Carranza (1503–76), Spanish Dominican canonist and archbishop. He spent the last eight years of his life as a prisoner of the Inquisition, before being finally acquitted. He had accompanied Philip II to England for the celebration of the King's marriage to Mary Tudor.

CASARUBIOS   Alphonso de Casarubios (154?–1615), Spanish Franciscan canonist and theologian.

CEPARIUS   Virgilio Cepari (1564–1631), Italian Jesuit philologist and historian. He was much employed in preparing the 'causes' of Jesuits proposed for canonization (Sommervogel, ii. 957).

CIACONIUS   Pedro Chacon (1525–81), Spanish priest and polymath who wrote a long list of commentaries on the Fathers of the Church, helped with the revision of the calendar, and served on the commission appointed to bring Gratian up to date.

CLAVASIUS   Angelo Carleti de Clavasio (d. 1496), Italian canonist and moral theologian. His *Summa Angelica* was reprinted many times between 1486 and 1610.

COCCIUS   Josse Coccius (1581–1622), German Jesuit theologian and controversialist. He was confessor to the Archduke Leopold (Sommervogel, ii. 1255).

COTTON   Pierre Coton (1564–1626), French Jesuit preacher and controversialist. He was certainly the best-known member of his Order in France; so much so that an attempt was made to assassinate him in 1604. He was friend and confessor to Henri IV (Sommervogel, ii. 1539).

CUDSEMIUS   Peter (born Samuel) Cutsem (158?–1649), a German Calvinist who changed both his name and his faith in 1608. The book Donne cites is a defence of his conversion. His other works are all anti-Calvinist controversy.

CUPERS   Rudolph Cupers, sixteenth-century Hungarian priest and theologian. His controversial works are mostly in defence of the papal primacy.

EUDAEMON-   André l'Heureux (1564–1625), Cretan Jesuit and
JOANNES   controversialist. He wrote in defence of both Garnet and equivocation (Sommervogel, iii. 482).

GALLONIUS   Antonio Gallonio (d. 1605), Italian Oratorian, historian, and controversialist. He wrote in defence of Baronius.

GERSON   Jean le Charlier de Gerson (1363–1429), Chancellor of the University of Paris. He supported the conciliar theory at the Council of Constance and on the same occasion spoke effectively against tyrannicide.

GRACIAN   Hieronimo Gracian (1554–1614), Spanish Carmelite and theologian. He was dismissed from the Order by Theresa of Avila and reinstated by Clement VIII in 1595. He served as confessor to the Archduchess Isabella in Brussels.

GRATIAN   Joannes Gratianus (twelfth century), a monk who, as the author of the *Concordantia discordantium canonum* (known as the *Decretum Gratiani*), was the founder of canon law.

GRETZER

Jacob Gretser (1562–1625), German Jesuit theologian and prolific controversialist who was for many years Professor of Theology at Ingolstadt (Sommervogel, iii. 1743).

HARLAY

François de Harlay (1585–1653), Parisian priest and controversialist who was later Archbishop of Rouen (1615–53).

HEISSIUS

Sebastian Heissius (1572–1614), German Jesuit philosopher and controversialist at Ingolstadt. All his writings are on controversial theology (Sommervogel, iv. 229).

KEPLER

Johann Kepler (1571–1630), German astronomer and experimental physicist. He was a pupil of Tycho Brahe and was instrumental in establishing the Copernican theories.

L'ESCHASSIER

Jacques l'Eschassier (d. 1625), French parliamentarian and strong defender of the rights of the Gallican Church, of Henri IV, and the Republic of Venice. He also wrote on Roman law.

MACER

Gaspar Schoppe (Scioppius) (1576–1649), German Lutheran who, becoming a Catholic in 1598, turned into a bitter and railing controversialist. It was Macer who revealed to James I Wotton's remark about lying ambassadors (*D.N.B.* lxiii. 51).

MARIANA

Juan Mariana (1536–1624), Spanish Jesuit and theologian. From his retirement in 1599 he wrote the *De Rege et Regis Institutione* which caused no stir at all in Spain, but created a furore against the Jesuits in the rest of Europe, particularly after the death of Henri IV (Sommervogel, v. 547).

MATTHEU

Pierre Mattheu (1563–1621), French lawyer and the historian of the reign of Henri IV. He also wrote on canon law. His work was put on the *Index Librorum Prohibitorum* in 1610.

MENGUS

Hieronymo Menghi (d. 1610), Italian Franciscan all of whose writings have to do with exorcism. Some of them were condemned for their exaggerations.

MESUES — Joannes Mesues Damacenus (Yahia ben Hamec 928–1018), Syrian physician and follower of Avicenna. His *De Materia Medica* was first printed in Lyons in 1548.

METELLUS — Joannes Matalis Metellus (1520–97), Burgundian lawyer, humanist, and friend of Osorius. He had been in England in 1555 on papal business.

MODESTUS — Military writer of the third century whose small work on military nomenclature, published at the end of the fifteenth century as part of the *De Re Militari* of Vegetius (q.v.), was popular with sixteenth-century soldiers.

MOSCONIUS — Isidro Mosconio (d. 1621), Italian priest who was Vicar-General of the diocese of Bologna. He wrote on controversial theology and civil law.

NIEM — Dietrich of Niem (1340–1418), a papal chancery official and partisan of Alexander V and John XXIII. His writings against the schism were taken up and republished by the reformers in the sixteenth century.

OSORIUS — Hieronymo Osorius (1506–80), Portuguese nobleman, bishop, and scripture scholar. His works include the history of the kings of Portugal, controversy with English divines, and commentaries on the Scriptures.

PALEOTUS — Alfonso Paleotti (1530–1610), Archbishop of Bologna (1597–1610) and author of several pastoral tracts.

PANCIROLLI — Guido Pancirolli (1523–98), Italian jurist, humanist, and historian. He was Professor of Law at Padua and Turin. Most of his writings are on canon and Roman law.

PARIS DE PUTEO — Petrus Paulus Parisius de Puteo, fifteenth-century Neapolitan lawyer who served for a time as Councillor to King Ferdinand I.

PLATINA — Bartolomeo Platina (1421–81), humanist, historian, and papal official. His *Vitae Pontificum* was the first scientific history of the papacy.

QUARANTA   Stephano Quaranta (d. 1640), Italian Theatine and
            lawyer, most of whose writings were on canon law.
            He was Bishop of Amalfi when he died.

RADERUS   Mathias Rader (1561–1634), Austrian Jesuit huma-
            nist who was celebrated as a philologist and editor
            (Sommervogel, vi. 1371).

REBULLUS   Guillaume de Reboul (1560–1611), French Calvinist
            who was reconciled to Rome and spent fifteen years
            writing against the Huguenots. He was executed for
            writing satires against Paul V.

RENSINCK·   Johann Rensinck, sixteenth-century German Francis-
            can who was Superior of his Order at Cologne. The
            work quoted is the only one he wrote.

RIBADENEYRA Pedro de Ribadeneyra (1527–1611), Spanish Jesuit,
            close friend and biographer of Ignatius Loyola. Most
            of his other work is historical or controversial
            (Sommervogel, vi. 1724).

SCAPPUS   Antonius Scappus (d. 1603), Bolognese priest and
            canon lawyer. For a time he served in Rome as a
            canonist.

SCRIBANIUS Charles Scribani (1561–1629), Belgian Jesuit, rhetori-
            cian, and controversialist. For many years he was
            Superior of the Jesuit house in Antwerp. His contro-
            versial works are mostly against Calvinists (Sommer-
            vogel, vii. 982).

SEDULIUS   Henry de Vroom (1547–1621), Belgian Franciscan
            official. His only controversial work was in defence of
            his Order.

SERARIUS   Nicholas Serarius (1555–1609), French Jesuit theo-
            logian and controversialist. He was for twenty years
            Professor of Theology at Mainz and Würzburg
            (Sommervogel, vii. 1134).

SOPHRONIUS St. Sophronius (560–638), Patriarch of Jerusalem and
            Greek ecclesiastical writer. The work Donne attri-
            butes to him is probably not his.

THOLOSANUS   Petrus Gregorius Tholosanus (1540–1617), French lawyer and *politique*. He was an opponent of the French Jesuits and wrote against the promulgation of the Tridentine decrees in France.

TORRES   Diego de Torres Vasquez (1574–1639), Spanish Jesuit missionary who was Provincial of Peru. He is claimed to be the first European user of quinine. The work Donne refers to is a history of the work of the Jesuits in Peru (Sommervogel, viii. 136).

VALLADERIUS   André Valladier (1560–1638), French canonist and hagiographer. He had been a Jesuit (1585–1608) but was released from his vows in 1608 by Paul V. Most of his printed work is pastoral with a distinctly Gallican flavour.

VEGETIUS   Flavius Vegetius Renatus, fourth-century Roman writer on tactics. The work Donne quotes was a compilation of other treatises and was printed in 1496. It became very popular as a military textbook in the sixteenth and seventeenth centuries.

APPENDIX C

Donne's Collaboration with Thomas Morton

PROFESSOR A. E. MALLOCH of McGill University pointed out to me that there could well be very real doubt whether or not the long accepted belief in a theological collaboration between Donne and Thomas Morton, generally assigned to the years 1605–10, was justified. *Ignatius His Conclave* cannot fully resolve this doubt: but it has some evidence to contribute.

In 1605 Thomas Morton was Rector of Long Marston in Yorkshire. During that same year he was made one of the King's chaplains and in 1606 was named Dean of Gloucester. In 1609 he was transferred to the Deanery of Winchester. During this period he published the following controversial works:

An Exact Discoverie	1605 (STC 18184)
Apologia Catholica, Pars I	1605 (STC 18174)
Apologia Catholica, Pars II	1606 (STC 18175)
A Full Satisfaction	1606 (STC 18185)
A Preamble unto an Incounter	1608 (STC 18191)
A Direct Answer unto . . . T. Higgons	1609 (STC 18181)
A Catholicke Appeale	1609 (STC 18176)
Encounter Against M. Parsons	1609 (STC 18183)[1]

Shortly after this Donne published *Pseudo-Martyr* (1610) and *Ignatius His Conclave* (1611).

Professor Malloch's doubts are based primarily on the fact that neither of the seventeenth-century lives of Morton mentions any such collaboration. The first of them, John Barwick's *A Summary Account of the Holy Life and Happy Death of . . . Thomas . . . Bishop of Duresme* (London, 1660) makes no mention of Donne at all. In talking of Morton's controversial works Barwick says, 'Only this encouragement he found, that as his great friend, *Arch-Bishop Bancroft*, put him upon the work, so *Dr. James* took the pains to

[1] STC 18188, *A Just and Moderate Answer to a Most Injurious Pamphlet*, 1605, is an answer to *An Exact Discoverie* and is not by Morton.

examine some of his quotations in the University Library of
Oxford . . .'[1] Later in the work, Barwick is careful to list the famous
people whom Morton knew or with whom he was associated,
especially his converts, but no mention is made of Donne.[2] The
second published biography was begun by Richard Baddily and
finished by Joseph Naylor: *The Life of Dr. Thomas Morton, Late
Bishop of Duresme* (York, 1669).[3] Baddily tells in great detail of
Morton's friendship for Donne and of his efforts both to help
Donne and to enlist him in the ministry. He even summarizes an
exchange of letters between them.[4] When, however, he tells us of
Morton's controversial writings, he gives substantially the same
story as Barwick with no mention of Donne:

. . . the examination of the testimonies of the Authors quoted in his *Appeal*,
was committed unto Mr. Thomas James (that indefatigable and laborious
keeper of the public and famous Library in *Oxon*) and to sundry other
Learned Divines of that University: but was afterwards finished in his
private library in the Deanery House of *St. Pauls London*, where he then
resided, *Dr. Overall* his reverend friend being Dean there.[5]

To this can be added that although Walton takes great pains to
describe the friendship between the two men, no mention appears
in his *Life of Dr. John Donne* of any collaboration between them.[6]
   The first clear statement of this collaboration comes in the
form of a conclusion in Dr. Augustus Jessopp's article on Donne in
D.N.B. in 1888. Speaking of the *Apologia Catholica* (which he calls
Christiana) he says:

. . . no one who should be at the pains to compare it and the long list of
authorities quoted and cited in its crowded pages, with Donne's *Pseudo-
Martyr* and *Biathanatos* could have much doubt that Morton and Donne
must for years have worked in close relations with each other, or
could avoid a strong suspicion that Morton owed to Donne's learning
very much more than it was advisable, or at that time necessary to
acknowledge in print.

[1] Barwick, op. cit., p. 132.
[2] Ibid., p. 164.
[3] The major part of this work was written by 1657, although it was not
published until 1669.
[4] Baddily–Naylor, op. cit., pp. 97–104.
[5] Ibid., pp. 35–6.
[6] Walton, pp. 31–8.

In 1894 Edmund Venables repeats much the same conclusion in his 'Life of Thomas Morton', again in the *D.N.B.*: 'Morton is believed to have derived aid from his younger friend, John Donne, afterwards Dean of St. Paul's.' At this point Venables cites Sanderson, *Works*, iv. 328. The page number is correct, because it describes Morton's controversial works, but there is no mention of Donne. In his short book on Donne in 1897, Jessopp takes the story a step further:

> Even if we had not been told that he gave Morton constant and valuable help, a comparison of the Authorities quoted and referred to in Morton's *Catholic Appeal* with those set down in Donne's *Pseudo-Martyr*, would have convinced a careful reader of the fact. The curious and out-of-the-way books cited in both works are very numerous and not to be found elsewhere.[1]

As Professor Malloch remarks, there is a certain irony in that 'even if we had not been told' coming from the first man to tell us. The main argument is, moreover, quite false. Even the 'careful' reader of seventeenth-century controversy will realize that books by Bellarmine, Gretser, Coccius, and Azorius may, to our eyes, be curious, but to the men of the times were certainly not 'out-of-the-way'.

In other words Jessopp is making a well-covered guess and to that extent the collaboration between the two men should not be regarded as a fact. I wish to urge that it is a shrewd guess; and that there is good evidence for making it.

There are two external reasons which support this guess. The first is the answer to the question Dame Helen Gardner asked when I informed her of Professor Malloch's objections: Why did Donne write *Pseudo-Martyr*? It is hardly the kind of book one would write without assurance that it would be accepted for publication. Moreover, theological controversy under James I was no field for amateurs: above all for amateurs not in orders. The Catholic adversaries were expert and would have welcomed with glee an ineptly done Anglican book. By 1609 therefore Donne must have had sufficient experience in controversial matters to be trusted with a major effort on behalf of his Church. There must

---

[1] Augustus Jessopp, *John Donne, Sometime Dean of St. Paul's*, London, 1897, p. 57.

also have been someone both competent to judge his work and interested in having him do it. Although Walton's account of *Pseudo-Martyr* is clearly wrong, much of his information about this part of Donne's life came from Morton;[1] and among qualified men of the time, Morton most clearly fits the description of someone who knew Donne's work and might have urged him to undertake it.

A second reason supports this conclusion. There is little evidence in Donne's earlier work, before his marriage, of any special theological competence. Yet we know that in 1607 Morton offered him the living at Long Marston.[2] This was, of course, two years before *Pseudo-Martyr* was published. From all we know of Morton it would have been most unlike him to make this offer to anyone whom he did not feel to be both worthy and prepared.[3] What else could more adequately account for Donne's theological studies between 1602 and 1607 than the assumption that he had worked with Morton; and would not the same assumption explain Morton's judgement of Donne's competence in 1607?[4]

Even the reason Jessopp advances is interesting, not in the sense he means it, but in the testimony it gives to Donne's access to a large and specially supplied library. The nature of the collection is more interesting than its individual items; and the collection could well have been the 'private library in the Deanery House of St. Paul's'. Morton prided himself in conducting his battles in the main from Catholic authors. Thanks to somebody's library, Donne is able to do exactly the same thing in *Ignatius His Conclave*.

When the Latin *Conclave Ignati* was entered on the Stationers' Register on 24 January 1610/11 the licensers were 'Doctor Moreton and Doctor Mokett'. The second licenser was Richard Mocket (1577–1618), who was regularly employed in licensing books from

[1] David Novarr, *The Making of Walton's Lives*, Ithaca, New York, 1958, pp. 71–3.
[2] Walton, p. 33; Baddily–Naylor, op. cit., p. 97.
[3] Barwick, op. cit., p. 162.
[4] Since this Appendix was written I have, through the kindness of Mrs. Bald, been able to see the chapter of the late Professor R. C. Bald's forthcoming biography of Donne which deals with the poet's years at Mitcham. He points out that a letter from Donne to Sir Henry Goodyer, dated 5 March 1607, shows that 'Donne was reading portions of [Morton's] *A Catholicke Appeale* a full eighteen months before that work was published'.

1610 to 1614.[1] The first licenser was certainly Thomas Morton, who was not one of the regular licensers. His name appears in the Register only once before this (in conjunction with Bishop King's) as the licenser of one of his own works, *A Direct Answer unto T. Higgons,* on 2 May 1609. His name does not appear again up to the end of 1611, not even for the entry of the English version of Donne's satire. Greg remarks that there are some 270 'irregular' licensers.[2] It is significant that the only books on behalf of which Morton's name appears are one of his own and one of Donne's.

I have noted in the Commentary several echoes of Morton's work in *Ignatius His Conclave* (e.g. pp. 124, 148, 151). There are certain not too common ideas which they share as well. An example is Morton's feeling that 'this proposition, *People, as subjects, were before their Governor,* doth taste too much of Machiavellism' (*A Full Satisfaction,* p. 28). Beneath the royalist sentiment of this lies Morton's perception, like Donne's own (see p. 115) that there is a strong republican element in Machiavelli's thinking. I have chosen this example because of Felix Raab's comment on how rarely early Jacobean commentators perceived this.[3]

There are many ideas and some books which both men dislike. Morton has several sharp passages on non-existent saints (*Apologia Catholica I,* 111–13; *II,* 217).[4] He objects to mystical phenomena (*Apologia Catholica I,* 360 ff.);[5] and to the extremism of the 'faction Jesuitical' (*A Full Satisfaction,* p. 95).[5] He uses much the same arguments as Donne against the claim that the Pope is superior to Councils (*A Catholicke Appeale,* pp. 289–94).[6] He makes the same gibes at the poetic proofs for Purgatory (*A Catholicke Appeale,* p. 498).[7] They both attack many standard Catholic books. Less usual is their almost identical mockery of the *Liber Conformitatum* (*A Catholicke Appeale,* p. 240).[8] They both give uneasy defences of Knox, Goodman, and Buchanan and connect them with Beza and Calvin. Morton does this twice (*A Preamble,* pp. 73–6; *Encounter,* pp. 165–74).[9]

[1] He later became Warden of All Souls and died of chagrin when one of his books was poorly received. See Miss B. Porter, in *D.N.B.*
[2] W. W. Greg, *Some Aspects and Problems of London Publishing Between 1550 and 1650,* Oxford, 1956, p. 58.
[3] Felix Raab, *The English Face of Machiavelli,* London, 1964, p. 68.
[4] See p. 7. [5] See p. 93. [6] See p. 11.
[7] See p. 9. [8] See p. 11. [9] See p. 77.

There are a good number of stories which appeal to both men. The boasting of Sixtus V (*An Exact Discovery*, p. 28; *A Full Satisfaction*, p. 75);[1] Pope Boniface, Gregory the Great, and the Emperor Phocas (*Apologia Catholica* I, p. 242; II, p. 299; *A Catholicke Appeale*, p. 32);[2] Spanish cruelty in the Americas (*Apologia Catholica* I, p. 339);[3] Pope Gregory raising the Emperor Trajan from Hell (*Apologia Catholica* II, p. 180; *A Catholicke Appeale*, pp. 3, 429);[4] animals worshipping the Host (*A Catholicke Appeale*, p. 435);[5] Plato permitting magistrates and physicians to lie (*Encounter*, ii, p. 59);[6] the Jesuit Acosta explaining the lack of miracles in the New World (*A Catholicke Appeale*, p. 419).[7]

There are even some purely verbal echoes, difficult as these are to evaluate. Morton refers to Paul II 'faciem sibi fucis concinneret' (*Apologia Catholica* I, 3 p. 65),[8] and to Jesuits as 'book gelders' (*Encounter*, 222).[9] He also uses a variant of the pseudo-Augustinian 'multorum nomina canonizantur in terris quorum animae cruciantur in Gehenna' (*Apologia Catholica* II, p. 333),[10] as well as the dispute about the two readings of St. Paul, 'servite Domino' and 'servite tempori' (*Apologia Catholica* II, p. 40).[11] One other echo is indeed tempting: Morton quips that 'the Pope and his minions by too much gazing on the moon are becoming lunatic' (*A Full Satisfaction*, p. 35).

All of these resemblances cannot make an absolute case for the collaboration between Donne and Morton. Both men were engaged in the same basic area of controversy and both must ultimately have relied upon sources which, if not identical, were certainly similar. The most serious argument against their having worked together is the silence of their biographers. Walton's is explained by his dislike of controversial matters.[12] But there is no such simple explanation for the silence of both Barwick and Baddily.

Ignatius His Conclave reveals similarities in the works of Morton and Donne. It thus adds to the arguments in favour of the guess Jessopp made. The similarities are however not enough to turn the guess into an accepted fact.

[1] See p. 77. [2] See p. 95. [3] See p. 69. [4] See p. 89.
[5] See p. 85. [6] See p. 55. [7] See p. 87. [8] See p. 42.
[9] See p. 67. [10] See p. 92. [11] See p. 44.
[12] D. Novarr, op. cit., pp. 124–5.

APPENDIX D

A Donne Discovery

IN October 1967, Professor Paul G. Stanwood of the University of British Columbia published for the first time a Latin poem attributed to John Donne.[1] Dr. Stanwood found the lines in a commonplace book in volume 27 of the Hunter manuscript collection in the Library of Durham Cathedral. With the permission of the Chapter of the Cathedral and of Dr. Stanwood, it is printed here. The attribution reads: 'Dr. Dun. Deane of Paules.'

Ignatij Loyolae ἀποθέωσις

Qui sacer ante fuit, sanctus nunc incipit esse
Loyola & in divis annumeratus ovat.

Sed queritur plenis a tergo & margine fastis
in minio, quo stet non superesse locum.

Repperit: expuncto multum Librarius audax
Germano, haud veritu'st substituisse nothum.

Lis hinc orta ferox, neque enim novus hospes abire,
cedere nec primus, nec simul esse volunt.

Quid pater hinc sanctus? qui vincit et omnia solvit,
Solvit et hunc nodum dexteritate nova,

State simul dixit, stabuloque quiescite vestro,
Ut Simon & Judas, quos tenet una dies;

Sin minus expectet quartani Ignatius anni
Februa, conflatum possideatque diem.

A relatively free translation follows:

The Apotheosis of Ignatius Loyola

Loyola for so long damned,[2] is lately canonized
and triumphs in the company of the saints.

---

[1] *Times Literary Supplement*, no. 3425, 19 October 1967, p. 984.
[2] Ibid., no. 3427, 2 November 1967, p. 1037. Mr. Carlo Dionisotti points out that *sacer* must in this context mean 'cursed' or 'damned'.

But he laments that the calendar is so full of rubrical
feasts that there is no room for him, even as a footnote.

So he makes room, by daring to play Recording Angel,
striking out Germanus and putting his own bastard name in his
place.[1]

Of course a brawl ensues: the new man won't yield, the
old won't leave and neither will co-exist.

What can the Holy Father do now? He who binds and
looses all, astutely unknots this one too.

'Stand', he says, 'yoked and still in your stall and
share it, as do Simon and Judas.

Otherwise, Ignatius can simply wait for every fourth
February, when he can have the fictional added day.'

The occasion of these lines is almost certainly Ignatius' canonization in 1622, as indicated in line 2. Dr. Stanwood points out that
the text was probably copied out by Thomas Carre, a Yorkshire
clergyman who was Vicar of Aycliffe (Co. Durham) in 1632 and
attended Strafford on the scaffold as his chaplain. From the handwriting it is probable that Carre made his copy in the early 1630s,
but there is no information on the source of the verses. Carre certainly had connections with friends of Donne, but there is no evidence either way as to whether or not he knew Donne personally.

There are, however, certain internal reasons for saying that these
verses could well be by Donne. The dramatic (and outrageous)
situation, the technical accuracy and the good-humoured wit are
all reminiscent of *Ignatius His Conclave* and very much in Donne's
manner. The use of *sacer* sums up the basic situation of the earlier
work and *nothum* echoes its 'French-spanish mungrell'.[2] The echo
of Matthew 16: 19 in *qui vincit et omnia solvit* is very like Donne's
other mocking echoes of serious expressions.[3] Finally, the genial
notion that Ignatius' feast could be celebrated on 29 February of
the disliked Gregorian calendar could also have fitted well into
Ignatius His Conclave.[4] Admittedly none of these similarities makes
for total certainty, but together they make the attribution of the
manuscript highly probable.

[1] Germanus of Auxerre was dropped from the principal place in the liturgical
calendar, when Ignatius' feast was fixed on 31 July.

[2] p. 25.   [3] p. 11.   [4] p. 19.

PRINTED IN GREAT BRITAIN
AT THE UNIVERSITY PRESS, OXFORD
BY VIVIAN RIDLER
PRINTER TO THE UNIVERSITY